CORYDON AND THE SIEGE OF TROY

ALSO AVAILABLE BY TOBIAS DRUITT

CORYDON AND THE
ISLAND OF MONSTERS

CORYDON AND THE
FALL OF ATLANTIS

CORYDON AND THE SIEGE OF TROY

TOBIAS DRUITT

SIMON AND SCHUSTER

For Ivan, Julie, Catherine, Hugo, Ben, Elissa, Jessica, Tabitha, Kate, Jacopo, Leo, Clare and Hermione: Corydon's first readers

SIMON AND SCHUSTER
First published in Great Britain in 2007 by Simon & Schuster UK Ltd
A CBS COMPANY

1 3 5 7 9 10 8 6 4 2

Simon & Schuster UK Ltd
Africa House
64–78 Kingsway
London WC2B 6AH

A CIP catalogue record for this book is available from the British Library

ISBN: 978-141-690116-7

Typeset by Rowland Phototypesetting Ltd, Bury St Edmunds, Suffolk
Printed and bound in Great Britain by Mackays of Chatham

www.simonsays.co.uk

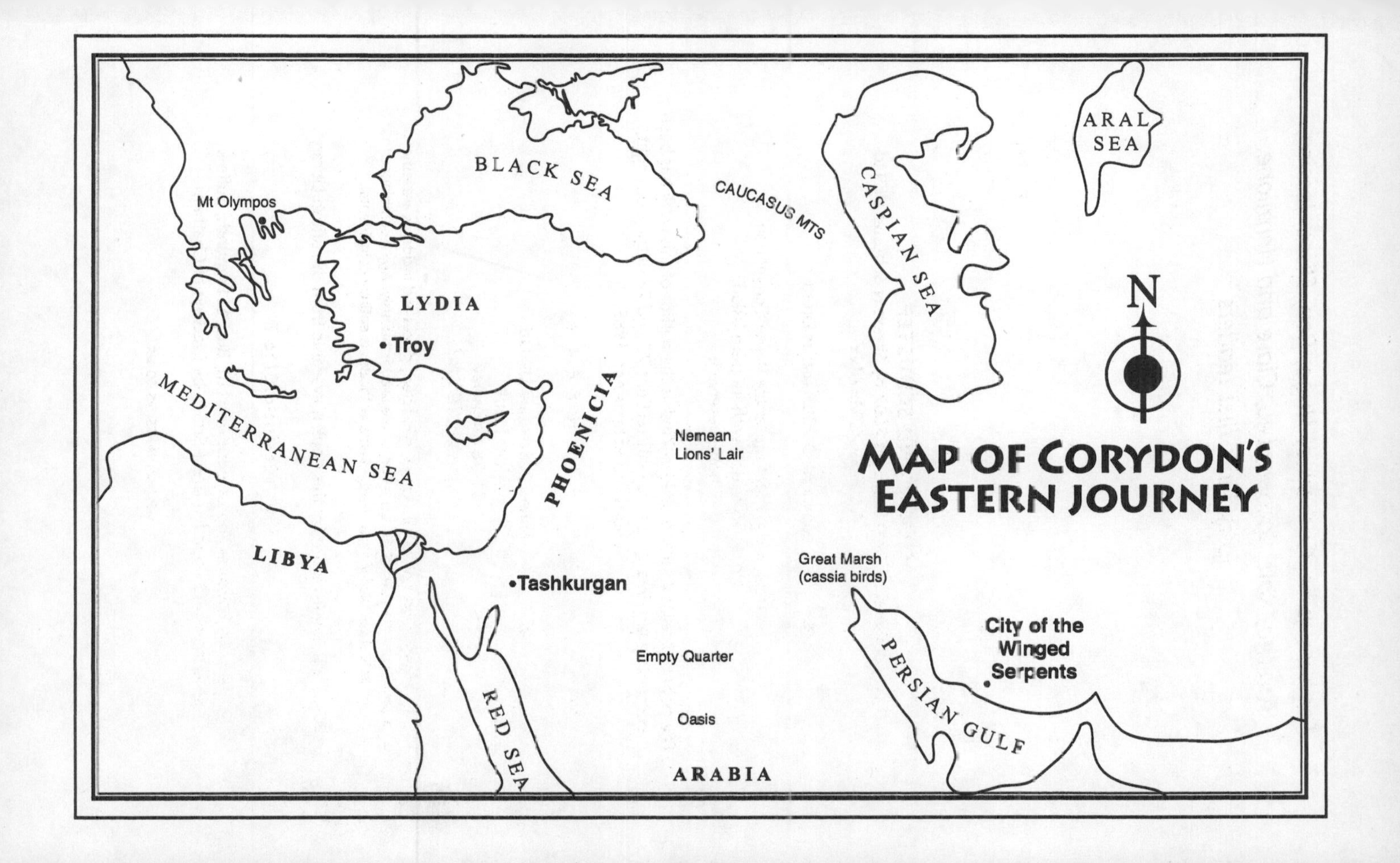
MAP OF CORYDON'S
EASTERN JOURNEY
N
ARAL SEA
CASPIAN SEA
CAUCASUS MTS
BLACK SEA
Mt Olympos
LYDIA
Troy
MEDITERRANEAN SEA
PHOENICIA
Nemean
Lions' Lair
LIBYA
Tashkurgan
Great Marsh
(cassia birds)
City of the
Winged
Serpents
PERSIAN GULF
Empty Quarter
Oasis
RED SEA
ARABIA

ἀλφα
One

Sthenno had been studying the magical papyrus all morning. It was one of the few that had been salvaged from the wreck of Atlantis, and the Trojan magicians were very interested in it. But Sthenno was not finding it easy to unlock its secrets. Sometimes she missed Euryale bursting in impatiently. Since she had discovered painting, her sister didn't do that anymore. Euryale was much more likely to stay in her own room and forget to eat than to rush in with half a deer on her shoulders. Sthenno had begun to notice, with concern, how thin Euryale was becoming. And she thought she understood. It was as if Euryale was trying to restore Atlantis through paint, restore that doomed and brilliant life by making it shine again on canvas.

Sthenno sighed. She saw that she was herself trying to do the same thing, spending a morning decoding an Atlantean text.

They all felt guilty. Sthenno wondered if that was why the mormoluke had stayed away from them. Did he think they were guilty, too? Restlessly, she got up and paced about, then retrieved a small piece of torn brown cloth from a box. With a gentle claw, she stroked it softly. It was all she had to help her remember Corydon, the mormoluke. But it brought him no nearer to her visionary eye. And the stars were silent about him.

A sudden loud noise pierced her thoughts. A messenger came running to say that the Greeks were bombarding the east walls again with their pathetic mangonels, catapults that fired small multiple stones, stones useless against Troy's great ensorcelled walls.

Sthenno thought about the Greek attack, her bird-like head cocked. She gave a shiver; her bronze feathers rattled. She felt she could not endure another war with any courage. But neither could she bear to desert the Trojans. It was only too clear that the Olympians had decided to blot them from the earth. In her immortal bones, Sthenno felt certain that Troy was the key to the conflict between the High Gods and the little gods of earth.

In Atlantis, they had lost. They had lost so much. This must be different.

Euryale was slapping thick blue paint on a canvas, trying to capture the exact tint of the Atlantean ocean. She added an angry streak of livid green to her picture; it represented the mouth of Vreckan, the Titan whose hunger had engulfed a city. Since the gorgons, the Minotaur, and Gorgos had tumbled abruptly into Troy's main square from the portal which had allowed them to evade the fall of Atlantis, the monsters were fighting shy of each other. Even the human refugees that Gorgos had led to safety avoided each other. The sight of a fellow survivor hurt because it made them remember what they had done and also what they had failed to do. The sight of the city hurt too, because it was so like and so unlike the Atlantis they had all lost. All Euryale could do was to keep on painting, seeking the quarry she loved, the truth her eye saw netted in paint. She knew it wouldn't help anyone but her, but the hunt for the eye's truth was a flickering Atlantean flame that she kept alive.

Several months earlier . . .

On the side of a sandhill, a shepherd boy watched over his flock. He still thought of himself as a shepherd, though his flock was composed of lithe goats, and its glory was his three milch camels.

He was not alone. The flock belonged to his gang, who had assembled it by a series of lightning raids on the people who lived on the vast desert's margins.

There were three other boys in the gang, and all of them were outcasts. There was Azil, who had been exiled for stealing a camel to try to win a race. There was Bin Khamal, who understood wind and weather so well that people had said he was a djinn. And, best of all, there was Sikandar, who had once lived somewhere greener, somewhere with sheep, but who now trod the lonely wastes.

Corydon didn't know why Sikandar couldn't go home. The gang didn't spend much time analysing things. They talked, of course, to pass the long desert days and nights, but they said little of the past. All of them were trying to forget their former lives.

Corydon was, too. There were still nights when his dreams tossed him from the sight of ruined cities and metal monsters to the screams of dying warriors. But the days kept him busy enough to ensure that such thoughts remained just dreams.

Sometimes the wind seemed to sing to him of a place a goddess had named. *Troios . . . Troios . . .* it sang. When the ghibli blew across the dry desert, it seemed to whisper of a city of towers . . . But Corydon tightened his blue headdress around his ears. Deaf and sullen, he would not hear what the ghibli wanted to tell him. Cities of towers . . . he was fatal to them. He knew that. And he knew in his heavy heart how right the people of his village had been to curse him and to exile him. He, Corydon, had destroyed an entire city, the greatest in the world . . . He had done the Olympians' will. Corydon tried to shut off his thoughts.

He loved the desert because it did not know his name. It was utterly indifferent to him. It might kill him, but it would do so without malice, just by being itself. He loved being forgotten. Disappearing into its vastness.

Sikandar approached him shyly.

'Lord,' he began. 'I must ask when we move. The camels must find more grazing soon. The goats also. And the tracks we saw . . . perhaps someone we might raid?'

'Don't call me "Lord",' said Corydon, a little irritably. 'I'm just a shepherd. And don't worry about the grazing.

Winter is fast approaching, and with it the rains will come. Till then, we can hold out by using the oases. As for the tracks, we must follow them cautiously, and attempt a raid when the moon is dark.' *The dark of the moon* – again his memories surged over him. He let them run into the sand like water. 'Are the animals all watered?' he asked.

They had stopped at a well. It had been called 'The Sweet', but the water tasted as if liquid iron and sea-water had gone into it. The taste was so bitter that only the camels drank it willingly. It tasted like the tears of giants. Again, Corydon tried to crush his memories. Sikandar's voice helped.

'Yes, lord,' he said. 'All have had water.'

'DON'T CALL ME LORD!' Corydon shouted. And then his heart filled with sadness. Sikandar looked forlorn, as if his last protector had struck him. 'I'm sorry,' he said. 'It's just—'

'I know,' said Bin Khamal. 'We are all in a desert of the heart, where the ghibli blows all day and fills our mouths with the sands of memory.'

Corydon smiled. Bin Khamal had the poet's heart that showed the true shepherd.

As they packed up the tent and stowed everything on the camels, taking a last drink of camel's milk, Corydon reflected. It was odd how difficult it was to escape from who you truly were. He was still Corydon, poet and shepherd, and because he was still Corydon, he couldn't escape for long from all he had done and suffered. But at least he felt sure he could do no harm here.

'Mount up!' he ordered. Each riding camel could carry two boys, though every time they came to dunes all had to dismount. The third camel was a beast of burden. One boy had always to be with the goats, too, which meant one of the riding camels had an easier time. It was still early, and the desert was almost cool. Corydon had always heard that deserts were cold at night, but this one wasn't, only less scorching. They had to move now, before the heat of the day began. The sun was only just below the horizon, and the stars had already paled. He had already scanned the camel tracks they were to follow. He moved his swift black camel into the lead. Corydon knew that a trot would be best for the early morning. A gallop would tire the camels, and when the sun appeared the camels would collapse, especially if they had to cross any dunes. All the boys followed.

It soon became clear that they were gaining on the other caravan. The tracks were fresher, and they saw a pile of camel dung. Azil examined it for a moment, then said, 'One hour. Maybe two.'

'What tribe?'

'Rashid,' he replied. 'And they have at least four camels. It may be a silk or spice caravan from far away. The camels are laden with more than men.'

A caravan, laden with spices! All four boys felt eager. With their bags full of spices, they could trade in a nearby town, and increase the herd. More milch camels and goats would reduce the hungry times, when all they had to eat was rock-hard sand-baked bread, or a few dry dates.

'Careful,' Azil warned. 'They are many. We must not

come too close to them until darkness can cloak us. Then we may steal in and – liberate some camels—'

'And some saddlebags,' put in Bin Khamal. 'Their saddlebags must be groaning in oppression. Only we can set them free!'

All the boys laughed. Spirits were high. Guided by Azil, they stayed carefully downwind of the caravan, and about a mile distant, until the hammering heat of day began to fade into the gentler heat of night.

Speaking low, Corydon took the initiative. 'I'll go ahead,' he said, 'and scout their camp. Make camp here yourselves, but be careful. Don't make a fire, and we'll all have to do without water for a while. Wait until the moon rises – luckily she's almost at full dark – and then follow my tracks. You know what to do when we get there.' They nodded, though inwardly all felt scared of robbing so great a caravan. Previously, they had mainly hit stragglers like themselves.

Corydon made his way cautiously in the direction the tracks showed. Though not a great tracker like Azil, he could follow a clearly-marked trail. After an hour of walking over hot sand, he could see the red star of the caravan's campfire. It helped to orient him in the vastness of the desert. There was no wind at all, and the hot air was motionless. He felt as if he were walking through stagnant water. He was also beginning to be very thirsty. Circumspectly, he took a small sip from his water-skin; it would be hours before they could water, because the caravan was occupying the oasis. Corydon hoped the caravan camels had been well watered, or they might collapse before the boys could lead them to a fresh well.

Now he was approaching the first date-palms of the oasis. He slowed, and dropped to his belly. There might be guards posted if the caravan contained anything truly precious. But he could see nothing, only the merchants sitting around an immense campfire, drinking coffee in tiny cups and listening to a minstrel telling a tale of the djinn. Under cover of the minstrel's song, he crept close enough to see that the camels were pastured on the opposite side of the oasis. Curses! Cautiously, he crept around to them, remembering to stay low. It was a big oasis, and he had to crawl on his belly for endless minutes before he saw the first picket-rope before him.

Corydon had learned about camels. They were irritable, but they were not stupid. Some camels would refuse to be ridden by anyone other than their owner. If another tried to mount them, the camel would fight them off with teeth and hooves. This was exactly the kind of disturbance they couldn't afford. He could see which camels were the best and fastest – that big black milch camel there, with her rangy legs, and the small white. But he couldn't tell if they were one-owner camels. Still, he might at least make himself smell more familiar; he wrapped himself in a saddleblanket that had been left lying on the ground, and rubbed himself against one of the saddles. It might not make enough difference. Corydon could only hope that Sikandar would be able to whisper any recalcitrant beasts, as he had before.

There was another problem, too. Beside them on the ground lay the heavy loads the men of the caravan had been carrying. The caravanners had unloaded them to make sure the camels were well rested for the morning ride, but had not wished to transport the heavy saddlebags far. He would have to discover their load.

Corydon crept over to the bags, slipping his hand inside. He reached into the first bag, and soft sand-like substances, seeds and other things were sifting in between his fingers, sand and seeds. He withdrew his hand, and caught a whiff of smells. Spices . . .

The second bag contained soft, many-coloured silk. The moonlight pacified some of the colours, but as Corydon held them up, one piece caught a gleam from the fire and grew strong, becoming molten gold. The impression was of a peaceful anger, as if the silks coolly restrained inner rage. But the third bag contained the greatest surprise. A hard stone. Then another. Jewels! Nearly a hundred rubies, sapphires, emeralds and diamonds. A gift fit for a king . . .

A flash of steel in moonlight caught Corydon's eye. Some weapons, perhaps . . .? He wasn't certain, but he crawled forwards, not sure of what he'd find. Just then something tapped his shoulder. Corydon spun around, and with infinite relief saw that it was only Sikandar. He put his finger to his lips hastily, and motioned to the boy to get down. Sikandar dropped obediently onto the sand. Behind him were the others.

Corydon motioned to the saddlebags. Understanding, the boys took one each, as Corydon dropped to his belly again, then slithered forwards to where the camels were tied. He hoped the scent of the blanket would fool them for long enough to allow him to lead two – or, with luck, three – away. But from his kleptis days he knew he must not be greedy. One was all they really needed, to carry the booty away. He approached the tall black. She snorted imperiously as he undid her picket-rope, but she did not resist as he put his hand on her bridle to lead her away. She followed him with that graceful camel-walk that looked as a tree might if it became mobile. He gave the picket-rope to Sikandar, who began soothing the camel's increasing agitation as Corydon crept back, elbows and knees to the sliding sand and small pebbles, to untie the small white.

But this camel was not fooled. As soon as she smelt his hand, she knew he smelt wrong. She gave a roaring gasp of fury and aimed a bite at his hand. The other camels, disturbed by the sound, had now got his scent and began to bellow. Now the animal noise was joined by the angry shouts of men, alert to the camels' raucous cries.

'Go!' shouted Corydon. He sprang to the unruly white camel's back, not bothering to try to persuade her to lie down so he could mount properly. As he'd expected, she was furious, and immediately tried to dislodge him, but using all his monster-strength on the bridle, he managed to force her to turn and to follow the black they'd already stolen. She set off at a fast trot, her feet thudding on the sand, and ahead he could see the other boys, insecurely mounted on the black, with the saddle-bags slung across her neck. Corydon urged his mount on until they were riding level. Behind him he could hear the men of the caravan mounting and setting off in pursuit. But he'd judged astutely; they were mounted on the fastest camels, and only a few of the men of the caravan had been able to pursue them. As they crested a rearing sand dune, and then another, Corydon began to breathe more easily.

'We must reach camp – your camel will founder!' he shouted. They nodded. Their makeshift camp was over a few more low rises, but Corydon was becoming less sure of the exact direction. 'Azil!' he shouted. 'Can you lead us to the camp?'

The black camel lay down in the lee of a dune while Azil began scouting for pointers to direction. At last he found one, a line of pebbles kicked by one of them on their outward journey. Feeling his shoulder blades prickle with the awareness of pursuit, Corydon urged everyone to remount, his unruly little white calmer now. They went on. The first faint light of dawn began to break, and still there was no sign of the camp.

Then they found where it had been. The charred mark of their small fire was there. But the camels and goats had scattered, and it might take hours to round them up. Corydon wondered why they had gone. Had something alarmed them? They had never strayed before.

It had been a long time since any of the boys had had water or food, too, and their overburdened beasts could not go on in that fashion for much longer. Bin Khamal cursed bitterly.

'Corydon,' he said, when he had done. 'There's a sandstorm coming fast from the east.'

The news was as bad as could be. A sandstorm would

cover their tracks – though that was the only good thing to be said for it, for it would also cover the missing animals' tracks. And they needed water and pasturage, which would be impossible to find in a howling cloud of sand.

'How fast is this storm coming up?' questioned Corydon.

'Very fast. In about thirty minutes its centre will be here. You can see it as a faint smudge on the horizon,' said Bin Khamal.

And there was a thick blot to the east, like a coffee stain on a good rug. It grew larger by the second, slowly moving back and forth, back and forth, like a snake trying to fascinate its prey.

Bin Khamal slid off his camel, turned to Corydon and the others.

'I think I know what to do,' he said. 'But I must be alone.'

What? Corydon couldn't quite bring himself to trust Bin Khamal to this extent. If his plan failed or if he were somehow planning to make off with the booty, they would be finished.

'I will stay with you,' he said firmly. 'The others must seek safety as they can. If they travel due west, away from the storm, they may reach the Bar El Kabir caves before it really thickens. There's an underground river deep within them, or so a trader once told me. Look out for a rock shaped like a man's finger; it marks the entrance.'

'No!' Sikandar exclaimed. 'Lord, I do not want to leave you.'

'You must.' Corydon was curt. 'Sikandar, I have seen many things worse than a desert storm. And I have lived through them all. I will not come to harm. Now let each man lay hold of a bag—' He passed his to Bin Khamal.

'What about you, my lord?' asked Sikandar, anguished.

'I do not need to keep my hands on treasure. I trust you. This is only a precaution lest we do not easily find each other again.' Corydon glanced at the sky. Already half of it was shielded by the greying, blinding storm. 'Now go! You have no time to waste.' The first hard rumbles of thunder rang out as the two boys galloped away.

'You should not have stayed,' said Bin Khamal.

'I had to,' said Corydon.

'So be it, then,' said Bin Khamal.

His face began to alter. At first it was a subtle rippling, a widening, as if Bin Khamal had had an unusually good meal. But there was a textural change too: smooth flesh began to dissolve, or to crystallise into a mass of moving sand so thick and so blown that it was like a solid dune rearing out of the desert. What had been Bin Khamal was now a dune seventy feet high, a dune made of sand thrumming violently with sound . . .

Singing.

Corydon had heard the sands sing before, but never at such close range. The cries were fierce, savage, a low keening that was more like the roar of mighty ocean waves than a sound made on land. He knew that the Arabs thought singing sands were the home of the djinn, but he had never realised that the sands themselves actually were djinn. It was clear that Bin Khamal's weather knowledge was indeed djinnish.

And he was singing to the storm. Enchanting it.

Already the storm had begun to sing back to him. The thunder crooned in rhythm with his song. The leading edge of the storm had stopped short of where they were, and flashes of lightning served only to punctuate Bin Khamal's deep, rich chanting.

Suddenly, Corydon realised that a face had begun to materialise in the sky, where the sand-clouds of the storm were thickest. Two blue bolts of lightning shot from the eyes, into Bin Khamal's eyes. Corydon reared back in horror, but the glowing light did no harm, seemed to radiate warmly from the djinn's face, from both faces. Then the storm's leading edge rolled up, and it began to move away, leaving only a small scatter of whirling dust devils in its wake. Bin Khamal gradually melted back into boyhood again.

'You *are* a djinn,' said Corydon, bluntly.

Bin Khamal blushed. 'I didn't want anyone to know,' he said shyly. 'I thought you would not wish me to stay with you if anyone knew.'

'Well, I won't tell anyone,' Corydon promised. 'But now you have told me your secret, I must show you mine.' He lifted the corner of his trouser leg so Bin Khamal could glimpse his goat-leg and -foot.

Bin Khamal was silent. 'Are you a djinn too?' he asked, after a long moment of thought.

'No,' said Corydon. 'I'm a monster, and the son of a god. The god Pan.' Bin Khamal looked blank. 'He is a god of shepherds,' Corydon explained. 'But we are not in his lands. Was the storm a djinn too?'

'That was MY father,' Bin Khamal admitted. 'But my mother is mortal, and human.' They both took a long drink of milk from the small white camel, which had waited disdainfully, caring nothing for sandstorms or djinn.

'Let us go and find the others,' said Corydon. They mounted, and pointed her head west, for the caves.

βήτα
Two

Seeing the storm dissipate, the other boys had taken time to find water, round up the camels and goats. Then they had waited in the cool dimness of the Great Cavern where Corydon and Bin Khamal found them. They had made a small fire, and killed a goat, which was roasting on a spit.

There was a river in the cave. Corydon and Bin Khamal were so hot and thirsty that they plunged straight into it.

'Why do you get thirsty when you are really part of the desert?' Corydon asked. 'Does it come from your mother?'

Bin Khamal said solemnly, 'Sand drinks water, Corydon. When it rains, and it does sometimes rain even in the Sands, the water is drunk very quickly. Sand is thirstier than any boy. It can drink a whole river. It could drink you.' And he laughed, and ducked Corydon.

When they emerged, cool and free of chafing grit for the first time in days, the smell of roast goat made everyone feel their hunger. Sikandar had rubbed it with a paste made of some of the seeds and nuts they had found in the saddlebags, and it smelt like paradise. They shared it, and shared, too, the remaining bread and dates.

They ran their hands unbelievingly through their treasures: jewels glinted in the soft firelight, spices poured out in scented streams. Emeralds and rubies, turquoises and moony pearls, purple shimmers of amethyst; amber, cardamom, cassia, spikenard and balm. Silks wove their vivid sheen into the light. Corydon picked up something scented, coiled like a papyrus scroll. He tried to unroll it, but it crumbled in his clumsy fingers. There were resins, too, frankincense and myrrh fit for a pharaoh's tomb.

They packed it all up again. They were rich beyond imagining.

They said nothing of their tender dreams and hopes. They did not want to break the spell. Each felt certain that such wealth would vanish, somehow.

They lay down to sleep. The firelight flickered on the walls. Just as Corydon's eyes were beginning to close, one log fell into the fire with a hiss, and the flames blazed brightly as its bark caught. Corydon caught a sudden glimpse of the cave ceiling.

It was painted with hundreds of small figures, black and red and ochre. Corydon could see a strange beast with spots and a neck longer than a camel's, and long, long legs. It was running from men who were chasing it fiercely. Then there was another picture: men were standing triumphantly over the beast and were plunging sticks – no, spears – into it. The painting reminded him painfully of Euryale's old hunting sketches, the ones she'd done before Atlantis had made her a grander artist. But even if Euryale had passed this way and done that picture, it seemed unlikely that she was responsible for the vast gallery of art that spread over his head. Corydon also saw hundreds of figures – yes, swimming, just as he and Bin Khamal had done. But most interesting of all was the depiction of a huge lion, mouth open, pouring out flame.

'The Nemean lion!' breathed Corydon. Now he looked more closely he could see that the lion was flanked by a lioness, and several cubs, all with tiny tongues of flame emerging from their lolling mouths. Not *the* Nemean lion, then. Nemean lions. A whole pride of them. Corydon wondered if there were any left in the vicinity. But when he sat up eagerly, he saw that the others were already asleep. He decided to wait until later before asking them.

The cave was so enclosed that there was no way of knowing when it was dawn without going outside to see. On the other hand, sleeping on rock made for a restless night. Corydon woke and went outside in what turned out to be deep night; the stars showed there were at least four hours till dawn.

The next time, it was Sikandar who woke, and who crept out to see golden desert sleeping under the tender blue of a morning sky. Full of sleep, water, goat, he felt fine and enthusiastic; he swung his arms and sang half a song as he looked out, pretending to be an emperor of vast domains, conscious of the king's ransom stored in the cave behind him. He felt a little lonely, too, shut out of the sleep of the others, and he decided that it was time to waken them.

He had just turned to go back into the cave's watery coolness when he saw a group of riders cross a rise far ahead. He shaded his eyes with his hand to see them better. They were all tall, superbly mounted on fine fast camels whose long legs swallowed yards of desert with every stride. All were wearing white headdresses, and the gold braid on their borders caught the light.

A rich caravan, perhaps. No. Too well armed. Sikandar's eyes were good. In the clear air, he could discern that each carried a heavy sword, spears, and a bow. Then – what?

Behind Sikandar, Corydon and Azil emerged from the cave, rubbing their eyes as the strong light hit. Sikandar pointed to the advancing line of figures. They were heading straight for the cave.

Bin Khamal came out. After one rapid glance, he said, 'Whatever goods they are trading, I do not think we wish to buy from them. We must go swiftly.'

All the boys rushed back into the cave, packed up frantically, brought out camels and goats. The line of heavily-armed men was much nearer by the time they emerged.

'Mount up!' said Corydon. He flung himself onto the large black camel's back, hardly caring for the jarring shock. He urged the camel forward just as the nearest rider hurled his spear. It landed less than a foot away, striking the sand with a dull thud.

'They mean to kill us!' Bin Khamal breathed. 'Go! Go!'

The goats and camels hurtled forward at a rough, bone-jarring trot. Another spear whistled through the air, striking a white nanny, who gave a bleat of surprise to find herself pouring out her lifeblood onto the sand. Corydon swerved as another spear thudded down.

'Bin Khamal!' he cried. 'Your other self! It's the only chance!'

Bin Khamal nodded. As he dismounted, Corydon caught the bridle of the riderless camel and led it forward as the boy began to dissolve into a thick, buzzing column of sand, then to spread himself over the face of the desert, howling, blocking out tracks, filling the air with grit. The pursuers checked. They tried to ride around the storm – they could see its edges – but the wild storm that had been Bin Khamal placed itself over and over again between the kleptis gang and its pursuers. Corydon and the others managed to put considerable distance between themselves and the men that chased them while Bin Khamal howled. Gradually, the small storm came closer to the boys, then dwindled into a boy again. Bin Khamal flung himself onto the camel's back, and all of them set off again at a fast trot, on the pebbly hard sand.

'I did not know you were a djinn,' said Sikandar. 'It was very useful for us.'

'I cannot do it again today, Corydon,' said Bin Khamal apologetically. 'If I take that form often, or stay in it too long, it will become my true form.'

'It *is* your true form,' said Azil stonily. 'You are a monster.'

Bin Khamal was silent. Corydon spoke sharply.

'Perhaps you would prefer the spears of those who pursue us! He has saved us all. And,' he added, 'he is no more a monster than I am. A monster leads you.' He displayed his goat-leg.

'You speak as if you were proud of it,' said Bin Khamal, puzzled. 'I have always been so ashamed . . .'

'I *am* proud of it,' said Corydon flatly. 'It means I am not like the Olympians.' There was a silence.

'Who are the Olympians?' asked Bin Khamal.

Corydon paused. 'Once upon a time the earth was ruled by kindly gods. The simple gods of earth, like my father Pan. They were not perfect, any more than men are perfect; they sometimes quarrelled or misused their powers. But they had no will to rule men. They asked for nothing more than friendship. But among their children rose up gods who wanted everyone to be like them, and who rejected all that were not like them. They imprisoned or murdered the kind old gods. Then they raised up the race of heroes to rid the earth of all who were freckled, or strange, or odd, or lame, or funny-looking. And ever since then they have tried to teach monsters to be ashamed. But we should not be ashamed that we are as we are.'

Everyone had been so absorbed by Corydon's story that they had forgotten to look over their shoulders. Suddenly, a gleam of light caught Corydon's eye.

It came from the point of a spear.

'They've found our trail!' gasped Azil. 'But how—'

'Never mind how,' said Corydon. 'Ride! It is our only chance!' All the camels shot forward.

They rode all through the dreadful heat, but the heavy footfalls behind them never slowed.

They kept on riding even after the sun went down, but the strong, relentless pursuers kept after them, out of spear range, but not losing any ground.

They kept on riding, on camels stumbling with tiredness. They paused at a well to allow the camels a snatched drink. It was almost dawn. This small respite lost them much of their lead. They mounted only just in time to avoid being speared.

'Who *are* they?' gasped Corydon. He looked back. The men's headdresses still looked immaculate. Their camels ran on tirelessly.

Bin Khamal spoke in the hard voice of one whose mouth has been dry all day.

'Corydon,' he said, 'I think they are heroes. But not Olympian heroes. Arab heroes. We have a great treasure here. I think someone wants it back.'

Sikandar spoke. 'We could give it to them,' he said. 'If it saved our lives.'

'I doubt that it would,' said Corydon, noticing their long bright swords glinting palely in the blue dawn light. 'And I am not inclined to surrender yet. They are heroes – well then, I have seen a bigger army of heroes than this, and have lived to tell the tale.' As he spoke, though, he noticed again that one of the riders was much taller than the others. He thought to himself that perhaps the heroes he had met weren't the very best heroes. Perhaps this tall man might be better than anyone he had ever faced.

Aloud, he said, 'We need to make a plan. We cannot simply blunder on like this.'

'We must trick them somehow,' said Bin Khamal. 'The weather will be of no help. And as long as they can see us we cannot mislead them through tracking tricks.'

Corydon thought. Then, without warning, he veered off to the left and galloped away, leaving the others to catch up. The bemused boys followed him.

'Where are we going?' said Sikandar.

'To a cliff I know of,' said Corydon simply.

The boys slowed the camels to a trot after a while, not wishing to tire their mounts under the ache and dazzle of the brutal sun. The heroes kept relentlessly on. Their camels were sweating, but they were not yet near the stumbling tiredness of the kleptis gang camels. The heat seemed to increase. Sweat poured down the boys' faces.

Corydon turned to see the tall hero taking a spear from his saddle. His face was twisted into a grimace of rage as he hurled it. A whistle of air. The boys stayed upright knowing they were out of range of a spear throw.

A foot in front of Corydon's camel, the spear hit a little kid, trotting along, looking desperately for its mother. It bleated a sad, surprised note, then fell down dead. Corydon saw its glazed eyes as he steered his camel around the spear stuck in the ground. He looked in shock behind him. The tall man had only a hard expression. Corydon was appalled. Did this man have no heart?

At last, when he was almost so thirsty that he could not bear it, he saw a shadowy shape ahead. He could only hope that it was the dune he remembered, the dune down which he had tumbled when the world-Tree and the goddess had finished with him, when Atlantis too had been over and done.

Corydon told the others his plan.

'We must stop at the top of that dune. There we shall wait, lying on the ground, with our camels down beside us, to avoid their spears. When they are close enough for us to see their eye colour, all of us but Bin Khamal must ride over the cliff.'

'What?' the other boys all exclaimed sharply. Then Bin Khamal asked, 'Why should we go over the cliff? Why not lure them over?'

'That was what I thought of first,' Corydon admitted. 'But they are too good. It wouldn't work. They are too clever, especially the tall one – see how he quests for our tracks even now, hot and tired and with no desert cunning or monster strength to sustain him? They would not be deceived. No, our only chance is for them to think us dead.'

'But – won't the fall kill us?'

'It might,' said Corydon. 'But the sea is below, and just there it is very deep. I once saw a whale, a leviathan, go by, blowing water. It is not the Middle Sea; it is some larger water.'

Azil spoke. 'This is the suggestion of a poltroon and a monster,' he said disdainfully. 'I would rather die with honour. I want to fight them.'

Corydon sighed. 'Azil, there are three times as many of them, they are well armed, and they are twice our size. How can we possibly fight them?' *As well*, he thought,

I am tired of fighting and battles. I never want to see or to be in another.

'Could we not pull up suddenly at the cliff-edge so that they alone went crashing over?'

'We could try,' said Corydon, 'but the cliff-edge is a sand and gravel slope. We would never stop in time.'

'We need a miracle,' said Sikandar.

Unbidden, Corydon remembered the other times he had been saved by miracles; the time Pegasus had come to his rescue in the underworld. He, too, was Medusa's son . . . If only he could be here now . . .

'I can't give you a miracle,' he said bluntly. 'And we must do it now, or throw ourselves on their mercy.'

'I would rather die,' said Bin Khamal, with a faint smile.

'I think we can oblige you,' said Sikandar.

'Now – ride hard!!'' Corydon shouted. 'When you reach the cliff-edge, do not wait for a signal! Slide off your camel – why condemn them to your choices? – and jump with the wind in your hair. Ride!' The camels leapt forward in a loping gallop, ungainly but amazingly swift. And yet their pursuers drew closer, till Corydon could almost feel the breath of the foremost rider on the back of his neck.

They were sliding, almost falling down the immense dune. Corydon could see the cliff-edge, much too close now. He tightened his grip on his treasure bag. Then he rolled over the side of his camel. He hit the ground with a bruising thud, rolled as best he could, then . . .

He stood up for one instant, shook a defiant fist at the

enormous hero looming up behind him. The hero was keeping his footing effortlessly in the slithery sand. His long golden hair streamed behind him like the tail of a comet of ill-omen. For a second, Corydon could see his eyes. He had thought Perseus's eyes cold. This man's eyes were not cold, but hot, white-hot with the longing to kill. His mouth was open in a battle-scream that transformed his face into a rictus. The hate-cry seemed to pierce Corydon's ears as the man raised his spear to run Corydon through.

And it was then that Corydon's miracle arrived.

Up from below the cliff-edge came a flight of sphinxes, sixteen of them, their enormous wings spread. They were so big that they cast a shade over the cliff-edge.

None of them spoke. That was not the sphinx way. But they placed themselves between the boys and the onrushing heroes. One huge sphinx reared up in front of Corydon, her wings spread to protect him. He crouched gratefully, glad not to see the hero anymore.

But to his surprise, the man's battle-cry did not cease. Instead, Corydon heard the whiffle as he flung his spear straight at the sphinx's face, aiming for the eye. She must have used her mind-powers on him, for next Corydon saw her settle down like a cat on a warm rock to play with him. He was still moving, still trying to attack, so his will must have been very strong, but he was moving as if thigh-deep in sand. Intermittently, he uttered groans that sounded like his war-cries slowed right down. He also began to look confusedly at the sphinxes, as if wondering why he hadn't reached them yet. He was clearly a man used to being abnormally fast; now he was incredibly and impossibly slow, but he didn't seem to realise this himself. Corydon saw that his painful progress *felt* like running to him.

'This one is the strongest,' the sphinx said. 'Some say a fleet of ships is best,' she added, 'some say a marching army of men, but I say it is the one you love.' Corydon was used to sphinxes, so he didn't ask himself what on earth she meant. He looked for the other pursuers. Each stood as stiffly as if he had been shrouded in linen. The camels, too, were utterly still.

'Don't look them in the eyes,' he hissed to Sikandar and Azil. Bin Khamal had already draped his headscarf lower, so that he couldn't catch their eyes by looking up at the wrong moment. It was clear that he too had met sphinxes before.

Corydon decided to risk one question. 'Why?' he asked. 'Why did you come?'

The sphinx did not turn her head. 'We are a miracle of rare device,' she said. 'You wished for a miracle. One of you. One of you must not die. Must not be lost. One of you –' she paused, and suddenly her claws shot out with a dull rasp on the sand '– one of you has a future.'

Not more prophecies! Not more being the Chosen One! I don't want it! I just want to be a kleptis leader! Corydon's thoughts ran on a familiar track through his mind.

As usual, the sphinx heard him, as if he had spoken aloud.

'Why do you feel so sure that I meant *you*?' she said softly, her eyes still fixed on the tall hero, who was moving so slowly now that it could barely be detected.

Corydon decided that he didn't want to know. At all. He wanted to get his boys together and go to a city and spend and buy and gather a herd of goats.

'Are you going to eat him?' he asked, pointing at the tall hero. Somehow, he would have liked to know that the man was gone for good. Those silver, raging eyes would haunt his nightmares.

'I will not,' she said. 'I will take him elsewhere. He shall be my slave.'

Corydon was satisfied; he didn't really want the man to die. He just didn't want to remember him or fear him.

The other boys were keeping their heads ducked. 'Come,' he shouted. And they set off in pursuit of their lost herd. If Corydon had looked back, he would have seen that the hero with silver eyes had turned his head, with an immense effort, to look after them as they went.

γάμμα
Three

The town ahead of them was the largest city of Nabataea. It is possible that if Corydon had not seen Atlantis, he might have felt overawed by Tashkurgan, city of white stone, whose name means the Stone Tower. It was as crisp and pristine as if it had been carved out of ice; all its buildings had an edge of newness. And yet this fresh-as-linen city was set in a ravine as red as the blood of sacrifice. The other boys looked awed – except for Sikandar, who seemed as unimpressed as Corydon. There was no time to wonder why. At the head of the ravine were guards.

'We come to trade,' said Corydon, quietly and respectfully, in the language of the Arabs. The guard looked at him quizzically. 'You are very young,' he said, 'to be trading in Tashkurgan. Does your father know?'

For a fraction of a second, Corydon wondered if his father did know . . . But he had long since stopped doing the errands of any god, even beloved ones. 'I have no father,' he said. 'I am alone.' The guard looked sympathetic. 'All right,' he said. 'Move along. But remember that you must make an offering at the Great Temple. All traders must do so.' The boys began the slow careful walk down a narrow cliff path into the deeps of the gorge.

Bin Khamal said, 'It is the temple of the Winged Lions. I am not sure what the offering is.'

Azil said, 'I have heard of it. More winged lions, like those who just befriended us, I imagine.'

Corydon opened his mouth to explain that sphinxes were not in fact winged lions, but then closed it again; he could see Azil had much more to say.

'I do not like it. For us, such djinn are evils of the desert. We appease them, but we do not befriend them.' He looked sidelong at Bin Khamal and Corydon. 'I know you as friends,' he said stiffly, 'but you are enemies to my people. The winged lions will be likewise friends and enemies. Sometimes the offering we must make to such creatures is too large.'

Sikandar took his hand. 'Azil,' he said. 'You lack ambition. You must walk with the immortals, and try not to feel fear. For if you die in their embrace, if they devour you, you will only be doing what you were born to do. Humans are made to seek out something too great for us to conquer.'

Corydon found this idea interesting. Suddenly he thought that it was because he was not human that he had spent his life yearning for the small things that did not content humans themselves: a fireside, a mother, a group of true friends. He supposed it was the contact with the sphinxes that had made everyone so thoughtful.

Now they were passing two huge gate-statues of lions, lions with thickly-feathered wings furled across their backs. The heads bore sharp horns, like those of a desert oryx, and heavy manes. The boys looked up at them in awe.

It was mid-morning, and a crowd was cramming itself into Tashkurgan. Carts of vegetables, carts loaded with grain, elaborately-veiled women holding baskets, black-swathed men of the desert leading strings of camels, blue-clad caravan men bringing in spice and silk on camel- and mule-back. Food traders were setting out their stalls, and a scent of spices filled the hot air.

'Aeee! The Winged Serpents! The Winged Serpents!'

Corydon looked up to see a black batwinged shape streak across the sky, faster than a swallow.

Everyone flung themselves to the ground. Corydon's mouth was in the dust of the street. But he raised his head. So he saw two immense shapes rising from the temple roof. It was the winged lions. They began to close in on the serpents.

It was an interesting battle because the serpents were much faster and more numerous, but the lions were stronger, though slow and heavy in the air. The lions' tactic was to drop on the serpents from high in the sky and crush them in their teeth, breaking their necks. Three serpents died that way; the crowd scattered as the broken bodies fell on the city. Corydon found it exciting, though he felt sorry for the serpents. He wondered what drove them to keep attacking. Then he saw that one of the winged lions was in trouble.

His flight had become erratic. One of his wings seemed to be almost paralysed; he could beat it only feebly. He was snarling in pain and fear. As Corydon watched in horror, he plunged from the sky, tumbling over and over. All around, people were whispering and pointing. 'It's the serpent poison,' said a blue-clad trader. 'He's done for.' As he spoke, the lion fell on his back onto a group of fine white houses, crushing them. Not knowing why, Corydon got up and ran to the spot. The lion lay broken, his body twisted, his eyes still open, his mouth a silent howl of surprise and shame. Then the great red mouth opened and the lion spoke.

'Corydon Panfoot,' he said. 'You cannot hide forever. You are needed. And my brothers will tell you what you must do. You must do it. You must. Must.' His golden eyes rolled back in his head as he slumped into death. Then they sprang open again. 'Where are your friends?' the deep voice asked. 'Where are they?' A single tear slid down the lion's nose. Then his eyes closed once more.

Corydon was blank with horror. He didn't want to be known, and he had been known. Worse, he had been accused. Of betrayal. And in his heart, he knew the accusations were just. The battle still raged overhead, but Corydon sat utterly still, holding the dead lion's head in his hands. He felt he had deserted a post of danger, and had been caught doing so by one who had given his life for others.

Suddenly he began to cry, and the tears poured out. Sthenno! Euryale! The Minotaur! He did not say the name of the Snake-girl to himself, then or ever. But the others!

How could he have – no, not forgotten, but neglected them? It was as if he had thought he might make new friends instead, as mothers buy their grieving children a new dog when the beloved dog dies, only to find it rebuffed.

As he wept for himself, for his friends, for what he now thought he was, the noises of battle above him gradually ceased. With a slow beating of wings, the other lion came and landed beside his dead fellow. The great creature ignored Corydon entirely. With an anxious pink tongue, it licked the forehead of its fallen comrade. The dead lion did not move. The living lion settled down beside him, paws regally outstretched, and threw back its head in a roar of grief and defiance. The fleeing serpents answered with shrill screams of triumph.

Corydon sat still and wept. He seemed to have a fountain of tears in him. After a while, he noticed that the living winged lion was weeping too.

Finally, Corydon's tears ran out into a sand of numbness. He wiped his face, and looked at the lion.

'Can – can I help?' he asked, uncertainly. He was pretty sure he couldn't, but something had to be said.

'Help?' The great beast looked down his nose. 'We are in dire need of help. But we do not ask it from those who abandon their friends and their fates.'

'But – we were separated—'

'And – you have searched?'

Corydon was silent. The lion looked down his nose again. Then he spoke.

'You always long for an ordinary human life, Panfoot.

But you know that is not your fate, can never be your fate. You cannot run or hide from who you are. If you do, you can never love anyone. In trying to betray yourself, you have also betrayed everyone you love, everyone who loves you.'

Corydon burst out, 'But do you truly know who I am? I am become Death, the destroyer of worlds! It was by my hand that Atlantis fell. I felled a city, a civilisation. I am more truly a monster than any. It is a pity my village did not kill me on the day when they made me their scapegoat.'

The lion said, indifferently, 'That is not the tale the stars tell. We gaze at the stars from our tower – that is how we know you – and they do not call you a murderer. In any case, what you say does not matter. What matters is that you love your friends, and they are your soul. And now you have another group of ragtags following you about and expecting protection. How are you to help them if you truly are Death, the destroyer of worlds? '

Corydon was appalled. He saw that he'd betrayed the desert kleptis gang as well as the monsters.

'But –' He wondered how to begin. 'I can't take action. Last time I made a wrong choice, a city died in pain. At least by living this simple life, I am not hurting anyone.'

'Look around you,' said the lion austerely. Corydon looked. The three kleptis boys were standing in a group, watching, listening, terrified of approaching the great lion. Azil's eyes were narrow with suspicion.

The lion said, 'Already one of your followers is powerful beyond your reckoning, and another carries a strange and terrible fate. And already, too, you and they have made powerful enemies.'

He stood up. A phalanx of winged lions was issuing slowly from the temple roof. They landed in the square, and were plainly about to bear their dead comrade away. They unfolded a white and gold bier, a kind of litter, and gently lifted the dead lion onto it.

'When you know yourself,' said the lion, 'then you may be of help to us. But now I choose to ask help of another.' Slowly, deliberately, he padded across to where the kleptis gang stood. It was plain the boys were terrified, but they stood straight, and waited.

'Alekhandros of Troios!' said the lion, in his deep voice. 'Stand forth. Your secrets are known, and they are not shameful. A task awaits you. It is difficult, but it is not impossible. Come.'

The three boys stood still, and their bodies made a kind of dreadful silence all around them.

Then Sikandar stepped forward. He lifted his chin proudly. 'I am Alekhandros, prince of the Trojans,' he said. 'What is your will?' His whole voice and personality had changed.

Azil drew in his breath sharply. His eyes widened. 'A prince!' he breathed. Bin Khamal, on the other hand, began quietly backing away. Corydon was astonished. Sikandar himself was almost in tears.

'I am sorry, lord,' he said to Corydon. 'I am sorry. I knew this might one day happen. Sooner or later. I could only hope for later.' He smiled faintly.

'But—' Corydon took his hand. Sikandar smiled again,

then gently let Corydon's hand drop. It was a gesture which seemed to seal him off behind a wall. The kleptis time was over, at least for him. But he turned for a last word. 'It is my fate,' he said, 'to resolve a quarrel between the Olympians. I hid because I cannot succeed. I can only fail. And when I fail I may take my people with me into darkness. Every day I was hidden was a day of peace and contentment for Troy. But now our time is done.'

'Then – don't do it!' Corydon called urgently, and Bin Khamal, too, ran and stood in Sikandar's way. 'Stop!'

'I cannot,' said Sikandar. 'Now I am discovered, I must judge. Must choose. If I do not, all the Olympians will unleash their wrath on Troy.'

Corydon shuddered. He knew what Olympian wrath was like. 'Then let me help you, if you must do it,' he said impulsively. 'Let me help. I know more of the Olympians than you do.'

'No one can help me,' said Sikandar. The great lion nodded. 'We too are compelled,' he said. 'Every day the winged serpents grow stronger. There are only a few of us left to guard Tashkurgan. This city too will go to dust and desert if the serpents rule it, for they will bring with them their king, the basilisk, and no people can live where he is. The Olympians are not our gods, but they have promised us that they will drive out the winged serpents if we can find the heir of Troy and persuade him to make judgement in their wars.'

'But you can't be stupid enough to believe them!' shouted Corydon. 'Surely by now you must know that they are liars. They will see you too as monsters, and they will break you too so that they alone may rule the people of Tashkurgan.'

'We have no choice,' said the lion, his voice sad. 'And we know that you too, Panfoot, have betrayed and abandoned your friends. I do not think you are on the serpents' side, but we cannot trust you. We cannot respect you, for you have run from yourself.' He and Sikandar began to move away.

Impulsively, Corydon spoke. 'Would you trust me and release Sikandar if Bin Khamal and I destroyed the nest of the winged serpents?'

There was a silence.

'How?' the lion asked pertinently.

Corydon looked up. Honesty was his only chance. 'I don't know,' he said. 'We might find a way. We must try, at least. If it will save both cities, how can we not try?'

'And I too am with you,' said Azil, to Corydon's surprise. Azil smiled, then shrugged. 'Well,' he said, 'the serpents are monsters. And I have no love for monsters. And if we succeed we will save cities of men.' Corydon found himself exchanging a grin of delight with Azil.

The lion was silent again. Then he spoke. 'Here is my say,' he said, and the phrase reminded Corydon sharply of the Sphinx. 'You have a whole moon to do as you promise – to find and destroy the nest of winged serpents. You must bring proof of your deed, the head of the serpent king. But the day after the moon is full, if even one winged serpent is seen over Tashkurgan, then Sikandar must fulfil his fate. He will remain with us. He will be safe.' He crouched, then sprang into the air, flying slowly towards the temple. His flight was heavy with sadness and foreboding.

Sikandar hesitated. 'Corydon,' he said, so perturbed that he forgot to say 'lord'. 'Corydon, do not do this. It will not save a single Trojan. And you will all die. And can we believe the lion? What if the serpents are right?'

Corydon could see his point. Both were monsters, of course, but monsters did not always get along. Both Talos the metal giant and Vreckan the Atlantic storm had been monstrous, but they had not been good. Monstrosity did not guarantee virtue any more than it forbade evil. He shrugged. They must judge when they met the serpents.

Now he moved to the side of the marketplace, where the camels were tethered, and began packing. His face was stern. He spoke curtly. 'Sikandar,' he said, '– or your highness,' he added ironically, 'you do not know what I did to Atlantis. This is my chance to make amends for the wrongs I did there. The Trojans are kin to the Atlanteans. Your city is crucial. Hera herself told me so. Atlantean ideas will one day defeat the Olympians. You cannot give your people up to the Olympians' anger.' Now his words came eagerly. 'We can hide you,' he said. 'Hide you in the desert. We are all hiding. We can go on hiding.'

Sikandar sighed. 'It is paradise to me,' he said, 'the life of a goatboy. But my heart tells me that it is over.'

Corydon finished packing the camel's saddlebags. 'Here,' he said. 'You keep the treasure. We will not need it, where we are going.' He handed Sikandar the bag of plunder. His last sight of his friend showed him climbing the temple steps, with the same slowness that had made the lion seem heavy in the air. Corydon hoped he could lift the unbearable burden of fate from both.

Another day out in the blankness of the desert, though this time their way was marked for them by the frowning hedge of the High Lebanon on their right. It broke the horizon, and Corydon didn't like it; he had relished the endlessness of the Sands, and his knowledge that out here no one would know him. The mountains reminded him too much of the Island of Monsters.

And his quest weighed on him. They were not directionless, joyous nomads now. They were a caravan, and their cargo – though no one could see it – was the life of two great cities.

The second day, they were riding along beside the mountains, when a sudden foul stench and a heavy sweep of batwings warned them that the winged serpents had seen them.

The creatures could breathe out as well as spit poisons so terrible that even Corydon and Bin Khamal were soon staggering from their effects. With no lions to fight them, the serpents kept coming; they flung themselves at the boys in waves of stink and sickness. Soon Azil was reeling in the saddle, his breath coming in gasps. Corydon's own lungs were burning, and his black camel was foaming at the mouth; he could barely keep her upright. They managed to bring down one – a superb shot from Azil's bow – but half a dozen took the place of the fallen one.

'Look!' cried Bin Khamal. Corydon saw that he was pointing to a crevice in the rocky wall of the mountains.

It might afford some protection. All three turned their mounts towards the gap, as the serpents plunged at them again and again; it was clear that their strategy was to weaken their prey systematically and to devour them when they had been overwhelmed by poison. They were mindless predators, who had learned that men were weak against them. Corydon was shocked; how could his fellow monsters be attacking so viciously? It turned his world upside down.

Corydon leapt off his mount, slapped her on the rump, hoped she would run fast enough to escape. Then he flung himself into the cave. He thought desperately that perhaps the serpents couldn't follow. The others landed beside him with heavy splashes; they lay in shallow water. Apparently the serpents were baffled by their sudden disappearance; Corydon could hear their raucous cries. Perhaps the water made it difficult for them to scent their prey, for after much swooping to and fro, their voices became more distant. The boys breathed a sigh of relief. But every time they tried to leave the shelter of the cave, they heard the ominous leathery swoop of returning batwings. Evidently the winged serpents hadn't given up.

'I think we should try to find a way through the cave,' said Azil firmly. He had never said so, but the others knew he feared the winged serpents to the depths of his being. Besides, he was right.

'If they can escape the serpents, the camels can run free. They will know us again. And we have a light,' said Corydon. He brought a small oil lamp out of his pack, and lit its wick with his tinder-box. Soft golden flame sprang up from its olive oil. He handed the lamp to Azil, hoping it would comfort the frightened boy. Then he scanned the rest of the cave. It was small and unimportant, but he'd noticed an entranceway, a hole that might lead them out, eventually . . .

They had been walking for hours in near-darkness. Corydon was certain that they were utterly lost in a vast underground maze of caverns that opened off each other like dreams. Most were the same red rock, big, small – some contained water so the boys didn't go thirsty – all were not warm, not cool. Corydon remembered seeing flutes of high rock soaring to the ceiling, bridges of rock as thin as silk. He remembered beaches of mud, and his shoes and clothes were soon coated in a kind of carapace of it.

But at last, when all of them were very weary and wishing earnestly that they had brought food instead of treasure from the camels, they came to a cave that was different from the others.

It was long and narrow, the shape of a man's throat, as if it were swallowing them. And it was striated with ribs sticking out from the crimson rock, ribs that were white . . . like shelves.

And that was when he saw them.

Row upon row of bottles in every jewel colour: opal and peridot and chrysophrase, agate and emerald and jade. Amethyst and ruby, garnet and turquoise. They were inlaid with gold and silver and every precious metal. Some were triangular, like tiny pyramids; others were square as dice. There were ovals and spheres, and every lissome lovely shape. Entranced, Corydon moved closer. Beside every bottle was a stopper of gold or silver. Each was shaped like a teardrop. Some bottles had their stoppers in them, as if something precious were already stored in there. The other boys gasped. It looked like their long and weary way had led them to unimaginable treasure.

Bin Khamal's gasp had not been a gasp of pleasure, however. It had been a gasp of horror. And as he looked at them more closely, he gave a scream, a dreadful sound that rang from roof and wall.

Azil turned to him. 'Why do you scream? These are riches enough to buy a whole city.'

Corydon sighed. 'It is not riches we seek,' he reminded Azil shortly. 'We seek to save our friend . . . Bin Khamal, what is the matter?' Bin Khamal was speaking in the tongue of his own people, of which Corydon had learnt only a few words; he caught the word for djinn, which he did know. 'Bin Khamal!' he shouted. 'Speak Arabic! Or Hellene! What is the danger?'

'The soul-traps,' Bin Khamal almost sobbed. 'Corydon, the soul-traps . . .'

Suddenly, to Corydon's astonishment, Bin Khamal rose into the air. He hovered there, as if lying on a comfortable bed. Then, with terrifying speed, he shot towards one of the walls. Corydon could see that his friend wasn't doing this himself; his mouth was open in a scream of terror. Also, as he flew, he was *shrinking*, and now already he was the size of a baby.

Corydon dived for the cave wall. Using all his kleptis climbing skills, he managed to scale the shelf-laden walls. His hasty feet sent bottles crashing to the cave floor, but he didn't have time to pause. He managed to fling himself at the now-tiny Bin Khamal as he hurtled towards the wall. But the boy was going faster than an arrow, and Corydon couldn't stop him from flying into the mouth of an open bottle.

The stopper leapt into the mouth of the bottle like a lover leaping into his beloved's arms.

Bin Khamal was gone. Corydon seized the bottle in one hand, holding desperately on to his shelf with the other. Climbing like a monkey, he reached the floor of the cave in seconds, and began trying to pull the stopper out.

It wouldn't budge.

Frustrated, he looked around.

Azil was crouched in the corner, plainly afraid.

And Corydon saw the smashed bottles from his hasty climb. He was about to hurl the bottle containing his friend to the ground also, when he saw . . . And what he saw made him freeze.

From each broken bottle, a thick mist was rising, condensing . . . There were ten or twelve of them.

Corydon began backing as soundlessly as he could until he stood against the wall. Then he extinguished the light.

The thin mists were casting their own glow. Now they were coalescing. Into a variety of forms.

They were djinn.

Corydon saw an elongated blue giant as tall as a

mountain rush past, his form strung out to such a length that he took five minutes to rattle by, faster than the fastest camel, a blur of movement. A troupe of stout pink djinn forced themselves through the entrance with a resonant squelch. A djinn flung himself into a whirlwind, and would plainly have been a sandstorm if there had been any sand to storm. Others simply made a harsh sucking noise, like a wave on sand, and flung themselves aloft.

'Wait!' shouted Azil suddenly, recovering his nerve. 'Aren't you supposed to grant us wishes?' But the djinn took no notice at all. Their one thought was escape.

Corydon remembered Bin Khamal because the bottle was agitating itself very slightly in his hand.

He flung it to the cave floor like the others, hoping Bin Khamal wouldn't just vanish into the cave as the others had. But although Bin Khamal raced twice around the cave in whirlwind form, he flung himself to the ground again. 'Run!' he cried. Corydon realised another bottle would trap his friend if they lingered, so he relit the lamp hastily as Bin Khamal rushed out of the cave end.

'Why don't they give wishes any more?' he asked, on Azil's behalf.

'Djinns give wishes only to lure people into releasing them. They are a promise. A golden lure. They are hard work; to make them come true, we have to put some of ourselves into each thing wished for, and that permanently ties us to earth and to humans. So we do it only when there is no other way. And you, Azil, should not be sorry. People began making traps like that one to try to force us to give them wishes, to harness our powers so that they might have bigger houses than their neighbour's, or more wealth, or prettier wives, or longer hair. Humans were willing to cage living things to be richer. Why should we of the Sands have any respect for that? And besides, human wishes always, always come to grief. The girl who wishes to be prettier than anyone else loses all her friends; the man who wishes for riches cannot sleep for fear that someone else is richer still. More does not mean more joy.'

After that, all they had to do was stumble through more spacious, shadowy caverns. Finally, after what seemed like long, hungry hours, Azil saw a faint light, and when they pursued it they found it was the last light of day, coming from an opening in the cave roof. They clambered swiftly up as the evening star emerged into the emerald sky of desert dusk.

It was too late to begin searching for the camels; they called a few times, but did not dare to make too much noise in case it attracted the serpents. They were all weary, but they were also all agreed that travel by night was safer than by day. They sat down for a short rest. Then they began walking, determined, sore-footed.

Corydon's heart was leaden. Why were they continuing? How were they to destroy the lair of creatures who had put them to flight so entirely? He didn't know. All they could do was go on, and hope, though there was no reason to hope.

δέλτα
Four

The cave opened on a slope, a scree of dry pebbles and sand. At the bottom, the light of the evening star showed the faint gleam of water. Corydon wondered if it was the beginning of the great marshes of the Two Rivers. He had sometimes heard traders speak of them, marshes so vast that the people who lived there built their houses on stilts and lived on fish, as their fathers had, with never a thought of books or jewels or silks. If so, it would be madness to venture into them without a guide, and he wasn't sure they led to their goal; the serpents were desert creatures. But skirting the outriders of the marshes might help to keep the serpents at bay. He said as much to the others.

Half an hour later, he was wondering if his decision had been the wrong one. The marshes reeked of death to a desert-lover; a stink of mud and spoiling fish. They were haunted by clouds of wailing insects which settled on their arms and legs and drank delicious draughts of their blood, leaving a raging itch as a present. The lamp seemed to attract them, and it was getting low on oil. Corydon thought that unless they were very lucky they would soon have to eat the lamp-oil, which had happened before, so he extinguished the warm fire, but that made it harder to see their way, and they all tumbled headlong into various deep pools so that all three were soon soaked. The coolness was pleasant to boys used to infernos of heat, but their clammy clothes slowed their movements. The moon was rising, but was in its last quarter.

Corydon struggled through the water, weeds and plants sticking to his feet. Azil followed. Bin Khamal was at the rear, fearfully looking around him. He was still stirred by the mad horror of the caves. Even his djinn-nerves were ragged, after the soul-traps.

A shadow shot past them, squealing furiously. The boys ducked. Suddenly a bat – no, something bat-like – hurled itself out of the darkness. It squealed ferociously, its claws flexing. More squeals reached the ears of the boys, and more of the bat-like creatures burst into view.

Corydon could see that they could not fight these enemies. There were too many, and it was too dark to use arrows. Azil, however, felt that they should, must at all costs, be fought. He drew an arrow, and prepared to use it as a dagger.

The beasts held back as if awaiting some sort of command. Corydon was able to get a better look at them. They were as large as a small child, and looked like a bat in every way, except for their long claws, about as long as his forearm, which were dangerously hooked, and glinted menacingly in the moonlight. There were three claws on each wing, he noticed. He also noticed that they were aggressive to each other as well as to strangers; they were pushing and shoving each other, waiting. It was as if they longed to fight.

Then, without warning, they charged.

Corydon had barely time enough to act as the first beast hurtled for his throat. His reflexes thought for him, and he managed to grab the beast's wingtip. It was hurled around in a circle, and then heaved itself onto his arm, trying to dig its claws in for purchase. He threw it from him into the marshy waters, flinging it as far as he could. But the creature rose from the waters effortlessly; it was plainly a swimmer.

'What are they?' Corydon panted, bracing himself.

Azil shouted, 'They are the guardians of a rare and fragrant spice called cassia. They are called the cassia birds. The marsh people gather the spice by wearing leather clothing and shielding their eyes.'

No wonder it's rare, thought Corydon wryly, *if that's what people have to face to get it.* Another cassia bird dived at him, trying to claw his head. Another sprang at his neck. Bin Khamal peeled the birds off, then threw them aside in disgust, as if they were detritus on the face of the desert.

'Here lies their treasure,' he said, pointing. They could see only a dim shrouded grove of bushes in the gloom, but the scent reached them, heavy and sharp, cutting sharply through the stench of the marsh.

All three boys backed slowly away from the cassia

bushes. As they moved further back, the cassia birds stopped their restless fidgeting and settled calmly.

'I think we're safe enough,' said Bin Khamal at last.

They left the swamp behind, at least. Many days' journey followed. And soon the yellow and grey sands swallowed them again.

And then every day was like the one before, only harder. Another day's journey in the sun of the desert. Another day of sand and parched mouths and dry tongues, and a longing for water so powerful all three boys felt they would sell themselves to get it. They had been able to carry little water with them, and it was almost spent. Nor did they know where water might be found; it had been Sikandar who was most adept at spotting the subtle signs – a greyish patch of sand, a sprig of dry grass, an old or withered tree. But when the boys tried to use his knowledge, it seemed to lead nowhere. Once they spent an hour digging in sand so hot it scorched their hands. And found nothing. They tried to rest in the heat of the day, but there was nowhere that gave shade.

Corydon began to wonder how long they could last.

Even the nights brought little relief. By now they were so hungry that they were forced to sleep on their bellies to quiet their growling protests. Their sleep was disturbed by the ache of exhausted, wasted bodies.

On the seventh day from the nests of the cassia birds, they saw a firelight on the horizon.

In their tired minds, there was only one thought. Fire meant people. People meant water. And food.

They began to stumble towards it through the darkness. Corydon felt he was moving through a nightmare. Azil had already tripped and fallen two or three times. Corydon's immense monster-strength allowed him to help the stricken boy from time to time, but he was himself in too much trouble to carry someone his own size. He could see that Bin Khamal was all right, and he could just about keep going himself, but Azil couldn't last long unless they found water soon. Water . . . Water . . .

Dawn found them and burnt their staring eyes as they crossed a salt pan. After just a few hours of sunlight, the temperature was so hot they could have fried an egg. If they had had an egg.

The firelight too had vanished. Corydon was not sure they were going towards it anymore. And he knew they must find water today, or Azil, at least, was doomed.

From behind the toiling boys, something black shot across the sky. Corydon strained his eyes to see what it was, but it was too fast for any shape to be clear.

'Winged serpent . . .' muttered Azil, in a dry barking voice, 'come to finish us . . .' He began trying to lay about him, as if he felt surrounded. It was exhausting his remaining strength. Corydon, his own mouth dry as an empty pot, tried to grab his hands. Both were distracted by low zooming sounds, as a hundred or so winged serpents sped overhead.

'Follow them!' Bin Khamal cried. He drew a line in the hard salt crust of the pan. 'They will lead us to water!'

Azil stopped fighting. 'Water . . .' he said, almost dreamily. Then he pitched forward onto his face. Corydon and Bin Khamal managed to set him on his feet again. By now he was clearly not himself. He kept moaning that he saw cascades of water, muttering about lush jungles and oases. Corydon found his words tormenting. He too could hardly help thinking of water all the time.

Something began to appear on the horizon.

It was – what was it? Something immensely tall. Taller than a man. Was it a column? A – a tree? Corydon strained his eyes.

A temple!

He remembered a map he'd seen in the city, a map which had shown the temple of the nymph of the desert, and he'd seen beside it the symbol for a permanent well, a well that was never exhausted or dry.

Corydon imagined the welcome the few sunbaked priests would give them; it was delicious to think of desert hospitality at its richest. They might even prepare a banquet. And most importantly, the water. Inside himself he questioned his own dream – how could a temple of nymphs have priests? – but he refused to let go of his ideas. He imagined the shade under the trees, by the cool stream that would lead them straight to the winged serpents' lair . . . Stream, said his remaining wits. What stream? This is the desert; a stream would run into the sand. But his mind clung to the bright glittering image. A stream. He could almost hear its voice, lulling and soothing his sand-rasped ears.

'A stream,' he said hoarsely to Bin Khamal.

Bin Khamal was puzzled. 'Where?'

'At the temple,' said Corydon. He pointed with his free

hand. 'There. The temple of the nymphs. With the kind priests.'

Bin Khamal took his hand softly. 'Corydon,' he said. 'There's nothing there. It's your mind. You're seeing a mirage.'

Corydon rubbed his eyes. He could still see the pillar. Then he rubbed them again, furious with them for deceiving him.

Hope fled. He wanted to lie down on the burning sand and die.

But he didn't do it. He kept on putting one foot in front of another. For just a little longer.

Rescue came unexpectedly, and from behind them.

There was a sudden thud of heavy camel footfalls. A pale camel came up so fast it almost cannoned into them. Its rider saw their plight at a glance. He stopped, dismounted, and offered the boys his water bottle.

Corydon handed the bottle to Azil first. He was delirious by now. Only water could save him. Then Bin Khamal insisted he drink. When they had all had a little water, Corydon discovered his true thirst again. He could have drained a river in spate. Oddly, he felt more thirsty than before he had had the water. But he also knew that the drink had saved his life.

The man who had saved them said nothing. He was obviously a trader. His saddlebags were full of cassia. Corydon decided not to say anything about their quest, but the man had already guessed something of their business.

'You're babes, you are,' he said. 'Get yourselves back

to a town. No one ever found any treasure but death out here. Take this,' and he handed them an extra water canteen. He flipped his reins on his camel's neck. The camel cantered away, and all three boys stood staring at the cool round of the waterskin in Corydon's hand. The sun burned down.

Corydon sighed. 'We must go on,' he said. Slowly, on heat-blistered feet, they began to move forward once more. No one asked to drink the precious water. They knew they must make it last. The landscape became hillier, and the dunes grew steeper and rockier; the boys slithered on pebble screes. Soon the dunes were not dunes at all, but hillsides, bare of almost all growth, blazing with silver stars of mica in the rockfaces where the sun struck them. Twice, the boys heard the thin cries of flying serpents. They knew they must be getting close. As the fierce sun gradually paled to red, Corydon saw something as he topped the great hill up which they had all been labouring. His head was light with hunger, but this time he felt sure that what he was seeing was no mirage.

'Look!' Bin Khamal's voice reached him at the same time as his eyes made sense of the sight. A narrow tower stood out from the folds of the hills ahead.

It reminded Corydon of Lady Nagaina's stronghold on the old Island of Monsters. Thinking of her hurt, so he tried to repress the memory – but surely that was a shattered dome on top of the tower, one just like the dome the hydra had made? Corydon realised that the tower had not been built by the serpents; it had been made by more ancient creatures, and the serpents were merely occupying it.

As the first stars rose in the east, and the sun dropped below the horizon, Corydon and Bin Khamal began cautiously to climb the clifflike hill below the tower. Azil had been told to wait for a day while they explored. He had been only too glad to curl up in camp; without monster-strength, he was almost spent.

As they climbed, as soft-footed as possible, Corydon could hear the hiss of the winged serpents' wings. He could also smell their odd spicy smell. It was clear that all of them were returning to the tower for the night. There were many loud shrieks of greeting; one coincided with the moment when Corydon dislodged a small stone, which rattled as if determined to give the boys away. Sweat broke out on their foreheads, but all was well. The serpent-shrieks grew so loud that they might not have heard if Corydon and Bin Khamal had begun singing to keep up their spirits. Soon the shrieking was so loud that Corydon and Bin Khamal would not have heard each *other* even if they had shouted. The noise grew so loud that Corydon felt his eardrums burning. But just as he felt he couldn't bear it for another instant, there was a single, long, imperious screech. At this, all the other screams and shrieks fell silent.

Bin Khamal and Corydon both felt sure there were words in that last cry, words of power, but they did not know the serpent-language. A long shriek began, with many different notes in it. They were certain now that a serpent was saying something important. Corydon tried to find meaning in the cry, and had almost worked out what it was that the serpent was saying when it abruptly stopped. Another cry began, and as the cries stopped and started Corydon began to feel as if it would never end. So when he finally reached the tower he was startled by the sudden intensity of the silence, only the hiss of wings as snakes flew to their nests, and settled down to sleep.

In the blackness, Corydon felt the rough stone of the archway entrance and stepped inside the building. His eyes adjusted to the darkness quickly, and as Bin Khamal stepped inside, Corydon saw that there were two large nests in the centre of the room. Inside them, two large serpents sat curled up, their long bodies intertwined; they were hissing softly to one another. The room stretched far beyond them; the boys could see a long line of burning torches receding into the far distance.

To his amazement, Corydon could make out a group of serpents clambering over the walls with some sort of paste in their – could they truly have hands? He noticed in amazement that they did have hands, a pair of fore-limbs that ended in a slender palm with long, malleable fingers. And what were they holding? Was it – could it be paint? As they drew lines with it, using very small, fine brushes, Corydon could see its slick blue gleam in the firelight. He looked at the walls around him, and was not surprised to see paintings there as well.

These paintings appeared to tell a story. First there was

a picture of many serpents painting and playing together. The elaborate curls and curves of the painting radiated pure joy. The second, however, was very different. The serpents had all stiffened, and it was clear why. In their midst stood three goddesses, all shouting and pointing towards a distant city over which lions were flying. Then there was a picture of an enormous snake cowering and bowing before the three goddesses, who all stood before what looked like a glowing egg; it was a jewel set in the wall. But it was the final picture that was the most frightening. The jewel had been split open. Standing in it were – well, what were they? Birdlike legs. Bright jewelled eyes. Vivid red scales. And two heads, one arising from each end of their long slender bodies.

'Amphisboena,' breathed Bin Khamal. 'Corydon, we must flee. Now. Amphis—' He choked on the word. 'We cannot stand against them. We cannot.'

His voice was low, but the heads of the two serpents whipped around. Their jewelled eyes seemed to pierce the gloom.

One of the serpents hissed softly, and the other put its tail to its thick red lips.

Corydon was puzzled. What was going on? Why were the winged serpents not attacking them, as they had in the desert? Something about the serpents' eyes – a look of anxiety, almost entreaty – caught and held him.

'They're asking us to be quiet,' he said softly to Bin Khamal.

'Why? We're obviously their enemies. Why don't they attack us? Or summon the amphis—'

The snakes repeated their gestures. Now they seemed urgent, even desperate.

One of the serpents began beckoning with his curling tail.

'They're trying to trick us,' said Bin Khamal.

'There is good in all monsters,' Corydon replied. 'Even if there is very little good, there is *some* good.' Bin Khamal looked abashed. If Corydon had not thought the same of him, how could their friendship have endured? He nodded silently. Corydon could see he had accepted the idea.

The serpents flew into a nearby room, wagging their tails comically, trying to beckon again. Then they flew out, waved their tails again, looked exasperated.

'I think they want us to follow them,' said Corydon, feeling stupid. Hastily, the boys moved through the sleeping serpents, stepping carefully over outspread wings and scaly tails, and into the room which contained the serpents who appeared to have befriended them. Almost immediately one of the serpents picked up a log of wood, and pushed it against the door, shutting out all light from the corridor, and leaving them in the dim light of a single orange torchflame.

Then both serpents turned and gave long, low, rhythmic hisses. Then snarling shrieks. Then low, ululating screams. It was obvious that they were trying to tell a story, but it was like watching a play performed in an unknown language.

'We do not know your language, if you will forgive us,' said Bin Khamal. The serpents looked baffled.

Then, understanding, one of them picked up a dry twig and began drawing a series of intricate pictures on the ground, in the thick dust and sand silted there.

First, they drew a picture of Corydon and Bin Khamal. Corydon could easily recognise himself by his goaty leg and his shepherd staff. Then they drew a pair of beaming serpents, looking insanely happy, with wings outstretched.

'You know,' said Corydon dryly, 'I think they are trying to tell us that we are welcome.'

'Great,' said Bin Khamal. He copied the serpents' cheesy grins as best he could, beaming and waving his arms. The serpents began grinning and waving their wings. Bin Khamal waved back. Corydon began to wonder how long this might go on.

Suddenly the serpents became far more serious. The one with the twig drew a picture of a crowd of happy serpents, drawing and painting. Corydon was abruptly reminded of Euryale. The memory ached, so he tried to concentrate on what the serpents were saying.

Then he noticed something else. The serpents in the picture were not in the tower. Instead they were living near rocks, and above them there was nothing but a starry sky.

'They were nomads,' Bin Khamal said. 'Just like us.'

The serpents drew a picture, under the same sky.

Then they drew a picture that was five times the size of all the others. It showed a huge serpent with fangs bared, tail stiffly upright, rearing up. A forked tongue was extended and the eyes were enormous.

Bin Khamal gave a cry of horror. The serpents, too, shrank back from their own drawing.

'Ahriman, Ahriman,' moaned Bin Khamal.

Corydon was puzzled. 'Who is Ahriman?' he asked.

The serpents had flung themselves away from the very sound of the word. Bin Khamal too covered his face in his hands, as if trying to blot out the fearsome sight. Between his fingers, he whispered, 'The Lord of the Dark. The Betrayer. The Evil One.'

Corydon was more puzzled than ever. 'Zeus?' he asked tentatively, remembering that Sthenno had once called Zeus 'The Ruler of the Darkness of This World'.

'No, not Zeus,' Bin Khamal said. 'Darkness itself. Not the one who rules it. The dark. The dark.'

Corydon felt lost. Why was dark so fearsome? He remembered the desert sky awash with silver stars, warm nights in the cave of the gorgons when the fire had shrunk to a single point of red. Why should darkness be terrible?

He looked at Bin Khamal. His friend, whom he had known for a year of joyous marauding. Corydon suddenly realised that he didn't know Bin Khamal. His thoughts were as foreign to Corydon as those of the serpents. And he suddenly realised that he himself was speaking a tongue that was strange to him. 'γνοθη σεαυτον,' he said very softly, in Greek. 'Know yourself.' Bin Khamal was staring too intently at the huge serpent to notice.

'It's just a monster,' said Corydon, loudly and clearly. 'Like me. Like you.'

'No, you fool!' Bin Khamal's voice was a hiss. 'This is

evil, itself. The father of all lies. Lies about monsters, lies about heroes. It all comes from here.'

'How can it all come from here?' Corydon asked, sceptically. 'These people are small in the large scheme of the universe.'

'Sometimes the small see what is hidden from wider walkers,' said Bin Khamal stubbornly. 'Listen, Panfoot. This is the Lord of Darkness, but he entered creation because of the Lord of Light. The Holy Fire God, Ahura Mazda, knew of the Lord of the Dark, and he yearned to do battle with him and expunge him. Because of that yearning, he bound himself in space and time, and in doing so he accidentally allowed his rival a being also. It is that being you see. He is here because the Lord of Light willed to defeat him. And he will go down to dust. But not today. Today he still has immense power.'

Corydon sighed. 'Bin Khamal, I have met the gods, and none of this rings true. The gods are not darkness, and they are not light. They are neither and both, just as men are.'

One of the winged serpents was drawing with swift urgent strokes. Corydon looked in astonishment at what it had made. A mountain, swathed in clouds.

'The home of Ahura Mazda,' said Bin Khamal.

'That isn't the home of Ahura Mazda,' said Corydon, after a long pause. 'That is Mount Olympos, where dwell the Olympian gods, who have sworn to expunge monsters from the earth.'

Bin Khamal scratched his head. 'Well,' he said, 'perhaps it is a different mountain.'

'It looks just like Olympos,' said Corydon stubbornly. 'And I will not take up arms against any whose enemy is the Olympians.' The serpents began to chatter anxiously, sounding more than ever like a flock of birds.

'But we have to kill him,' Bin Khamal pointed out. 'He is their leader. In a way. We can make a bargain with them; if we kill him, they stay away from the city, and we take his head to the winged lions. And then release Sikandar.' He sounded stubborn, but Corydon wondered where all his optimism came from. First Ahriman was dreadful darkness, and now suddenly he was a beetle to be crushed?

Corydon saw Sikandar's pale and fragile face in his mind's eye. He wanted to save his friend, his vulnerable friend. But not this way. Not by contributing to the plans of any Olympian, whether they were led by Zeus or someone with a different name but the same plans for the world.

'I can't,' he said simply. 'I can't do it. I want to help. But this is not the way.'

The winged serpents stopped chattering and stared at him, shock, sadness, and surprise on their reptilian features. Bin Khamal too looked hurt. 'I thought you would help,' he said sadly. 'But you won't. You won't even help these monsters,' he said, gesturing at the serpents, who were writhing in coils of sadness.

Corydon felt a familiar pang. *Corydon the Betrayer*, he thought. *Corydon the destroyer of worlds.* But he had learnt one thing from the wreck of Atlantis: no gain, no friend, was worth obeying an Olympian. And he felt sure this was all a crucial part of an Olympian's plan.

'We are being moved about like gaming pieces!' he cried. 'Can you not see it?'

'It is you who are blind!' shouted Bin Khamal. 'How can we do anything other? Of course what we do is controlled by the great gods!'

By the Olympians, thought Corydon. His heart was as heavy as a sack of grain. Had all these months hiding in the desert been in vain? *I might just as well have gone straight home to Sthenno and Euryale,* he thought sadly. *At least I would have seen them.* Thinking this made him remember the aching gap that was Medusa, and suddenly the impossibility of the choices before him overwhelmed him. He sat down abruptly. 'Do as you will,' he said to Bin Khamal. 'I can do no more.'

'You cannot escape your destiny that way,' said a new voice.

Corydon looked up. The voice had come from a vast winged serpent, forked tongue lolling. It had the deadly face of the drawing. Corydon smiled in bleak recognition. But he couldn't bring himself to care. It was clear that his escape was over; he was entangled in an Olympian web again. But he could at least struggle.

'Yes, I can,' said Corydon.

'I will kill you,' said the serpent.

Corydon shrugged. 'Yes, you can,' he said. 'Do it if that is your will. But it is no victory.'

The serpent's lolling mouth gaped wider as he smiled. 'You are right,' he said. 'For me to attain victory, I need to win you to my allegiance.'

'I have no allegiances,' said Corydon flatly. He was

thinking of Atlantis. The last time he had formed an allegiance, thousands of people had perished.

'Yes, you do,' said the serpent. 'And by them you can save what remains of your people.'

'I have no people.' He thought of the village where he was born. He thought of the monsters, of Medusa's pale dawn-lilac skin, of Sthenno's brassy wings. He thought of the warm rumble of the Minotaur's voice. He thought of the old kleptis gang and the new one, of Bin Khamal standing tense and furious at his side. He thought, *They are all my people.* 'I have no people and I have all people,' he said. 'I do not have an allegiance.'

'But though you may think all people are yours, they do not agree,' said the serpent, smoothly. Somehow Corydon found himself thinking of the heroes. Of Dolphin and Shell leaders. Of all the humans who had looked at him with horror and hatred. Even among monsters, there had been Vreckan.

He lifted his head. 'They may not agree,' he said steadily, 'but they are still my people.'

'So simple,' said the serpent calmly.

'I *am* simple,' said Corydon. 'I'm just a shepherd. I'm not a god or a sphinx.'

'But you are the son of a god,' said the serpent. Its eyes flashed with a sudden hot light.

Corydon thought of his father.

'That is what makes all people mine,' he said, 'because I am myself of many kinds. Many-minded. Because my father himself is goat and man, all god, and my mother is—' He paused. He wished he felt more certain about his mother.

'Do you have a mother?' Now the serpent sounded solicitous. Kindly.

'I have many,' said Corydon stoutly. To himself he added, *many and none. But for a while I had Medusa. And Sthenno, and Euryale.*

'Many is not the same as one,' said the serpent. 'Nor is it as good.'

'Perhaps,' said Corydon. 'But since you are not yourself my mother, of what use are you to me in this matter?'

'Ah,' said the serpent, with a long, melancholy pause. 'But I know. I know many things. I know, Corydon Panfoot. I know the name of your true mother. I know where you can find her. And if you will become my servant, I will tell you what I know in exchange.'

Now Corydon paused. 'Become your servant?' he said.

'Do me a service, at least.'

Now Corydon turned his back. 'I serve nobody,' he said. 'And I make no bargains.'

The serpent-voice was unexpectedly gentle. 'Because your last bargain went awry. But it does not follow that all bargains will do so. Why do you find it impossible to trust me, when you have trusted this boy beside you, and your other friends, and your friends the monsters?'

Corydon spoke curtly. 'I have known you for only a few minutes. I have known them much longer.'

'But it was your heart which told you to trust them. What does it tell you now?'

'It tells me that I do no service for anyone.'

'You are no longer a monster, then,' the serpent purred, 'for you are not as we are. Monsters, little shepherd boy, are the ones who can feel.' When it said the word *feel*, it came out as a long hiss. 'We are soft and muddled with feelings. But you have shut yourself off to feelings. Now you might as well be an eidolon.'

Corydon suddenly snapped to attention. 'What do you know of eidolons?' he said.

'Ah.' The serpent gave vent to a soft venomous sigh, a breath of poison. 'That is something else I know. I know where your missing monster is. Yes, I do know. The girl with snakes. I know very many things, little boy. And if you will serve me, I can give you knowledge. For there is so much, so much you do not know about what and whom you love. So much.'

Corydon was struggling with curiosity. But he was also halted by glaring realisation.

'I know about temptation,' he said. 'I know about tests. I have been tempted by the waters of Lethe. By death itself. Himself. You have no knowledge,' he added. 'You have only information. But I will hear you out. What service do you want from me?'

'It is a simple matter,' said the serpent. 'I would like you to kill me and take my head to the winged lions.'

Corydon strove to conceal his amazement. What did the creature mean?

'I will explain,' said the serpent. 'By dying and rising again, I will become a god. When my head is nailed to the gate of the city, I will live again. And I will be able to influence multitudes, sway thousands – Corydon, perhaps I might even overthrow the Olympians in due course.' A glinting longing shone in his eyes.

'But you would only replace them with your own tyranny!' Corydon shouted in a burst of realisation. 'You are not an earth-god – you have no place, as my father has a place, or as the Lady of Flowers has a place. You have no link to the earth, nor to water. You want only power over men's minds.'

Viciously, he added, 'It's all rather sad, actually.'

'Oh, yes,' said the serpent, with apparent calm. 'Very sad that you will never return home.' He gave two shrill whistles, and the creatures they had seen on the painting in the corridor stepped out from behind them.

Amphisboenas. A small courtesy from one of the Olympian goddesses. Just to make sure Sikandar would be forced to choose.

The serpent's grin widened. 'You see,' he said. 'I do know things. I know, for example,' he said, 'that you are about to die without knowing your mother's name. *That* is what I call sad.' He pressed his long forked tongue close to Corydon's face. The stench was horrible.

There was a sudden sound, taking Corydon by surprise. With a slither of scudding feet, Azil flung himself into the room. Corydon guessed that he had been worrying about why the party had not returned, and had come to see for himself. He had seen the winged serpent king, and before Corydon could stop him, he gave his high, strange war-cry.

'No! Don't!' Corydon could see that Azil was about to grant the serpent's wish. He had spoken too late. Azil had already fired two sharply-barbed arrows at the serpent's jewelled eye. He was too good a bowman to miss at such a short distance. Bubbling black blood poured out. But the serpent gave a chuckle of triumph.

'I shall be . . . a god . . .' he whispered. 'Panfoot . . . a god . . .'

Corydon bent low. 'My mother!' he said, his voice fierce and urgent.

'She is . . .' But life was ebbing from the serpent's body. His head lolled. Then fell to one side, as his body coiled itself one final time, then stiffened. The amphisboenas closed in. Corydon could see the birdlike legs, the brilliant eyes. They glowed red as poppies. Their two heads swayed like Nile serpents, as if trying to hypnotise the boys. Their long slender bodies were poised like the bodies of cats.

Bin Khamal and Azil were ready. The amphisboenas plunged one of their heads into the mouth of the other head, and tucked in their legs. They had formed themselves into hoops, like children's toys. Then with incredible speed, they rolled forward, straight at the boys. One of them reached Corydon in less than a heartbeat, and knocked him to the stone floor with the force of its impact. The amphisboena had somehow uncoiled in midair, so that one of its heads was free to strike savagely at his throat. Corydon summoned all his strength and pushed violently at the creature, flinging it away from him; by good luck it struck the flying hoop-form of the other amphisboena aiming itself at his prostrate body. For a second or two they were entangled, then with a spit they separated, hissed, and formed themselves into hoops once more, aiming now at Bin Khamal and Azil. They had found Corydon too tough a morsel.

Quickly, Corydon drew an arrow from Azil's quiver, and hurled it at one of the rushing hoops. The squeal of the amphisboena was a fierce scream of pain. Bin Khamal rushed forward and clove it in two. Grimly, he shouted, 'Look! I have restored it to nature!' It was true. Each end now had its own head. But the serpent was not able to enjoy it; after a few feeble thrashes, it lay still in its noisome blood.

Then Bin Khamal and Corydon remembered the second amphisboena. Turning, they saw it, crouched on Azil's chest, its claws sunk into his body. It was rearing back to strike his neck. Corydon and Bin Khamal grasped its two heads. Each one took a thin neck. They flung it from them, against a wall. It slumped, unmoving. Bin Khamal ran it through with his dagger.

Bin Khamal spoke soberly. 'It is easier to fight them in a confined space,' he said. 'In the desert they will follow a horse or a camel for days in their swift hoop form. And they wait for you to make camp. Then in the blackness they attack . . .' While he listened to his friend's desert lore, Corydon had not noticed that Azil was on his feet, oddly triumphant. Shouting his strange war-cry, he drew a knife from his belt and began hacking off the head of the great snake.

'No!' The cry came from Corydon.

'We have to save Sikandar,' said Azil, and went on cutting doggedly.

'But he said that when his head is hung on the gate of the City of Winged Lions, that he would become a god, with the power to control men's minds,' said Corydon. 'Azil, you do not want that.'

Azil averted his head. Without looking at Corydon, he said, 'Friends come first.' He gave a last slash with his knife, and the head came free. Dark algae-green blood spurted onto the floor, and the stone hissed under its power. Corydon looked into the serpent's dead, jewelled eyes. His spine prickled. The serpent was no Olympian . . . but might it be true that he shared their aspirations?

έψιλον

FIVE

The exhausting journey back to the city went by in a walking nightmare. He was always aware of the presence of the serpent's head, its eyes unsleeping. Somehow the head connected his dreams with Medusa. But she did not come to him as he had last seen her. Instead, he lived her death again and again, and woke to cold stars and the icy finger of the serpent's unseeing gaze on his back. And yet . . . All his instincts told him to run, but he was curious; would he truly become a god? And would a monster-god be different? As his father was different? Or would the serpent-lord be just another Olympian behind his scaly mask?

Not for the first time, Corydon longed for his father's voice, for his friendly touch. But out in the desert his father was all but silent; the desert was not his place, Corydon realised, for the first time. His father's place was the land around the Middle Sea, its pastures and hills. He had been almost silent in Atlantis, but for one dream . . . So it was here. Corydon had no wish for his father to seek control of the earth entire, like an Olympian. His absence was proof of his truth.

They reached the Winged Lions' city of Tashkurgan at dawn on the second-last day of the month. Its remembered white walls were flushed a faint red by the rising sun, so it looked as if it were tainted with blood. They had to wait for the great gates to open when the rays of the sun turned the topmost tower to molten gold. Then the guard on duty ushered them in. Carrying their poisonous, heavy burden swathed in a blanket, the three boys made their way to the white temple.

The lion on the steps opened wide his golden eyes. 'Good,' he said. 'You have met your fate.'

'Take me to the priest,' said Corydon evenly, 'for your city must choose rightly or you shall meet yours! And it will be terrible,' he added.

Bin Khamal abruptly raised his voice in what sounded like a song of bitter lamentation. 'Your temples will lie broken into pieces, and your houses will be empty and roofless,' he said sternly. 'You will be the sport of those you once called slaves. No voices will sound in the streets of Tashkurgan, but only the scream of the wind. Your old men will take their wisdom to the grave, and your young boys will be forced to beg for bread in strange lands, and the jackal will roam in the streets of Tashkurgan, and—'

'Bin Khamal!' Corydon spoke sharply. 'This does not help us.' Already the guard was looking angry. But he ushered them into the priest's presence.

He was an immense lion, evidently venerable, with a mane turned as white as the city walls. The lion who had brought them whispered urgently in his ear. The priest's long tail twitched twice.

'You threaten Tashkurgan,' said the lion. 'You have helped us, but now you menace us?'

'It is not we who menace you,' said Corydon. 'But if I have truly helped you, I would like to speak to you, that I might beg for a boon.'

'We will allow your friend to go,' said the lion-priest.

'That, yes,' said Corydon, feeling his courage balling inside him, hard. 'But I also wish this serpent's head to be immediately destroyed, not raised as a trophy.'

The lion opened his mouth a little, showing his teeth. It was a movement of surprise, but it had the effect of intimidation. Bin Khamal, as always, reacted to his own fear with angry bravado. 'You must,' he said fiercely. 'Or your city will be the abode of djinn.'

'The mouth is near the heart,' said the priest after a long silence. 'I know what you are, my friend. An abode of your kind . . . The sands are your abode, and all night you hear their siren song. An abode of djinn. So you would wish, I see.' Corydon could also see. He could see that the priest thought that destroying the head was a conspiracy. He tried desperately to sound calm and reassuring.

'No,' said Corydon. 'It is not our wish—' But the priest was not listening. Waving his paw gracefully, he motioned at the blanket bundle, green and glistening with slime. 'Take this and nail it to the gate of Tashkurgan,' he said.

'No, please—' But the lion was already leaving the room. Corydon had no choice. He flung himself at the winged lion who bore the head, and tried to retrieve it. Azil held him back, but Corydon, using his monster-strength, managed to wrest the stiff, horrible head from its covering. He threw it to the ground, and was about to stamp on it, when Azil managed to knock him sideways, as the winged lion pounced on the head. Battered, stained with blood, its eyes still compelled. Corydon got to his feet, but it was too late; the lion had taken off, his slimy burden clutched in his paws.

Corydon ran to the gate.

And reached it just as the lion was fastening the serpent's head into position with a long iron spike.

There was a hard flash of green. And the serpent's head began to grow.

The lion sprang back in amazement.

The serpent's head continued to swell venomously, like a coiling snake about to strike down its prey. The eyes were alight with the livid, sick hue of death. Rank poison streamed from it. And yet Corydon felt that it was putting on an act. Because he was a song-maker, he understood that the serpent was making itself into a story, the story of absolute evil. The creature was making it up, though it was also real; the serpent wanted to impress everyone, wanted it so badly that he was willing to kill an entire city to make sure they were truly and properly impressed.

Perhaps the Olympians were no different. Making themselves. Were all gods poets, in an odd way? It gave him a feeling of dreadful kinship with the serpent, and with the gods, too. Making themselves. Poesis.

He spoke to the gathering and swelling horror.

'You don't have to do this!' he shouted. 'You can be anything! Why be a nightmare?'

'I choose to be a monster!' the terrible voice said, hoarsely.

'You are not a monster! You are a servant of the Olympians! The Olympians care only to be worshipped, and so it is with you!'

'You cannot change the rules to suit yourself! I am a monster. It is I who am your true father now, your true mother also. I am the true father of us all. The father and mother of all monsters.'

Corydon went on speaking steadily as the green darkness thickened. 'You are not a monster. You are merely the Olympians' mirror image. You do not deny them. You confirm them. You are only their shadow. Monsters are themselves, beyond the high gods.'

The green darkness flickered briefly, then deepened to near-black. Corydon felt he was standing at the bottom of a dank pool. The sun was invisible.

'Fool!' boomed the voice, growing in strength. 'Yes, I am their servant. I serve because I will share thereby in their power.'

Corydon raised his own voice. He felt his knees begin to shake as the serpent's power gathered, but he held himself upright. 'My father has a power you can never understand. My mother, too, whoever she was; the power to make life rather than to devour it. I am not your son. You have no son.'

Now the voice was silky. 'Look and see my family,' said the serpent.

Corydon turned. The people of Tashkurgan were standing behind him, lions and men and women. All were still, silent. All had their eyes fixed on the serpent's eyes, which now lit up the green darkness like white torches.

'Your father has no power here,' said the serpent. 'He is bound to the Middle Lands. The High Gods, the Olympians, rule everywhere.'

'My father does have one power here,' said Corydon. 'He has me. I am his son.'

'You can do nothing,' said the beast-head. 'And now your friend Sikandar has a choice to make.' Its mouth opened. The dry forked tongue writhed, and it gave a rusty laugh.

Sikandar was suddenly beside him, materialising in the darkness.

The boys' mouths dropped open in astonishment and horror. Their journey had been for nothing. For nothing. The words seemed to hang in the heavy air. In the midst of his nausea Corydon suddenly realised that the serpent himself was nearly nothing. It was pretending. It was speaking and acting as it thought a god would. From the stories about Ahriman, the serpent had formed an idea about absolute evil. Now the beast had thrown its dry heart into the part.

Corydon knew how hopeless it was to regret his actions, but he felt haunted by the crying ghost of the fresh dawn for which he had hoped: four boys riding away into the peace of emptiness. The clear pale light. The setting moon.

He thought of his father, longing for the warmth of his embrace.

Then he remembered.

'You are no god,' he said clearly. 'I will never worship you.' He drew in a breath. The fetid air seemed to choke him. 'Tell me about my mother. Tell me who she was,' he said.

The serpent gave a horrible, hissing laugh, a laugh that sounded like pebbles being pushed into a bottle. 'Why,' said the rasping tongue, 'should I tell you? I have no reason to do that.'

Sikandar put a cold hand on Corydon's arm. 'I must end this,' he said. 'I must make the choice.'

Bin Khamal spoke too. 'Corydon, he may not even know. He is just trying to taunt you.'

The serpent spoke again. 'Of what use would it be to know? You know who your father is, but it is of little use to you. He has not helped you, he has –' the serpent's laugh rattled out again '– he has *deserted* you.' The pun delighted him. 'Out here, his kind have no power. Here there is only blackness, or white light. Nothing between. The sky gods understand this. That is why they gave me power. And now, little friend,' its voice became a sibilant hiss, like stones rattling in a dry riverbed, 'now you must make your choice.'

Sikandar spoke again. Corydon could see that he was shaking with fright. But he controlled his voice. 'Tell my friend who his mother was,' he said. In the imperious tone, the other boys could hear for the first time the voice of a little prince, used to getting his own way.

'Have you not learned by now that you cannot bargain with the immortals, little princeling?' the serpent sneered. 'You would rather make the fatal choice than see every winged lion die?'

'You have no power to do that!'

The mouth smiled. 'I see you require proof.' The forked tongue flickered. The green-dark lifted. Into white brilliance stepped two winged lions. Their jewelled eyes were open, but it was clear that they saw nothing. Corydon saw that the mouth of one lion gaped a little, and his tongue lolled, like that of the serpent head. The serpent god gave a prolonged hiss. The lions took off in a wobbly, shaking flight. Then, as they drew near the high wall of Tashkurgan, they collapsed into it, smashing themselves against it repeatedly as they fell. They landed, twitched once, and were still. The white wall was stained with their blood. The serpent's nostrils twitched as if it were drinking in the smell of death. 'I enjoyed that. Would you like me to do it again, but with passengers?' said the serpent. Sikandar gave in at once. 'I will choose,' he said, gazing at the immobile bodies. From somewhere among his robes, he drew an apple, shining gold.

'Great Ones!' the serpent cried. 'I am among you now. I have done your will.'

Abruptly, the darkness vanished. It was bald, ordinary morning. The people of Tashkurgan blinked in the light. But they still stared at their new god as if their eyes could not drink enough of him. Thus, they missed the arrival of three female figures, who appeared with stunning suddenness in front of Sikandar.

One was Hera; Corydon's stomach gave a sick squirm as he saw her blonde helmet-hair. The second was Athene. Her grey gown was spotless, immaculately ironed, set in clean folds over her ample, solid bosom. Her hair was plaited very neatly. She had a scrubbed, very *healthy* pink-and-white face.

With sudden loathing, Corydon noticed that she wore a kind of elaborate shawl, or scarf, around her neck. On it was what was obviously meant as a portrait of Medusa's severed head. He almost retched.

'I must choose the fairest,' said Sikandar. 'I must decide what all men desire most.'

To Corydon, neither of them was remotely beautiful.

The third goddess was also a stranger. To his surprise, Corydon saw Sikandar smile feebly at this one.

'Have you chosen her?' he asked urgently.

'No, but I may,' Sikandar said.

Corydon looked at her. 'Why?' he asked bluntly.

'Because I know her, at least,' said Sikandar desperately. 'Her name is Aphrodite and she's a sort of aunt.'

Aphrodite did not look like any aunt Corydon had ever seen or imagined. She was tiny. She looked dark and sulky, with full ripe lips, full ripe body. Full ripe hair. She preened a little. Corydon was reminded of Fee, but Fee had been much prettier.

With her came a mirror, and in it Corydon could see the figure of another woman brushing long flaxen hair in front of another mirror. It made him dizzy. Too many mirrors.

'That's Helena,' said Sikandar. 'She will give her to me

if I choose her. I have to choose her, really. She's my aunt. In my family, we always help other family members. 'We're – well, we're the Family. We always help out other family members,' he repeated.

'But Sikandar,' said Corydon, 'the others are far more powerful. And they'll be really angry if you choose her. I've seen the wrath of Hera. She sank Atlantis. And Athene transformed a friend of mine into a snaky-haired goddess.' *And she chose to stay that way,* he thought suddenly. Which didn't justify Athene's action.

Sikandar shook his head again. 'I have to choose this one,' he repeated stubbornly.

'It's not that you actually want the girl, is it?' Corydon asked anxiously.

'Of course not!' Sikandar said scornfully. 'Who would? I know she's pretty, and I see why men like her, but she's a grown-up and a nuisance, too.' He dismissed her with a wave of his hand.

Corydon was not so sure. He thought that in the silvery mirror Helena had looked rather dangerous. Magical, and powerful. And as if to confirm his thoughts, she spoke again.

'Sikandar,' she said, and Corydon admired the clever way she had caught Alekhandros's name, 'Sikandar, if you choose me I can have adventures too. I won't be a nuisance. I'd love to roam in the desert like you. I don't care about clothes, or jewels. Sikandar, my husband is three times my age. I just want to have the kind of good times you have. Please.'

Sikandar hesitated.

Corydon turned to the image of Helena.

'Listen, Helena,' he said. 'Be careful. Be careful about your wishes. You are trying to escape from who you must be. I know; I too wish for that.'

'But why must I be it?' she said. She was almost crying. 'Why can I not choose? I want to be a child, to play and hunt and have adventures. Why must I always be a woman, a wife?'

Corydon suddenly saw that she was as caged by her fate as he was, perhaps more caged than he had been when the pirates had shown him as a freak. She saw the image in his mind, and smiled. 'Yes,' she said, 'it is like being a monster in the freak show. I want to go where people cannot *look* at me.'

Now he was reminded abruptly of Medusa. She too had hated being seen. He felt a warm rush of pity.

And Sikandar evidently felt it too. 'All right,' he said. 'All right. It is clear that all my choices will bring doom. But perhaps I can give one person a few days of happiness by one choice, and I can see no prospect of that in the other choices. I choose Aphrodite. And I shall take Helena as my – companion.' He held out the apple to the goddess.

Aphrodite gave a smile of pure triumph. She stuck her tongue out rudely at the astonished Athene and Hera, snatched up the apple, and took a huge bite of it. It did not seem to worry her that it was made of gold. Her white teeth snapped gleefully.

And as she bit, the other two goddesses gave loud shrieks of fury that did not die away. Instead, they grew louder and louder and louder until they sounded like the howling of the wind.

The serpent head tried to cast his green darkness again. But the eldritch shrieking somehow clawed it to thin tatters, which were blown away by sharp gusts of wind.

Athene's voice rose, steady, calm, a little reproachful. 'It was not for this,' she said, 'that we allowed you to be a god.' Her voice rose again in a cry of fury.

'We did not give you a city,' said Hera, 'so that the harlot could be awarded the prize.' Her voice too rose in that thin scream.

The serpent's darkness refused to re-form. Corydon saw his tongue twitching, and then his head beginning to writhe. A sudden gust of stormy sand blew into his eyes, and their glitter was dimmed.

'Godling,' said Athene, and now her voice was almost caressing, 'little godling. You have not served us.'

'And now,' said Hera, 'we shall keep our promises. You shall be a god, and you shall have your city. But now we shall raise the djinn against you and they shall engulf your city in sand in a storm that lasts for ten years. No one shall hear you. No one shall know you. No one shall see you. You will be a god, but you will be buried under all the sands of Arabia. You shall know your fate. And all men shall know the fate of Tashkurgan, the city destroyed, scrubbed clean by the sand of the High Gods.'

Already, Corydon could hear the high whine of the approaching djinn. He motioned urgently to Bin Khamal, who stood with his face white.

'As for you,' and now Athene turned to Sikandar, 'as

for you, princeling of Troy, Zeus has decreed your doom long ere this, but we shall be its messengers. Your tallest towers will fall, and flames shall engulf you; you who seek to walk in the footsteps of Atlantis shall die in fire as did she in water.' Her voice held an anger that was greater than the sounds of the gathering sandstorm.

'It is fitting,' said Hera, her voice full of spiteful satisfaction, 'that Atlantis perished in water, Troy will be ruined in fire, and Tashkurgan in air and earth.'

'You who had faith in the little gods of place,' said Athene, her words sharper than the sting of the sand, 'shall die in their elements. Do you understand? It is we who command.'

'Bin Khamal!' hissed Corydon desperately. His friend reached his side.

'Corydon,' he shouted, raising his voice above the scream of wind and sand, 'I can do nothing. These are not the djinn of my tribe, but the efreets of the far south. I can do nothing – I do not even speak their tongue.'

And it was true. The clouds that were encroaching on the city's walls were different from the other djinn Corydon had seen. And he was reminded suddenly of Vreckan; the efreets looked greedy, and their burning sand made earth and sky the same substance, as Vreckan had united sea and sky.

He knew no one would hear him well above the roar of the efreets, but he spoke all the same. 'Bin Khamal, run! Find your father. I pray we meet again. Sikandar – Prince – you must warn them in Troy. Go!'

'I will help him,' said a low voice that could be heard

below the shrieking winds. The small, dark goddess was there, her eyes slumbrous. 'If Troy is to burn,' she added, 'it will burn with the flames of love.' She took the mirror, put it in Sikandar's hand, and led the way into the gathering sand.

Corydon turned to Azil. 'Go,' he said, as gently as the wind allowed. 'Have the life for which you were born. Be a shepherd.'

But Azil ignored him; perhaps did not even hear him. He had already put his bow to his shoulder, arrow on the string. Sobbing, he fired at the oncoming storm.

A hand made of cloud and sand came out of it and tore him from the ground, hurled him up into the air. Then the hand let him drop. Corydon saw the tiny black shape falling, falling. A cloud of sand obscured the terrible landing. Though he ran towards the place, the swirling clouds hid it from his eyes. The wind's roar now held a trace of laughter.

Azil was gone. And yet Corydon's own eyes were dry. If he had wept, it might have been for the boy his friend should have been. The firelight on his face. The songs. The glory and insanity of the kleptis game. But his tears had been dried up by the storm. He turned away from the broken body. He felt the weight of his uselessness. He could not even cry.

Bin Khamal swallowed, a handful of dust. 'Corydon,' he said. 'I must go. The efreets . . .' he had to raise his voice above the wind – 'the efreets will know. They will know me.'

'When shall we meet again?' Corydon remembered

Medusa saying that. He couldn't decide whether it was a good omen or not.

Bin Khamal shrugged. Both glanced one last time towards where Azil's broken body lay. Both glanced away. Neither said anything. The gathering sand stung their eyes.

It was not worth saying things like, 'There are only two of us now.' Both knew the kleptis life was over. Neither could speak. Bin Khamal put his hand on Corydon's arm for half an embarrassed second, then turned and ran from the bruised plum clouds. Their livid colour reminded Corydon of Medusa's skin, and there was something stupidly comforting in the thought, as if she were with him.

ζήτα

SIX

He did not go into the desert. As the storm hit the city outskirts, he turned and walked deliberately, slowly, back into Tashkurgan.

Slowly the air went solid with sand. Corydon groped his way through the almost invisible streets; people jostled him, blinded, and his eyes, his nose, his face were prickly with sand. He wandered without purpose, his only thought that he could not watch another city go to destruction while he was safe outside it. He hoped to be buried here by the stinging sand, beside his hopes.

Through the swirling sand-wind, he caught a glimpse of a light, surrounded by the black vortex of the storm. Jinking himself suddenly sideways towards it, he found himself in a tavern.

It was shelter, anyway, he thought, as the swirling sand filled the streets. Inside, it was crowded with others seeking refuge. Squirming, Corydon managed to find a quiet corner. The talk buzzed and swirled in six different tongues.

And then he heard a conversation that gave him a jagged shock, as if a bolt from Zeus had run him through the ear.

'– a girl who could make snakes come out of herself; half-snake she was, too. I dunno why he wanted her so much, but he couldn't look away. Yes, she's out at the Old Palace, with all the others. Upsets the other girls, you can imagine. So ill-omened.'

Corydon listened desperately. But by now the two men had moved on to talking of a black racehorse, and he heard no more. Still, he kept watching the men until they got up and left.

It couldn't be. The Snake-girl was dead. She was gone. He thought of the bronzy scales of the eidolon, its kisses, its pleas for life. And he had loved her. But it wasn't her. Now he didn't know what he felt. If there was a real Snake-girl, what would she think of him?

A man brought round a pitcher of a thick white drink. Corydon supposed it was camel's milk, but when he tasted it he realised his mistake. It was sweet and rich and delicate all at once; he'd never had anything so good. It seemed to drive the sting of the sand out of his throat.

He looked up over the rim of his beaker, hoping for a refill.

But he couldn't see the servitor. What caught his eye instead was a tall figure swathed in a deep blue hood, the hood of the desert people. Through the blue stuff, he could see the glitter of eyes. The man was watching him, unwaveringly.

Corydon stared back. He knew the rule of the island

villagers among whom he had grown up; never, ever be the first to look away. But it was hard to go on holding the gaze of a man whose face was hidden.

Then the man began, slowly, to unwind his headdress. He bared a fierce hard mouth, a high-bridged nose like a hawk's beak. Last of all, he unwound the blue covering from the rest of his face.

It was the man with silver eyes.

Corydon knew he was in trouble. The storm raged ferociously outside, but he began to think of its roar with pleasure in comparison with the silence that enveloped him in the tavern.

The man stood up, and flung back his cloak. Corydon saw his sword's gleam. Then he spoke.

'I could have killed you minutes ago, if I had chosen,' he said, in a voice which rang through the tavern. Behind Corydon, the bartender was hurriedly stowing any precious-looking pottery vessels out of harm's way. The other customers were backing away too.

Corydon said nothing. His dark eyes met the man's silver eyes. 'I cannot run any further,' he said fiercely. 'Do as you will. As you and your kind have always done. Butcher me if you must.'

The man was silent for a whole minute, thinking. Then he spoke again. 'Do you not know,' he said slowly, 'that Rashid al-Haoud has put a bounty on your head so large that every bounty hunter in Arabia is out searching for you? You and your kleptis gang stole the dowry he sent with his daughter – yes, you know well what I mean, the jewels, the cloth, the spices. You have put him to shame.

His shame will not be undone until he sees you on a spike in the sun in front of his house.' His silver eyes flashed fire.

Corydon shuddered inwardly at the terrible death that confronted him. But he spoke bravely. 'At least my friends have escaped,' he said. 'And if I must buy their lives at the cost of my own, I consent to that.' *After all,* he thought, *I'm tired. Tired of running from heroes.* A vision of Medusa's cottage came to him, very sweetly. *And perhaps,* he thought, *I deserve death.* He thought of the thousands of dead Atlanteans.

But the hero with the silver eyes was silent once more.

'Come,' he said at last. 'I will take you.'

Corydon stood up. It was obvious that fighting was useless. He was weaponless. This was very clearly the greatest hero he had ever met.

As they moved towards the door, it seemed that someone didn't think so. A man in a black cloak turned from the bar, and drew a dagger, pressing it sharply into the hero's throat. 'Give me that boy,' he said hoarsely. 'I've been watching him all day. I need that bount—'

That was as far as he got. In a single movement, the hero's sword rippled out of its sheath and found a new resting-place in the man's belly. He looked down at it with a gasp of surprise. Then his soul went crying to the realm of the many. The hero's face did not change. His eyes looked just the same. He wrapped his face and head again, to protect him from the wind. Corydon did the same.

When they stood outside in the roaring wind, the hero spoke.

'I am a fool,' he said. 'I cannot kill you. You are a thief, but you have acted honourably. You were willing to die for your friends. And there is something about you that is noble. Something I had almost forgotten. But if we ever meet again,' he said, and those astonishing eyes lit again from within, like marsh-fire, 'if we ever meet again, you must die on my sword.'

Corydon stood still. Then for the first time, he said two words with sincerity. 'My lord,' he said.

'My name is Akhilleus,' said the man with silver eyes. 'Now go.'

Corydon took a breath of stinging dust. Then he drew his cloak about him and ran into the deeps of the storm.

Its scouring sand led him, but also hit him in the face like a horde of angry wasps. Despite its buffeting, all he wanted was to get as far as possible from those silver eyes.

He had never met a hero like this one. Perseus had been a hero, but he had also been an idiot, frightening because of his stupidity. Pirithoos, Lysias – only Kharmides had been of normal intelligence. But this man was very, very far from stupid. Very far from Perseus's nervous fumblings. He was . . . Corydon groped for words, wishing it was possible to play his pipes in the driving wind; it helped him think. This man was as an Olympian god should be . . . It was as if everything evil and disappointing in them, everything twisted, had somehow been smoothed and straightened. And Corydon had also sensed a great loneliness and depth of solitude more profound even than the Minotaur's, but here it did not go with the Minotaur's soft-footed bumbling, but with hardness and strength.

The thought stung him like the sand. It threatened his world. How could a hero be so like, so like . . . well, so like a monster?

He pushed on into the darkness, oblivious to his own danger. Somehow he knew the answer lay in the blinding darkness, the itching sand, and not in the town. He must trust to his instincts.

Hours of stinging pain went by. Corydon's eyes were almost swollen shut when he began to feel the wind lessen against his sore skin.

As the darkness began to lift, he stumbled against rock. Where was he? He scraped his forehead against more rock, then obeyed an instinct to crouch low, finding his way forward free. He crawled into a space that smelt oddly familiar, though he didn't try to put a name to the smell at first. It was enough that his nose and mouth and eyes were out of the tormenting flying sand. He collapsed onto the cave floor. His mind gave a few last bright flickers before he fell into sleep.

He woke thinking of the other monsters, thinking he was in Lady Nagaina's stronghold. Thinking he heard Sthenno's voice. But it was only the cry of some large bird outside the shallow cave in which he had lodged. A pang of sadness struck him as he felt the full loss of that past.

It roused him, though, and he sat up. As he did so, he

became aware of the thick sound of breathing all around him. Of the condensation in the cave. Of the rich spicy smell of fur that had haunted him. He remembered in a sudden rush where he had smelled that particular odour before.

The Nemean lion . . . One night Corydon had slept next to his old friend in the stronghold, enjoying his scented warmth. In a flash, he recalled the images he had seen in that other cave . . . As the memory flooded him, he saw them. The humped backs of a huge adult, and near the dam, the softer outlines of three cubs.

Nemean lions hated killing, but they also had terrible tempers, and Corydon remembered how fiercely his old friend had loved and guarded his rock. What if the thing he had stumbled on in the dark was *their* rock? And they might not welcome an intruder in their cave . . .

Just as Corydon realised that he might be in danger from a people among whom he had once numbered a dear friend, one of the cubs stirred. He rolled over onto his tummy, sat up, washed his face, and noticed Corydon.

'Hello,' said the cub. 'What are you?'

Corydon held out his hand for the cub to sniff. 'I'm a mormoluke,' he said. 'And you are a Nemean lion cub.'

The cub tumbled backwards in surprise.

'How do you know that?' it asked.

'I have met one of your kind before,' said Corydon.

That was quite enough information for the cub. 'Oh,' it said, satisfied, then butted its mother fiercely. She woke too, in a swirling rush of gold and amber fur, and her vivid jewelled eyes caught Corydon's steady gaze.

'You go,' she said. There was no room for discussion in her firm voice.

Corydon got up obediently.

'I will go,' he said carefully. 'A Nemean lion is my friend. I honour your people. I will tell no one.'

She bared her teeth very slightly. 'You go,' she said firmly. 'Go now.'

'I'm going,' said Corydon hastily. He couldn't stop his heart from aching a little. He had hoped for the furry warmth he remembered so vividly. He realised it had been a very long time since anyone had hugged him or ruffled his hair or played games with him or teased him. Perhaps it was because of seeing the cubs, but somehow he felt like a cub himself. He chided himself: how old are you, Corydon? Then he realised he had no idea of the answer. As he ducked through the entrance, he began to cry. He felt hideously ashamed. But he longed for his mother's arms. Or Medusa's. Arms to hold him. The salt tears burned his raw face.

And he felt a heavy paw on his shoulder.

The mother lion had heard him, and with simple wisdom she gathered him softly against her wide furry body. Her cubs gambolled around him, patting him with their soft paws too. He relaxed into the scented furry warmth. His tears dried. She tickled him a little, and he began to laugh instead. Monster-warmth, monster-love. The love of his own kind. He sat up, and she did too. She met his eyes, and he saw that hers were full of tears too.

'We too cry,' she said in her soft rumbling purr.

Corydon realised that there was no father lion.

'Where is your mate?' he asked.

All the lions burst into a long ululating howl. A long sound that rose and fell. As if the rocks themselves wept stone tears. Corydon felt his own eyes beginning to fill again; he remembered the Nemean lion crying like this after the battle, and it was partly grief for his friend that made him want to weep himself. But as the howl went on, became almost a lament, he felt scoured clean of the past, lost in a loss that was forever present, inescapable for all but a second. He knew that somehow the father had been lost to them. How did not matter.

He began crying softly again. This time his tears were for them. The cubs pressed against him.

After an ageless time, they all felt entirely empty, white and clean like new snow. 'Hungry,' said the mother lion. She tore a piece of meat from the carcass she had been saving and brought it to Corydon. He thought of the old days with Euryale, when she would devour bleeding chunks of meat while he and Sthenno watched the heavens . . . His heart thrummed again, a new song was being born in his mind. He knew he had to go to them. He had to find them. However dirtied he was by what he had done in Atlantis, he had to face them. He had to trust their love as he had been forced to entrust himself to the clemency of the lions. Even to the clemency of Akhilleus – a hero who was also a monster . . .

But how could he find them?

He knew it would be of no use to ask the lions. Nemean lions generally knew only their own territory. They were not offended by his refusal of their food; they were eating hungrily, and he wondered if food might be scarce.

'Are there other monsters here?' he asked. The mother lion shook her head. 'Now you are here,' she said. 'We too.' One of the cubs rolled over, and Corydon saw a flash of unexpected intelligence in its face. 'Once,' said the cub, 'I saw a bird-lion. Flying. And once a snake. Flying.'

'You're a fibber,' said another cub, pouncing.

'He-is-not!' said the third. 'Anyway, I saw a monster. I saw one. I saw one. Big, big, big. A girl. A girl who had a tail like a desert serpent.'

Corydon's head whirled. The Snake-girl? Lamia? Careful not to alarm them, he asked slowly, 'Where did you see her?'

The small lion was obviously trying to think. It scratched its ear. 'I think,' it said carefully, 'it might have been on the oasis. I remember her lying on the sand. I think she was trying to get warm. Sometimes you see snakes doing that in the morning. But you mustn't touch them because they can hurt you with one bite. So I didn't go close.'

Corydon forced a warm smile. 'Thank you,' he said. 'Which oasis might that be?'

The cub frowned. It looked up, its eyes fully of worry. 'I think it was the one where you go that way, then that way,' it said, gesturing with a small golden paw.

Without drawing breath, Corydon began to run in the direction the lion had indicated.

The Snake-girl . . . why had he never asked about her before? What could have befallen her, while he idled away his time in the desert? He remembered her sweetness, her intense shyness, her hatred of anything that impinged on her delicate world. From her inexact copy, the eidolon, he had learnt something of the misery that had made her the monster she was. He had also learnt a little of love from that machine, though the memory made him wince that he had been so tricked.

And yet, as he ran, his heart was full of dread, abrupt dread that came heavy-footed, like a surly robber who knows his own might. He also felt as hollow as an eggshell. Open and empty.

He reached the oasis in a skid of sand, after running all night, sleepless, wild-eyed, with the voices of the sandwinds singing in his ears.

Of course, there was no one there.

There were the hoofprints of many camels, many hundreds that had drunk the sweet waters and left refreshed. Discarded dateseeds lay all around. But there was no way to know which were the tracks that might lead to the Snake-girl.

He sat down to wait. And he waited. And waited. Waited while the moon waxed to a fat silver drachma, then deflated to a thin wisp of ice. He ate dates. He grew thin. But no one came.

At last his stubborn heart admitted it. They had just been passing through. And he only had a cub's word even for that.

He felt a sudden longing for the lions, their comforting warmth. Time to move on. He must hope for the guidance of dreams. Somehow he knew he and the Snake-girl would meet again.

ήτα

Seven

He travelled all night again, his mind filled with an image of warm golden fur.

When he arrived in their pridelands, rosy-fingered dawn was caressing the sky. He ran on, tireless in his strength. His hunger was a steady pain.

Then, abruptly, he skidded to a stop. There in front of him was a small, pathetic bundle of golden fur.

His mind refused what his eyes saw.

It was the head of one of the Nemean lion cubs.

The eyes were open, as if the baby had seen its death. The baby body, legs splayed, lay on top of a rock, as if trying to catch the last fleeting warmth given out by the sun. Corydon noticed how big the paws were compared with the short, sturdy legs. The cub hadn't had time to grow into them. He hadn't had time.

Corydon looked around. A blood-trail led across the sand. He followed it numbly, and it led him to the mother lion, foam on her jaws. She had died defending another cub, whose torn body still nestled at her side, as if she could still feel it.

Who? Nemean lions were difficult to kill, almost impossible. Their skin was like bronze armour.

Corydon looked at the mother's body and noticed for the first time that a spear still pierced her side. It had broken off in her death agony, but he could see the red shaft. He could see it was a Greek battle javelin, the kind thrown rather than thrust at a foe. He withdrew it from her, wincing as if she could still feel its barb.

Then he examined it. The barb was made from a lionclaw.

So. Whoever had done this had killed Nemean lions before, and knew much of them. A Nemean lion's skin could be pierced only by one of its own claws. And the killer was a Greek.

He sat still, dry with grief. Dry as a desert heart. Who? Who? Who?

He jumped when he heard the bored voice from behind him.

'It was Ares,' said the wingfoot god. 'He does many such deeds.' The words were muttered sullenly. Hermes hated doing errands. One of his sandals tried to untie itself and frisked angrily from side to side. He glared blackly at it. Slowly it settled back to the ground again.

'I shall go now,' said the god. 'High Olympos awaits me.' Awkwardly, he shuffled his feet. 'Boring, isn't it?' he added, in an almost friendly voice. Corydon saw that he was looking at the outstretched paws of the smallest lion cub. He stood still for a moment. Even the restless sandals were motionless.

'I liked them,' he said, abruptly. Then he leapt into the sky.

Corydon stood, astonished. Then black fury took him, and he cursed at the retreating figure. What good was an Olympian's pity now? The lions lay in their blood.

He made a pyre for the lions, digging a deep pit, bringing scrubby bushes, kindling a fire. The bodies were consumed by the quick hot tongues, and he remembered Medusa's burning and could still find no tear, no song, no words for the griefs of the world. His heart was as bare and black as ashes. He didn't even know what to wish for any more; he knew only that he must find a way to end the Olympians' rule and all its cruelty, or die in the attempt for he could live no more in a world which left them free to destroy the innocent.

If I am to die, he thought, *I could be with Medusa,* and his heart lifted slightly. He was glad she was not here, though, glad she could not see the lions' deaths. It would have made her cry with rage.

He set out and began to walk towards the sea.

He ate no food and drank only from the few brackish wells he came across. He needed nothing but his searing hate to sustain him.

On the fourth day, a great shadow passed over him, and he thought wildly of a story Bin Khamal had once told, the story of the roc, the eagle-bird so vast it was said to blot out the sun. Then he thought of winged lions, and brushed away the question of whether any survived. But a white-and-gold and Lapis-blue body alighted in front of him.

It was a Sphinx.

She lay down regally, paws spread forwards, wings folded. Around her sprang up the white pillars of a temple. Grass rippled outwards from her reclining body. A fountain leapt suddenly skywards. The air turned cool and fresh, and there was a scent of flowers. Soon she was surrounded by her own dream-landscape.

She was bigger than he had remembered. Was it the same Sphinx, his own friend – no, not *friend* – from the Island of Monsters?

'Does it matter?' she asked, in a voice like sliding water, a cool ripple of a voice.

'I suppose not,' he conceded, then rebellion welled up in him. 'Yes,' he said. 'It does matter. What happens to us matters. What she knows and what some other sphinx knows – they are different.'

The Sphinx was silent. In the silence he could hear the plaintive splash of the fountain.

'Not to the Sphinx,' she said. 'To the Sphinx all knowledge is indivisible. All is one. There is not you, I. There is only the Sphinx.'

'That's—' He realised he'd been about to say 'monstrous'. He stopped abruptly.

'I am here to give you some knowledge,' she said. 'Here it is. You have asked the right question to obtain it. The quest to be someone is the root of all evil,' she said, and he sensed something like irony in her look. 'It is of the

Olympians. Each one wishes to insist upon himself, or herself.'

'But they don't want anyone else to do it,' said Corydon sharply. 'And so our insistence that we *are* must be a way to anger them. To thwart them. I will thwart them, Sphinx.'

'For this you were born, Corydon Panfoot,' she said tranquilly.

'But all I have managed so far is to survive. To hang on. I redeemed the underworld, true, but what of this world, the world where mortal men begin and live and die? Can it not be redeemed?'

'You do not have another staff,' she said.

'No,' he said. 'Is there another way?'

'There is,' she said. 'But think, mormoluke. Think. If once I speak of it, you will not be able to forget it. It will haunt you, shadow your steps. It will become your *moira*, your fate. You have spent long times running from your fate, into the desert places of the world. A long time longing for nothing more than to be allowed to be, to be Corydon, a boy with a few friends and some sheep.'

'Still I will hear,' said Corydon.

'And I warn you, Panfoot. This life cannot be utterly redeemed. Men will still choose wrongly. You must think, too, whether redemption is truly what you seek. What would it mean for the world to be redeemed?'

'No Olympians,' said Corydon, through clenched teeth. He thought of the warm dead bodies of the Nemean lions lying on the hard unfeeling sand. The wide look of staring surprise in the eyes of the smallest cub.

'No Olympians,' she repeated.

'No Zeus, then!'

'But will that be enough?'

'No, it will not,' Corydon agreed. 'But it will at least be a start. It will be something.'

'Very well,' said the Sphinx. 'You know what you must do.' Her golden eyes began to close.

'No, I don't.' Corydon spoke urgently. 'I'd have done it by now if I knew. Please.'

'You *are* the Staff now, Corydon Panfoot. You have it in your body to redeem this world, as you once had it in your hand to redeem the realm of the many. Your mission was once to plant a seed . . . now, somehow, you are *yourself* the seed. If you become the land, if the land becomes you, becomes your monstrosity, your monster-self, then the Olympians will be unable to bind and twist and deform it. Men will see, and they will act. There is a riddle in the land. You must follow the thread. Understand the land, and the gods who live in it. But I too do not know what act can bring this to pass.'

Corydon remembered what to ask. 'Then,' he said, 'if you do not know, who can tell me more?'

'I can tell you to go to the city of Troy. Find your friends. That, I know, is the beginning of your story. Your revolution. The earth turns, and it shall be Corydon who makes it turn. But I do not know how.'

'Could Kronos help?'

'Panfoot, he might help if he knew the need. But you cannot ask him.'

'Why?'

'You no longer know the way. The way to his realm has been closed. You do not have the Staff. It was the key. Once the key is gone, who can open the door?'

Corydon felt annoyed. Of course no one could enter a locked room without a key; why did oracles always tell him simple things a village child would know?

He began to wonder if oracles were of any use at all. What could they tell him?

'Yes, you are beyond us now,' said the Sphinx. 'You know yourself. You know that there can be nothing in excess.'

She was smiling slyly. He felt he was being tricked again. 'What I want to know,' he said, evenly, 'is why no god or monster can answer a simple question with a simple answer.'

'Because that is not the way meaning is made. Meaning is in you. And in me. But we must make it ourselves, or it will not truly have meaning for us.'

Corydon smiled too. This time his smile was a sly echo of hers. Had he known it, he would have seen his father's face mirrored in his own.

'Then tell me,' he said, with a small bow of freezing courtesy, 'tell me how to get to Troy.'

'There are many ways,' the Sphinx began, but this time he cut her off, his eyes fiery with tears. 'Yes,' he said, 'but tell me. Which one. Should. I. Take.' His words were spaced as exactly as tombstones. A shudder ran over the Sphinx, like a cat's quiver in a cold breeze. Corydon barely noticed, but she was remembering other angry, impatient heroes.

'You can take a ship,' she said, and her golden eyes widened. 'A fleet follower of the foam.'

'Yes,' said Corydon. 'But would it be the quickest way?' He remembered Sthenno's prophecy. He had no wish to spend a year and a day at sea. The war would be over before he got to it.

The Sphinx opened her huge golden eyes. Her white body stretched out, like a lion's in the sun. 'You are in time,' she said, and he caught both the meanings. He was inside time. He would be in time in her eternal present.

A sudden thought struck him. Carefully, he asked, 'Are the Olympians in time?'

Her eyes opened wide again, then narrowed. Somehow he knew that what he had asked was tremendously important. 'They are above it,' she said, 'as the dead are beneath it.' Her golden eyes were very bright. He was so surprised that she had offered him an answer, in prose, that he hardly knew what to think. 'Is that true?' he asked.

'It is,' she said. 'But what is truth? You must find the truth, as you did before. The place. And much that is true will not come to pass.' And before he could stop her, she had broken into verse again, singing in a voice as delicate as a silk thread, 'Call no man happy, for the turn of the wings of a dragonfly cannot outmatch the speed of fortune ... See, that man who sits next to you seems to me a god, for your eyes are on him ... He is entangled in the magic of her thighs ... The moon is on the clear waters of home, but I sit here on the mountain-side, lonely, lonely.' Her singing was still clear, but he lost the thread of it, and it was abandoning him into a labyrinth of feelings for which he had no time and no words. Still, he saw how choice was about blindness; you could only choose by choosing not to see all the richness of the possible.

'Choice,' he said aloud, 'is easier for heroes. Monsters are too many for it. We are too many in ourselves.'

She was almost asleep, her eyes nearly shut. In her singing voice, she whispered, 'But the sons of men choose and choose, and so the world shrinks to a slit of light in boiling darkness. Follow the light. To the height. These courts of mystery.' She blinked, then added some more half-murmured lines. 'The ice-gulfs that gird his secret throne, bursting through these dark mountains like the flame of lightning through the tempest.' Corydon sighed. Her brief impulse to speak clearly had vanished. Her voice went higher, like a lark soaring. 'And from the sky, serene and far/ A voice fell, like a falling star,/ Excelsior!' She said this last in a high silly voice.

Corydon knew the oracle was over. He had a kind of answer. He must get to Troy, and he must go upward. That night, he lay down by the Sphinx's fountain as it faded, but he slept little, and what sleep he had was dream-laden. He was rocked on the back of the swift black camel he had stolen, and the rocking spoke to him of ships sailing for Troy, sleek as dolphins. In one dream he saw Medusa, and her eyes were full of unshed tears as the dead streamed past her into the Kingdom of the Many. Then as he lay half-sleeping, his eyes dazzled by the vivid desert stars, he drifted into a dream of a thickly ridged peak whose snowy top lightly touched the white clouds that hung low in a vivid blue sky. He seemed to be rushing towards it as if borne on a gorgon's wings. As he came nearer, the clouds thickened, and heavy lightnings began to gather; the peak turned dark and menacing. The dark clouds swirled lower, and he felt himself caught in their whirl; now he was back in Tashkurgan, seeing the desert engulf him and many others, weighted by hatred and impotent rage. And the mound of sand that had once been Tashkurgan grew and grew, until it became a child's copy of that lonely, forbidding mountain.

Corydon awoke to the thought that the Olympians had made another image of themselves.

It was the chill hour before dawn. He set off to walk to the sea.

Many days passed, days of tired, restless sleep riven by ancestral voices that screamed out one word that could not be distinguished, by dark clouds and voices in agony. He saw a tall city with towers like Atlantis, burning. And black ships beyond counting. And Helena, smiling and holding Sikandar's hand, and Sikandar shy and unhappy. There was something odd about Helena, something he couldn't understand. He woke many times, walked a few more miles, fell into sleep again, and woke again after being tossed by more dreams. His eyes were wide and glassy with exhaustion and dread by the time he stumbled at sunset on the fifth day into a tiny fishing-port. He stopped for neither food nor water, but went straight to a stocky seaman who was pulling his boat onto the beach. Corydon pulled his treasure-hoard from his pocket and held out a ruby to the man.

'I will give you this now,' he said slowly, 'in exchange for your boat and for you to sail it. When we get to our destination, I may have more for you. But try no tricks. I am stronger than I look.'

The man looked at his boy's face, with its faint whisker-growth, at his white staring eyes, at his dirty feet, his ragged clothes. He took a second look at the feet. His eyes opened wide, and he began babbling.

'Please spare me,' he said simply. 'I have two children.'

Corydon spoke simply too. 'I will not harm you,' he said calmly. 'But I need your boat.'

The man motioned him aboard. Then he said, 'And where do you wish to go, sir?'

'You need not call me sir,' said Corydon. 'To the city of Troy.'

The man began setting up his sail fussily. 'Sir,' he said urgently, 'sir. You know about the army? The fleet?'

'I know,' said Corydon. 'I must go.'

'But it is death, sir!' The man was almost wailing. 'The Akhaians – they will kill us . . .'

'Not if we are careful,' said Corydon.

θήτα

EIGHT

They sailed for four days to reach the city. Before they could see Troy itself, Corydon saw a shoreline covered with the sparkling lights of what looked like fallen stars. They burned hot yellow and vehement orange, and as they drew near the stars spread out, further, further, a wide net of flaming stars.

It was the Greek watch fires. There were thousands. As many as the stars. Corydon realised he'd been expecting an army on the scale of the force Perseus had used to attack the Island of Monsters. But he was now facing an army a hundred times larger. The watch fires were fierce and unblinking.

As they drew towards the shore, Corydon could see the black ships of his nightmares. They were like great cormorants who wait with folded wings for an unwary fish to jump. Men moved about their decks, their armour bright and their javelins brighter still. The watch fires lit up the many tents on shore, a tent city.

The man insisted they land a half mile from the edge of

the camp, fearing that any closer would bring death to him and his passenger. However, when he saw the forbidding rows of guarded palisades around the edge of the camp, he became uncertain. Corydon took no notice. Handing the ruby and a bag of spices to the man, he sprang over the side of the boat and splashed to shore. The man tacked hastily to get away as quickly as possible. Corydon realised that he had never heard his name. But he turned resolutely towards the shore and its silken, cruel fires that made the water seem to burn.

Now to get into Troy itself. But how? It was clear that the Greeks couldn't get in. Corydon slipped past watch fire after watch fire, noticing how dejected everyone seemed. He heard fragments of talk: 'The landing was all very well and good, but now they've got us pinned down.' 'It's the generals. They don't seem to know what they're doing.' 'They know, all right. They take all the gold and all the girls, and leave us with nothing but blood and scars to show for being here.' At another fire, he caught at different words: 'What's it about, anyway? Some girl captured by a Trojan. Nothing to do with us.' 'They say there'll be a Big Push tomorrow. Some new leader and a new army. Called the ant-men. Brought over here specially.' The others laughed at that. 'Ant-men?' said one. 'What use will ant-sized men be against that?' He gestured at the frowning wall that towered above their heads. 'No, but they say the greatest of all heroes—'

Corydon heard no more. He slid along until he was out of range of the firelight. He could sense the men's anger and misery hanging in the air, and he knew enough of armies not to want to be caught by men so unhappy. They would think him bad luck. He had not come a long way from the Pharmakos Rock for that.

Now the wall towered above him. Corydon crept cautiously along its line, noticing the cressets streaming out orange fire atop its vastness. Even in Atlantis he had not seen a wall so high, so thick. The wild west wind blew torch smoke wildly before it, and his heart lifted. The Trojans were holding out, which meant his friends were still safe inside – Sikandar, but also the Atlantean refugees who had come through the portal with the monsters . . . so he hoped. He hoped for Sthenno, for Euryale, for the Minotaur. The last monsters. And maybe even Gorgos?

And the real Snake-girl . . . why should he think of that now? Suddenly he knew; his keen ear had caught the soft slither of a snake-belly on stones, captured a faint hiss. He looked down, and a slender red-and-gold snake slid into view in a sudden flare of torchlight. Corydon could remember the Snake-girl making a snake exactly like this during the battle against Perseus.

The snake did not slither past, as he expected. Instead, to Corydon's amazement it reared up abruptly, its eyes fathomlessly black. Its tongue flickered. Corydon could see it was trying to speak. There was a kind of striving in its face. Finally it gasped, 'LLLlllaaaammmiiiiaaaa.'

Lamia! Was she here? The snake fell back to the pebbly strand, and tried to curl its tail into a beckoning finger-shape. Then it glided forward, and Corydon, understanding, followed it as silently as he could, his panfoot extended to help him avoid rattling pebbles. The snake slid straight towards a tent, silk-sided and more splendid than most, scarfed with the red pennants of a hero or leader. Crooking its tail again, the snake slipped under the tent-flap. Corydon took a deep breath, then very slowly lifted a corner of the flap. Bending double, he could see into the tent.

Lying on the ground on a pile of silken cushions was the Snake-girl, her serpent body gloriously gold and peacock green, her glossy black hair shining bluish in the lamp-light. Corydon was amazed, delighted, and strangely shy all at once. Then he realised why she was lying so still. She had been bound, was tied to the central tent-pole. Her eyes compelled him, and he crept forward, began working swiftly on the knots, untied them, and released her. Swiftly she put a finger to her lips, and now Corydon saw that they were not alone in the tent. On its other side lay a tall, big black-bearded man, asleep and snoring, a winejar beside him. He looked like a villager after a festival, but his clothes were rich, and Corydon could see that he was no peasant. His hand was on his sword-hilt.

The Snake-girl looked back at him, and then very softly slithered over to him. She spat gently into his eyes. Corydon saw his face begin to change; his mouth opened in a yell, he lifted his fists to his face like a furious baby, his eyes opened, but they were – clearly – blind. 'Come on!' cried the Snake-girl, and they did not dare stay for more. The man's cries were rousing the camp; servants came running. Corydon caught the Snake-girl's hand; they ran silently into the friendly dark against the walls, within arrow-shot of them . . .

An unwise decision. The Trojans on watch had heard the yells, too, and plainly thought an attack was in progress. With shouts of rage, they began hurling arrows and javelins into the darkness. Corydon and the Snake-girl swung back towards the Greeks, but now they too were arming, and the air was rent by the clash of bronze weapons, the twang of bows. They wove their way through men brandishing swords, spears; one warrior cuffed Corydon sharply, ordering him out of the way. The Snake-girl was breathless, and terrified that her shimmering scales would show up all too clearly in the firelight.

They plunged down the beach, felt cool water splash their feet. Without a word, both sank deeper into its friendly darkness. At least they were safe for the moment . . .

Just as Corydon thought this, something told him to look behind him.

Over the water, the cold pink shell-light of morning was faintly visible. Against it Corydon could see a boat, swift as a seabird, pure white, skimming the water as if drawn by dolphins. In the prow stood the figure of a tall man, his scarlet cloak whipping in the sea-wind. He wore no helmet, and Corydon could see no armour, but something told him this was the man the soldiers had spoken of, the leader of the ant-men . . . The boat drew ever nearer. And as the man scanned the water with a cold sweeping gaze, calm and exultant, Corydon saw his face clearly.

It was Akhilleus. The man with the silver eyes.

Instinctively Corydon ducked, low, so that only his

eyes were still above the waterline. Beside him a faint swirl of water showed him that the Snake-girl had followed suit.

But it was no use. Akhilleus had seen him.

His words flashed through Corydon's mind. 'If we ever meet again . . .'

The boat swept towards them. With a crack like lightning, Akhilleus drew his sword. It glinted argent in the dawn light. His eyes never left Corydon's.

He raised the sword high for a killing stroke. Corydon dived desperately. As he did so, he felt the Snake-girl's body slide past him, as she flung herself in front of him. He surfaced, desperate to prevent her, and caught her around the waist, trying to thrust her out of the way. While they struggled, the boat reached them. The sword flashed down like a diving fish, silver. Corydon pushed the Snake-girl clumsily out of the way, but she was a dead weight, her eyes fixed, her head flung back, inviting death. The sword caught her arm; bright blood flooded into the water, staining the dawn radiance. Akhilleus's boat sped on, and ground on the shingle. He leapt out, his silver eyes searching the water.

Clinging to each other, Corydon and the Snake-girl waited shivering for his death blows. In a last effort, Corydon flung himself under the surface again, dragging the Snake-girl with him. Her serpent tail thrashed like a mermaid's and they were engulfed in her blood, making them an obvious target. He knew he couldn't hold his breath for long; desperately he swam for the deeper water, and came up hard against a rock he hadn't noticed because it was entirely submerged. Feeling in the gloom with his hand, Corydon realised there was a small sea-cave that might afford a few seconds' shelter, while his breath held out.

He flung himself into it, dragging the Snake-girl, her body heavy and reluctant. To his surprise, it was larger than its opening suggested; he swam on, in darkness, and came to a place where faint dawn light was visible . . . there was a little beach . . . and then his tortured lungs broke into air . . . the Snake-girl too took a gasping breath, and both almost cried with relief.

But now that they were beached, his lungs no longer sending black-and-red warnings to his brain, Corydon noticed again how badly hurt she was. He tore off his cloak and ripped it into strips, tying one tightly above the vehement orange-purple wound from which blood still poured. She was white, whiter than snow, and her black hair was like the wing of a bird of death.

'Lamia,' he said, using the true name which for him had become poisoned by the touch of the eidolon.

'I want to die,' she said, answering his question. 'I want to . . . Corydon . . . Neoptolemos . . . I cannot go on living. After what he did . . . I cannot bear it. I am for the dark, Corydon. My bright day is done.'

Corydon did not answer her. He flung his arms around her. Her body felt small and fragile, like the birds she doted on.

He knew what she was trying to tell him. He did not know a good answer, but finally he said, slowly, 'I love you.' He didn't feel sure of what he meant, but he knew the words were true, and he also knew that it wasn't the same as his love for Medusa, for Sthenno, for the Minotaur. He also knew he needed her to stay. So he could find out what he had meant, and tell her. One small monster, from the wreck . . . He was sure, at least, that he meant he could love a monster who survived the spite of the Olympians. To love other monsters was to be at peace with himself.

Her bleeding had slowed. Now her body curled towards him. She began weeping softly, and her tears ran down his arm.

'Corydon,' she said. 'You cannot know. And I cannot say.'

'I don't need to know,' he said. 'I know I love you. You are a monster, and you are my friend. I am here to defeat the Olympians.'

She laughed, shakily. 'You haven't begun very well,' she said. It was a tease, but her voice was growing fainter. Corydon knew he needed help, needed it desperately.

And as he thought this, the water at the edge of the sea began to heave, unexpectedly. Out of it came the oddest head Corydon had ever seen, in a lifetime of meeting monsters.

It was huge and brown, with scales, and with a full row of gills along the ridgy neck. One eye was blue, the other brown, and both were staring. Sharp teeth were visible around the tight frog-mouth.

'Help us!' Corydon cried.

The creature's mouth opened and the terrible head nodded. Then it disappeared in a splash and ripple. *That was useful,* Corydon thought. Blood seeped from the Snake-girl's arm, ignoring the boundaries of his temporary dressing.

Then the sea began to boil again. The frog-mouthed creature was back. With him was a man so ancient that his skin hung in folds, long and dragging on the ground. His arms were deflated sacs of skin, his beard a bushel of seaweed.

It was Proteus.

With him was a herd of yelping seals.

Corydon was uncertain. Proteus had not been enormously helpful the last time they had met.

'No,' said the Old Man. 'I am not Proteus. I am Oceanus, his full brother. The sea has its chthonic past, as the land does. I am the shepherd of the sea, as your father is of the land. I and my brother are the second and third oldest of the children of Gaia and Ouranos. In order there is Kronos, firstborn and killer of our father, then I, then Proteus, then Rhea, Kronos's wife, then . . .'

The Old Man continued to talk about his genealogy. The Snake-girl's blood fell on Corydon's hand, and he wondered if Oceanus was going to go on talking while she died before his eyes. It might be fatal to interrupt him, though. He chewed his lip in an agony of impatience. The Old Man was a Titan, and the earth-powers didn't like to be interrupted . . . Finally he mumbled his way to silence.

Corydon burst out, 'Please help her.' A sob caught at his voice; he swallowed, ashamed. The Old Man looked at the Snake-girl for the first time. Her eyes had closed and her breathing was ragged. Her lips were white.

'She wanders between the worlds,' he said in his high old voice. 'She is lost between. Driven there by Neoptolemos. You know? Yes, I thought so. This wound comes from his father's sword, but the deeper wound is within . . .'

Corydon was taken aback. How could the shimmering hero be the father of the bearded snorer he had seen in the tent? Next moment he was regretting asking anything like a genealogical question, even in what was normally the privacy of his mind. It launched the Old Man on another long ramble.

'Begot him when he was barely out of nappies, on Deidamia, who was the daughter of the king of Skyros, Lykomedes, now *there* was a great king . . .' He rambled on. Corydon finally pointed to the Snake-girl.

'Heal her,' he said. 'Please. Then I shall hear all your tales.'

The Old Man held out a stick as wizened and shaky-looking as he was. He touched its end to the Snake-girl's forehead.

Her eyes opened. Her wound did not close, but it ceased to bleed profusely.

'I cannot heal her mind and heart,' said the Old Man, sadly. The frog-mouthed creature clambered unexpectedly out of the water, touched Lamia with the tip of a webbed finger, and gave a croak of sad agreement.

Lamia sat still, silent. Two more tears trickled slowly from her wide eyes. Corydon took her hand. Then they settled back while the Old Man told them tales, bewildering tales of men called Lysias and Lykabettos and

Lysimakhos and Lysandros. Tales in which human names and identities flowed into each other like the waves.

It was tiring and boring, but it was also a song, and Corydon could see it was a rich one; he imagined kings and heroes listening to it, listening for their own names. As he thought this, he heard his own, 'Corydon Panfoot, son of Pan, son of the goddess . . .' The Old Man clapped a hand to his mouth. Without another word he flung himself onto his frog-mouthed creature, and his herd of seals leapt into the waves with him. All of them disappeared with flicks of their tales.

'Oh, great gods,' said Corydon. 'I wanted to ask him about my mother.'

'What does it matter?' said the Snake-girl tiredly. 'You are who you are. Whoever your mother is. And it's Medusa who is your true mother, and you know it. I don't mean she is really. Not in the way she is Gorgos's mother. But you and she belong together. In your heart she is your mother.'

She had changed, Corydon saw. The old Snake-girl would have been too shy to say all that. And now an awkward silence fell. Corydon seemed to hear the words 'I love you', ringing around the cave like a harsh bell.

'I love you too,' said the Snake-girl. She curled a vine-like tendril of snake tail around his wrist. The touch felt light, like a plant's caress, and cool even to his goosefleshed skin. 'But I am no use to anyone any more. I am all used up. Like a cup of wine drunk by another. I have nothing left to give you, Corydon.'

He bent hesitantly towards the caress of her tail. 'Well,'

he said, stoutly, trying to ignore his own crushing shyness, 'I love you and you will always be my friend. And I think that's useful. What could be more useful than a friend?'

She gave a very soft hiss. Two seasnakes slid out from under her glossy black hair, and cavorted in the small waves. He decided to take this as a good sign. 'Come on,' he said, taking refuge in sturdy commonsense. 'We have to find the others, warn them that Akhilleus is here.'

'Is that his name?' asked the Snake-girl. And then, more urgently, 'Corydon, have you met him before? He seemed to know you.'

'Yes,' said Corydon. 'I've committed a crime. I stole a dowry. Jewels and spices. He came to take me, but somehow he didn't. He's not like Perseus, you know.'

'I know,' she said. 'He is not a fool. Corydon, he reminds me of – well, of us. Can a hero be a monster, too?'

Corydon nodded. Together, they dived into the shallow bay, and began groping their way back through the deeps to the open sea.

As he swam, Corydon tried to take his mind off his heaving struggle to hold his breath by thinking about Akhilleus. He had had the same thoughts as the Snake-girl himself. Was this what a true leader of both men and monsters might be like? Perhaps Akhilleus might somehow bring peace instead of war. But that felt wrong; Corydon could see that Akhilleus *was* war. But war as men know it to be, a mixture of the best and worst in themselves. Flaming bright courage and dark acts of violence. It was so beautiful that men would always, always love it too much to give it up for peace. Only monsters like himself wanted peace.

ιώτα

NINE

Corydon could see the light of morning now, the water a thin shimmer of silver silk above them. They broke the surface with gasps, in the lee of a big Greek pentekonter. Luckily, no one noticed them, and looking at the shore, Corydon could see why. A Trojan sortie was attacking the Greek camp. A contingent of sphinxes had launched itself from the high walls of Ilium to give battle to the Greeks, who stood gazing at them, their eyes whirling with hypnotic sphinx-gold. And in the sky, Corydon caught a flash from bronze wings as Sthenno and Euryale harried the fleeing Greeks from the air. His heart lifted too, soaring in pure relief. They lived; they were real. Then as his eye was drawn upward, he saw the familiar dark shape of the Minotaur, directing the Trojans as they hurled flaming shafts down into the rear of the Greek army. He felt as if his heart might explode with joy.

From Troy's open gates came a flood of chariots. Corydon saw their wheels, scythed to slice off the arms and legs of warriors. As they drove into the fleeing Greek cavalry, there was a horrible scream from a horse, and Corydon saw blood spurt up like grain flying under the thresher's flail. He felt suddenly sick. He had forgotten war, he realised, in just the year he had been in the desert.

He looked up at the sky again. As he watched, Sthenno changed direction with birdlike speed, jinking towards him. He could hear the remembered clash of her feathers. Her birdlike voice rose in a thin scream.

And she shot down from the sky, dropping like a stooping falcon.

'Mormo!' Without a pause, she swept Corydon and the Snake-girl up in her claws. They dangled over the seething battlefield as Sthenno flung herself straight upwards into the heavens. Arrows pelted them as Sthenno's great wings laboured for height. Corydon felt the familiar exultation as the gorgon's wings lifted them all high. Memory flooded him: the gorgon's wings, sweet safety of his childhood. But he saw that the Snake-girl was white with dread as the air around them grew cold.

From their zenith, the battlefield was no longer frightening. It was a child's toyworld, its small racing figures comically frenzied, neither sad nor important.

Perhaps, thought Corydon, this was how the world looked to the Olympians.

The thought hit him as hard as a blow. Of *course*.

His own father was an earth-god; he saw the world from where men stood. But all-father Zeus (mentally, Corydon spat the name out) was lifted above all fray. He looked *down* on men, and so he despised them. And – now his mind was racing as the cold air blew in his face, as Sthenno vaned to avoid battle-smoke – the Atlanteans and Trojans built towers to give themselves a little of that divine power. There was this airy coldness even in Sthenno, much as Corydon loved her. She lived on earth, but could escape it at need, and the stars were her realm. Men could not escape except in thought.

Sthenno banked sharply down towards a second flashing bronze figure. Euryale. But was it really her? She seemed thinner, and oddly, less warlike. He could see the artist in her sweeping flight rather than the huntress. But when she saw the two figures clutched in Sthenno's claws, she gave a harsh ringing-bronze cry of welcome, and Corydon knew it was her. *But if I am right*, Corydon thought, *Euryale would have this coldness too.*

And yet she didn't. How could that be?

They were over Troy now, the thickness of the ribbed walls behind them. It was a towery city, like Atlantis, and it was branchy between its towers, textured with thick leaves and thrusting twigs. The roofs were all flat terracotta tiles, red and ridged. The houses were white, rambling. It was like a brighter, leafier Atlantis.

Looking down, Corydon could see green courtyards where fountains played in the sunlight; they flew above a children's playground and the clear voices rose to his ears like birdsong. It was a dusty city, too, and in its wide marketplace men sold silks and figs still, despite the war, and carpets and pots and scented trifles.

The port had once been full of ships bringing cardamom and cumin and cinnamon from greater jungles and deserts to the east. Ivory, peacocks, sandalwood, cedarwood, diamonds and emeralds. Sacks of moon pearls, and amethysts of the deep sea. Crisp gold and ambergris. All that is original and strange. But now it was almost silent, only a few shipwrights braving the Greek army to put thick tarry pitch on their ships to stop them rotting. One man had a tiny toddler with him, a child with golden skin and blue-black hair. A stray Greek arrow caught her. Corydon turned his head.

He thought of Atlantis, and of Tashkurgan, and he wished he was an Olympian so that he need not give his heart to things he was powerless to save. Not again. For the air was still ringing with the clang of battle. Before the thick walls, men were disembowelling each other. He was glad he could no longer see.

They swooped down a narrow twisting side-street, dusty and hot-looking, and then they lurched under a low archway. Corydon landed hard, and Sthenno's remembered talons caught him, set him right. Then he was enfolded in the prickle of her great wings. With a clatter, Euryale landed too, and he felt her talons rake lovingly through his hair. She extended her other talon to the Snake-girl, and as she did so Corydon saw that it was dyed red.

He had expected questions, explanations. But perhaps his year in the desert was like a long evening to the gorgons, for they spoke to him as if he had been gone only for that long. Euryale noticed him looking at her claw.

'Not blood,' she said. 'I was mixing paint when the muster horn called us to defend the city. Come inside, and I'll show you.' She led the way into the house. Inside it was cool and the stone gave off a soft dampness that reminded Corydon of their cave. Sthenno bustled about, scrabbling for food for them, and produced a dryish hunk of bread, and a few figs. Corydon looked surprised, and the Snake-girl politely refused all of it. More quickly than he himself, she had seen that the city was running short of provisions. But Euryale gave her a piece of the bread.

'Yes, we are on short rations,' said Euryale. 'When we can, Sthenno and I hunt on the hills, and so do the sphinxes, though it doesn't come very naturally to them. But the slopes of Mount Ida are exhausted now. The city has eaten its own land bare. And now the Greeks have stopped the trade-ships—'

'But the Minotaur has a plan,' said Sthenno. 'He has invented a flying machine, and if it works we may be able to range further. Euryale and I cannot be spared from the battle for a long journey, you see.' Her voice was falsely bright, and Corydon could tell that she didn't altogether believe her own words. It was obvious that no flying device could feed a whole city that had once been nourished by grain-fleets from all over the Mediterranean.

He nibbled his fig quietly. Euryale drew him aside. She was golden-eyed with curiosity. 'How?' she said pointing to the Snake-girl, who sat pushing a piece of bread from side to side. 'Is she real, this time?'

Corydon suddenly realised with a cool shock that he didn't know. This could be another eidolon . . .

No. 'I know she's flesh,' he said. 'She was wounded. Bled. And Oceanus healed her. He would have known if she were an eidolon.'

'Where has she been?'

The Snake-girl looked up. 'Ask *me,*' she said without heat. 'I hear you. I hear as acutely as a snake. I was sold into slavery. From Hephaistos's island. I was first the slave of Dionysos himself. He fed me with apples and poems and pomegranates from the Lady's tree of death and dreams, until I was sick with his love. I spat him up, and he hated me. So he sold me to a new master.'

Her eyes flared wide, like the eyes of a hunting cobra. Her voice went low, its hiss hard as baked desert. 'His name was Neoptolemos. He consumed me, then he flung me onto his dungheap. He delighted in my pain. I shall not rest until one of my pets sinks its venomous fangs into his flesh, till I see him turn black with the pain of my venom. I live only for that day.' For a second her eyes closed. She looked like a baby drunk on the sweetness of its mother's breast. She smiled, drugged by the distillation of imagined revenge.

Corydon found his eyes full of tears. One precious monster . . . but no longer the person she had been . . . where had her gentleness gone? More than the Nemean lions had been lost. More than Atlantis. Why should they survive if it was only to become mirrors of the huge egos of those who sought their ruin?

But he said nothing. And the others, looking at his gaunt, tanned face, his sun-blasted hair, his hard eyes, felt the same ash on their own tongues.

He was a stranger, as she was. And looking at Sthenno and Euryale, he saw that they too were not the same. They were like great bronze statues; their gleam had comforting timelessness. But Euryale was far thinner, and Sthenno's thinness now had a worn quality, as if the metal that made her was wearing in use, like the armour of a doughty warrior who ventures the vanguard in every battle.

He had imagined that the metal of which they were made could never change or be destroyed. That it was forever, like the rocks of the island.

But it was written on their faces that this was not so.

His heart suddenly accepted it all. They were all still his friends, even if they were not the same. He still longed to save them.

'How goes the war?' he asked.

With a bright birdlike glance, Sthenno looked at him hard. 'For now, mormo, we can say we still live,' she said. 'We have so many advantages.' Her voice was drier than desert sands.

'We do have the walls,' said Euryale eagerly. 'Do you know how they were built?'

Corydon and the Snake-girl looked polite. Sthenno clattered over to a small coffer and began rummaging for a parchment. Not everything had changed, clearly. 'Not now,' she said, absently. 'I shall not tell you now. It is a long, heavy tale. But mormo, there are so many on our side. The sphinxes. The Selene Amazons are here, in force, led by their queen, Penthesilea. We have the Minotaur. And his many devices. And then there are the daimons. I have been using magic. Some of the gods themselves fight on our side. And yet – we only suffice. Only barely. Every day we go weary from the field. The Greeks – it is as if an inner fire drives them forward . . . Not desire of gold. Not ambition. Something stronger.'

Corydon's heart felt like a heavy cold lump. He looked at this new, tired Sthenno and fought to make his face smile into hers. He squared his shoulders, and knew he must find out more to help save the city. 'What are daimons?' he asked, warily. The name made him uneasy. He thought of the hateful serpent whose vanity had destroyed Tashkurgan.

'The Airish Ones,' said Euryale.

'The People of the Stars, the asterions,' said Sthenno. 'They have told me much I did not know about some of the darker stars. Such as yours.'

'I have a star?' asked the Snake-girl in confusion.

'Yes,' said Sthenno. 'All living beings have a star. It can tell their fate.'

Corydon began to close his ears to the gloomy prophecy he could see was about to be flung at his head. 'What use are they?'

'They do not really have a use in war, but they can sometimes predict the future,' said Sthenno. 'They have a priest called Khryses, and his priestesses are visionary too, and they say one has ensnared Apollo in love so that he fights for us. They all brew a mighty magic against the Greeks . . . I know what it is, but others do not. I cannot tell even you. But we all place our hope in it.'

Hastily, almost at random, he said, 'What plans are there to break the siege?'

'*Break* the siege? It is all we can do to keep them at bay,' said Euryale. 'The Trojans could give Helena up, but we all know she is just an excuse; one has only to meet her.' She gave a rich chuckle. 'Agamemnon cares nothing for his brother's wife. He is here because Troy is a rich prize. And because the Olympians will that her towers fall.' Her voice was plangent with sadness, and Corydon could tell that she was remembering Atlantis.

'And Gorgos?' Corydon couldn't imagine Medusa's son sitting patiently around, waiting for Sthenno to brew up a spell.

'He has left the city to seek Philoktetes.' Euryale's voice was a mixture of eagerness and fear. Corydon didn't understand either. He felt, as often, shy and rustic in the face of the deep wells of knowledge of the immortals. He might be a monster, but he did not share their knowledge as a birthright. He looked up questioningly.

'Philoktetes has the bow of Herakles himself,' said Sthenno. Corydon could hear the complex shudder in her voice as she said the name of the monsters' greatest foe. 'It bears arrows of –' her voice sank to a whisper '– hydra venom . . .' Everyone was silent, for a moment, thinking of the death of that hydra, and the death of their own friend Fee.

'We do not do well to make use of a weapon so ill-gotten,' said the Snake-girl firmly. Corydon noticed how much braver she sounded.

'But,' said Sthenno, and her voice rose eagerly, 'there is a prophecy—' Corydon and the Snake-girl both groaned. Euryale gave a metallic sigh.

'Not another prophecy, sister,' said Euryale. Sthenno's

protests were interrupted by the blaring of the trumpet.

'The Akhaians are trying another attack,' said Sthenno. 'They press closer and closer. Usually we can count on a few hours at least between attacks.'

Akhilleus! Corydon had to warn them. It must be he who was intensifying the attacks. He saw in his memory those silver eyes. Sthenno was plainly preparing to take off, but there was no reassurance in her ten-foot bronze body; he felt certain Akhilleus was a match for her and for Euryale as well, and his heart also knew that Akhilleus was clever enough to want to knock them out of the battle . . .

'Beware,' said the Snake-girl abruptly. 'The Greeks have been reinforced. Pyrrhus is here. And his great father. Akhilleus.' Her voice was colder than her snaky skin. Sthenno stopped in her tracks. She folded her wings, despite a second furious blast from the trumpet. She bent down, and took the Snake-girl's small face in her claws. 'I can hear that you have been hurt,' she said gently. 'I do not know this Akhilleus. But there is a black night in your eyes.'

'He is – a hero like a monster,' Corydon spoke hesitantly. 'Like Perseus wanted to be. Only he actually is. Real, I mean. As we are. Not a sham. See?' His tongue seemed to rebel, as if he didn't want to conjure Akhilleus up – or as if he didn't want to give the silver-eyed man away. Which was it? He shook his head.

Sthenno looked interested, but Corydon could see that he hadn't frightened her enough. Euryale was frowning at the Snake-girl. 'You seem different,' she said to the

Snake-girl. 'And I don't mean what you said about Pyrrhus. There is something else. What is it?'

Corydon could see that Euryale was right. She did seem different. Her boldness was strange. Sthenno too turned her bright bronze gaze on the Snake-girl, who didn't shrink or duck her head as she once would have. She stared back, her black eyes fathomless. The trumpet sounded a third time.

'Yes,' she said evenly, with a faint hiss in her voice. 'Yes, it is true. Yes, I am with child. A child I do not want to bear. It is the child of Pyrrhus Neoptolemos. I shall kill it when I can.' Corydon saw a small flare of madness in the deeps of her eyes. His heart turned over with sadness for her.

He flung his arms around her. 'Lamia,' he said, using the forbidden name, 'it will be yours too. And I will help. We all will.' She seemed passive in his arms. But she didn't hug him back. She looked at him, and her face was like cool marble.

'Corydon,' said Sthenno. 'We must go.'

'And I shall come too,' said Corydon. He smoothed the Snake-girl's hair, smiled awkwardly at her, and then fumbled for his slingshot, felt its soft hide, and slid a pebble into it. He did not welcome war. But he could not let Sthenno and Euryale face Akhilleus alone. And perhaps he might find the Minotaur on the walls.

They all ran out into the streets, jostling with a kind of swarm of men and women shrugging on corselets, checking swords, grasping spears. Corydon squirmed between two immense fighters, following Sthenno and Euryale as they clove a path through the throng. Many stopped and saluted them; it was obvious that they had proven their value to the city in battle.

One immense, blue-glazed building was clearly the king's palace. From its great cedarn gate issued a troop of armed men, and behind them the captains rode in gilded chariots drawn by prancing horses. It was clear that they intended a sortie, to risk opening a salley port in the walls to allow men out onto the plain. Corydon could see that this was where Sthenno and Euryale were vital; he himself would deploy them to guard any such breach in the defences . . . and for now he intended to join them.

A strange noise that was not the horn began to sound faintly in the distance. It was the terrible even drumbeat of spears on shields. Corydon had heard it before, but this thunder was far louder. There must be hundreds of them – perhaps thousands. The beat went on, inexorable even and rhythmical. It said, 'We are trained men. We will not break in a charge. We will hold forever, at our lord's command.'

The sound filled Corydon's heart with fear, but a grim young captain riding in a chariot galloped up to them. His hair and beard were black, his eyes were wilder than the island wolves, and his teeth split his face in a grin of joy. He was already half-mad with battle, before the fighting had even begun. He wore a tall helmet crested with gold and blue feathers; Corydon could see he was a leader, brave and reckless. He waved an arm at the gorgons.

'Fly! We prepare a sortie. I call on you to break their

line. If you fly in their faces, they cannot hold. No man can!' He clapped Euryale on the shoulder, reaching up to do it even from his chariot-platform.

Corydon knew it would be a waste of time to speak; this young prince was in no mood for argument and was already moving off. He also knew, none better, that for men warfare was all about breaking the other's shieldline; once the overlapping fence of hard shields that cradled soft human flesh fell to pieces, the enemy could be picked off easily, like wayside berries. But he listened to the ferocious regularity of the beat, as regular as the turning of a watermill, and he felt sure the men making that sound would not be broken easily, not put to flight, any more than the millstones . . .

'Take me!' he called to Sthenno. Too late. In a bronze flash, the gorgons had sprung into the air. The press in the streets had lessened, but Corydon could not see the tall prince anymore either. He decided to make for the top of the walls; then he could observe and also use his slingshot if at all possible. He began to run towards the tall walls, sure he would find a stair to the top somewhere.

Κάππα

Ten

At last he saw the stairs, covered in milling archers and observers. Leading a phalanx of archers up the stairs was a figure that Corydon knew well.

'Sikandar!' he called.

Sikandar turned round. 'Who called me?' The crowd fell silent.

Corydon gulped. 'It is I, old friend,' he shouted. Then he added, carefully, 'Corydon,' since Sikandar was still looking bewildered.

Sikandar gasped then shouldered his own troops aside, and quickly embraced Corydon. 'Old friend! Lord!' he exclaimed. 'Why are you here? See, our doom nears. Have you not had enough of doomed cities?'

'I have,' said Corydon calmly. 'And I have had enough of the gods tormenting or killing all my friends. I am here and I will save Troy, somehow. I do not know how, yet. But I know that I will do it.' As he said it, he realised that he sounded as young, as silly as Gorgos – boastful, wild. And yet as he heard his own voice he knew this was an illusion. He had come to these words through a desert of despair. That made them true. They were like iron that had been through the fire of the forge.

There was a strange ringing silence, in which even the beat of the Akhaians seemed muffled. Sikandar heard the iron in his friend, and he felt it in his heart like a spear. 'What has happened to you, old friend?' he asked softly.

'The last straw,' said Corydon. 'Only a family of dead lions. But it is the last unjust death the Olympians and their followers will cause without opposition.' Springing to the walls, he shouted to the sky, 'All-father Zeus! You and I are enemies, and I will thwart you and destroy all you love if you pit it against the city!' He heard a very faint, nearly inaudible rumble – thunder? Then all the Trojans around him broke into cheers. The louder thunder of the fierce shieldmen grew, as if in response.

And Corydon saw the menace pitted against Troy.

There were uncountable numbers of them, arrayed with the precision of a line of Kronos's parchments, each upright, each armoured, each the same distance from the other. Their helmets gleamed deeply from much polishing; the crests stood up black and white, like the feathers of a heron. Each wore a bronze corselet, each carried a short stabbing spear, and swords glinted at their sides. On their shields were emblazoned the most comic, ironic portrait – a small creeping black ant. And they were ant-like themselves, marching to the music of their drums with ant precision. But Corydon had seen how a nest of ants could strip a sheep to the bone in a day.

And then he saw who rode ahead of them.

He was alone, driving his own chariot, as if he despised having a driver as soft. Armoured like the moon in silver, his helmet bitter with brilliance like the stars, his spears like sea-light. A white light seemed to radiate from him. He stood and raked the battlefield with his silver eyes. Corydon saw the exact moment when he picked out the salley port opening. His argent eyes lit with an inner light, and he gave a sharp call: 'Chelonia!'

The machine-like forces following him responded with terrifying swiftness. The whole formation swung around like an opening door, then coiled on itself, forming several small mounds. Unanimously, they lofted their spears, and somehow each group lifted shields too to form a tight overlapping wall, like the shell outer casing on a great reptile. Then Corydon realised that Akhilleus had shouted 'tortoise' and that the men were obeying. Now they were equally impregnable. The multitude of ants, apparently so easy to crush, had become seven vast impregnable reptile-creatures, lumbering towards Troy. Any attack would beat in vain against their heavy armour.

Corydon had expected the great man-tortoises to stop, but somehow the ants who made them up kept moving towards the walls – slower than before, it was true, but keeping up a steady pace, exactly like ants carrying grains – staggering, but persevering.

Then he saw the bright flash of Sthenno and Euryale's wings in the sky. They had banked around to get themselves in line with the sun, increasing the surprise of their attack. They swooped down upon the lumbering, prickly tortoises. The men hadn't noticed the menace, and continued to lumber forward, urged on by that high voice, those argent eyes. Corydon saw Sthenno pounce, but she was rebuffed by the heavy shield-wall, and Euryale fared no better with her tortoise, forced to jink to evade a thrust from a spear.

The two gorgons battered hopelessly against two of the armour-plated tortoises; they managed to slow progress, and to kill a few men, but the other five tortoises crept inexorably on to lie in wait for the sortie when it burst through the salley port.

It was evident that Akhilleus had devised the tortoises precisely to defend against the gorgons. And it was also obvious that it was working. Akhilleus came forward in his swift chariot, too, and sent up a rain of spears at Sthenno; she was forced to leave the ground and dodge to and fro in the air, as spears struck and loosened her bronze feathers. Corydon's heart was in his mouth, and he felt a black rage.

He lifted his slingshot. Akhilleus was very nearly under the walls now, and Corydon heard the hard twang of Sikandar's bow beside him, as he aimed arrow after arrow at the hero. But none found a secure mark. Corydon took aim, and a stone shot from his sling, straight at Akhilleus's eye.

His heart sang, watching the stone's flight, swifter than Euryale's and curved, perfect . . . It hit, and as it did crumbled into stony powder. Akhilleus looked up, his face showing the mild annoyance caused by a fly buzzing about one's head. His uninjured eyes met Corydon's, and he smiled, a fierce battle-smile. Then he turned back to the battle.

Euryale, infuriated, was still picking at a tortoise of men, darting to and fro, but they were not afraid of her. They kept their shields high, knowing she could not penetrate. She tried prising the shields apart, using her strength, but the men had developed a strategy for that too; when her claw was inside the shields, they slammed their shields together. Bronze met bronze with a harsh scream of tormented metal. Their bronze was just as strong as hers. Her claw was bent and buckled in the collision, and she was forced to withdraw, nursing it.

Corydon's eye was caught by a small troop, obviously Greek, moving purposefully towards the walls. They were trying to avoid attracting attention; they were light-armed, carrying the wicker shields of slingmen like himself. They were peltasts, the light-armed with their slingshots and frail wicker shields, the poorest and weakest troops, and with them were archers. Leading them was a man hard to notice, harder to remember, a man with a patient, lined, ordinary face. Something about his plainness was oddly restful after gazing at glorious Akhilleus until the eyes were tired of silver. Corydon looked at the man's solid comfortingness, and thought he too had a little monster in him; he recalled the Minotaur, dark and furred and full of plans.

He had a plan now, Corydon was sure. He was busy not being noticed, while the flaunting ant-men took up all the attention. A shepherd's eyes were useful in battle. Corydon decided to watch this seemingly-ordinary man.

There was a grinding noise as the salley port opened to allow the sortie out. It was so narrow that only two fighters at a time could emerge. Corydon could see how difficult the sortie would be, with the ant-men and this other strange man on the alert.

At the front were the prince-hero Corydon had met and a woman who looked familiar; her long silver hair was tightly braided, she wore a black pelt around her shoulders, and ahead of her paced a panther and a leopard, clearly battle cats; they lifted their heads at the smell of blood. The woman was related to the Selene Amazons; her hair and gear were the same. He turned to Sikandar, who was still raining arrows down on the Greek tortoises; he was such a good archer that he'd actually managed to find a few gaps in their defences.

'Who is that man?' he asked.

'My older brother,' said Sikandar, his hands still busy fitting his bow with a fresh arrow. 'His name is Hektor. He's bossy, but he's brave. It's just that in battle he works by going completely mad and screaming at the enemy at a full charge.' Corydon looked at Akhilleus and could see that this tactic was likely to lead only to death if Hektor tried it. 'The other one is the queen of the Amazons – they're our greatest allies. She's a warrior, but they also have witches and magewomen – you'll see in a minute. The queen is called Penthesilea.'

'Are they Selene Amazons?'

'They worship the moon, if that's what you mean, but all its phases – the young goddess, the full moon and –' his voice dropped to a whisper '– the dark moon. We do not like to speak her name.' Corydon didn't like to speak it either. He recalled the hate-filled madness of the Morge-mage only too well. 'We may need their powers,' said Sikandar, then saw one of his arrows strike down an ant-man whose shield had slumped a fraction.

Corydon clapped him on the shoulder, then turned to him. 'Sikandar,' he said, 'Atlantis fell by using the powers of the dark moon. You must not.'

Sikandar shrugged. 'It will not be my decision,' he said. 'And it would be worse to be overrun by men like that.'

Corydon knew it would not be worse. It would be the same. But he also knew that it was he who must find a way of defeating the Olympians. As he looked at the seething mass of soldiers spread on the plain, he felt sure he could almost see the shadowy forms of the gods among them. There was Athene, her owl heavy on her shoulder, whispering to one of the heroes. He knew he was seeing what they were thinking; that the Olympians were *inside* as well as out, that they were ambition and pride and lust for gold and women and a belief that anything you wanted was yours by right – Zeus's rule.

Sikandar spoke again. 'We have another plan,' he said. 'Khryses is brewing something terrible.'

As he spoke Corydon could see that the sortie party was emerging from the salley port. They were forming up, ranks of Trojans and Amazons, and an array of fierce leopards and panthers. Nine sphinxes flew from over the walls to join the attack group. As they all formed up, Corydon saw the tortoises changing to an attacking formation; bristling spears sprang out all over them, and the lumbering reptiles were suddenly sinuous silver snakes of men with fierce fangs.

Akhilleus was still at the fore, and Corydon saw his teeth flash in a smile, the happy smile of a farmer who is bringing in an expected harvest. His men turned, and he gave a high cry. They ran forward suddenly with the ferocious speed Corydon had seen earlier. It was apparent that Akhilleus at least had been expecting the sortie all along. Somehow, the Trojans had entirely lost surprise.

Elsewhere, the Greeks were battering the gates, assaulting the walls with ladders. Almost every ladder that hit the wall was either too short, or slithered from the stone. Defenders dropped buckets of burning sand on any Greeks who ventured up; it was work for the women and children not trained to arms, and they seemed to relish it. But Akhilleus was blind to all that. He saw only the sortie party, ripe for his sickle.

But then something happened to disrupt his plans. Along the wall to his right, Corydon saw a party of Trojans straining to lift some kind of war machine, a great ballista that could fire arrows at the attackers from above like a deadly rain. Accompanying it was the familiar furry figure of the Minotaur. Corydon gave a cry, but the great beast didn't hear him above the roaring of battle.

With the Minotaur was a small man in heavy dark robes, and a girl so tiny that Corydon thought she must be a Selene. The man carried a brazier, and lit it. Fierce black flames rose, piercing the hazy blue sky, and down the smoky spiral a god began to descend. Corydon was sure it was a god. But it bore a man's head with thick curls, and the body of a serpent, long and sinuous and golden.

'Come, Loxias!' cried the man. The girl held out her arms, and the snake-god slid into them. Then he breathed on the bundle of arrows she held. Instantly every arrow turned black as night. The arrows themselves seemed to tremble in her quiver, as if terrified of what they had become. She and the Minotaur began loading them into the ballista. Then, at a signal, the ballista fired, straight at a rushing platoon of Greeks trying to reach the walls with their ladder.

The sky was almost darkened by the arrows' flight. The men looked up, flung their shields over their heads. But these arrows seemed intelligent; like an angry swarm of wasps, they sought the joints in armour, swung and twisted, until each had stung a man. Then they fell to the sparse shoregrass. Where they landed, they dissolved into black puddles, then disappeared, leaving only a circle of burned grass to show where they had been.

At first, the men seemed unharmed. They reacted as if stung by insects, then smiled to find themselves still alive. They re-formed, and began moving towards the walls once more. But it became clear that something was wrong. Corydon could see that they were staggering, apparently weak. 'Is it poison?' he asked.

'No,' said Sikandar, his voice hard. 'It is plague.' As he spoke, Corydon saw that the air around the men was thickening into a black buzzing dark. A stench drifted towards him on the wind. The stricken Greeks dropped to their knees; Corydon could see one turn a white face to the sky, and stretch out his hands, as if asking the gods how they could do this to him. On the walls, the snake-god gave a rustling sigh, like dry scales rubbing dust. The man apparently heard it somehow, over the din of battle. His face slumped into pain and despair. He slid to the ground, lying full length, and his eyes emptied of life as they turned to the indifferent heavens. Along the walls, Trojans were cheering.

The sound made Corydon sick. He saw the people of Troy bend to pay homage to the god Loxias, and his heart was dead; Loxias was too like the serpent king, eager to destroy worlds that he might rule them. But as he thought this, something astonishing happened. Where Loxias had been, a shape reared up, tall and terrible. It was not a serpent, but a hero-shape, slender and strong and golden like sunlight. It was manifestly a god, and in his hand was a black bow, the arrows of pestilence clattering at his back. He held too a black lyre, the strings shook and gave out a vast discord as the god leapt to the slope of Mount Ida, his feet making no sound, treading down and plashing the snow into the slurry of mud as he went, with his terrible arrows booming on his back.

As the god abandoned the city, Corydon noticed the only one who had not bowed to his serpent-form. The Minotaur sat with his great furred head on his knees, his arms shielding his face. His heart went out to his friend. Corydon knew he was deeply ashamed of helping an Olympian even for a moment. He hurried to the great beast's side as the people around him began to straighten up, as cries of pain came faintly from the Greeks below the walls. He put a shy hand on the furry shoulder, remembering its warmth saving him in the Land of the Many. The Minotaur looked up, and Corydon saw that his huge black eyes were dimmed with tears, which clung starlike to his long lashes.

'I know it is not simple now,' he said, his warm dark voice as comforting as Corydon remembered. 'The Trojans are not perfect, but they are better than their foes. And they deserve better than to be first robbed and then butchered. Even if they keep making mistakes. But though I know this,' he said, and Corydon could hear a faint low sob in his rich voice, 'though I know this, I hate what I know. I want them to be perfect. So my hands will be clean. Clean of blood.' They looked at each other with wordless sympathy. To Corydon it seemed as if the Minotaur and he had come upon different roads to the same desolate turnpost. At least now neither was alone there. They clasped hands.

'I want only to destroy the Olympians,' Corydon was saying, when a movement on the plain below caught his eye. The ant-men were staggering under the arrows of far-shooting Apollo, their skin growing black with death. Akhilleus was trying to rally them, and Corydon could see his grief for them in his desperate movements. But the other little group of men, under their seemingly-ordinary leader, were untouched. They were creeping along, so close to the walls that arrows could not reach them. They crept on silent feet, ignoring the plague-victims as sternly as if blind and deaf. Their moving glitter of eyes was all fixed on the salley port.

Where was Hektor? Corydon looked wildly around. Hektor and his forces were exultantly pursuing and slaughtering the plague-struck Greeks. The plain-looking man and his men were on the point of breaking into the city! And if they got in they would open the main gates to the rest of the Greek army . . . Who would bring their plague in with them . . . The plague had been a perfect diversion. The ordinary man had used their own attack to surprise them.

A hero with brains. Perfect.

He shouted to Sikandar, but the little group were too close to the walls for a bowshot. The Minotaur looked up, and Corydon saw him rallying his own men, but by the time they devised a weapon that could reach the group, it would be too late. Only Sthenno and Euryale could stop the city falling. He sent up a long singing cry, and saw a small golden dot, far out to sea, wheel and begin to return. It was Sthenno, and he could see that the wind was against her and that she did not really see the need for hurry. Euryale was nowhere in sight. He called again, then saw that there was no one but himself. Telling Sikandar in a fierce shout to shut the salley port, he seized one of the ropes from the ballista, slashed it free with his knife, and clinging to its end like a monkey, swung himself out from the walls and then, taking a deep breath, slithered down its full length . . .

And let go.

He thought in the second that seemed to last ten years that the surprise of his fall might distract them for long enough for Sikandar to shut the gate.

Then all the breath was driven out of his lungs as he landed right in their midst. What saved him was the men's surprise, and the fact that he was only lightly armed. Seeing in dazzles of red and black, Corydon held up his slingshot, flung a pebble almost randomly, and ran in the direction of the salley port. The men followed.

But it had been enough. Sikandar and a group of guards were there. Corydon squeezed inside, and watched the little Greek party resume its prowl around the walls. Everyone could see that they were waiting for night to leave their shelter; they had no wish to be shot by plague arrows. The Trojans hurled spears, but couldn't touch them. Corydon stood next to the Minotaur as he watched the dark man lead them carefully, like a father shepherding nervous children. 'He reminds me of you,' he said to his old friend.

The Minotaur sighed, a long warm breath. Then he spoke. 'He is many-minded, great with devices and desires of men's hearts. They call him Odysseus. He may be the greatest of them all.' Corydon looked at the ordinary man's plain blunt face, his hunched shoulders, and he recalled the searing eyes of Akhilleus. Yet he did not disbelieve the Minotaur. How could the monsters hope to survive them both? He had no illusions that anything other than blind luck had helped him prevent Odysseus's cunning attack.

The battle was over for the day. But the war would begin again tomorrow.

λάμβδα

Eleven

The Trojans held a council of war that evening. It did nothing to help.

The large throne room was crowded to the gold doors. A heaving mass of diverse humans and creatures was barely contained. Corydon could smell the sweat of fear under the courtly reek of incense and spices. It was the custom in Troy for every man or woman who wished to to have a voice in momentous state affairs. Corydon had thought this sounded fine and fair, until he saw the bitter reality. Frightened people do not judge justly. Each man and woman in the room felt the war could take everything. Each was full of rage.

Some of them yelled and quarrelled about their troubles: sons killed, farms outside the walls destroyed. Others expressed their grievances about Troy's rulers. A tall man complained that Sikandar did far too little. 'He stands safe on the walls while we risk our necks on the plains!' he shouted. 'And it's all his fault!' screamed another citizen-woman. 'He offended the goddesses. He chose Helena. And what use is she or her goddess? The attackers have mighty Athene and renowned Hera, and we have a sandy-haired pasty-faced whore with a dirty—'

King Priam, looking very tired, silenced her with a wave of his hand. Raising his thin old voice to be heard over the tumult, he spoke out. 'We are not here to discuss the causes of the war, but how to win it!'

Prince Hektor spoke out too. 'We are not beaten yet, friends. As long as the walls hold out—'

'But the Akhaians nearly got inside them today. Because of your stupid foolhardy sortie,' said a dark-faced man whose apron proclaimed him a smith.

'You forget the plague,' shouted the priest and his daughter. 'Did you not see how Loxias's magic brought them to their knees – yes, even the Myrmidons, the ant-men?'

'The army of Agamemnon will not run because of a mere plague!' shouted another belligerent man, wearing the breeches of a labourer.

'And our hero Gorgos is on his quest to find the bow and arm of Philoktetes,' said Priam, in his high voice. At Gorgos's name, the angry people were briefly silent; it seemed they respected him. Then one of the citizens banged his goblet on the table. 'The bow will do us little good if we are all dead when it arrives!' he said. The brief peace was shattered, and fresh outbursts of fear came from all present, together with fresh solutions.

Corydon's head rang. It was even worse than the councils of war the monsters had held when Perseus came.

'We need to study their battle tactics,' he said suddenly, remembering the Sphinx's careful battle drawings in the sand, at Lady Nagaina's tower.

A cool voice from an unnoticed corner chimed with his thoughts. 'The boy shines, with his feet on the sands of prophecy,' said a large silver sphinx. On the sphinx's back was Penthesilea, Queen of the Amazons. They had been so still in the noisy, hot room that Corydon hadn't seen them. Now the queen spoke.

'They have new leaders,' she said, her soft precise voice somehow audible amidst the hubbub. 'Akhilleus, who is guarded by a sea-daimon that some say is his mother, and a man called Odysseus. I know little of him, but I do know that High King Agamemnon was so eager to have him that he sent an argosy to his home in Ithaka . . .' Her voice tailed off.

'Then', said Hektor, 'we defeat these two in plain battle. Call each to single combat.'

Corydon's heart lurched. Single combat hadn't helped Medusa. He could see a little of her in this wiry young man, who had leapt onto the table to volunteer.

'I will fight him,' Hektor cried.

'And you will die if you do,' said Sthenno calmly. 'The stars speak clearly. And Akhilleus is virtually invincible. Have you not seen spear and arrow bounce off his flesh as if it were made of the metal of the stars themselves? His mother is a sea-daimon, and she has made him proof against any weapons forged by holding him in the dark waters of the River of Hades' lands; his body drank death there, and so it cannot be pierced by death.'

'But Philoktetes' bow—'

Sthenno interrupted curtly. 'That is nothing to place faith in. The poison cannot hurt him, I tell you.'

'How did she hold him in the Styx?' Euryale asked. Sthenno shrugged. Sikandar was sitting nearby; he seemed about to speak. But his great father had moved on.

'What is Akhilleus, what is Odysseus, without followers?' he said. 'He may be made of metal, but those who serve him are of flesh and blood. We do not need to destroy him. We need patiently to destroy his followers. This will break his heart, too. For indeed, I think he has one, this hero. He is not a metal man, nor a man of straw.' The wintry chill in his voice shook Corydon. Did Akhilleus really deserve to have his heart broken? Perhaps the king saw him wince, for he gave a wry smile. 'Little one,' he said, 'I do not seek any man's destruction. But I do seek to keep my city, and in peace.' Corydon bowed his head. But in his heart a rebellious wish for an end to all this continued to flicker like a wavering flame.

'Sire,' he said, 'have any tried a peace embassy? Since all here think Helena a bad buy, why not return her to her vendor? Then Agamemnon would have no excuse to attack.'

There was a long silence. There were doubtful murmurs. Sikandar spoke. 'I would gladly do this,' he said. And then fell silent.

Hektor spoke. 'But, friend, there is a disadvantage,' he said. 'If we return Helena, we will earn the hatred of the goddess who entrusted her to my brother. And have you ever seen what Aphrodite's wrath can do?'

'No,' said Corydon staunchly, 'but I have seen Hera's. And Athene's. And you yourselves were saying only a moment ago that their anger was worse.'

Hektor turned his wine cup in his hand; the firelight swirled over the black figures of two wrestlers on its side. 'Aphrodite can send men mad,' he said. 'There were once two cities on a great plain, much as ours. Beautiful, with slender turrets piercing the blue sky. Someone offended Aphrodite, and the men of the city began running mad with love. Not even the children were safe. Eventually a great djinn of shrivelling fire came and the city was ash on a wind that blew for five years, to destroy forever the memory of what they had done. The cities were called Sodom and Gomorrah. I have seen where they stood.'

Corydon said no more. He still felt unreconciled. He wanted to tell them what Hera's anger had done to Atlantis, to Tashkurgan. But of what use was it to make them hopeless? He was still turning over in his mind the idea of some kind of truce with Aphrodite – a really huge sacrifice? – when the Snake-girl, utterly silent till then, pressed his arm with her tail. She lowered her voice to a hiss so soft it was like shifting sand.

'They are right. Pyrrhus is mad with Aphrodite's madness, and it is much more dreadful than you know.' Corydon noticed that she held her hands across her softly scaly belly as she spoke. A sudden recollection of Medusa cupping her womb ripe with Gorgos pierced him, and he understood her gesture. It was the same. His heart swelled with hope; perhaps she could love and accept the baby after all.

'I will care for you,' he said, trying to sound firm and confident. She took his hand in hers and placed it on her belly. Faintly, within, his monster-sense felt the small insect-flutter of a life within. A rush of protective love welled up in him. With it came a sharply ironic awareness; here was he, holding between his hands Pyrrhus's child, ready to die to protect the seed of a man who was ready to die to kill him and his friends.

'Well, a battle plan is needed, then,' said Penthesilea. The sphinx nodded. Corydon wondered how she had tamed it.

The sphinx heard his thought, and swivelled her yellow eyes to his face. Then she spoke calmly, cutting across someone's long speech. 'Little monster-boy, I do not serve. I am her companion. My people cast me out, long ago. The Amazons took me in. Now I have persuaded some of them to help. We do little to avert doom.'

Everyone stared, and Corydon felt shamed. But he spoke up. 'Can you not use your magic powers?' he asked. 'Enchant the army?'

'I have only small might,' she said. 'We cannot turn entire armies. An army has a will many times the weight of the individual men in it. Training, collective motivation . . .' Her voice was mocking.

'But what of the leaders?' Corydon persisted. He remembered all too well the sphinxes charming the heroes on that cliff, only a few short weeks ago. 'Could you not break that will by controlling those who lead it?' The sphinx was silent, and Corydon could see her turning over the plan.

'It might be possible,' she said. 'The memory of my colleagues shows it would be possible if they were all separate and alone. But they are guarded night and day, and in battles they are always near their troops. There would be no chance to get near them.' Her voice rose in song. 'The silence, the deep quiet of all the stars . . . The love that moves the spheres and the glinting stars . . .' Sthenno smiled in delight, but other people began drumming their fingers and sighing. Corydon wondered why she'd said it. Sphinxes usually meant something by their songs. He thought about the stars . . . was she talking of fate? Then he remembered. The daimons of the air . . . could that be it?

'What of the daimons of the air?' he asked abruptly, interrupting a long speech much as the sphinx had done. Some of the Trojan warriors were plainly wondering if the monsters were more trouble than they were worth. But Hektor and Priam looked interested.

'Yes, the daimons!' Hektor said. 'Our friend is right. They have power. It is their power Khryses called initially, to make the plague. But they were too pure. So he called on Loxias. Even now, they stir up winds that keep the airs around the Greek camp as a kind of wall, so that Loxias's plague may not menace Ilium or its people.'

'But the daimons have often spoken of the stars.'

'Why can't they tell the stars to fall?' said Priam sadly, his royalty an unbearable weight of sorrow. 'Let us end in silver fire.' Everyone was silent, but Corydon's whole body rebelled. Priam caught his eye, and noted its fierce refusal. He smiled faintly. 'Some still have the will to resist, it seems,' he said.

'Many,' said Hektor firmly. He caught Sikandar's eye, and he too nodded, though Corydon could see that he truly agreed with his father.

'And I have an idea,' said an old, grizzled man in a leather apron. 'Did any of you ever see Gorgos's sword?'

There were some nods, and the smith continued. 'It was his mother's, astonishing though that seems to us even in Penthesilea's company. It was made of a strange metal. Not bronze. Its blade was black, and Gorgos said it had been made from a star that fell from the sky. It was far harder than anything I have ever seen before.'

'But philosophers say the stars are but matter like ourselves,' said Sikandar quickly. He could foresee the next step, and he evidently disliked it.

'Perhaps they are transformed by flight, or perhaps philosophers are wrong. They have probably not been to look,' said Hektor. 'I see your plan, Eumenides. What if the daimons ask for some stars to fall? Then we too could have better blades.' His eyes shone. 'Then their metal would make our swords.'

Corydon was shocked, and Sthenno outraged. 'King Priam,' she said, her high voice sweet. 'King, you do not wish the stars to begin destroying themselves to preserve your city. You do not wish that. The years of men are few, but the stars go on forever. We cannot destroy the immortals to save ourselves.'

Priam nodded gravely, and Corydon could see that he respected Sthenno's words. But others murmured. 'They are immortals themselves,' Corydon heard one man say. 'They all hold together. We are but dust to them.'

Corydon knew he had to stop them. Extinguishing the stars to win a war would make the Morge-mage's acts seem wise.

'No,' Corydon said, anger conquering shyness. 'I have another plan. Friends of Troy, the Greeks are not your true enemies. You know not what you are, nor what is being done to you. Your true enemies are the Olympian gods themselves. It is they who have decided to destroy your city, because you are too wise. Because you have too many knowledges. Because you have poets singing in the streets, and artists making paintings that are even more beautiful than the real world. All this challenges their power, and they will kill you for it. The Greeks are but their weapons, like a man's spear in his right hand. It is the man who must die; if the spear's wood makes its shaft too tough to break, then we must aim our own spear at the man's throat. Allow me to think of a plan to end the Olympians' reign. You must hold the Greeks off until I succeed. But do not bring more of the gods' enemies to destruction in the battle. The stars spell out the ending of the reign of Zeus. Sthenno has seen it. Haven't you, Sthenno?'

Sthenno bowed her head. There was a long silence.

'Even if that is true,' said Priam, at last, 'what can mere men do against the gods?'

'Mere men, mere men! Do you not know the gods need you, and not the other way about?' said Euryale impatiently. 'Why be so humble? Without you they would wither like leaves. They would fade into the common light of morning. It is you and your worship that burnish them and gives them lustre.'

'But what of the old gods?' asked Sikandar. 'They do us no harm, and much good. Can we still have faith in them? Can they have faith in us?'

Priam spoke from deep weariness. 'We have invited our household gods many times to defend our homes, with incense and prayers. They do nothing. They wait for us to act. Because they are not gods of war. They act to make our homes feel warm and safe to us, not to *make* them safe. They make our houses homes; they cannot make them citadels. And it is the same with the little chthonic gods of wood and stream and hill. They are mighty in their own domains. They have no might to oppose the will of the heavenly powers. To outlast them, perhaps. To survive them. But not to master them.'

Corydon's thoughts ran deep, to his own father. Mighty in his own domain . . . 'Then how,' he asked, 'how did the Olympians come to fill the sky? For it was not always so. Once they too were little gods. How comes it that they now rule all?'

Priam sighed. Euryale spoke sternly. 'It was men's doing,' she said. 'As men spread out over the earth, they took their little local gods with them. They wanted every place to be the same. So gradually the dominion of a few gods grew great. Men called the gods of others by the names they knew. Every sky god became King Zeus. Every hunter became Apollo. So a few gods came to rule more and more land. They longed to see their own extended lands, and so they ascended the mountain, becoming forever separate from the land . . . And so there was nothing left to connect them with the men who loved them, feared them. Not even the earth under their feet.'

'Spread out against the limitless sky, they block the light.' The sphinx's cool voice was assenting. 'When the stars threw down their spears, and watered heaven with their tears, Zeus he smiled his work to see.' She smiled herself. No one knew what she meant, or what they might do to help. But a germ of an idea was growing in Corydon, a cunning kleptis idea. The Olympians had become mighty by combining their strength with that of many other little gods, by becoming supergods. What if the monsters and the little gods of earth could do the same? He wasn't sure it was truly possible – and monsters had never combined well, being already precarious blends of snake and girl, boy and goat, metal and flesh – but wait! There was Gorgos, who was both monster and god, and whose body was less unstable than most . . . Could the little gods of field and hill and river somehow come together in him? If so he might be a champion for Troy . . .

And repeat his mother's fate, said a voice in his head. But he squelched his dread. His mouth was opening to tell his plan to the council, when the sphinx spoke again. 'Out of the mouths of babes and sucklings,' she said, and, 'your young men will see visions.' She looked directly at Corydon with her huge golden eyes. Corydon felt as if he were drowning in them. She withdrew her gaze. And now she spoke clearly. Corydon felt exposed, as if a wind had blown away all leaves from an autumnal tree. 'He knows.'

Priam looked at Corydon. He could see that the sphinx's endorsement meant that he would be heard.

Haltingly, Corydon explained his idea. Sikandar's face lit up, and Sthenno and Euryale began talking excitedly. Priam's face was full of hope, and he began eagerly questioning the sphinx and the gorgons. The priests and priestesses began arguing about how to proceed. One priestess asked how they might summon the wood and field gods, and another how wood, earth, water and fire might occupy the same space. And who should they occupy? Already the Trojan princes and heroes were outdoing each other, trying to volunteer to be the hero possessed by the gods. But the Minotaur was silent.

Corydon put a hand on the great, softly furred arm.

'My friend,' his soft voice rumbled. 'The little gods combined may win. And then we will truly have made a monster. We will depose the Olympians, and have another such in their place, one not constrained even by lust for power. All that wildness . . . Do you remember Vreckan? Then we will have to set about destroying our own creation. Have you not seen enough of that?' His great head drooped. Then he went on, his voice so soft it was like a faint murmur of wind.

'And if we lose, the little gods will also be lost. And men will lose forever the sense of a home, the sense of their own place.'

He gave a great bull-like roar. 'It would be better for

Troy to fall.' There was a shocked silence. Sthenno clashed her wings for attention.

'If this is to come,' she said, 'it is Gorgos's destiny. And he cannot fight the Olympians, but only the Akhaian champion. Akhilleus. We must wait. Until he returns. And in the meantime we must think of a means to attack the Olympians themselves.'

'And we must hold,' rumbled the Minotaur softly. 'Tomorrow I have a new machine. And another plan. Khryses has a healing herb that will cure the plague. If we offer it to the Akhaians in exchange for their withdrawal . . .'

'No!' Trojan voices broke out from all sides. Levelly, coldly, Hektor spoke. 'Let them die,' he said. 'They have taken many a brave man's life. The more of them who die, the better.'

The Minotaur bowed his head. It was clear that he was unhappy. And Corydon could see that they all resembled their foes too much already. He thought of the choking, screaming troops. This was no longer even warfare. It was vengeance. But wasn't vengeance what he had wanted himself? Vengeance for the lions . . . for Medusa . . . for Atlantis . . . Wasn't that what he wanted too?

No. He wanted a world in which such things no longer happened. Not a world in which the only way to prevent them was to do them himself.

'We must find a way to destroy them,' he said. 'When Gorgos returns. Till then we must hold on as best we can.' He looked at Priam, at Hektor, and saw their fear, their pain, their frustration. What would have to hold was their patience, and he could see that it was thinning. Suddenly he remembered a night on a kleptis-raid. The other boys had burst out far too soon and the shepherds had caught two of them and beaten one until he died.

The Snake-girl put a soft coil of her tail on his hand. It was warm and he felt a flicker of comfort; she had not lost the power to give in her troubles.

Priam stood up. 'The council is over,' he said. 'Tomorrow we begin the battle again. My friend' – he turned to the Minotaur – 'are your machines ready?'

The Minotaur looked up. Without additional formality, he said simply, 'Yes.' It was clear that he did not see Priam as a king or as special. There was some murmuring, but Priam didn't seem to mind. He smiled. 'We all rely on you, my dear friend,' he said warmly. The Minotaur looked down. Everyone else got to their feet and the Minotaur took Corydon's hand.

'Come,' he said. 'I want to talk. But I must go and make sure my machines are all right. Would you come with me?' He still sounded shy. Corydon smiled warmly, waved to the others, and together they left the meeting room.

μv

Twelve

Corydon followed the Minotaur through the long twisting corridors of Priam's palace. 'It reminds me of my prison,' said the great black monster. 'It's very old. But I liked my own home much more. I could smell the thyme everywhere.' His face was still, dreaming. 'They've given me a room, though.' Their way led them past many staring faces. Corydon felt the eyes skinning him; was he friend, foe, good or ill omen? He kept his head bent. He didn't want to make any silent promises to the hopeful eyes.

They reached a series of storage rooms. Corydon saw that the food store was guarded, and realised what it meant. 'The corn dole is down to half a measure a day,' said the Minotaur. 'The Greeks have destroyed the harvest. The port is blockaded. Much came by sea. Now we rely on the slow land caravans. And last week they took one of these, too. No one is starving yet, but the children begin to look hungry.' Corydon shivered.

Though he had seen much, he had never before seen starvation, or plague, the accompaniments of war.

'But my machines might help,' said the Minotaur hopefully. 'They are not only war machines. They may make it possible to gather food from further away than Mount Ida.' He turned several keys and flung open the door to the last storeroom, an immense wood door with a complicated shutting mechanism. Corydon lifted the cresset from the hall.

But the room was utterly empty. The Minotaur looked around as if he couldn't believe it. Like a puzzled dog, he searched the room with his eyes. Then he turned, and a roar broke from him, a great bellow of rage. Then he sat down and put his great head in his hands.

'They've gone,' he said, in a simple, hurt voice. 'Gone. All ten of them. And my plans for using them. And the launchers. All gone.'

Corydon was shocked. Quickly, he asked, 'Could someone have moved them?'

The Minotaur shook his head, as if the question was a distracting fly. 'I alone have the keys. It cannot be.' The Minotaur examined the door lock. 'All is well here,' he said. Then he turned to one of the guards, who had heard his cry and had come in to investigate. 'Did you see them? Did you?'

'I was sent to escort the royal ladies to the council chamber,' said the guard, swallowing; it was clear he feared the Minotaur.

The Minotaur looked around. 'But they were here,'

he said. 'They were here. They were. I came late to the council, while a man accused Sikandar of causing the war.' The council had been well underway.

'How many people knew they were here?' Corydon asked.

The Minotaur put his head in his hands again. 'Each machine had two man trained to use it,' he said. 'But they did not know where the machines were kept. And I had two assistants. Euryale sometimes came. I saw her paintings and some gave me ideas.'

He stood up. 'Corydon, the battle. We must not stop to resolve this matter. I must go to Hektor so we can remake our plans.' And with a sigh, he left the room. Corydon stayed, searching for some clue. But the place was swept clear. The thief or thieves had left nothing behind.

It was, however, obvious that Troy had a new problem. Someone within the walls of Troy had done this. There was a traitor within the gates.

Corydon hurried after the Minotaur. Grimly, they went to report to Priam and Hektor that the machines were gone, and that the Greeks probably had them. Priam, his face set, called Sthenno, Euryale and the sphinxes to him, and warned them of what they would now have to face.

Euryale tried to encourage him. 'King,' she said, 'do not fear. We shall suffice. We always have. We will study the plans of these things with the Minotaur and determine how to best them.' Priam sighed, but the others nodded, the sphinxes keeping their heads lowered so their eyes did not enchant the king.

The Minotaur went to get his sketches, and when he returned all the flying monsters bent over them. 'When we have studied them,' said Sthenno, 'we will summon the daimons, and then the other leaders. We will instruct them.' But Hektor, angry and flushed, insisted they search for the thief, and Corydon explained again that there were no clues at all. As he did so, he began to wonder if any mortal could have done this; not a footprint, not even the dust disturbed . . . Maybe the daimons might know something?

He suggested this, and Hektor clapped him on the shoulder, a little too hard. Corydon lurched slightly. 'Good boy!' cried the prince. 'A fine idea. They see everything.'

'But they may not choose to reveal it,' said Sthenno. 'Like the stars.' She was hunched over a sketch that showed a kind of giant wasp-machine, a stinger in its rear that could evidently spew out flame. As Corydon watched her, she gave a sudden shiver. He moved to put a hand on her shoulder, and she turned her head. Her usually calm bronze face was somehow troubled. She put a wing around Corydon, however, and stood up, the sketch still in her hand. The Minotaur was explaining how to destroy the weapons on the various crafts, how to block up their fuel pipes so that their flame-throwers would not work, and all the monsters listened attentively.

As they did so, an astonishing thing happened. The air in the room turned blue, like the sky of evening. Drifting about in it lazily were a series of shapes, like the papery cutouts of men and birds, floating rather than flying in the smoky torchlit air. One large shape detached itself from the others and was wafted towards Priam, like a leaf on the wind.

There was a sound like shrill song, not unlike the song of Sthenno herself; a kind of lark's song that eddied and swirled.

'That is their speech,' said the Minotaur. 'Only a few understand them. Priam is one; he was an acolyte in their temple as a boy.'

Priam was singing to the blue daimons as the Minotaur spoke, telling them their need. The tall one stood in front of him, and Corydon could tell it was angry; its bluishness had a hard shimmer, like the hot blue of a huge star.

Priam turned to the others. 'They are angry about the plague,' he said. 'They say the work of Loxias has made miasmas in the air which is their food. They say that if we pollute the air then they cannot be our friends. They also say they cannot fight for us. But they say they will try to disable the machines without hurting other men.'

He produced a burst of grateful-sounding song. No one else felt especially pleased. It was plain that the daimons could eliminate the Akhaians if they felt like it. Penthesilea, who had been summoned with the other war leaders to plan for the disaster, looked mutinous. She seemed on the verge of speech, but Sikandar plucked at her arm and she subsided.

'Ask them if they know who the thief was,' said Hektor urgently.

Priam spoke, and a long fluting birdlike song broke from the daimons. Priam turned. 'It was the god with winged feet, Hermes,' he said bluntly. 'They knew because they saw him, but they say we too should have guessed from the comic way he did it. A kind of joke. Now you see it, now you don't.' He looked surprised. 'But now the Akhaians have even the Olympians running their errands, we can have no hope. None.'

Corydon thought of Hermes, and his response to the lions; which side was he on? Could he be trying to stop the war, prevent the machines from dealing out more death? Aloud, he said, 'We too have gods, and ours will help us. Just as the daimons have. And my plan may work. Tomorrow, however, our task is to keep the flying machines from landing in the city.' It was abruptly clear that no one had realised that this was the risk, but that they now did. Priam and Hektor seemed silent from despair, so Corydon spoke again. 'We must place a sphinx on each tower,' he said, 'to intercept this threat. Minotaur, how many machines are there?'

The Minotaur spoke softly. 'There are ten. Though the Greeks may begin to build them themselves by copying my design. But I made ten.' Corydon longed to hug him, his voice was so sad. He could feel the thoughts, so like his own. *I meant to help . . . Only to help . . .*

Euryale spoke. 'Sthenno and I, together with the sphinxes, will try to destroy these machines over the field of battle. And the daimons have promised to disable some of them. But all troops must wear bronze breastplates, and we must station buckets of water and sand about the city in case they manage to set fire to it. The men must also guard against smoke.'

It was plain that the preparations would take all night. Corydon turned to Sthenno, who was unusually silent. 'Is something wrong?' he asked.

Sthenno put her bronze wings around him, and hugged him hard. 'It is difficult for an immortal to face death,' she said. 'I have seen so many deaths. In parchments and on battlefields. Now I see something . . . but it may be just fear . . . I wish I could be on the island again with you, mormo.' Corydon felt a cold shudder down his spine. Was Sthenno truly saying she feared for herself? She had never said that before, despite the dangers she had faced.

'This is not the place you will die,' he said. 'Somewhere so far from home.'

'Wherever there are stars,' she said, 'I am at home.' She spoke briefly to the daimon leader, having plainly learned his speech. His response sounded like a mourning cry, but died away peacefully. Sthenno turned, resolutely. 'And now we must help with buckets of water,' she said.

As Corydon left the palace he couldn't help thinking that Sthenno knew what might happen in the battle, and that that was the reason she was so afraid. Maybe some of her parchments would help him understand. But he realised that although he had been to Euryale's studio-house, he had not seen Sthenno's parchments; she had obviously found somewhere else to study them. So he asked a guard simply and plainly where Sthenno lived.

The guard laughed. 'She lives up in that tower,' he said pointing to a rickety structure that leant like a spear at ease. 'But you had better be careful. She does not like being disturbed.'

As Corydon hurried through the lamp-lit streets to reach the rickety building, he wondered whether he should be doing this. Sthenno was his friend. Should he really be searching through her papers? Also what might a guard think if he saw someone rifling through her belongings?

The tower was unlocked, and he climbed the wooden steps, carefully dodging the missing boards and gaping holes. Then he was at the top, a small round room with its roof torn away to reveal icy stars and a jet black sky. All round the room were piles of parchments, spread on a table and on the floor. On the table were a round metal disc and a piece of parchment. Corydon moved closer, and noticed four symbols: a whirlwind, a wave curling fiercely, a flame, and what looked like a lump of something. Around the rim were some hastily scratched symbols. Corydon examined the parchment and noted that it was a kind of key; the same symbols appeared, but beside them was a Greek translation. He read, 'Earth . . . Water . . . Fire . . . Air . . . These are life itself. When all life is done, the city must fall and rise again beyond the seas.'

So the city must fall . . . but what did it mean about rising again? He knitted his brows, and as he did the air turned sharply blue, like the way moonlight looks on snow. There was a cold breath of air, and a light singing sound. He looked up to see one of the papery daimons floating above him. Slowly it drifted down to stand before him. It sang a long garbled phrase, and Corydon thought it was trying to tell him something, but he had no idea what. Then with a sharp movement, the creature began twirling rapidly in its place, like a spindle. As it twirled, it rose to a sharp point, then with a furious buzz its point touched his ear, and it vanished into his head. Corydon felt it buzzing there, and suddenly a clear bell-like voice spoke inside him.

'It is the prophecy of the city's fall. But you should not be here. This room is that of great Sthenno, watcher of the stars. We honour her because she guards the secrets of the universe.'

'I know she dreads the battle,' said Corydon aloud. 'So I decided to visit her room to find out why. I want only to protect her.'

'I can see that,' said the voice, booming in his ears like wind in a clearing, 'but you have no business here. You should ask her.'

'I did,' said Corydon.

'Very well,' said the voice. 'The stars show that the theft of the machines is the beginning of the end for Troy. It means battle in the air, and when there have been battles in air, water, earth, and finally fire, Troy too will be destroyed, as Atlantis was. But from that death it will rise again, far greater than before; it will be reborn as an empire so great that all the gods will marvel at it.'

'And will this empire last forever?' asked Corydon hopefully. He felt he'd been asked to pin his faith to Troy after Atlantis had fallen; now he was being asked to hope for yet another city.

'No,' said the spirit. 'No. But its greatest city shall

endure. It will last for thousands of years and will rule the lives of many countless millions.'

'And will it be like Troy and Atlantis? A place of ideas? A menace to the gods?'

'The Olympian gods will fall,' said the spirit. 'And I see your dream. They will fall by your hand, Corydon Panfoot, though it will take some years for mortal men to see that the gods are dead stocks and stones.'

By *his* hand! But how? He knew enough about prophecy to know he was unlikely to get a direct answer.

'You will find the way,' said the daimon in his head. 'You must know by now that all immortals answer questions so. But you must also have found it true.'

Corydon had another, more pressing question. 'Can you help in the battle?' he asked urgently.

'We are not warriors,' said the voice firmly. 'We do not fight. But we can help. Not by killing, and not by knowing. We can awaken others who can help in the ways you hope.' It was plain that it would say no more. It withdrew from him with a slight pop, and floated away, just a leaf on an autumn wind.

Corydon sat down on the floor and pulled an old cloak over himself. The moon rose, hard and bony white. He fell asleep, his hand around his knees, and when Sthenno came in she did not have the heart to wake him, though she felt a sharp longing for comfort, tonight. She looked up at the stars, and felt a kind of cold comfort from them. Whatever happened on earth, they would continue their great and fiery dance.

*

The morning dawned chill and foggy. Corydon woke at first light, and at once became aware of a terrible sound, like a dissonant version of Sthenno's clashing wings. Then there was a grinding sound, like metal wheels clashing.

The flying machines! Were they already overhead? Corydon looked up, and so did Sthenno, who sprang aloft. She peered back in through the tower window.

'They come,' she said grimly. 'Go, Corydon. Help the peltasts, and the sphinxes.' And she flew off. Corydon tore down the stairs and ran through the streets. Already men and women were looking up fearfully. He took the stairs up to the walls three at a time. The machines droned. Ahead, he could see Sthenno and Euryale flying out to meet them, the rising sun catching their wings.

The machines were long triangles like dragons, with tails hanging behind them. One of the tails somehow twitched itself over the creature's head, and a thin thread of flame came from it. So the daimons had not managed to disable all the weapons. The Minotaur spoke beside him. 'They stopped the ballistas,' he said. 'They stopped them from firing spears. And they told me they blocked the fire pipe with small stones, and bent it. But the Akhaians must have noticed and fixed it somehow.'

Now it was as if ten dragons were converging on Troy. Sthenno and Euryale flew steadily towards them, but beside the lumbering metal giants, even Euryale looked puny. The gorgons suddenly swept upward to try to come down on the machines from above.

A piercing whistle sounded from one metallic creature.

All the tails turned forward, then swivelled upward. Ten bursts of conical flame combined, and then shot towards the gorgons.

Euryale swerved suddenly, crashing heavily onto a flying machine and managing to grab another with her claw. Both lost height abruptly, and the one she'd caught began hurtling towards the plain below, while the other too lost height, forced to land and bury itself in flying dirt. The Trojans cheered. That left eight.

But Sthenno had not fared so well. As she pounced hawklike on one clumsy beast, the pilot managed to turn his flame-thrower upward. At such close range, it emitted a fierce high-pressure geyser of flame, beating against her right wing. To his horror, Corydon could see the bronze melting like wax. Sthenno tried to control her flight, but with one wing all but useless, she was helpless to do so. Flapping desperately, she tried to reach the walls, but already she was below their rim. One of the guardian sphinxes dived for her, and managed to get beneath her, singeing herself on the melting metal. She grimaced, and Sthenno lost her precarious hold. She slid from the sphinx's back and crashed to the ground, her damaged wing broken into shards during the fall. She lay exposed on the plain. She tried to rise, fell back, her eyes staring at the sky as if seeking a last sight of the stars she loved.

The flying machines closed in for the kill. Frantically, Euryale stood over Sthenno's body and tried to beat them off; she snatched one from the air, tore off another's wing. But there were still six of them. Four peeled off to attack the city. The others dive-bombed the gorgons, evading Euryale's claws. It was plain that whoever was piloting them was becoming better with practice.

Corydon was frantic, but it was clear that the sphinxes, less manoeuvrable than the gorgons, would find it very hard to prevent them entering the city.

They tried. One sphinx flew down to help Euryale defend Sthenno, while the others strove frantically to block the metal machines. One sphinx used her hypnotic gaze on the pilot, but thick flickering flames from behind soon set her alight, and she fell, screaming horribly. Euryale rushed to put out the fire, exposing Sthenno. Sthenno gave a faint cry, and Corydon sensed that she was groping for a spell, but then pain made her lose consciousness and her head rolled – or was she dead? Corydon took aim at the nearest metal beast to him. Its gleam reminded him of Talos, who had destroyed another feathered creature by fire. So with all his hatred he aimed, and his stone hit the pilot's hand; the man cursed, but his machine drove on, low, towards the walls. It dived over them into the city.

Troy's defences had been breached.

THIRTEEN

There was a low thrumming wail. At first Corydon thought it was the people of Troy, but then as it increased he realised it was the walls. They were humming louder and louder, until it was impossible to hear anything above the shrill, hard sound. Men stood with their mouths open.

And an answering hum came from far away. Straining his eyes in the direction of the sound, Corydon could see something like golden rain in the desert, something gathering and massing and forming in the emptiness. It grew larger, swelling with song and sound. And they came, seven djinn, golden cloud-kings of the desert, bringing their empires of sand with them. Each paused outside the city.

Then they noticed the flying machine. Each formed a thin golden thread and poured themselves over the walls, which cried out in welcome to them. Then they ballooned into clouds again, and closed in on the flying machine. It tried to fly beyond them, but Corydon could see that it could not climb sharply enough.

The djinn drew closer and finally blotted the machine out altogether; they were singing so sharply that Corydon could not even hear the machine crash to the streets of Troy. But he knew it must have done so, for now it lay, twisted and gnarled, its pilot turning his dead eyes to the thankless sky. The djinn gathered themselves together, swept beyond the walls, hurled the other flying machines to the ground, and withdrew.

No. One thin golden streamer remained. It hurtled towards the walls – towards Corydon himself – as if bringing some urgent message. It poured itself onto the ground in front of him. And slowly it grew into someone Corydon had not expected to see again.

Bin Khamal gave a wintry little smile. 'I was near Wabar when we all heard the call. I knew it must be to do with you.'

Together they bent over the walls. In the city people were running and cheering raggedly, but Corydon had eyes only for the limp form of Sthenno, carried from the field in Hektor's own war chariot.

'Is she dead?' he called.

'No,' said Euryale. It was clear that she would not leave Sthenno's side. 'Her wing is damaged, though. We must think how to reforge it. If we cannot, she will not be able to fly again. But she will not die of this wound.'

Corydon gave out a long breath of relief. He felt certain that Euryale would find a way to reforge her sister's broken wing. 'I'll come and see her soon,' he promised. He thought with a jolt of Sthenno's own fear before the battle, of what the daimon had said. It was obvious she had had a prophecy about herself. He decided that he must ask her more when she was better. Waving to Euryale, he turned to Bin Khamal.

'What called you to Troy?'

'The walls of seven cities in the world were built by my people, the djinn. All of them have a secret. In each a djinnish sacrifice is imprisoned; when any enemy of the city breaches the walls, that djinn sends out a call to his brothers, and we hear it and come even from the ends of the earth. Troy is such a city, endowed with our magic.'

'What are the others?' Corydon asked.

'Not all still stand; some are gone like the Cittavecchia of old Atlantis. But some stand yet. Wabar, which I visited before rushing to Troy's aid, is another such. But I cannot reveal more. It is a secret of my people.'

'And will you stay now, and help?'

'For a night and a day. Such is our vow. I am with my people now, though it is not the freedom of which I once dreamed. But I would like to see Sikandar again as well as you.'

'I am here, old friend,' said a voice from behind them. Sikandar seized his friend's hand, then looked shy. 'I came to help the peltasts, just as you did.'

They smiled at each other. For a while at least the survivors of the kleptis gang were united, though Azil's absence was a wound. The Minotaur shambled past, his dark head bent. He looked sad and forlorn, so Corydon introduced him to Bin Khamal.

The Minotaur spoke in his low rumble, obviously much

shyer than even Sikandar was. 'I help with the machines. Those that you destroyed were stolen, and I am glad that you stopped them. But I can never forgive myself . . .' His voice trailed off.

Corydon patted his arm. 'You were right to make them,' he said. 'What you said was true.' At the same time he wasn't sure that the Minotaur had been right to want to save Troy at this cost; was it ever right to make a killing machine? And Sthenno . . . 'Let's go and see Sthenno,' he suggested.

'I am too ashamed,' the Minotaur rumbled softly. 'Give her my greetings.' He stood on the walls, his face turned towards the plains. 'I shall keep watch,' he said. 'They may have learnt the secret of making them. It is difficult but not impossible to learn. I will watch them.' It was obvious that he couldn't face Sthenno now.

Watching his face, Corydon saw its haunted sadness change to grim resolution. Suddenly the great monster gave a bellow of fury, and ran for the stairs.

Corydon watched in dread. Was he going to his workshop? No. It was plain that he had suddenly reached a deadly resolve.

The Minotaur emerged into the streets moments later, wearing his breastplate and carrying his axe and shield. It was obvious that he was going to attack; maybe even to kill himself to end his shame and grief. He disappeared from sight, and Corydon thought he'd gone towards the salley port. He hurried to follow the huge beast, accompanied only by Bin Khamal and Sikandar. The salley port was closed, but they flung it open and closed it behind them. The Minotaur was ahead of them, his great head lifted, as if he were trying to smell out the Akhaians.

Then he lowered his head, and charged, his legs pumping furiously. Corydon could see the bull was uppermost in him, the angry bull that had been goaded again and again until all he feels is a killing rage. He ran straight for a line of the Akhillean ant-men, and with a fierce toss of his head he scattered their too-neat ranks, turning them to mere hay tossed by the thresher. He ran on, and brought his axe down on a man's head, swung, pivoted, struck again and again and again. His horns were dark with the blood of men. The Greeks fled before his rushing charge like sheep fleeing a wolf.

A huge man turned to face him, a man as tall as the Minotaur, and as thickset. He carried a huge shield, bigger than any Corydon had ever seen, the size of a cartwheel. Beside him was a tiny, nimble man holding a bow. The Minotaur's axe flashed down, but the little man swerved elegantly and pivoted to arm his bow; it was so graceful that it could be mistaken for a ballet. Corydon, seeing the danger, armed his sling and fired. The little man was hit on one elbow; it spoilt his aim and his arrow went wide.

By now, the Minotaur had begun to fight the giant with horn and axe, and the plains rang with the bronze clash of their weapons. The giant himself had a long stabbing spear, and he had already goaded the Minotaur with it; black blood ran down the monster's bare arm, its passage slowed by his thick black fur. Corydon saw Sikandar draw his bow and send a flight of two arrows straight at the giant; one pierced his knee behind the greave, and he gave a howl, but did not stop his fighting. His teeth were set in the fierce grin of battle.

A swift movement caught Corydon's eye. The small bowman had knelt to draw his bow, and now he fired, catching Bin Khamal in the arm. Bin Khamal gave a cry, and sank to his knees; though his djinn-flesh closed up almost at once, he could still feel pain. Corydon bent to help him, but the fight was now all around them as Greeks and Trojans heard the battle and ran to join the fray.

Then Corydon heard it. The swift, unmistakeable footfalls of Akhilleus, running towards them, almost silent, and deadly as a shorebound wave, bearing on its shining top a white crest foaming and free. His steps grew impossibly swift, and he extended his spearshaft to leap over the combatants and confront Corydon and the wounded, cursing djinn-boy. Sikandar fitted an arrow to the string with a trembling hand. He fired, but Akhilleus's jump was far swifter than he had anticipated. Then Akhilleus struck the ground, as delicate and precise as a landing waterbird, his feet outstretched.

But one of them struck the little man's spent arrow, and great Akhilleus gave a roar that silenced even the Minotaur as the arrow pierced his flesh – a roar of amazement at feeling any pain at all. He cursed, and with his wounded foot began to limp back towards the camp, supported by the ant-men who had come hurrying up to help their leader. Corydon sent a single slingstone after them. It missed, and he wondered briefly why he always found it difficult to make up his mind to want to kill this terrible shining man.

But now the big man saw his chance while the Minotaur stood dumbfounded. He prepared to thrust his swift and deadly spear at the great beast's throat. But reflex saved the Minotaur; his axe flashed down, and the spear fell in two pieces, its end bouncing on the sand. The giant was left holding a stump. He threw it down and ran into the camp, ran and ran as if heading for the ships themselves. With another bellow, the Minotaur followed.

Corydon started after him, but Sikandar spoke. 'Corydon, it is his *aristeia*.'

Corydon didn't know the word. Sikandar explained. 'All warriors have a day or an hour when they are unbeatable and triumphant. It comes from virtue, *arete*. Not the kind of virtue that makes you obey; the virtue you were born to do. Your true nature.' He stopped to kill a warrior. 'Then they are like gods, though only for an afternoon. This is his *aristeia*. His time.' They began trying to fight their way out of the press, using their stones and arrows.

When they were clear and making their way towards the walls, Corydon thought about it. An *aristeia* did not truly mean that the Minotaur was like a god, Corydon thought. Or if he was like a god, perhaps he was like the wrong god. His virtue was not a warrior virtue, but a dark furry kindness and a gift for solitude. So in triumphing on the field of battle, he was not doing what he was born to do, but something else.

The battle raged for much of the day. Corydon saw most of it.

The Trojans had cleared the Greeks from the plains, and confined them to a small line of beachhead around their ships. Corydon had seen the Greeks running all afternoon; without Akhilleus to lead them, they were on the defensive. Eventually, after much fighting, the arrival of dusk forced the Trojans back to Troy.

The Minotaur came last, his head lowered. He did not look like a triumphant warrior, but like one who had been defeated: his horns were stained with blood; his own and that of those he had killed; his fur was thick with it from wrist to elbow. He looked at his axe, its blade dripping with gore, as if wondering how he had come by it. Then he put it down softly. Corydon picked it up and was amazed by its weight. The Minotaur had been wielding it as if it were a light blade. Corydon began to wonder how strong he really was.

Wearily, Corydon resumed his place on the walls. No one had told him he must watch there, but he knew his monster sight could see trouble further off than human eyes could hope to do. Sikandar and Bin Khamal stood with him. After an hour of cold and tiredness and growing dark, Euryale came up to relieve them, saying that Sthenno was mending from the shock but that her wing would need careful remaking.

Just as they were turning to go, they heard a long low horncall from the plains. A great sea horn, fierce and clear and true. Everyone rushed to look out into the gathering dusk, and at the Greeks' fires more distant than before, piercing it like counterfeit stars.

A small group of horsemen was galloping towards the

city. The leader blew his horn for aid, and Corydon could at once see why; another and much larger group of horsemen were closing in on them fast. At their head, Corydon could see the white plume of Akhilleus shining in the darkness, and his armour gleaming like the sea on the shore. He had not been disabled by the wound, then, unless . . .

There was something wrong. Corydon couldn't see the hero's strange silver eyes, but perhaps that was the dust lingering, the dusky air. The newcomers sped towards the small party with the speed of a thrown spear. The hornbearer swung his horse around to face them, then set him to a full gallop, so that he seemed to fly over the plain.

The rider was Gorgos. Corydon couldn't see his face, but only a son of Poseidon, breaker of horses, could so manage a horse.

The leader of the Greek horsemen also turned – not quite so immaculately; could it *really* be Akhilleus, who never did anything less than perfectly? The two raced towards each other, their followers also charging more slowly. Corydon saw the moment when Gorgos's spear left his hand; it flew in a perfect line straight at the white-plumed hero, who raised his shield only just in time. But Gorgos had another spear, and he flung it at the hero; to Corydon's amazement it found the space between greave and saddle, and a gush of warm red blood stained the silver armour.

The hero looked down for a second, and Gorgos seized the moment to draw his sword. The hero's sword appeared in his hand, and the two blades clashed, like lightning in the sky. Gorgos's horse reared up suddenly so that his rider could rain down blows on his opponent from a height. The hero had his shield over his head now. Gorgos's attention was fleetingly caught by one of his band falling, and it infuriated him. He drove his sword into the hero's throat, where the gorget met the breastplate. Black blood bubbled from the mouth, and the white plume began to tilt, then to fall, till the hero lay prostrate on the windy plain, looking up at the sky with eyes grown dim while his lifeblood poured onto the sand. Then a sortie appeared from Troy, and Hektor led it; he kicked the hero's body once, hard, and then plunged his spear time after time into the hero's belly, till it poked out from his back. Then he and the others began systematically stripping off the stained silver armour, the helmet, the shield.

Gorgos was indifferent to plunder. He was watching the fleeing Greeks, riding to their camp with their terrible news. The Trojans all turned for the walls, and rode back hard, passing through the salley port. Gorgos was mobbed by the many friends eager to congratulate him, to greet him, to tell him he had killed great Akhilleus. 'And I have Philoktetes,' said Gorgos happily. 'Here he is.'

He galloped up to the walls to show Philoktetes the Greek camps. Corydon and the kleptis gang went too, trying not to notice the peculiar smell that came from Philoktetes. 'They say his wound never heals,' whispered a Trojan boy. Corydon's heart was in turmoil; here was

Gorgos again, as irresponsible as ever . . . but now a great hero too.

Gorgos flung himself cheerfully at the Minotaur, gave him a hug, and pointed to the camp. Everyone chattered and laughed. Corydon, as always, did not know what to say to Gorgos, or how to return the thump on the shoulder that Gorgos gave him, nor his cheerful, 'I knew you were safe, somehow.' He watched Gorgos caught up in a cloud of merry greetings, and hoped he didn't look sulky. The Minotaur, still shaking from his battle fury, stood close by. Neither found anything to say.

And, because they were silent, they were the first to hear the sound from the Greek camp.

It was not a wail. It was not a scream. It was not a song. It was a cry, high and controlled and clear. As clear and defiant as Gorgos's horncall, but bursting from a terrible grief. The Minotaur looked up as if it at last expressed what he felt. It was a series of sounds made by a naked anger fully controlled and turned like a spear at the throat of Troy. The poet in Corydon thought he had never heard a better lament for the painful mortality of all things.

'It is Akhilleus's war-cry,' said Priam behind them.

And as he said it, they all saw a sight that was the most dangerous any had ever seen. Akhilleus, naked, not even holding a sword, stood in the Greek trench, his hair lit by a brilliant silver flame, as dazzling as lightning, which flickered and ran over his whole body. He did not even have a dagger. But everyone could see the murder in those silver eyes.

'But he died . . . We all saw him die . . . Dead. He's

dead. See, his corpse.' They pointed to the stiffening body spread below them on the plain.

'Only his armour died,' said Corydon. It was as clear as a written scroll. 'He sent out a friend in his armour because he was wounded. His goddess-mother healed his wound. Now he is back. And he wants revenge on us all.'

Gorgos smiled. 'I can face him,' he said, easily.

'Not yet,' said Corydon, finding words for Gorgos at last. 'We have a plan. We will discuss it in council.' He smiled. 'You shall face him, my friend. But you cannot face him alone.'

ξι

FOURTEEN

The council was the same muddle as before. The Snake-girl slid in beside Corydon, looking white and ill. Corydon pressed her hand quickly. Then he banged imperiously on the table; he had had enough of the silliness of Trojan councils and the complaints and grumbles, so reminiscent of the monsters' councils. 'We need to talk of the old gods,' he said. 'All priests and priestesses must come to Sthenno's tower this evening to discuss how to summon their masters. Then we must arrange for them to be summoned or invited to the same place, where Gorgos must await them. And you must ask the Akhaians to send forth their greatest warrior for single combat. We already know who it will be.'

His tone was almost stern. He was amazed to find that the day of battle had left a thread of hard metal in him. He no longer feared to bend these people to his designs, though he knew – none better – that his plan might fail. And said as much. 'Of course we cannot be sure that Gorgos and the small gods can together defeat the

Akhaian champion. But there is at least a chance. And if it fails we can try other plans. And others, and still others, until they weary of their work and go home. We cannot surrender, but we *can* make them stop.'

The Minotaur nodded sturdily, his great head heavy. He was the toast of Troy tonight, even though it seemed their greatest foe had not been removed, and yet no one was more deeply unhappy than he.

'Gorgos,' he said, 'are you willing? Consider. I myself had my own *aristeia* this day. It is not as you think. It is possession by another, a terrible burning from inside. If many gods possess you, you will be changed, your seemly simplicity lost. You will sag like a woman who has borne many children. You may be worn out. You may even die. Is Troy worth all this to you?'

It was a very long speech for the shy Minotaur to make. He sank back ashamed. But his deep eyes met those of Gorgos unflinchingly.

Gorgos smiled. 'I care not for bricks and stones,' he said. 'Troy is not worth all this to me, but my friends are. And if I choose this path, there is a good chance that I may somehow defeat the Olympians, and avenge my mother.'

'We do not even know if it is possible,' said Priam.

But Khryses, priest of the gods, spoke at once. 'Oh, it is little more than most priests and prophets attain,' he said. 'All the gods can take possession of a willing man or woman, and most can force an entrance where none wish to receive them. Inaction is not the risk. The risk is that if he opens himself to many nameless little powers, then some evil spirits or evil gods may find a foothold too.

I can try to protect him by calling only upon those who can be named, but it is still possible to be mistaken. As were we in Loxias. He was truly a local god once, but we know how the Olympians take and take and take the power of such little gods, just as King Agamemnon absorbs the kingdoms of little kings. We cannot be certain we are not making the same mistake twice.'

'It is especially risky that Gorgos is the son of a god who, though not precisely an Olympian, is not exactly *not* an Olympian either,' said Euryale thoughtfully.

'My father will not interfere,' said Gorgos. 'I am still on terms with him. I was his champion in Atlantis, and not even my friends here preferred Vreckan to him, when all was said, and done.' He grinned, and Corydon thought, *But I blame them both, Poseidon and Vreckan. And Gorgos too.* He smiled back, as if in agreement.

'But our great father seeks dominion over Troy,' said the Minotaur heavily. 'And to blot from the earth all who dissent. He is cunning, as we know to our cost.'

'I will safeguard Gorgos as I can, and Sthenno will help me,' said Khryses. 'Any weapon we make may be turned against us, as this day showed only too well. Yet we cannot sit here and wait to be starved out; already the corn dole is down to half a measure, and the children in the streets beg for bread. We must try. Come, Gorgos. You must undergo a cleansing and a ritual before you can be offered to the gods.'

Gorgos got to his feet. With a little smile at Corydon, he followed Khryses. Corydon wondered if he would see his friend again in private; there was so much to say. He felt a familiar cold dread. Would Gorgos's life end in single combat with a hero, like his mother's? But he also felt a strange calm. If that must be so, then so be it.

Quickly, talk in the council turned to Sthenno. One short stumpy man asked, 'How are we going to reforge her wing? It is obvious that this is what we must do.'

'I think that with the help of a blacksmith, the Minotaur and I could reforge it,' said Euryale hesitantly. It was obvious to Corydon that she was scared that Sthenno might remain flightless forever. That down in some deep well of thought Euryale was in terrible anguish over Sthenno's wound. She was reacting to it now as if it were an artistic matter; she evidently found this obscurely comforting.

'Are *you* a blacksmith?' she asked. The stumpy man said he was, but he said that she should approach Volkos, the greatest of the Trojan smiths. He did not come to councils. *A sign of good sense,* thought Corydon. But he did make weapons for all of Troy. Euryale said she would go at once. Corydon followed her to the door, and Bin Khamal and Sikandar went with them. The Snake-girl looked wistfully after them, but remained in her seat. Corydon felt a little snubbed by Khryses; there seemed no place for him by Gorgos's side.

But in this he was wrong. Khryses was waiting for him outside. 'Gorgos must have an esquire,' he said, in his stern priest's voice. 'You can serve as one, if you wish.'

'I am no esquire,' said Corydon. 'I am a simple peltast shepherd.'

'But a leader,' said the priest. 'A leader of boys and also

of men. I have marked you and your followers; one a djinn, one a prince of Troy. It takes a strong will to make a whole of such parts, and I have come to see that the will is yours.' His deep eyes seemed to burn into Corydon's.

Bin Khamal laughed. 'But Corydon does not always lead us,' he said. 'He has most ideas, and so we fall in with them. His wits are good. You are doing the same. Falling in with his plan. Do not make a mystery of sense, good priest.' His tone was tinged with dislike.

Khryses smiled, a smile full of knowledge held by men, as opposed to little boys. It irritated all of them.

Corydon spoke. 'I will do all that is required,' he said. 'I will help Gorgos. Has he gone to prepare already?' The priest nodded. 'What ritual is needed?'

'First he must be bathed in seven waters. Then he must watch all night in the temple of the Great Goddess, to placate her.'

It sounded very boring and Corydon couldn't imagine Gorgos sitting still for any of it. 'Is all this truly necessary?' he asked.

Khryses nodded solemnly. 'It is a courtesy a man does to the gods,' he said. 'Boredom too is a sacrifice,' and here he smiled a little.

'Can you organise the priests and priestesses in time?' Corydon asked.

Khryses nodded, evidently enjoying himself. 'Yes, I can. I have already made contact with them through the daimons of the air. Everyone in Troy and all the Atlanteans will bring their household gods to the square outside the temple next morning. Then Gorgos must go out to wake the gods in the woods and rivers, with the appropriate priests and priestesses.'

'How will we get out?' asked Corydon. 'What about the Akhaians?'

'There is a hidden way, of which I may not speak,' said Khryses. 'But it will be safe.'

Corydon questioned him no more. The priest led the way to a dark temple that Corydon had never seen before. It reeked of earth-magic; he could smell the stink of pigs and the smell of gathered wheat. *Demeter*, he thought, remembering her daughter, the Lady of Flowers. He remembered, too, the tests he had undergone in the Land of the Many. It seemed obvious that somehow Gorgos would be tested too.

And he was right. After the ritual washing, Gorgos and Corydon were led into a large room. In it was a table, and on it was the most complicated twisting of rope that Corydon had ever seen. No not rope, but corn. Lengths of it with the golden grain still attached in places. Impossible lengths of wheat tied and twisted together.

Khryses smiled. 'You will sit on the floor for an hour and observe this knot,' he said to Gorgos. 'When that time has passed, we will come and ask you to untie the knot.' He glanced in distaste at Corydon. 'Your esquire may stay with you. But there is to be no talking. No noise or communication with one another. That will make you impure.' With a swirl of purple cloak, he turned and left the room.

Gorgos looked at the knot. He probed it with his hands and tugged here and there. He picked it up and put it down. Then he smiled, curled up with his head on the knot, and went to sleep. Corydon didn't dare to wake him because he couldn't speak or touch him without making the test invalid. But how was Gorgos going to manage?

Eventually, Khryses came back into the room. When he saw that Gorgos was asleep, and that Corydon was anxious and close to fury, he could not forbear a quiet smile of triumph. The dark eyes flashed. Corydon, already tense as a lyre's strings, couldn't help wondering if this man were truly on their side.

The priest woke Gorgos with a tap on his shoulder. Gorgos rolled over sleepily.

'Now,' said Khryses, in his musical voice. 'Unlace the knot.'

Gorgos looked calm. He stood above the knot, then bent low, crouching on his haunches in front of the low table.

Then he drew his shining sword and swept it down on the tight mass of wheat.

The bright blade cleft the knot in two. It cleft the table in two as well, and the halves fell with a sharp clatter. Working briskly, Gorgos effortlessly untwisted the wheat ends until before him lay a mass of crinkled sheaf-pieces.

Khryses scowled. It was obvious that Gorgos had passed a test meant to defeat someone of his abilities. In his sheer simplicity he had proved more than a match for cunning.

'Very well,' said the priest. 'But you must now face a second and harder task. You must enter the maze, and you must find its centre. There you must perform a ritual in honour of the goddess. If you make any mistake, you will know her wrath, and if you do not find the centre, you will wander forever in her realm of underearth, until the ending of the world. Will you try?'

'I will,' said Gorgos.

'And you, will you go with him?'

Corydon shrugged, a tiny part of him wincingly reluctant. Then he smiled. 'Yes,' he said. 'Gladly.'

The priest led them to a low tunnel blocked by a stone. 'Help me move this stone,' he said. Gorgos lifted it clear easily. Gorgos and Corydon entered a dark tunnel.

'May we take a torch?' Corydon asked.

'Yes,' said the priest. 'But it will not burn for ever.'

Corydon took a pine torch from the wall. Holding it aloft, he and Gorgos saw a long tunnel curving away to their left. It had no corners and no junctions. To their right was a similar tunnel. Gorgos stood still, and lifted his head as if he were sniffing; all Corydon could smell was the damp earthy smell of the goddess, and a faint odour of pig. Then Gorgos, who appeared to be listening, turned right.

They walked for some time without passing any junctions, without making any choices, without seeing any living being. The curve seemed to go on forever, like the curve of the earth itself. Perhaps they were to walk all around the world. Corydon could see the walls, slick with mud, and he felt hideously imprisoned, a grain of wheat caught in a furrow. He was not a farmer; he was a shepherd, and he longed for the pale sunlight on upland pastures, the clean winds of his home. What was more, his stomach had begun to rumble. It could not yet be reasonable to be so hungry, but Corydon found thoughts of roast pork and fresh barley bread with honey stalking his imagination.

Gorgos was still listening and smelling when the torch began to burn lower. Corydon knew he must say nothing, but he looked as imploring as he could. Gorgos shook his head, as if to brush off a fly. Then he stopped dead, and suddenly began burrowing into the left-hand wall of the tunnel, as if he were a dog who had hidden a bone there. Earth flew from his fingers. As he scrabbled, he called, 'It's all right, I'm coming.' It was clear that his words were not addressed to Corydon.

Corydon began to help him, dropping the torch. In the utter blackness, he was forced to rely on touch and smell, and to his surprise he found it less terrifying than the dim light of the torch. The echoing tunnel was reduced to a handful of earth, then another handful. It was as if the touch of the earth itself took away his fear. But he still felt wildly hungry, as if he had not eaten for days.

In a rush they broke through the wall, to be all but dazzled by the glare of a thousand thousand torches.

They were in an immense cave, bigger by far than an Atlantean palace, stretching upward into darkness further than they could see. All around it stood women. Old women and young ones, pretty and plain. All wore grey robes daubed with ashes and dark red streaks of what looked horribly like blood. All wore their hair unbound. With one voice, they spoke.

'Men!'

'They shall die,' said a tall woman.

'They shall die hard,' said another. 'And their bones will be thrown into the pit.'

'You greasy stinking zetas, you fat white leering lard-laden louts!' 'You bad-breathed snot-nosed retards!' 'You Kretan liars!' 'I was looking for fools when I met men!' 'If we can send one man over the sea, why can we not send them all?' 'Fat as you are, we could find whole countries out in you!' 'You eat so much that women can smell your farts from a league away!' 'You run so fast from battles that the ground bursts into flames behind you!' The insults broke out from everywhere. Gorgos grinned easily, Corydon uneasily.

Gorgos stepped forward. 'Greetings,' he said. 'I have come to sacrifice a pig. I have spoken to her and she goes consenting. I am the appointed slayer, and afterwards we may all feast.'

There was a roar. Then all the women rushed fiercely upon Gorgos, waving crude iron weapons, roasting irons and pig-knives. But they were stopped by a shout from the grey-haired priestess. 'Wait, sisters, for he speaks the truth!'

'If he can find the pig,' said another slyly, 'then we will let him go.'

The women began chanting softly. 'Find the pig, find the pig, find the pig.' They eddied around Gorgos, their clothes stinking of blood and earth and pig. Corydon saw that *they* were the true maze.

Gorgos closed his eyes, and seemed to be concentrating. Then he opened them again. Then he walked straight forward, jinked suddenly sideways, shoved aside four women, and emerged from their midst with a small piglet in his arms. It squealed frantically. Corydon could see the stripes on its back, the huge eyes; it was a wild boar piglet, and that explained why Gorgos could hear it. Now the women drew aside, making a narrow pathway for Gorgos. Corydon followed him. As he walked forward, the pig still bleating, the women threw blood and ashes at them. Corydon was nearly blinded, and choked by the terrible iron smell, the press of unwashed bodies. Nevertheless his belly roared with furious hunger.

Gorgos stopped, very suddenly. And Corydon saw why.

In front of them was a chasm in the earth. Cautiously Corydon looked over the edge. It seemed to go down forever and forever, and he took a stone from his pouch to check. It seemed an hour before he heard the faintest *plink* as it hit the ground.

He looked a query. Gorgos nodded. He held the pigling over the terrible drop. The piglet looked calm, her large and liquid eyes fixed on his face. It might have been a last plea, or gratitude.

Gorgos opened his hands. Soundlessly, the piglet dropped. Corydon heard a soft crunch when she landed, and turned his face away. He could only hope that Gorgos had been right when he said that the pig had consented to her death. But there was a low hum of approval from the women.

'So she will be reborn as corn . . .' said the priestess. 'Reborn, corn, corn, reborn . . .'

All the women took up the chant. Suddenly it was like a dream.

Gorgos waved a friendly hand, shouldered some women out of the way, and began to move towards the opposite wall from where they had entered. They emerged into a new passageway, this one straight and lit by torches in wall cressets.

To his disappointment, Corydon found he'd brought his famished hunger with him. He could have eaten the earth itself.

With a faint bursting noise, something green and wriggling exploded out of the ground. At first Corydon thought it was a green shoot, growing at a magical rate. But as a second, and a third burst out too, the answer struck him. He saw the heads. He saw the glossy black eyes.

Snakes. Green ones, with black lines running down their backs. Some were thinner than string, others fatter than a ship's cable. Most looked hungry.

As the thirteenth snake erupted, Gorgos spoke in a low hissing voice, evidently trying to talk to the snakes. Then he seized Corydon's arm and began running, Corydon keeping up without difficulty. Corydon glanced back. Most of the snakes were wriggling away, looking for food and shelter. A few larger ones were sitting peacefully, but the largest of these was wriggling away into the tunnels. It shoved several smaller snakes out of its way, and bit one who was not fast enough to escape in time.

The small snake gave a pathetic hiss, then sped towards Gorgos. Perhaps it sensed his sympathy. He had always loved lizards, and snakes meant his mother. Delightedly he bent and picked the little creature up. It twined itself lovingly around his arm.

Slowly the other snakes emerged again and slid slowly towards them. All of them made for Gorgos, who was soon engulfed in a happy mass of hissing and slithering as the snakes expressed their adoration of him and claimed his attention. Corydon wondered if they were hungry too. His own steps were becoming almost unsteady with hunger.

Gorgos stroked as many of the snakes as he could, then set off festooned with them. Corydon thought how pleased the Snake-girl would be if he could somehow get them back to Troy.

But now the passageway was widening, its walls stone instead of raw gleaming earth. Corydon could make out faint drawings on the wall, ancient ones like Euryale's hunting pictures. He saw a full-breasted goddess suckling a baby, a field of stiff wheat, a woman crouched over an oven.

And he smelt something different from the reek of earth and pig and snake. He smelt the most glorious and appetising smell.

It was roasting pork. Plainly the sacrificed pig was somehow to be consumed.

As a very much shunned shepherd boy and thief, Corydon was used to inhaling delectable scents from feasts to which he had not been invited. But this smell seemed to tear at his body. He could not give up hope that it might be for them. And when he saw a table laid out before them, with a fair white cloth and a lordly bronze dish and pottery goblets as fine as those in Priam's hall, he felt a rising excitement.

Then two of the priestesses, now changed into clean and seemly white robes, bore in a dish, and on it was the small body of the piglet Gorgos had sacrificed – or if that were impossible, a creature of the same size. Its rich brown flesh caught the light.

Corydon could have died for a taste of that piglet. He leaned forward eagerly . . . water rushed into his mouth.

And was stopped by Gorgos's restraining glare. The snakes were hissing a warning, a wail of horror. Corydon frowned. Why shouldn't he eat it? Everything was laid out for them. For *them*.

An old, old priestess moved out of the shadows. Her face was so wrinkled that Corydon could not even see her eyes. She beamed a toothless smile. 'Eat,' she said. 'I know boys get hungry.'

And suddenly, despite his roaring belly, Corydon felt a sense of warning tingling in him. He remembered the Kingdom of the Many, where he had been told not to eat. This too was a realm of the dead. As well as the delicious scent of pork, there was a dank earth smell, like an open grave. And the reek of old blood under that.

And he looked at the pig, its bronzy skin, its delicate little upturned nose. He could imagine it running and playing. Did he really want to eat it? His stomach said an eager yes. But now his head was awake.

'No, thank you,' he said. Gorgos squeezed his arm. He meant it kindly, though Corydon knew there would be a bruise tomorrow.

'Then leave us, you feeble sons of whores, you snivelling relics of what should have been men!' The old woman's voice rose to a scream, and she flung the roast piglet down on the table. It broke apart before their eyes. And, with it, the illusion broke.

With a heavy lurch of his stomach, Corydon could see that it was no pig. It was a baby. A roasted baby. Its skin was still bronzy, its nose still sweetly upturned. But it was a baby. A little girl baby.

'It is the goddess's daughter,' the old woman said. 'And when she is eaten, she is later renewed. But only if she is eaten by the goddess herself.' With that, she tore off a hunk of meat – Corydon turned aside to retch – and crammed it into her mouth. One of the other priestesses spoke. 'Do not fear. This is as old as the world. Older than men. But it is not for you. Had you eaten, it would have been a curse to you. For her it is a blessing, and the babe will live.' The firm clear voice held certainty, and Corydon believed it. So did Gorgos. They had both seen stranger things.

'Now you must face one more test,' said the younger priestess. The old woman was still cackling and mumbling and nibbling. Corydon still felt sick at the sight. But Gorgos turned to her.

'*You* are the goddess,' he said. 'You are a monster. You are of our kind. We offer you our homage.' Corydon was astounded. Suddenly Gorgos was learning true wisdom and discernment. Truer than his. It was his turn to squeeze Gorgos's arm.

The old woman slowly put down the bone she was gnawing.

'Yes, you are of my kind,' she said. 'All food is a monster, a changeable terror for men to fear. Anything can kill or heal. Men fear food and its loss more than a three-headed dog, and food has more power over them than love. Your friend Euryale knows all this. It fuels her art. She too is of my kind.' She chuckled. 'I will help you if you pass the final test. You must meet three old women and wrest from them a great secret. If you can do that you will be free.'

She laughed again. 'Do not tell Khryses what you have seen,' she said. 'He does not have the wisdom to understand it. He would hate you for your knowledge.'

Now she moved forward, a tiny bone still in her hand. She moved towards Corydon. 'It is you who must remember,' she said. '*You must remember.*' And she touched his forehead with the bone.

For a few seconds Corydon was caught in a vision which seemed to burst onto the stone walls.

The terrible sacrifice was reduced to a heap of chewed bones, and now all three priestesses circled about the pitiful heap, throwing on herbs: the gingery smell of rosemary pierced him, and he saw the rich purple flowers of hyssop and the yellow of ragwort. They chanted something, strewing the mass with something Corydon couldn't see. Then one of the women took a lump of pinewood from the breast of her robe, lit it, and used it to set fire to the pile. It burnt with a strange sweet smell, and all the women cried out. At first Corydon could not understand a single word of their song. Then it changed, and he heard, 'Let the Goddess-child be whole! Let the Goddess-child be whole! Let the Goddess-child be whole!' At the third cry, the fire died abruptly, and in its centre, glowing like a rose, Corydon saw a live baby. It was naked and crying with hunger and one of the women picked it up and opened her robes to give it food. 'Feed and keep, feed and stay, feed and live,' they all crooned. All were smiling.

The vision faded. It had taken only a second. Gorgos had not even noticed.

The old woman pointed to a long corridor stretching away into the blackness of another room.

'Go. Find the women. Do as I said.'

Still wreathed with snakes, Gorgos strode towards the archway into the next passage. Corydon followed him, tracking the noise of happy snakes; they were like cats purring.

Corydon wished *he* felt so contented. The vision had made him uneasy. What did it mean? And what was this secret that they were meant to discover? He was still musing on these things when he heard the muttering.

It sounded like birds fluttering for nesting space. But like sharp-beaked seabirds on a cliff-edge, not little hedge-birds crooning.

To Corydon's amazement, he could hear the sound of waves too, and smell a rough saltiness in the air. The light grew stronger, greyer, bleaker. It was not torchlight, but the cold light of day. He burst out into it.

He stood in a huge cave hollowed out from the soft

sandstone by the groping fingers of the sea. The walls were pitted by long generations of hungry waves, sculpted so that they made homes for shells and seaweed and other denizens of Poseidon's kingdom. Gorgos, stroking the suddenly chilly snakes, took a deep, happy breath. But Corydon had noticed what looked like a bundle of seaweed or driftwood in the corner, a black tangle of ragged fragments. The muttering came from there.

He touched Gorgos on the arm. Gorgos turned. The muttering grew a little louder.

Corydon could hear individual words, but he couldn't understand them. *'Farra deae micaeque licet salientis honorem. Detis et in veteres turea grana focos,'* said one voice. What tongue was it? Something barbarous; not Hellene, not one of the tongues of the desert peoples. And not that of the people of the Western pirating empires.

He looked a question. Gorgos shrugged eloquently.

From the untidy heap of seawrack, a figure drew itself up. Corydon caught a glimpse of a face so terrible it dwarfed all monstrosity. This face was old age itself. It made the ancient priestess of Demeter look like a young girl. The face was like the cave; worn to smoothness and folds by the beating waves, but these were waves of time, not sea. The eyes were blind, shut by eyelids with a thousand thousand creases. The voice was a low shifting mumble, coming from an ancient soft mouth with no teeth: *'Et, si tura aberunt, unctas accendite taedas: parva bonae Cereri, sint modo casta, placent.'* If Corydon had not been a poet, he would never have been able to hear words in it at all.

Now another ragged shape rose up. It too sang, *'Venerat ad sacras et dea flava dapes'*. It swayed softly to and fro, and Corydon noticed the bristles on its chin, the nose and chin nearly meeting. But this one gnawed something with its mumbling mouth.

Finally, a third shape rose. *'Est specus exesi structura pumicis asper, non homini regio, non adeunda ferae,'* it sang. And Corydon saw the face. This one was not blind. It – she – had an enormous eye, blue-white and rheumy with age, but huge, set in one socket. And the eye roved, and saw them.

Laughing manically, she flung up her garments in the kind of rude gesture a child might make. Bending, she showed them her bottom. Gorgos and Corydon made faces of disgust, and she laughed again, a cracked old cackle. The muttering rose, and it was plain the others were asking what their sister saw.

'Two boys come here,' she said. It was plain that she at least knew the language of the Hellenes. Corydon felt a rush of relief.

'Give me the eye,' said another. 'I want to see them. Give it to me.'

The ancient woman who had been speaking sighed, then she put her long gnarled fingers up to her face. Using her talon-like nails, she prised the eye out of her head, as one pulls a wine stopper out of a bottle. It came out with a thick, slithery pop. Corydon saw it lying in her hand, jelly-like and slimed with rheum. It shone with white, sick light. Corydon's still-hungry stomach heaved. Then the woman bent and offered it to the other shabby black figure, who grasped the air several times, muttering, 'Where is it? Give it me, sister!' before closing her fist on the eye. She held her hand up to her collapsed eye socket. With a sucking sound, like a sea-creature slurping, the eye slid into her face. She swivelled it to look at Corydon.

'Oh, a boy. Give me the tooth, sister. I have been hungry lately. The bones we gnaw are old. Fresh meat would taste sweet. Yes, juicy . . .' She smiled, a child's happy toothless grin when offered a sweet.

'Come here, little friends,' said the one with the tooth. She held out a bone. 'See, we have food to share . . .' She tried to make her voice sound coaxing, but the greed under it was only too obvious. Her greyish tongue came out and licked her lips.

'No, not just now,' said Corydon, feeling ridiculously as if he were at a village party. 'We need to ask you a question.' He paused. How could he ask them anything? What could he say?

Gorgos had no such qualms. Smiling, he said simply, 'Tell us your secret.'

There was a terrible silence.

'Only if you let us gnaw off your hand first,' said one, in a quavering voice.

'And your head too,' said the one with the eye, fixing them with a steely glare.

'Give me the eye, sister,' said the third. 'Let me look upon this sweetmeat that asks us so impertinently for our treasure.'

'I have only had it for a moment,' whined the old

woman, but the others began long querulous moans, and at last she reached up and began to loosen it, then held it out. While it was out, all three were blind.

Quick as a panther, Corydon pounced on it, trying to take the eye as he had seen the women do. He felt he might die of fright if those terrible old fingers caught him, but he danced silently out of range before any of them were even aware he had been there. Then they began calling out and begging for the eye. 'Sister, I cannot see it. Where is it?'

'You've dropped it, you stupid old woman. You're in your dotage. Feel for it on the ground.' They all began a dreadful groping hunt for it. Gorgos drew his sword with a sharp slither, took the eye and stood in front of Corydon; neither wanted the hunt to discover them. At last, when the old women were wailing more and more frantically, Gorgos spoke.

'We have your eye,' he said. 'And I will crush it under my foot unless you tell us your secret. Now.'

The voices were raised in screaming abuse. It was clear they were saying a very firm no.

'All right,' said Gorgos, moving to the cliff-edge. The drop to the ocean below was sheer, many thousands of feet. The snakes reared back in dread. 'I'll drop it, then. It will give some fish a good meal.' The eye sat on his palm, unable to wink. It was warm, and it pulsed faintly, as if still alive. It looked at him piercingly. He wanted to be rid of it. One snake made a movement to eat it, attracted by its warmth and movement. Gorgos had to stop himself feeding it to his pet.

'No, no!' one of them cried out. 'The secret is in our song, that is all. In our song.'

Corydon spoke gently. 'But we cannot understand your tongue,' he said.

They cackled. 'It will be the language of the world one day. And the language of the gods. It is a light that comes from Troy. From Troy to light the world. But you do not understand it now. Not now. Of course not.' She blew a long, rude raspberry with her naked rump, right at them. Gorgos held the eye over the cliff.

'You wish me to throw it,' he said. The eye gave a small, terrified leap.

An idea struck Corydon. Taking a burnt stick from the centre of the cave, where the old women had once had a fire, he began to write down the letters of the words he had heard as best he could. Then he snapped his fingers, and Gorgos gave him the eye, which was desperate to save itself, flopping like a trapped fish. Holding it still, Corydon moved it – not without a shudder of revulsion – to his own eye.

At once the letters rearranged themselves into Hellenic words. Corydon did his best to read them, though the letters were as blurry as the ones he had scrawled. 'There is a cave, rough-formed, of corroded pumice, a place neither man nor beast may enter . . . You may honour the goddess with spelt, and dancing salt, burn grains of incense on ancient hearths . . . light some pitchy torches. Little things, if pure, please the good goddess-mother Demeter.'

They must find a cave, then, and make an offering.

And that would open Gorgos to the little gods.

Now there were only two problems left. One was what to do with the eye. The second was how to get out of the cave.

'Grey women,' he said. 'I have found out your secret. I will restore your eye if you tell us the way out from here. A safe way, and a comely way. No other will do. Tell me, and I promise that I shall restore the eye you lost.'

There was a furious scrabbling and a kind of clacking sound, like the fighting of angry birds. Then one of the sisters spoke.

'We must tell him or be blind forever. We must. And besides,' she said, 'I can see that their destiny is already marked out for them without any eye to help me. Mormoboy, you will die in the high places. Snakeboy, you will die on the ringing plains. You will both die. But you will also be victorious. As you have been today.' She pointed to the wall behind Corydon. 'Place all four of your mortal hands on it and a way will open,' she said. 'Go with the blessing of the goddess.'

Carefully, Corydon crept over to them and placed the eye on the floor in front of them. The eye immediately began hopping frantically, as if trying to reach their faces. It made a noise like a plopping frog, and the one who had spoken captured it quickly. Even from a distance, Corydon could see that it was quaking with pleasure. She inserted it and gave them a last appraising glare, blue-white and spare.

'Go,' she said. 'Troy's need is very great.' For a second Corydon thought her voice was different, younger and firmer, the voice of Demeter. But he did not remain behind to find out. He and Gorgos placed their hands on the wall and at once felt them reaching into darkness. They fled down a short corridor, and emerged abruptly into the temple.

όμικρον

FIFTEEN

The torches they had left had barely burned. They had been outside time. Or in many different times, but not this one.

Gorgos settled himself in front of the altar. His eyes were open and he was glassily calm, talking to his snakes and hearing their songs. Corydon was less at ease. Had they done enough? He paced restlessly, unable to give way to sleep; he must watch beside Gorgos despite his tiredness. Luckily he was no longer hungry. No one could stay hungry after seeing a baby being devoured and an eye being passed from hand to hand.

In the darkest hour of the long night, he heard a clatter below. It was the messengers galloping back from the Greek camp, with their answer. He did not dare hail them; they must assume the answer was yes.

Which meant that the morning would bring the anger of Akhilleus down upon them like an unstoppable storm.

*

They were still there at dawn, grimy and very tired. Corydon made sure the sun had risen. Then he and Gorgos gave a great whoop of laughter, and gave each other a quick hug. Corydon found that he had come to love Gorgos in a more intelligent way; he loved his courage and his simplicity and his fearless inability to be deceived by glitter that held no gold.

Khryses came in. 'Well done,' he said.

It meant nothing to Gorgos, who knew that Khryses's approval made no difference now that he had done as Demeter wished. She was the mother of all the gods of earth – not literally, but spiritually. Khryses was just a kind of porter and self-important, as porters often were. He gave a little shriek and drew back when he saw Gorgos's snakes, who had all found warm places to sleep while the boys remained awake. Now they poured out and crept up to Gorgos, climbing him as if he were a tree. Corydon looked tiredly at the man before him.

'Did you ever pass those tests yourself?' he asked bluntly. It was a Gorgos kind of question, he knew, but he felt irritated by the man's air of knowingness.

'No,' said the man. Corydon saw that he was ashamed. 'I am acceptable to the goddess as her priest,' he said, with a sigh. 'And I can speak with her and with other gods. But that is all.' Sudden tears came to his eyes. Corydon and Gorgos moved towards him, and Corydon awkwardly patted his arm.

'Try,' urged Gorgos. 'We can give you knowledge of what you must do. Not much knowledge, because the goddess forbids. But some. You must seize the adventure before you.' The priest looked up hopefully. Then he nodded. 'I shall not do it today,' he said. 'For at dawn tomorrow I will be at your side in case I can aid you in your combat. Perhaps I might not return from the testing in time; I am not young, like you and your friend. And now you must go and see your other friends; they have been anxious about you.' He smiled.

Outside the temple, Sthenno was waiting. Corydon and Gorgos hurled themselves at her. The snakes, too, entwined themselves around her, sensing Gorgos's love. Her bronzy wings went around them with a crisp rattle.

'Your wing!' It seemed as good as new, though now Corydon looked he could see that the feathers were a little smoother and sleeker than on the other wing.

'Yes, I am healed,' she said encouragingly. Her claws stroked their hair.

But then Sthenno broke off the joyful hug. 'Gorgos,' she said. 'There is a prophecy—'

'I know. That I will die tomorrow morning. I know I will. But Sthenno, if I do, follow Corydon. He knows what to do if that is my fate. But he cannot speak of it. Do you promise?' Bewildered, Sthenno nodded. Corydon hoped he knew what Gorgos meant. He also hoped it would work.

'Don't worry if it doesn't work,' said Gorgos soothingly. 'It will only mean that I am in Elysium. All heroes long to be in Elysium. And I will see my great mother. And be truly my father's son.'

He seemed genuinely calm. But Sthenno fluttered. 'Yes,

I know the prophecy of which you speak,' she said. 'But that was not the one I meant. I wished to speak of the four battles of Troy. It says that Troy will fall when it has endured the battle of the air, of water, of earth and of fire. I have a clay disc that shows it all.'

She pulled a disc from her bag. Corydon examined it; it was indeed the same disc that he had seen in her room – but wait! The whirlwind symbol had vanished. And Sthenno too was frowning at it. 'There should be a fourth symbol; where did it go?' She caught her breath. 'Of course! The battle of the air is over and done. So its symbol has gone too.'

'And soon Troy may be gone,' said Corydon. 'We must learn from the fate of Atlantis and from another city I have seen destroyed, the desert city of Tashkurgan. We must make a plan to rescue as many of its people as we can, and lead them to safety.'

'We should ask the Snake-girl. Her powers might be useful. If she can enchant people and tell them where to go . . .' But Corydon felt no confidence in his suggestion.

They went back to Euryale's studio. Sthenno had already retired to her tower.

The Snake-girl was sitting at a table, surrounded by a mess of feathers and small bones. Before her was a tray on which Corydon could see at least a hundred songbirds. They had been limed, and struggled pathetically to be free, their wings flapping weakly. As Corydon watched, the Snake-girl picked one off the tray, brushed off the lime, and without even bothering with its song popped it into her mouth and crunched hard. Then she picked up another and shoved it in too, spitting out bones and fragments of feather.

She looked around. 'Aroo, Cooydong,' she said. Her mouth was too full of bird to make much sound. Swallowing hastily, she added apologetically, 'I'm so hungry. I need to eat them all.' Sitting on a chair beside her were two empty trays. Corydon could see that bird-song was unlikely to wake the city early for many a long day. He could also see her swollen belly for the first time. It was now very clear that she was expecting a child.

She crunched up a protesting robin. A wren on the tray made panicky tweets. It gave an abrupt squawk when she grabbed it.

'What happened to singing with them? To their graves?'

She shrugged. 'I'm just hungry,' she said. Euryale bustled in with twelve boiled stuffed dormice to tempt her; she knew the Snake-girl would be full of regret in a few minutes' or a few hours' time.

She looked at them. Then she grabbed three screaming larks at once and bit their heads off. Corydon saw her chewing. He suddenly felt unhappy. Medusa had been so horribly changed – even killed – by childing, by being a mother. Was the Snake-girl now to lose all tenderness in fierce, serpenting greed?

But she was still the same in other ways. When Gorgos brought in his snakes, she gave a soft welcoming hiss, and forgot the birds completely. The snakes folded themselves around her, hissing back.

'They are hungry,' she said reproachfully. 'You should have fed them, Gorgos.' Now she picked birds off the tray to feed the new pets, who responded eagerly. Then they all went to sleep in a contented warm huddle. But the Snake-girl woke after a quick nap. Corydon told her that the fall of the city could not be prevented forever. He asked her to help assemble people to escape when the Akhaians got in.

'But this is the royal family's business, King Priam's business,' she said. It was clear that she did not like the idea of leading, nor of leaving the city. 'And I cannot control so many people.'

'If King Priam tells people to leave, it will be seen as surrender,' said Euryale. She had provided Corydon and Gorgos with a good supper – cold lamb, an egg apiece, hunks of cheese, a spoonful each of precious honey, plenty of bread she had made herself. It was crisp and caramel-crusted, and somehow its savour seemed to recall Demeter herself, as if she were blessing their feast. She was the corn-woman – and suddenly he thought of an old song about the corn as a king who ruled for a day and then was cut down, then beaten down, then buried – only to spring up into the light. Resurrection . . . Corn was resurrection. And the bread made with fresh rich wheat gave life. He took another huge bite. It was as if it strengthened him magically. Gorgos laughed, and Corydon saw the same bright vitality in his friend's eyes.

'Euryale,' said Gorgos, 'what did you put in the food?'

'Food always makes me feel like this,' said Euryale calmly. 'But it's better when you are really hungry. Look,

Gorgos. What is going to happen to you is what happens to every artist. You have to empty yourself to be possessed by the work. And you were empty with hunger, too, and now you are becoming full. It's the same kind of thing.'

'Is it?' Gorgos looked doubtful. 'If you say it is.'

Euryale fetched a painting she'd been working on. 'It's called "The Goddess's Spring"', she said. It showed a pink girl lying on the ground, surrounded by blurring flowers. She lay under a softly painted apple tree. One huge apple hung down over the girl's head.

'But if the apple is ripe,' said Gorgos, 'then it cannot be spring. It must be "The Goddess's Autumn".'

'Things can happen in art that are against the rules in real life,' said Corydon.

Euryale beamed. 'And in the realm of the gods, too,' she said. 'There too, art is like life.'

Taking another healthy draught of the deliciously honey-sweet wine that seemed so much a part of Troy, Corydon found these words revolving in his head. He thought of art, and the gods . . . Of how artists tried to contain a god in their works. To harness his or her power.

Then he thought of the djinn, and how one had sacrificed himself to remain behind, to be part of the city's defences, incarnating himself, taking on flesh that could be hurt and could be destroyed, and that even intact was a burden past bearing. And of how Gorgos tomorrow was to bring together all other incarnations, all the little gods who dwelt in one fountain, one riverlet, one tiny tree, one man and his children, one family hearth. And of how the good seemed always limited by being incarnate, while the wicked were free to stride over the entire earth and call it theirs. Because they were not part of life? They could rule life because they stood *outside* it. So they gained power. The djinn unleashed were like gods, but they could be held in a bottle the size of a man's hand.

'What a pity,' said Corydon, 'that you can't put the Olympians in bottles. Like djinn.'

'Perhaps you could,' said Euryale. 'If you knew how to. It would make an interesting installation. Live gods in glass bottles.'

'It would make them as they once were,' said Corydon. 'Little gods of hill and river. No god should rule the whole world, and no man either. And it would be fun to see them struggling to get out.'

'Beating the sides of the bottles with their hands,' agreed Euryale, smiling.

'Maybe even trying to push out the stopper,' added the Snake-girl.

They all stared dreamily into the fire, enjoying the thought of a world where the Olympians were in bottles. Perhaps it was the wine, but their own spirits felt freer and more released than at any time in Troy. But it was also the knowledge of tomorrow. Euryale and the Snake-girl, as well as Corydon, found themselves noticing things about Gorgos they had never noticed before. He was full-grown now, not a boy in shape: a tall man, lean and very strong-looking. But his dark skin had kept a boy's softness, his eyes a boy's brightness.

When Sthenno clattered in again, she made for Gorgos

and hugged him; she had been at work on prophecies in her tower. It was plain that this was an act of love. She also had a small spell to offer. 'It will make your weapons sharp,' she said shyly. Gorgos's sword was always sharp, but he didn't say so for once; he was learning a kind of care with people's feelings. He thanked Sthenno warmly. But the old Gorgos was still there. At the end of the meal, he pushed back his stool and said, yawning, 'Well, I'm going to sleep. If I die tomorrow, please don't worry. Corydon knows what to do.'

'What do you mean?' asked Corydon desperately.

'You'll know if it's the right thing to do,' said Gorgos. 'The little gods will help, and so will their mother.' The Snake-girl looked puzzled, and Sthenno scrabbled for a parchment that spoke of the fight. But Gorgos, with another wide yawn, was already heading for bed.

None of the others could sleep. Corydon dozed and tossed, fragments of dream reaching him . . . the dead baby . . . the live baby . . . the smell of earth and blood. When the dawn trumpets sounded, he was deeply asleep for the first time in the night, and woke with a horrified start.

Gorgos was already up, and was putting on his armour. 'I have to take it with me and on me is the best place to carry it,' he explained. 'I'll take it off when we get to the cave.'

Corydon noticed Gorgos assumed he was coming too, which was warming. 'Shall I wake the others?' he asked. The Snake-girl was snoring softly, and as he looked at her tired and tender face he felt a wave of protectiveness.

'No,' said Gorgos. 'Let's just go.'

The fight was scheduled for high noon, in a dusty roadway on the plains south of Troy. No one wanted to let Akhilleus into Troy, even for a fight they hoped he would lose. But Corydon felt he could sense Akhilleus's rage and impatience licking at the strong stone walls like a fire.

He and Gorgos slipped out of the south gate. There was still stiff green grass on this side of Troy, though the cattle and sheep had been pillaged by gorgon and Greek. A few wildflowers lined the path with bright pinks and purples. On Mount Ida was a morning mist, turned to faint pink by the sun's dawn light. The river Skamandros shone and twisted nearby, and a few birds that the Snake-girl had spared sang. As they began to climb, Corydon followed Gorgos. The knowledge of where they were going seemed embedded in him, and he was following some inner direction.

They reached a narrow slit in the rock. 'We are not men, nor beasts,' said Gorgos, and ducked his head to insinuate himself into the slot. Corydon followed suit. It was dim and grey in the cave, damp and shaly, though the walls were full of huge holes blasted by some wrath of the earth's. The ceiling had a huge gap torn in it, mainly overgrown by vines and cyclamens, but giving faint light. Through this gap appeared the anxious face of Khryses.

'I cannot enter,' he said. 'I am but a man. But I will be here. Stand in the cave entrance, Gorgos. And you must be naked. You will resume your armour later.' Gorgos smiled. Khryses had to feel as if he were in charge. But he was not.

Glistening, dark, naked, Gorgos took up a piece of bread he'd brought with him. He broke it.

There was a long, deep rumble of thunder.

And Corydon heard the sound of many thousands of feet moving towards the cave. He went over to Gorgos and stood by his side.

They streamed up the hill in the mist, taking shape as they grew closer, and the shapes were strange – the shadow of a blossoming tree with long hair like a girl; little squat faun-men with stout goat-legs; tall half-horses; some satyrs swishing long tails. Here was Faunus, with his thick pelt of fur. Pomona and Vertumnus came in hand in hand. Pales came with her fleecy shepherdess's coat, giving Corydon a fleeting smile. Maiden huntresses of the desert came, tawny and golden-eyed like lions. The rivers flowed uphill, took shape as solid beings, and poured themselves into Gorgos like long drinks.

Out of the city came a new flood of beings. These were the family gods, the Lares, and since every family had a Lar, there were every kind of people: glossy blue-black Lars and russet Lars and Lars with golden skin, pale pink Lars with linty hair, male and female and everything in between. One that was only half-made sped past; Corydon recognised Euryale's work, and wondered why anyone who could have no children would make a Lar.

As each god or goddess arrived, they saluted Gorgos, and then, somehow, merged with him.

Gorgos stood bolt upright, as if someone were holding

him by the hair. He looked just the same, but he radiated a new kind of power, and Corydon could see that he could have transformed himself into any of the gods, in the manner of the sons of the ocean, Proteus and Oceanus. In that way he was truly making himself more Poseidon's son, even as he sided against his father.

A kind of fight seemed to be going on over the surface of Gorgos's skin. First Faunus's soft fur seemed to be mirrored in it, then it turned to a reflection of soft petals, then to tree branches. Then a raging waterfall seemed to erase him altogether. Then his own dark skin emerged like a black wet rock, and he seemed to step out of the water. Gorgos's expression was thoughtful and concentrated, as if he were trying out weapons or armour.

'Are you all right?' asked Corydon anxiously.

Gorgos paused. 'My own form is best,' he said. 'Their strength is in me. I can take their forms, too.' His voice sounded odd, as if he were speaking in a vast and echoing cave.

'Are you ready?' Corydon asked, when they had strapped on his armour and his sword.

For answer, Gorgos picked up the heavy plumed helmet that he normally didn't like to wear.

As he turned towards the doorway, the old woman in black he had been half-expecting came and put her hand on his arm. Immediately an ear of wheat erupted from his skin. His hair turned to straw. Then it all went back to normal.

'You carry my powers too,' she said. 'Though they are not really like a warrior's powers. The power to make things grow is not of immediate use in battle, but it is also the only reply to battle. Without that power, it would not matter who won or lost.' She took his hand again, and briefly Corydon saw that his face was made of small loaves of bread.

Gorgos ran swiftly down the hillside, burdened though he was. Corydon followed him. Already the sun had melted the morning dew, and the hillside grew pale. The air was very clear up here, above Troy, powdery with dust.

'It's like the island,' said Gorgos wonderingly. 'I wonder how Mother Wolf is. And your sheep,' he added kindly.

Corydon had long since resigned himself to the fact that Mother Wolf had eaten his sheep. It didn't seem the right moment to say so. 'I miss the island,' he said, instead.

As he spoke, he felt a fresh new wind, which brought a scent of thyme and crushed herbs with it, a scent of the island. A swirl of dust built up, and from it stepped his father, Pan. Corydon ran to him, feeling his usual mix of love and dread.

'I am not truly here,' his father warned. 'This is only my image, and it is only for this place, which is pasturage, my domain. The other gods have been willing to sacrifice themselves to be Troy's defenders because they are Trojan. I am not willing. I must be what I am.' His face was both sad and comical. 'I wish you well, Gorgos,' he said, 'though you are none of mine.'

'Join us!' Gorgos's face was bright. 'We fight for Troy.'

'She is not mine either,' said Pan. 'I cannot take what is not mine.'

'Everyone else has,' said Gorgos simply. He raised his hand. Millions of tiny faces swarmed in it like ants.

Pan laughed his sly laugh. 'If you have so many then you do not need me,' he said.

'I do not know what I need,' said Gorgos. 'In Troy – in all my life, in truth – we are like men piling up defences against a sudden flood, building the wall of sand high lest the tide overwhelm us.' Corydon could see this idea wasn't at all Gorgos-like, and nor was the language. Plainly his passengers moved in his brain and heart as well as in his body.

'You do not need me now,' said Pan. 'You need me later. To make a threnody for the fallen,' and again his face was sly.

'Who will fall? You know and I know. But you also know what will happen next.'

Now Pan was serious. 'Yes, I know. But do you understand what it means? You will be cut off from normal human joy. You will be an exile.'

Gorgos laughed. 'So have I always been,' he said joyously. 'So are we all. And I do not really care if my joys are normal or not.'

Now Pan smiled. 'And what of you, my son?'

Corydon spoke sturdily. 'You know we must save something of this land. You yourself said it. If its defeat is swift, more of what it stands for will be lost. If the battles for it are worth a song or two, men may remember it for ever. That is the best way to defeat the Olympians.'

'Not the best way,' said his father. 'But it is a good way. Remember that songs can lie.'

'Show me anything else I must do!' begged Corydon. His father's eyes were deep green wells of sadness as he said, 'Do not run, my son. In a few days you will know. You will know. And you will act. I will see you again, soon,' he promised. 'For now I leave you an additional weapon.'

He led up a man who walked as if he were old. He wore a robe of a blue so dark it was almost black, a precious colour, but it was as plain as ash. He carried a black staff, and Corydon saw that he was using it to feel his way. 'Where is my boy?' he asked in a high shrill voice, a voice of power that didn't sound like a human voice, but like one of the daimons of the air.

'Your boy is here,' said Pan. 'A new boy to lead you to this day's great battle.' The man shuffled over, and Pan placed his hand on Corydon's arm.

Corydon looked in amazement at the softly folded old face. The man was blind, his eyes sealed as if by some giant hand.

'Has he always been blind?' asked Gorgos.

'I have not always been blind,' said the man, clearly and directly. 'But it is only since I was blinded that I have been a singer of wars and heroes. My sight was taken in order that I might have other gifts.' His voice rose sweetly in a song: 'Sing to me, muse, of the courage of the swift-footed son of Poseidon, the ebony-skinned one, Medusa's boy . . .'

'How do you know all about me?' Gorgos demanded.

'I know everything that I need to know,' said the blind man. 'That is my gift. And now you too are large, and you too contain multitudes.' His smile was not sly like Pan's, but open and direct like Gorgos's own. Pan himself gave Corydon a last smile, and melted into the hillside.

'Are you ready?' Corydon asked Gorgos, but the old man replied:

'He is ready. So am I. Now for the battle. Already the eagles have gathered, and the fat wolves of the Ida woods, swollen with the bodies of dead men. You contain their powers. Their wildness.'

Corydon looked around nervously. He could see no wolves. Then he looked at Gorgos and could see what the old man must mean. Gorgos himself was the wolf and the eagle . . . 'You see well,' he said.

'You do too,' said the old man. 'You are of my kind. Not his. It is not your metier to fight the Olympians but to sing songs about those who do.' His voice was hypnotic. Corydon thought he sounded more and more like Pan, and like the daimons, too. The old voice ran up in a strong arc. 'Sing, muse, of the shepherd boy who saved the dead, of his hurt when he could not save a city. Sing of his vow, great muse. Sing of his war against the Olympians. How he sent many men to the realm of the dead. And the kites picked their bones.'

Corydon shuddered. The song had caught perfectly his own sense of who he was; the melody weakening under the weight of the words, just as he felt himself weak in the face of the gods. Then the blind eyes somehow seemed to flash. And the man grinned.

'Sing, muse, of the boy who hates himself,' he said. Corydon forced himself to smile back. 'And soon I shall sing of another. Of him. Of the rivers of gods who pour through his veins, course through his heart. He is mighty beyond the lot of mortal men, but this day's battle will not be lucky for him. You have invoked your gods. So too has the Akhaian champion.'

SIXTEEN

They had been moving at the old man's slow pace down a level road, now white with dust in the late morning light. And it was through a hot white haze that they saw him. Akhilleus.

His armour was all black now, the hard black of obsidian. His helmet still bore a silver crest, but the plumes of light were now interwoven with black feathers, and even at this distance Corydon could see the plumes were dyed with blood. He bore a new shield, splendid in painting and carving, but he bore it as a weak impediment, one he did not want or need. His true shield was his eyes. Corydon had thought their silver fierce before. Now they had the ferocity of burning sunlight on metal; they gave off silver lightnings like great storm clouds. And his spears too were thunderbolts. His mouth looked as if he had never smiled.

As they approached, he was absolutely still, as if he were truly made of stone.

Gorgos greeted him when they reached hailing distance.

'You are the champion of the Akhaians, I of Troy. We fight to determine the city's fate.'

The severe mouth opened. 'I care nothing for Troy. I never have. Once I did not kill; I only captured. I fight you because you killed my friend, and stabbed him where he lay. For that I will gladly tear out your lungs.'

Gorgos was silent. He had killed many on the field. 'Which one was your friend?' he said.

'He wanted to wear my armour into battle. He took my place when I was hurt. Now I take his place. See? Enough words. We are warriors, not actors.' He jumped nimbly down from his chariot.

He and Gorgos began circling each other, like stags who fight in springtime. Slowly.

Then Akhilleus reached down his spear and threw it swifter than eye could see, all in one movement. Gorgos leapt aside. Corydon saw the spent spear on the dry ground, a flash of black at its tip.

Obsidian. Someone had told Akhilleus about Gorgos's vulnerability.

Now Gorgos flung his own light spear, and it hit the shield and broke. Both swords flashed out.

Now the two swords clashed, and it looked as if they were animate, fighting each other while the strong men watched. The blades were equally strong; again and again they drove against each other. Akhilleus's blue-black blade thrust to and fro, and Gorgos's own black blade leapt to meet it. It was as if the swords were friends or lovers who could not bear to be apart. Akhilleus tried to overbear Gorgos by strength, but Gorgos pushed him away. He tried speed, but Gorgos was equally quick. Akhilleus leaped to the top of a small tufty hillock to rain blows down on Gorgos, but Gorgos managed to trip him and he stumbled. The Trojans cheered frantically from the walls. But Akhilleus recovered his balance as swiftly as a cat.

It was plain that neither man could easily overcome the other. The battle might come down to sheer luck. Or the will of the gods.

Now the gods within Gorgos did seem to take a hand. Corydon saw the shadows of their forms and faces passing over his friend's face. At last, a cunning little Lar looked out. In the next second, Gorgos had somehow jerked Akhilleus's sword around so it twisted, and then he brought his second spear down on the blade with a thud like a falling tree. The blade shivered, but did not break. But a splinter shattered from its side. It was very slightly weakened.

In a burst of white light, a young man appeared at Akhilleus's side. He held out a new sword, exactly like the old one. Gorgos tried to keep the Akhaian so busy he didn't have time to grab it. But at last Akhilleus managed to land a blow on Gorgos's shield arm, and he used the precious second to take the blade. The boy who had held it gave a satisfied smile. With that smile, Corydon recognised Athene. Her smile widened and she vanished to the sound of boos from the watching Trojans. The Olympians were always cheats.

Now Akhilleus pressed forward eagerly, hitting at Gorgos repeatedly. Gorgos parried again and again with his sword but Corydon could sense some of the gods in him turning away, horrified and afraid. He thought about it: trees and rocks and woods had some power to resist battle, but not much. Eventually if men fought over and over in the same place, the pleasant landscape would become a blasted wild with wizened trees and no clean water.

Now fragile landscapes were trying to stand against the face of War itself.

As Corydon looked at Akhilleus, he saw a terrible grinning rictus, far uglier than Medusa, more dead than any shade. His horror was shared by some of the gods who inhabited Gorgos. As he watched, a sobbing dryad distended Gorgos's skin. With a soft popping sound she materialised beside him, her leafy hair dripping with tears, and then stumbled away, searching for her tree. Her gentleness made him think of the Snake-girl, and he was abruptly angry, thinking of her fate, left with a monster who looked like this when he was angry.

And now, too, his heart was black with a sense of disaster. For with the dryad's defection, other gods had begun to leave Gorgos. Corydon saw some small Lares patter back towards the city, crying with fright. One huge boulder-god slid out, then began running back up Mount Ida.

Akhilleus's grin widened. And Gorgos's strokes grew swifter. Was he getting too desperate, might he blunder?

There was a flick of Akhilleus's sword. And everyone

saw a trickle of blood running down Gorgos's arm. Gorgos himself stared at it in disbelief. He, who had withstood lava and seas and monsters of the deep, had at last had his skin broken by a man's sword. Then he looked up, and met Akhilleus's eyes. They stared at each other for a long time. And slowly a smile curved on Gorgos's face. A death smile. A smile that made the two terrible faces, streaked with dust and sweat, strangely alike.

Then he turned, twisted on the spot, seemed to stretch, his armour slipping off him, his arms slowly merging into his sides and his legs cleaving together. Again and again he wrapped himself around Akhilleus as his skin turned into watery scales. His face became that of a shimmering snake, his eyes two blue pools with shells for eyelids. His hair grew long and weedy, greener than his mother's snakes had been, and in it gasped little fish-lice.

Corydon realised that Gorgos had allowed one of the river-gods to possess him completely. It must be Skamandros, the chief river of Troy.

The serpent-river flung many coils about the hero's body, trying to trap his arms against his side, then trying to choke him. Akhilleus managed to free his sword-arm, and the Gorgos-river roared with fury and tried to squeeze his arm so that he would be forced to drop the sword. But Akhilleus held the sword aloft and brought it down against the watery body. It was silly, like a child angrily hitting a tree with a stick. But it kept his head above water, and the Gorgos-body within Skamandros's watery carapace felt the blow resonate, and shivered. Nor was he immune to the hero's sword.

Plainly, the river could not overcome the hero like this. He tried a new tactic. Skamandros had borne many a Trojan to the shore on his broad back. His waters had run red with blood as he meandered into Poseidon's realm. He felt polluted. And now he heaved up from his whole being the power to summon those dead who wallowed in his waters.

A tidal wave of half-decaying corpses surged at Akhilleus, as the river rose and charged against him, churning, surging, all his rapids rising in white fury. Then the river drove the mass of corpses against the shield of Akhilleus. Skamandros – or Gorgos – was bellowing like a bull as the river flung out its dead.

To the amazement of the onlookers, the dead were animate; they thrust broken spears and swords at the great hero, impelled by the riverine frenzy. Akhilleus beat them off, but now his eyes were staring with horror as men he himself had killed strove for revenge, strove to force him too into muddy, bloody death. Thrashing over Akhilleus's shoulders the river formed itself into a wall, a wave that hurled itself at his head. The tremendous thrust of it slammed into his shield. He staggered and lost his footing. A corpse was on him, shoving him deeper into the water. He managed to grab a tree, but the branch was ripped from his grasp by an avalanche of dead, mud, and water.

Akihlleus fled, with Gorgos-Skamandros at his heels, roaring and immense. 'Gods are stronger than men!' roared the voice of the river. 'Gods are stronger than men!'

Now Akhilleus turned. His brilliant eyes flashed. 'I see that there are many gods in you,' he cried. 'Fight me as a man and we shall see who will triumph.' Again and again the mighty crest of the river kept coming, but Akhilleus leapt and ran, desperately, as the river kept on dragging his knees down, cutting the ground from under his legs. He looked at the sky. 'Why have you abandoned me, Lords of Olympos?' he cried.

Instantly the youth that was truly Athene was at his side. 'Do not be afraid,' she said, contemptuously. 'I bring the blessings of Zeus. That river will subside. You know it is not your fate to die in the embrace of a little, local mud-god. You chose glory, Akhilleus. Glory rather than length of days.'

'Help me!' The words were torn from Akhilleus. Corydon could see that he hated to ask even the gods for help, and Athene smiled. Suddenly Hera stood beside her.

Hera's voice was shrill and severe. Corydon shuddered as he heard it coming from the goddess, she who had looked on the fall of Atlantis with a satisfied smile.

'My son! Hephaistos!'

And a little man came running on his lame leg, his body black and sooty. He came limping down from the mountains, running so fast that the ground behind him was bursting into flames as he ran. 'Mother, I come!' he cried eagerly. Corydon remembered his love for his mother.

'Burn that river!' his mother screamed. 'Destroy it!'

The little man somehow lifted the flame of his own

running and flung it directly at Gorgos-Skamandros.

The fire poured over the whole plain like water. The dead burned, the living dead crying out in pain. And the bright coils of Skamandros shrank, turning to billowing clouds of steam. The earth shrank too, its moisture drying out; cracks appeared in the ground, arid and hard. Trees by the river caught too – elms and willows and tamarisks and lotus and galingale – and Corydon heard many dryads shriek in agony and crumble into ashes from within his friend, who stood in the midst of the turmoil, bewildered. But no doubts held Akhilleus, his foe. As plain Gorgos emerged from the steam and the water, Akhilleus wasted no time.

'You will die now,' he said, in a low soft voice that carried to the watchers over the crackle of flames.

Soon they were at it again.

Hephaistos was running desperately towards his already vanishing mother. 'Mother! Don't go!' he cried. But she had gone. The dwarf-god gave a wail like an abandoned baby. 'Come back!' Athene turned away in distaste. Hephaistos huddled small on the ground where his mother had stood.

Then he turned to look at the contesting heroes. 'I made both swords,' he said to the air, since no one was beside him. 'I made them both. I think it will be difficult for either to triumph.'

But it was plain to everyone else that Akhilleus was winning now. Steadily he drove Gorgos back. Gorgos was somehow depleted by the magical energies he had exerted; his simple plainness was scored across by the gods' possession of him. It was as if he were stretched thin by Skamandros's use of him. And now Athene took a hand.

She slid out a foot, and tripped Gorgos up. All the Trojans booed, but Gorgos fell.

'Get up,' said Akhilleus. 'I will kill you on your feet.'

Gorgos got up, smeared with mud and blood and ash. He did not know how to stop fighting or how to despair. Or how to die. It had to go on. And it did. From time to time a little god would appear in Gorgos, with a plan. Faunus with his strength. The wild cunning of a hunter staring out of a boy's eyes. But Akhilleus was always still standing. Still there. He killed the hopes of a thousand thousand gods, but he could not seem to die.

Now Gorgos looked tired. He wasn't as quick. He didn't look as strong; his blows lacked force. Akhilleus was wearing out that godlike confidence. Fighting the Akhaian hero was like attacking a statue; every time Gorgos managed to land a blow, there was a dull clang, and the weapon bounced off. Normally Gorgos too was impervious to weapons forged by mortal men, but Akhilleus had an obsidian sword. Hephaistos had betrayed Gorgos's secret to him, and now there was no salvation in it.

'Gorgos!' Corydon shouted it. 'Gorgos! Retreat!' Sthenno and Euryale stood nearby now, ready to sweep him away.

But Gorgos didn't even turn his head. Beside Corydon, a dark-haired woman said in a low voice, 'It must be now.' Corydon turned and saw it was Demeter. He began a rebellious protest, but was silenced by her seriousness. 'Do not fear,' she said. 'It does not end here.'

As she spoke, Akhilleus finally saw the opening in Gorgos's defences that he had been seeking all day. His sword flashed forward. And Gorgos was broached on it.

Gorgos looked down and saw the black blood of his death. More black blood gushed from his mouth. He made a choking sound.

The little gods gibbered and bubbled inside him.

Gorgos looked at Akhilleus's sword, still incredulous. He drew the sword from him and threw it at Akhilleus, who caught it easily. And smiled. And smiled and smiled as Gorgos's knees gave way, as he fell to the ground like a wave collapsing. Corydon ran over to him, withstanding Akhilleus's silver glare.

'Do you wish to die too?'

'Rather than let him die alone I would oblige you,' Corydon shouted recklessly.

This seemed to give Akhilleus pause; a shadow crossed his silver eyes, as if he was remembering. Sthenno and Euryale moved forwards protectively, but Akhilleus didn't seem to fear them. Instead his eyes were all for Gorgos. He bent towards the boy, still with that terrible smile. 'Little king of monsters,' he said. 'You are for the dark. Find my friend there. His name is Patroklos. Tell him Akhilleus sends him a slave, the man who killed him.' He clapped the dying Gorgos sardonically on the shoulder. 'And now I go to find Hektor. For he too helped to kill my friend.'

Corydon took no notice. His eyes, too, were all for

Gorgos. He took the bloodstained hand; it was slick and sticky with blood. To his amazement, he felt the Snake-girl slither up beside him, under the defiant shelter of Sthenno and Euryale's wings.

'Can you help?' Corydon asked desperately.

She shook her head. 'He's dying, Corydon. There's nothing we can do.' Gorgos's breath was rasping now through the blood that was choking him. The Snake-girl wiped it away, but it bubbled back. She was joined by the dark-haired, dark-robed woman, who wiped Gorgos's brow.

Now Gorgos found enough breath to speak. 'Corydon . . .' he said. 'Remember. Remember. You can.'

Corydon nodded and pressed his hand. His own tears were falling fast, but he barely noticed because he was so busy drinking in Gorgos. Imprinting him on his mind. Sealing him there forever. Even now, he could hardly believe his friend was dying. Had been defeated.

Gorgos tried to give him a final smile, but death caught him and his eyes rolled backwards. His head flopped into the lap of the woman in the dark robes. She stroked his hair and very gently closed his eyes.

He was gone.

Akhilleus was exultant. He split the skies with a shriek of triumph.

'I shall enter Troy tomorrow at dawn,' he said. 'With my Myrmidons. And I shall be remembered forever.'

ρω

Seventeen

They bore Gorgos home, shoulder-high. His body lay in state in the palace. And all Troy came to visit him. For hours people walked slowly down the long corridor, then into the receiving room where he lay. Huge piles of flowers furtively gathered from gardens and hillsides piled up around him, and they smelt not of scent, but of rot and decay.

Corydon had not left him for an instant. It was for him to brush away the flies that came.

At last the city quietened. And Gorgos still lay motionless.

Corydon knew he had to try now. Try something impossible. He had to try to raise the dead.

Resurrection was what the little gods did, after the small annual death of winter. This was Gorgos's winter. And he, Corydon, was a shepherd. This was a kind of transhumance, a seasonal movement of his flock from pasture to pasture. But he said all that to himself because he knew he was breaking a law that was far older than the Olympians. Man is mortal.

Sthenno understood. She too had stayed. She knew what had to be done.

As the stars wheeled and the great Hunter sank to the horizon, she met his eyes. She took Gorgos in her arms; he was stiff, like a wooden doll. She called Euryale, shrill and birdlike; it was like the cry of a hunting nightjar. Now Euryale came, and took Corydon, and together the two gorgons flew.

They landed on the bare hillside just beyond the cave of the goddess-shrine.

They gathered wood in silence. Sthenno spoke only once. She drew the clay disc of prophecy from her wings. 'See,' she said.

Corydon looked at it. 'The water has gone,' he said. 'There are still earth and fire to come.'

Then they laid Gorgos on the pyre.

They flung on rosemary, hyssop, ragwort, and a knot of pine. Gorgos was buried in an avalanche of flowers. Then Corydon bent and looked at his face. It might be the last time and he wanted to make sure he did not forget.

He threw the torch he had carried from Troy.

He spoke the words he had heard in the dream. The fire sprang into greedy life, and its glow lit the entire hillside, so that grass and flowers stood out, their long shadows black behind them. From somewhere, a ring of dancers appeared, and flickered around the pyre – or were they nothing but the shadows of the flames? Corydon's heart was full of a terrible mixture of unbearable hope and ashy despair. He remembered the burning of Gorgos's mother. He wanted to fling himself onto the pyre, but the wide greedy turrets of fire also terrified him with their heat.

Out of the pyre poured more of the little gods; not all of them had left Gorgos alone in death. Some sleepy pasture gods didn't seem to know he had died, and only now awoke with the pain of burning at their backs. A few left nursing bruises or burns. It was clear that they could never make a force to rival the Olympians. It was also clear that no one would ever persuade them to take action again. A pastoral nymph of a spring shook her fist at Corydon as she fled.

The flames closed around Gorgos after these exoduses.

And then it became obvious that there was something magical at work. The fire stopped giving out heat, or crackling. And its centre slowly changed colour, like a cloud filling with rain. It had been red and orange and gold; now it deepened to a dawn-green, and then – slowly – to blue, the clear pale blue of winter skies. It stopped feeling hot. Gorgos was invisible inside it; this flame was not transparent, but a cloak behind which the gods were at work.

The flame turned rosy. And inside it Gorgos stood up, and with flame shining on his skin and spurts of flame clinging to his hair, he walked out of his own pyre, and stood on the hillside before them.

The dark-haired goddess stood beside him. Had she been in the fire, too?

She held out her hand. 'Bread,' she said. 'It will hold you to earth.' She broke the bread and gave a piece to Gorgos, who took it and ate it solemnly.

'Now,' she said, 'I do not do this so that you may fight. That would break the laws of battle. I do this that you may save the idea of the city. It must fall, and you cannot prevent it. But you must lead the Trojans to a new place. And it is there that your destiny will be fulfilled. For now,' she said, 'you must remain with me. In my temple. You,' she spoke directly to Corydon, 'can visit him once a day. And when the city falls he will return to Troy, to lead the people.' She took Gorgos's hand and led him away. Corydon saw her body sway in grace like that of a young girl. Suddenly he saw that she was looking at Gorgos the way a bride looks at a groom.

Corydon was stupefied. Now indeed Gorgos belonged to someone other than the monsters. They had not even had the chance to talk to him.

And Troy was to fall . . . today? Such had been Akhilleus's vow.

How could there be a battle in earth? For that they must somehow prepare. Akhilleus had spoken as if he knew he could enter the city . . . so he might know a way, somehow. But what way could there be?

They went to King Priam's palace, where the blind man was singing a long account of the battle to the king. Corydon listened for a while, his heart stirred by the marvellous weaving of words – though he noticed that the man had not mentioned Gorgos at all, seemed to think

Akhilleus had just fought a river. Priam looked up with tears streaming down his face.

'What of Gorgos?' Corydon asked the old man fiercely.

'You do not truly want the Olympians to know your plans,' said the man serenely.

Corydon asked Priam if they could do anything. Dismissed, the monsters went home.

They gathered around the table, morose, feeling prickly and uncomfortable. Gorgos was a card they had played. Now it looked as if the whole game was lost.

No one said, 'What now?' They all thought it, but rejected half-formed plans. No one wanted to do more than meet what might come with stoic courage.

Euryale was working on a bronze sculpture, slowly carving the wax form that would be destroyed when the hot bronze was poured into it. It seemed depressingly symbolic of their failed plans; working on a shape that would melt away to nothing.

Sthenno hated to see everyone so defeated. She scuttled to and fro, talking eagerly of the plan to evacuate a remnant of the people of Troy. She had already organised muster-points for key Trojans: a priest, an artist, 'and of course about fifty astronomers,' said Euryale rudely. But Corydon felt pleased that this small idea was in hand. It made the struggle to raise Gorgos seem more valid.

'How does that work, Euryale?' he asked idly, watching her press the wax with her scraper. She had made an eye.

She explained. 'Well, the wax melts in the heat of the molten bronze and pours away. See? And in its place we cast the bronze. You can't carve or change bronze because it's so strong. But wax is weak and you can change it.'

'What is it? A statue of what?'

Euryale looked down. 'It's Gorgos, when he was full of the gods.'

She showed Corydon how on the wax, faint shapes of the other gods could be discerned – a shadowy nymph peering from his chest, a satyr in the line of his belly, a thousand dryads caught in his curly hair. Corydon admired the conception. Gorgos would truly look full of the little gods.

And yet it seemed ironic for Gorgos-and-the-gods to be so . . . fixed. It reminded him a little of the eidolon of the Snake-girl. The real Snake-girl was coiled up asleep after absent-mindedly eating a supper intended for them all. It didn't matter. No one else had wanted it. The eidolon might have curled up, too, but it would have kept to the Snake-girl's normal diet. It was rigid. Like the metal of which it was made. While Gorgos had been like a roe or a young stag. Not rigid, but fierce with instinct. Now he was in the hands of the goddess who had brought him back to life. The goddess who was kin to the gods who had filled him.

Full of the gods . . . the phrase rang in Corydon's ears. Suddenly and reasonlessly he remembered the silly conversation about the Olympians in bottles, like djinn, and Bin Khamal's story about a djinn confined in the walls of Troy. Maybe that djinn would help again tomorrow . . . It was a pity about statues of the gods; if they really contained the god all the time, as some priests said, then the god would break when they did. He remembered the fractured statue of Poseidon in Atlantis City.

Then, suddenly, he stood up, pushed back his chair vehemently, and seizing his cloak went out of the house. He had an idea and it was vital to think it through thoroughly. Using one of the small tunnels, he crept out of Troy on the Mount Ida side, and under the paling stars sped up the hillside. Sitting where he could see the Great Hunter spiralling towards the earth, he thought hard.

The idea he had had was to catch Zeus himself in a kind of eidolon. This would ground him, incarnate him, make him as he had once been, as the little harmless local gods still were. He would be not destroyed but *limited*.

What he needed was an eidolon, and the power to persuade or force the King of the Gods to enter it.

Euryale! She could make a beautiful Zeus and Corydon need only suggest he inhabit it to delight his loyal followers. Could it really be that simple?

His thoughts were rushing now, like the tumbling river he sat beside.

Someone else would need to tempt Zeus. Who? Gorgos would be too tactless even if he were available. So would Euryale herself. He wished Fee were with them. Would the Snake-girl do it, with her hypnotic powers? She might not be quite quick-witted enough.

'I think you need my help,' said a voice beside him. 'You seek a woman in your mind. I will help you. But there is a price.'

Aphrodite! Corydon had almost forgotten Sikandar's aunt. There she stood, still looking like a fishing-girl in a port, forced into whoredom when a cargo went down. Sulky and pretty.

'You don't see me as beautiful because you have not yet learned to want what I offer,' she said. 'You are young and your heart is full of dreams. Later you will know me as part of your heart, and then I will seem much lovelier.'

Corydon didn't like the idea of this monster being born within him . . . He thought of the Snake-girl, of his warm and tender feelings for her, his longing to protect her, and imagined himself becoming like the man who had hurt her, Akhilleus's son . . . But he could see what Aphrodite meant. The Olympians were extreme about love; Zeus seemed to want to do only one thing with every nymph, while Athene refused all desire. Perhaps moderation would be wiser.

She spoke again. 'I will help you because I too hate them.' And she looked murderous enough.

'Why?'

She laughed. 'They spoil all my fun,' she said. 'And they killed my father. I was born from a very special part of him. Their father killed my father. That stupid old man in his stupid old library.'

'So . . . You remember before there were Olympians?'

'The gods did not always live on Olympos. That you know. And I like being a goddess on earth, not all cold among the snows.' She laughed. 'Though the cold damp snows certainly suit those frumps, Hera and Athene.'

Despite his hatred of Athene, Corydon did not have to listen to Aphrodite's irritating laugh for long to begin thinking a bit of restraint would be a relief. He wasn't sure he wanted someone like her on his side. Except . . . she was like a less-clever Medusa, in some ways. Somehow it made him feel fond of her. There was something warm-hearted about her.

'What is the price?' he asked her cautiously.

'Well,' she smiled coquettishly. 'I need a husband.'

A husband! Who could she be thinking of? 'There are no men among us,' he said bluntly. 'Only boys and monsters.'

'I know that, silly,' she said, in what she evidently hoped was a wily and seductive tone. 'But I want you to find me one. I have one in mind. Someone really big, and very strong . . .' Her voice went dreamy.

'Who?' Corydon had a sinking feeling.

'That lovely boy of yours . . . your friend . . . He's just sooo cute I could bite him. Fit . . .'

'Who?' Corydon was horribly sure she meant Gorgos. But that wasn't possible. Corydon could see he belonged to Demeter – or the Lady of Flowers – or whoever it was who had taken him to the cave, perhaps the land herself.

'That handsome wretch . . . you must know . . . such a fine archer . . . And I know he's my nephew, but pooh! You're not stuffy like some people, darling Corry.'

Corry!

Corydon was doubly aghast. 'No, you can't have Sikandar. He's too young, for one thing.'

'He is *now*,' she said. 'But it will only be a few years before he is ready for me.'

'And I can't give him to you. Why don't you ask Priam, or his mother, the queen?'

'They would be much too stuffy to say yes. And anyway he'd listen more to you. He trusts you.'

Corydon could see that she wasn't stupid, really. Perhaps she even had a kind of wisdom.

'If you help,' he said, 'I will talk to him. But it must be his choice.'

'For that I will help you,' she said. 'You can call me when you are ready to tempt the gods.' She smiled, a smile that chilled him because it was so greedy. Then she drifted off into the brightening mist. Corydon saw her give a little skip at the end – a skip of glee and triumph – and it made his blood freeze.

σίγμα
EIGHTEEN

He returned to the city grimly prepared to face the day. The first thing was to find Euryale and persuade her to work on the eidolon.

Over breakfast, he explained. Both gorgons looked startled, then more and more thoughtful. Sthenno felt a surprising prickle of affection for Corydon. Her dear mormoluke. Always seeking to heal the universe.

'There is no prophecy of this,' she said severely.

'But that's the whole point,' said Corydon. 'The Olympians won't know we're coming. If there was something written across the stars, the Olympians could find it out as well as you. Also, don't you think this is a moment when monsters might free themselves from their fixed fates? Can we not say, "This shall be so because I will it?" Must we always creep about under a freight of prophecies?'

'We do not have as much power as that.'

'Are you sure? Is it truly our stars that are at fault, or ourselves, that we are underlings?'

'Akhilleus would agree with you,' said Sthenno, very dryly.

'He would,' Corydon agreed. 'Because he is the most monster-like hero we have ever met. I can sense some kind of conflict in him, as if there is something in him which shames him.'

'Perhaps his *agon* will end today,' said Sthenno. 'Philoktetes has given his bow to the House of Priam in honour of Gorgos. The princes of Troy will try to destroy him today. They have named Gorgos an honorary member of their family in death.'

'They may succeed, or not,' said Corydon. 'We hold these desperate last stands about the city, knowing it will fall nevertheless. Why do we do so? Is it not obvious?'

'No, or not to me,' said Euryale. Corydon noticed that she was not eating her posset of stewed grain. Admittedly, it tasted like glue, but the city had grown used to it after the flour grew scarce. It was not like the Euryale he knew not to eat.

'It is because of duty and necessity,' said Sthenno. 'And if you do away with them entirely, men will be less than animals, who know them well.'

'It is, but it is also because the Olympians use all that is good in us to make us their sport, so that they can watch us fall and suffer and strive. For nothing.'

'For something,' Sthenno corrected. 'For our homes. For our friends. For this bowl of tasteless gum that sustains life. These too are necessary.'

'And I have found a new way to protect them,' said Corydon. 'Let me try.'

'I will try too,' said Euryale. 'I will make you an eidolon of astounding beauty, one that will tempt a god with an exaggerated reflection. One that will convince him he will be loved.'

'Is that what Zeus wants?'

'I do not know. But I shall guess as I work,' said Euryale. 'Sister, I must leave the war to you.'

'No,' said Sthenno. 'I will go to my tower and find all I can about the journey Corydon must make. To Olympos. To the very summit. And I will also look out on the battle. And join it if I must.'

'And I will go with Corydon to Olympos,' said a deep voice from the doorway. 'I heard your talk. I will travel with you again, as I did to the underworld.' Corydon smiled, and put his hand on the Minotaur's furred hand. It would be wonderfully comforting to have him on the journey. It was good to see him again; he had been aloof, recovering from his *aristeia,* helping by caring for the children of Troy.

'There is one slight problem, though,' he added.

'What?' said Sthenno

'Well, Aphrodite.'

Sthenno flapped her wing in a gesture the peasants used to avoid the evil eye. Then her face tried to look kind. 'Oh, poor Corydon. I suppose we forget you're growing up. Euryale was saying only yesterday that it was a pity about the Snake-girl . . . so difficult for you . . .' She patted his arm.

Corydon laughed. 'No, not like that! I mean, she's agreed to help us if we help *her* to marry Sikandar.'

'She wants to marry *Sikandar*?' asked Euryale, after a startled pause.

'I suppose we're lucky that she doesn't want Akhilleus or Hektor,' retorted Sthenno. 'But Corydon, have you spoken to Sikandar yet?'

'I will,' Corydon promised. 'But there are the trumpets. Euryale, can you start work on the sculpture today?'

'I have already made a plan in my head,' she said. 'Sister, call me if the battle gets too hot. Corydon, go with her. Don't let her do anything silly.' Corydon wondered how he was supposed to stop a ten-foot metal gorgon from doing anything that occurred to her, but he remained silent.

A hiccup came from the end of the table. It was the Snake-girl. She had just eaten everyone's pottage. 'Oh, I am sorry,' she said. 'Did you want it?' Then her eyes bulged, and she slid to the door. Hideous sick noises were heard. When she returned, she was marble-white, and her eyes were full of tears.

'I keep doing that,' she said. Then her tongue flickered. 'I hate this stupid baby,' she said. And burst into tears. Corydon put an awkward arm around her shaking shoulders. Savagely, she turned away, then seemed to relent and let him hug her.

'I promise I'll look after you,' he said uncertainly. Through her tears, she almost laughed. 'But Corydon, you can't protect me from something that's already happened. This isn't your baby. I wouldn't mind it so much if it was. It's the baby of a perfectly genuine monster. A real one.'

The trumpets were still blaring brazenly. The city was full of hurrying feet. Sthenno stood in a huddle with Euryale, then brushed apologetically past them and took off with a brassy rattle. Euryale bustled off to her art room. Yet Corydon still held the Snake-girl in his arms. His chin touched the top of her head. Daring, he stroked her soft scales. She looked up at him, and he kissed her, just as he had once kissed a girl he thought was her. It was a quiet, sad kiss; gentle and permanent, as if he himself had been sealed inside her like a djinn in a bottle. Now he too would be bound by her for as long as he lived. It didn't matter if she liked him, or just needed comfort. He would always be there. That was all he knew, and it came from being a shepherd.

'I shall like the baby,' he said. 'It's your baby too.'

Now she kissed him again all by herself. 'You are very sweet, Corydon,' she said. 'But I think you are making a mistake. I'm not a girl any more, really. I've been spoilt. I'm *truly* a monster.'

He kissed her very firmly this time. 'Shhh. Things might have been spoiled for you. That doesn't mean YOU'VE been spoiled. Of course you're still a girl. And I like your snakes. And I love the way you eat birds. Really, I do. It's you. You're still you.'

'I just can't love the birds the way I did,' she said sadly. 'It's as if my feelings are worn out. Worn thin.'

Corydon said gently, 'We all feel that way. We saw a city fall. You yourself are a kind of fallen city. But one day, in the kingdom of Hades, Atlantis will rise again. If people want it badly enough. As Gorgos has. And so will you.'

He kissed her again. This time both knew they were clinging together for warmth against the terrible sucking cold of dread that had invaded their lives.

The trumpets sounded again. Corydon let her go, giving her rounding belly a pat. She smiled at him and he thought that her smile was a small, warm miracle. That she could still smile at all.

'I go,' he said. 'If Akhilleus comes, you know what to do.'

'I wish I could help,' she said. 'But I can't seem to make snakes any more. It's the baby, I think.'

'You can help if the city falls,' he said reassuringly. 'Rest now.' And he ran off into the hurrying, frightened city.

Even from the street, Corydon could hear the approach of the Akhaians and their ant-men. The ground seemed to shake with the rhythmic pounding of their feet. Just as when a farmer is chopping wood, each split log falling with precision onto the woodpile that will ignite a long-burning fire, so the *tramp-tramp* of the Greeks' marching feet was regular and disciplined. The sounds from inside the city were frantic and chaotic. But that was why his heart was suddenly full of a longing to defend the place. Chaos was better than that unnatural rhythm.

Reaching the top of the walls, he saw that Hektor was leading a defensive force that had formed a shieldline in front of the broad wooden gates. On the walls stood Sikandar, who was organising the archers so that all could fire together. They were dipping their arrows in a vat of poison.

'Look,' said Sikandar, smiling ingenuously. 'I have it! Philoktetes' bow. He is with the healers; Khryses hopes to cure his lameness. So he lent it to me.'

Corydon found he couldn't quite meet Sikandar's eyes. How was he to tell his friend of his bargain with Aphrodite? He hoped passionately that Euryale would finish the eidolon today. Then they could get it all over.

They were interrupted as a large silvery sphinx landed beside them, the one that bore the Queen of the Amazons. Penthesilea was astride the calm monster, bearing in her hand a long, sickle-bladed spear; its point was like the horn of the new moon. 'I bring you our bows of the moon,' she said, gesturing behind her. Perhaps two dozen women in brightly-coloured doeskin tunics were readying their bows. 'We have our own poison,' said Penthesilea. 'Do not touch our weapons. The poison paralyses instantly.'

To prove her point she drew her own slender bow, took aim, and fired at an Akhaian who had run out ahead of his regimented shieldline. The arrow pierced his forearm where the greave didn't cover the skin, and the man looked down in surprise. Then he stiffened, as if he had been turned to stone, gave a gasp, and fell backward clutching his throat. 'They have also been blessed by my father, the god of war. He often helps me.'

Looking at Penthesilea, Corydon wasn't surprised that her father was so violent; he could sense the same raging blood in her. He turned once more to watching the man as he finally stopped twitching.

Sikandar winced, and turned to Corydon. 'My brother's chariot just tipped over. A spear knocked one wheel off.'

Corydon looked over the walls and could see that he was right; Hektor's chariot lay on its back, the horses standing surprised by the wreck. Standing beside it stood Hektor, wearing Akhilleus's old armour, his hate-filled eyes turning to the chariot constantly circling him. Akhilleus's chariot.

As they watched, Akhilleus leapt nimbly out of the chariot and threw his second spear all in one fluid moment. A sudden wind blew the spear straight into a passing bird, killing it instantly. Corydon could see that this was not fair play, that a goddess was taking a hand. Beside the wreckage stood the semi-transparent form of Aphrodite, smiling girlishly. Hektor shouted an insult as he prepared to throw his spear: 'Hunting birds, are we, my friend?'

A sudden fog encircled Ahkilleus, and a silvery, smiling Athene stood behind it, weaving it stronger. Hektor shouted in frustration, and lost his temper. He flung his spear into the centre of the dense cloud. There was no thump of a body falling. Then Hektor seemed to go berserk. Drawing his bright sword, he rushed into the cloud, shrieking, 'Akhilleus! Coward! Come out and fight!'

The cloud turned silver, the hard silver of Akhilleus's eyes. It burnt away like a tattered piece of paper. In the centre stood Akhilleus, a faint smile on his lips, his black sword shining. He waited for Hektor as a lion waits for a wounded deer to stumble into his path. He waits and waits, then springs, and the deer is no more. So great Akhilleus waited, his smile deepening.

And Hektor ran straight at him. All Akhilleus needed to do was raise his sword. And Hektor ran right onto the blade.

Blood blacker and glossier than the sword burst from Hektor's mouth. Akhilleus bent to whisper something in his ear. Hektor gasped. And Akhilleus laughed as he gripped the prince of Troy, drinking in his death like a long draught of cold water in a desert.

Then he flung great Hektor's corpse into the dust, and kicked it, and climbed triumphantly upon the prostrate prince. And again his war-cry sounded and sounded. And he cried out in a voice clearer and fiercer than a hawk's. 'Have you any more of these little princelings of Troy? They are my meat and drink.'

Penthesilea cried out in answer. 'Nay, but we in Troy have a princess of the moon and a daughter of Ares. Will you give battle?'

Akhilleus's face closed, as the helmet of control replaced his momentary exultation. 'I will.'

In answer, Penthesilea gave a slight tap on the sphinx's shoulder.

The sphinx rose into the air, wings spread, and drifted down to land in front of the mightiest of the heroes. Corydon pressed his knuckles to his mouth as the warrior queen sprang from the sphinx's back. He could see

Penthesilea's fragility; Akhilleus was taller, and his arms were three times the size of hers, bulging with muscles that were sickeningly visible through his golden tanned skin.

But the queen did not seem to have noticed that she was overmatched. She looked directly into Akhilleus's eyes. Even from the walls, Corydon could see her eyes were blazing, her mouth a tight line.

'You stupid bully! You just don't care, do you? How can we go into Troy and say that Hektor's dead? King Priam will be struck to stone. Hekabe will weep so much she will be a fountain, not a queen. How can I say it? Better that they say that Penthesilea died too, and lies beside him. But before I die,' and here she sucked in breath between her teeth, and fumbled with her helmet strap, 'beforehand I shall see you too lying in the dust, coward and bully. Die now upon the spear of an Amazon!'

She flung her helmet from her, and her long hair poured down, a torrent of tossing red.

Akhilleus was still, just for a moment. Corydon could almost have thought him tangled in that red net of shining hair.

And in that moment, the great spear given to her by her father flashed upward. It caught Akhilleus's face, slashing his cheek; only an enchanted blade could have marked his skin with a thin line of red blood. But the blade could not withstand the contact; it jagged, as if the queen had driven it against a hard stone, and its crisp edge was blunted. Penthesilea snatched it back in horror. And

Akhilleus used that moment to bring his sword slashing down. She got her shield up just in time, but his strength nearly broke her shield-arm; she stumbled, catching her foot, and almost fell.

Akhilleus waited, his eyes never leaving her. It was almost like a lover watching his beloved when she is unaware of him. Yet not quite, for next moment he brought his sword around in a wide sweep, so swift it was like the winged curve of a bird's flight. The black blade sank deeply into her throat. And her blood came out in a gurgling rush. She sank like a slender tree felled by a woodsman's axe, and lay in the dust beside Hektor.

Her silver sphinx swooped in desperate rage on her slayer. He waited, poised; he now seemed immune to her eyes and her magic. Then his spear arced upward, and caught her between her forepaws as she wheeled over her mistress's body. She fell like a hunted bird, and lay in agony beside her still mistress. Akhilleus left her to die slowly, ignoring her harsh cries of pain. He seemed less callous than preoccupied. To the surprise of the watchers on the walls, Akhilleus remained beside Penthesilea's body as her last breaths gurgled in her lungs. A Trojan who had been in Hektor's party, his voice shrill with loathing, cried out, 'So! Mourning over your girlfriend!'

Akhilleus turned. His fist flashed out. The punch was so hard that his taunter's skull seemed to collapse, his brains splayed on the ground.

Akhilleus looked around, as if inviting any other man to come and talk to him. His cold eye was caught by Penthesilea's sprawled body. He reached up and unpinned the dark cloak from his shoulders, and dropped it over her. The gesture was like a man throwing away an old coat he doesn't need. And yet the man had done it, had singled Penthesilea out from the nameless dead on the field. He stood still for a moment, his head bent. If Corydon hadn't known better, he might have thought the hero about to weep.

Then his head went back, and he looked at the sky, like a man staring down a foe. He gave his great cry again. A silver flame flickered over his bare head.

The Trojans were terrified; they ran back towards Troy like frightened babies seeking their mothers.

Akhilleus didn't even turn to see them run. The other Akhaians were doing great deeds – Corydon saw the plain snub-faced man leading a troop up to the very walls – but Akhilleus stood by the body of Penthesilea like a man stunned by grief. The Trojans were routed, but the hero was too preoccupied to enter the city. As the sun went down, he was still standing there; occasional silver flares of his anger shot up into the night sky.

By then he was alone: the Greeks had returned to camp through a sea of Trojan blood. And in front of the city lay its prince and princess, shining Hektor down in the dust, and the Amazonian queen with her silver sphinx dead beside her.

It was then that Corydon had his second idea to defeat the Olympians.

Hastily, he put his cloak over his head, clattered down from the walls, tore a branch from an olive tree, groped his way to the salley port tunnel, and crept out onto the plain. The stench of death was overwhelming. His hood well down over his head, he crept towards the still dark figure that was Akhilleus.

He stood next to the hero. Out here, his eyes by now used to the dark, what struck him was Akhilleus's great stillness. Usually he was a man who moved as fast as a striking snake, but now he had the snake's hunting immobility. He was watching Penthesilea as if he were hoping that she might come back to life. Corydon thought of the ritual he had helped to perform on Gorgos, and at once knew it couldn't work.

Akhilleus didn't turn his head as Corydon touched his shoulder tentatively. But he spoke. 'I would rather be the lowest serf on my father's fields than king of all the restless dead,' he said.

'It's not like that anymore,' said Corydon. 'I have been to the Land of the Many. It is what men and women choose to make it. No longer a land of shrieking shades.'

'I replanted the pomegranate tree from Hades' staff,' he added, hoping Akhilleus would know what he meant.

It was plain he did, but he frowned, and the silver eyes lit. 'My mother told me of it. But what will befall me, small goat-boy, when I enter the realm to which I have sent so many before their time? Will they greet me with joy? I think not. And you, goat-boy. What will the dead of Atlantis say to *you*?'

Corydon spoke up. 'I have seen them in a vision,' he said. 'They were angry at first, but now they are reconciled. You will see.'

Akhilleus smiled. 'But will I? Am I not immortal, like

the great winged creatures that fight for Troy? Am I not capable of resurrection, like your friend whom I sent screaming to his death? Suppose for me there *is* no death?'

'There is death for everyone. For me too. But I do not fear it. It will be for me a meeting-place with old friends.'

'I have no friends any more,' said Akhilleus. 'Patroklos was killed because of me.'

'And some of my friends were killed because of me. But it doesn't matter. Your friends will still be your friends.'

Now the hero turned and looked at him. The light eyes went through him like daggers. 'You have something I do not, boy,' he said. 'Hope. I have no hope for myself. I do only what I must.'

'You don't have to make war on the city,' said Corydon steadily. 'You could go home.'

'Home? To what? I have no home. I want to be remembered forever as the greatest of the Akhaians. Because it is just, for I am indeed the greatest. But I do not wish to die. If I must die, I wish to die on the rubble of Troy, killed by the last Trojan as I kill him. Not by some eager boy before I see it burn.'

'You are truly the greatest hero,' said Corydon truthfully. 'And I see that you are also a monster, for you understand necessity and fate, and also you kill as my friend Euryale did, because you truly wish to kill something in yourself. I once knew a hero, but he was a coward. Now I see that not all heroes are so.'

'That was Perseus,' said Akhilleus. 'A coward, yes.

But a son of Zeus.' He said the name Zeus thoughtfully.

'Do you serve Zeus?' Corydon asked curiously. 'I have seen Athene at your side.'

'I see that you do not altogether understand the Sky-Father,' said Akhilleus. 'I do not serve him. He serves me because I am going to win. Thus he gains prestige. He never helps the helpless.' He smiled. 'And neither does the Grey-Eyed Lady of Victories.'

'Will you help me fight him?' asked Corydon suddenly.

Now Akhilleus truly turned his head towards him. The stars burnt blue and silver overhead. There was a long silence.

'You are going to fight the king of the gods?' His head went back, not in a laugh, but in true amusement. His smile became a grin. 'Oh, I like you, herd-boy, I truly do. You have enough courage for a regiment of my Myrmidons. Shall I give you the command of a group of them and, after the war, a farm of your own? I do not like to see courage wasted.' He looked briefly down again at Penthesilea and her sphinx.

Corydon found himself smiling back, but then became serious again. 'Lord,' he said, surprising himself, 'I cannot forgo this quest. Soon there will be none of us left. Monsters, I mean. We have lost so many. And soon too Troy will fall, and it has become our last refuge. The ideas of Atlantis live on only here. How long shall I wait? Until every city is laid waste? Zeus will not let a new empire grow.' He grew more passionate. 'Sthenno said one day men would gain the power to throw lightning bolts that could burn the whole world. Shall I wait till then? I must act now to save my friends, however rash and foolish it seems to a hero.'

'You must,' said Akhilleus. 'And I must die here. But before I do I would like to help you against Zeus. You have a plan? Do not tell it me. But listen. Zeus wins men to his side because they do not want to be forgotten. To be forgotten is a kind of double death. I am a man like this too. Zeus promises the immortality of fame. Do not be entranced by it. Your songs might live forever, but to beat him you must give up the idea that your name will echo down the years. Men will not know that you have suffered and died for them. The story will be twisted, as the story of Medusa was twisted. You must be content with your quest. No laurel, no bays. Do you see?'

It was a long speech for Akhilleus, and to his dismay Corydon found himself unnerved. Did he want laurels and bays?

'I just want to go back to my sheep,' he blurted out.

Akhilleus smiled. 'Such simplicity! Do you truly think that everything would be the same if you did? You yourself are not the same.'

Corydon pondered. It was true. But he held on stubbornly. 'I would not weary of it,' he insisted. 'I do not want anything but my sheep, and friends to visit.'

'Do you not want to be loved?'

'I gave up that wish long ago.' He thought abruptly of the Snake-girl, but that was different. He knew their brittle kisses, cautious and spiky with shyness, were not the cosy mother-love for which he had once hoped. 'What do *you* want?' he asked curiously.

'I wish to be remembered forever, but I no longer know why I hold to that wish. It has caused so many deaths. I have swum in blood. I hate the High King of men and the High King of the gods. All kings I damn. I now seek only an end to it all. And yet I do not want to die.' He smiled. 'What a fool I sound. And this day my folly cut down beauty and valour and worth.' He looked sharply at Corydon. 'When I die,' he said, 'I wonder. Do you think they will forgive me?'

For just a second his face was naked with a child's need for reassurance.

'You do not want fame,' said Corydon, suddenly. 'You want absolution. You are trying to drown the memory of blood in blood. Give it up. Go home. Embrace your father. End it now.'

Akhilleus hesitated. Then his back straightened. 'That would be dishonour,' he said simply. 'I honour your quest. Honour mine.'

'I cannot. You need to know and understand that you are truly a monster, and to love yourself. I cannot make that happen, and nor can many more deaths. You need the healing only the Lady of Flowers can now bring. I leave you to seek her.' Corydon put out a hand that was no longer tentative, and brushed Akhilleus's shoulder. In a rush, he said, 'Thanks. Goodbye. Maybe we will meet in Hades' realm.' Then he turned and ran back to the city just as the first rosy fingers of dawn light arrowed across the sky.

TAU

NINETEEN

As he ran through the city, Corydon noticed an unusual sound; great drums beating, instead of the shrill bray of trumpets. And, ahead of him, in the wider main street, he saw an extraordinary sight. Riding along on stubby, stripy horses were tall men with skin the same colour as Gorgos's glossy black. But while his had blue and green in its hues, theirs had hues of gold and red and brown. In their right hands they carried long eye-shaped shields made out of the same hide as that of their mounts with a bronze rim. In their left hands they held long, finely-pointed spears. They wore little armour, just a kind of kilt made of more hide, studded with metal.

Behind them marched more men of the same kind, this time on foot. And more men. And more men. Among them too were men dressed entirely in skins, with huge masks to cover their faces. They were priests, perhaps. At their head, riding on a larger stripy horse, rode one who was wearing Greek armour, but it was festooned with the skins of strange striped and spotted beasts, and he bore a great darkwood spear hung with the tails of beasts and birds. Corydon looked at them, astonished. Here were men who seemed to want to be monsters; they liked the blend of animal and man. They were also heroes, though: slender and upright and very proud. Prouder even than the Amazons.

He wanted to watch them forever. He liked the way the men moved, with the same grace as their beasts. But they were not regimented like other armies. When they felt like it, men would stop and talk to the crowd. They sang songs of great strangeness. Did they speak Greek? The melancholy of Troy was lifted by their delight in the city. They jostled each other, looking up at its towers.

The tall man in the Greek armour was looking around, puzzled, as if searching for a missing face in the welcoming crowd. As the army came closer to Priam's palace, he came to look almost hurt. And Corydon, running along through the crowds, had a thudding moment of realisation. *He's looking for Hektor,* he thought. He squirmed his way to the front, and caught the man's bridle.

'Hektor is dead,' he said. 'He was killed yesterday. We cannot even bury him. Akhilleus stands by his body.'

The man's face went still. Then a great howl of fury and lamentation rose from his lips. He turned to his men, ordered them to halt. Then he dismounted, handed his strangely marked beast to his squire, and strode into the palace. Corydon followed.

Another council? No. This man was stamping along, bellowing; calling on Priam and Khryses and the Trojan princes. He wanted simply to attack. Now. Sikandar, his light armour half on, came running out. 'Old friend,' he said shyly, 'Memnon.' And Memnon grasped his arm. 'Old friend. How can we bear it?' Corydon could see Sikandar was torn by grief. His hair stood on end, rumpled from a night of sleepless tears. And something kind had gone from his face.

The man put an arm around his shoulders, firm and quiet now. 'Then it's true? As this boy said?'

'Yes, it's true. He lies dead. Dead in the dust. But none have been able to perform the rites of burial. Akhilleus stands on the plain as if he were a lover longing to court the city. He too lost a friend.'

'And now this day he shall lose his life,' said a high clear voice behind them. Memnon swung round, and looked up in some awe at ten-foot Sthenno.

'I came to tell you,' she said. 'The stars are clear. He will die today.'

'And by my hand,' said Memnon grimly. Sikandar looked grim too.

Somehow Corydon couldn't bring himself to offer them help. How could he conspire to kill a man he'd come to know – and – yes, like? Akhilleus was – well, difficult – but he'd come to understand how he'd become what he was.

He felt like a traitor. But no one noticed him. They were all too busy eagerly planning the attack. Corydon, listening, found himself tired of wars between the Olympians' victims. He patted Sikandar on the arm, smiled at Sthenno, and went off to see how Euryale was doing. As his plan rushed back into his mind, he took a last look at Sikandar; he couldn't tell his poor friend about Aphrodite just now, when he was still knotted with grief over Hektor. But he also couldn't help grinning a little.

Euryale was carving a layer of wax on an immense clay statue. It looked horrible, obscene and blobby and thickly bodged with a kind of yellow snot. Surely no Olympian could want to inhabit it? As he watched, she began sticking little tubes and pipes all over it. Then she took an armful of clay and slapped it on over the yellow gobs. It spread smooth and thin, but just as Corydon was thinking it looked better, she pulled out much stiffer clay and began covering it with that. The thing looked as monstrous and crude as the Olympians were inside their hearts.

'You will see,' promised Euryale. 'When it is fired.'

'Euryale,' said Corydon gently. 'Isn't it a bit big?'

'It will need to be big for Zeus. He has that kind of mind. Sthenno will make it small with a spell so you may carry it. Now we will fire it. Very slowly. Then we will pour the bronze, and polish it. I have also asked the women in the palace to make a silken robe for the god to wear, with much gold stitching. They are working on it now.'

Corydon tried to conceal his impatience. 'How long?'

'Art is slow, little mormo. I know that Troy cannot stand. But I hope that our plan may at least make sure the Trojans get away safely, with the secrets of art and of life, with the city's powers of thought. We must have courage to hold on until all is ready.'

Corydon realised as she spoke that it was a long time since he had made any songs. The old blind man was making the songs for this war. But he missed the making. It had not been quiet enough to make songs. He needed the stillness of a grassy hillside. Thinking this, he understood Euryale's need to take her time, and smiled. 'I do see,' he said. 'Your work is good.'

Then he told Euryale about the coming of Memnon and his strange stripy beasts, his tawny-skinned proud men. 'I wish I could paint them!' she exclaimed. 'A few sketches. Just while the clay is baking slowly. When it is fired I must be there, ready with the bronze.'

They flew to where Sthenno stood on the top of the wall to see Memnon and his tall troops assembling in a spear-pointed formation. They were not waiting for the Akhaians to attack, but preparing to attack them. Strange desert-coloured sphinxes and great spotted cats were with them. These were not leopards, but a dog-like beast with impossibly long and agile legs, and thick ruffled hair. The head of the spear-point was formed by the men riding on their stripy horses, but with them were men riding on grey animals the size of oxen, with two grey horns sticking like knives out of their foreheads, one small, one so great it looked fit to cleave anyone open. Their thick and folded grey skin reminded Corydon of the clay statue Euryale had just sent to be fired. Were they too armoured within? And they had tiny eyes, like the eyes of wild pigs. One gave forth a deep lowing noise, like an immense cow. What kind of beast could it be?

'It is a monoceros,' said Euryale. 'Some men call it

rhinoceros, for its nose is certainly horned. I never saw one before. How wide the world becomes.'

And now they saw the most astounding sight of all.

They were grey, taller than the monoceros, with the most amazing noses, longer than tails, longer than their legs, noses that twisted like serpents. They were grey and bald and they too had the small intelligent eyes of pigs. Their weight shook the ground, and yet they trod as delicately as little girls. There were ten of them, and each carried on his back a little tent of fighting men. The beasts wore heavy bronze armour. The men carried spears, and bows too, but the beasts had their own weapons, two long curving fangs of ivory that stood out from their faces. Corydon also saw that they had vast flapping ears like huge fans. One of them took a long draught from a pool, and then spurted it all back into the air with its nose – how could such beasts be? They were much stranger than any monster. As he watched, Corydon saw a sphinx fly down to greet one she evidently thought of as a friend.

'What are they?' The question burst from Corydon and Euryale at once.

'Pakhudermos,' said a sphinx as she vaned past their turret. 'The thick-skinned ones. Their skin isn't thick really. It just looks heavy. Incised with hard wrinkles, embossed with wide ears, invincibly tusked, made safe by magic hairs.'

Magic hairs? 'Are they safe?' Corydon asked.

But the sphinx had gone. Where was Sikandar? Corydon had become used to fighting with him and his archers. But he was nowhere to be seen.

'Down there,' said Sthenno. 'He must lead them now Hektor is gone.'

It felt wrong. How could an archer lead armed men? Sikandar wore little armour; could not withstand a charge. He would be killed.

'Get me down there,' said Corydon tersely to Sthenno. He could not let Sikandar go out like this so nakedly into the very jaws of death.

Sthenno swooped, seeing Sikandar. He had acquired armour from somewhere, but it really looked no more fitting than it would have on Corydon; he looked like a boy dressing up in his father's things. A squire held one of the great heavy helmets that made men into birds of prey. Corydon called to him, 'Sikandar!' But when he turned, Corydon could see that his friend the shepherd boy had gone forever. The face he saw was as alien as the Ethiop men's, a face set hard, all his smiles buried in the grave of his brother.

'Don't—' But he stopped. It would be no use. And he meant nothing to this man. This man had never known him, had never galloped wildly on camels through sliding sands. This man was a prince of Troy, nothing else. Perhaps he might marry Aphrodite after all. He looked like the kind of man who might find the sweetness of forgetting more important than anything else.

'I have the bow,' said Sikandar in a hard dry voice. 'I shall kill him, Corydon.' Corydon could find no words. And he was no longer certain of what he wanted. Was it Sikandar he wanted to save, or was it that he didn't want his friend to kill Akhilleus? To send him down into the Realm of the Many?

It was clear that no one could save Sikandar now. He was already lost.

He turned his back on Corydon. Without apology. He took a flaming torch from a servant, waved it in the air. 'Memnon!' he cried in a shrill voice that carried to every corner of the field. 'Ethiops! Men of Troy! Today we will put an end to this war! We shall kill Akhilleus! And after that we will burn their ships! They will die on our spear-shafts, on our swords! We shall attack them, not defend ourselves! Are you with me?' A large chorus of eager shouts answered him. The strange grey pakhudermos trumpeted ferociously. Some of the beasts snarled. 'Charge!' cried Sikandar.

And they did. The cats streaked out in front, a blizzard of spots, before leaping over the palisade wall of the Greek camp. From there they heard wild whinnying as the cats terrorised the Greek horses, and then an avalanche of horses poured out and ran wildly back, trampling the half-armed Greeks who were still stumbling into armour and arms. Then came the monoceros. They didn't know about palisades. They just ran on, treating the Greek palisade like tall grass, and it bent and broke as grass would. Two men were impaled swiftly on the leader's horn, their purple blood maddening the beast further. The stripy horses followed, the wild creatures fighting and kicking, while the men were using spears and darts, holding up their huge oval shields to deflect the blows of the Greek spears and arrows, their teeth showing white in laughter.

But best of all were the pakhudermos. They ran right into the Greek camp itself. With a hard rain of arrows hailing down from their backs, their enormous feet plashed and crushed everything in their path. Tents and pavilions went down. One creature's nose snapped out and snatched a running man, breaking his neck before he could escape. Then he was flung aside like a broken twig.

But suddenly one of the great beasts stumbled, and then toppled forward. It crashed into another pakhudermos, which gave a great squeal of fury and ran wildly, causing its own side to flee from it.

The man who had cut the pakhudermos's tendons was gleaming in his shining black armour. He gave a quick harsh shout. For the first time, Corydon noticed his long hair; it had escaped from his helmet, so that he was like an ill-omened, streaming comet. In his train came his hard-running Myrmidons, and they scattered the Ethiops like leaves in autumn.

But fierce fights erupted everywhere when the men turned to give battle; it was not clear that the Myrmidons had the upper hand. Corydon saw a swarm of them go down under the trampling feet of a pakhudermos, another little hillock of men plashed to ruin by the great monoceros. The Greeks could not master their horses, which were wild with the scent of all the strange beasts. The tawny dog-cats sprang fiercely at Greek throats. And the Ethiops used their long spears with real wildness, too.

But with a sinking heart, Corydon saw that the

Myrmidons' steady attacks were wearing away at them. The plain seemed strewn with bodies, the many hides of beasts. Then Corydon noticed Memnon. His horse was gone, but he went on with wild courage, jabbing with his spear, flinging huge boulders among the Greeks. He would not give way.

Corydon shouted to him to rally his men, retreat. But Memnon would not hear him. He was fighting his way towards the man he had come to kill, the man who ran dealing out death in his black armour, a storm cloud lit with silver lightnings.

Memnon leapt through the circle of dying attackers and defenders that surrounded his quarry. With him was one of the dog-cats, which sprang at Akhilleus's exposed throat. Almost scornfully, Akhilleus caught it in one hand and flung it out of the ring. Corydon saw it limp away, puzzled. Memnon grinned, then attacked with his spear; Akhilleus thrust it away with his shield. Akhilleus recovered, and thrust his great spear at Memnon's throat.

The spear juddered, as if he had pushed it into a rock. Akhilleus frowned to discover one who shared his own invulnerability. Memnon gave a great laugh, his teeth showing, and spun round to force his own spear into the hero's throat. But his spear too was rebuffed as if he had hit a tree. He grinned again. 'I will enjoy finding your weak spot,' he said. 'I know you have one.'

'I know you have one too,' said Akhilleus evenly. Now they circled each other slowly, delicately. They had dropped their spears, swept out swords. Each watched the other's eyes. Then each would make a sharp thrust at a different part of the other's body, frowning as their weapons met rock-hard skin. The shock jarred their arms; stabbing a rock hurt the stabber.

Memnon's rage could find no outlet. He stopped, and picked up a huge boulder, bigger than a man. Holding it in his immense arms, he flung it at Akhilleus's head. But it was no use. Akhilleus simply headbutted it away, as easily as a man shaking off a fly. It broke into millions of pieces, some tiny as insects, some bigger than wild wolves. One of the large pieces struck Memnon himself squarely in the belly, and he fell over with a cry of surprise and pain.

Akhilleus smiled coldly.

'I have you now,' he said evenly. He paced calmly towards Memnon. And bringing his sword down in a shining arc, he stabbed him in the belly, choosing the spot marked red from the impact of the stone, just where there was a gap between corselet and kilt. Black blood gurgled out and Memnon looked down in astonishment. And his life ebbed onto the sand. His Ethiopian warriors gave deep cries of mourning; many of them too had been struck down, and the plain was littered with the fierce and outlandish bodies of their beasts. Corydon heard the great drums beating for a retreat.

An early gale was gathering, and the light of dawn was blotted out by heavy clouds. It was as if Memnon's mother Dawn was weeping for her dead son. He lay in his blood, his eyes still open. Above him stood his conqueror, methodically cleaning his blackened sword.

The sight was too much for Sikandar. Ignoring the

drums' command, he charged forward, entirely alone. Corydon saw him putting an arrow to the string, his hands sure and steady. He muttered something between his teeth. He was behind Akhilleus, and the hero hadn't seen him. Hardly knowing what he did, Corydon shouted to Sikandar to stop, but the man lifted his bow, and as he did so Corydon saw his quarry look up, as if hypnotised, as a great stag looks at the hunter who is about to vanquish him and take from him his sweet life. Akhilleus's silver eyes lit, but he didn't move. Then he closed his eyes.

Sikandar's arrow flew, swift, and it found the mark. He had seen Akhilleus's weakness in the hero's battle with the Minotaur. Now his arrow sped like a hound for that very place on his left foot, the place where his goddess mother had held him as a baby when she dipped him in Styx to make him like iron. The arrow plunged in, ripping a path through tender mortal flesh. Bubbling black poison, the deadly poison of a hydra, burnt his flesh, frothing, before working its way into his body.

Akhilleus gave one cry, one hard cry, as the arrow hit. Then he fell forward, conquered by the hydra's ferocity. Grimly, Corydon thought that it was ironic that the greatest hero should be defeated by a monster at the last. But as he looked at Sikandar, he could see that the boy who had once been his friend was now more fierce and cruel than ever Lady Nagaina had been. He was smiling as he watched the poison ravage the hero's body.

He was smiling so much that he didn't notice the

Greeks behind him. They were led by the snub-faced man. Odysseus.

Without any fuss, Odysseus took in the sight: Akhilleus dying, Sikandar standing over him triumphantly. He said something to one of his men. Then he scuttled sideways, like a crab, until he could get to Akhilleus directly. Meanwhile, four of his men's bows twanged. Corydon shouted, but Sikandar didn't even turn as four Greek arrows pierced his body, finding every joint in his ill-fitting armour. He toppled onto the sands, plucking feebly at one of the arrows.

Corydon leapt from Sthenno's claws, hit the sand with a hard jarring impact, and rushed to his side. He took the dying man's head into his lap, as he had seen too many others do with their friends. But Sikandar was already past speech. He had just time to hear Corydon's, 'Farewell, my friend,' before his head rolled in death.

Looking away from his friend's sightless eyes, Corydon saw Odysseus, with Akhilleus's head in his lap. Akhilleus's face was stiff; all his superlative energy was ebbing into a battle for breath. He fought death as he had always fought, expecting to triumph. But death was going to win. Corydon could see it in the yellowing of his skin, in the restless hands that clutched at air. He was trying to say something, something precious. Corydon found himself lunging forward to hear him. But then he gave a fierce gasp, and his soul went out of eyes that could not know defeat even when they looked on it. Corydon looked at his sprawled body, its severe dignity crushed into dust, and wondered why the gods feasted on forever while courage and energy melted into air. He looked at Odysseus, cradling Akhilleus's head as he himself held Sikandar.

Their eyes met. In the hero's dark face he saw as in a mirror the image of his own anger and sick bewilderment. But when the man spoke, his words were light, having nothing to say to the glittering tears in his eyes.

'You do seem to love leaping from high places when I am in sight,' said Odysseus. Despite his casual words, there was a sadness in his voice, as if he found the entire war sad, even hopeless.

Reading Corydon's thoughts, the man said, 'No, I am not sad for myself. For him. He was not truly my friend. He didn't truly have friends. He was too great for earth. Who are you, leaping boy? Friend of Prince Paris?'

Paris? 'This is Alekhandros,' said Corydon. 'Yes, I am his friend. I am Corydon Panfoot, and I come from the Island of Monsters.'

Odysseus smiled. 'Then Perseus did not conquer you,' he said. 'Ah, well. I thought not. Now I must lead the Greeks against the city, Panfoot. Perhaps we shall meet again, before the end.'

He lifted the dead body of Akhilleus to his shoulders. 'He must not lie here to be despoiled,' he said, and strode off, towards the Greek camp. The hero's arm flopped down from under Odysseus's cloak, and Odysseus bundled it up again as if it were a piece of stray washing. It was comic and undignified and unimaginable. Corydon felt a twinge of real grief, almost fear; how could someone so alive be dead? It was for his friend that he mourned, but his friend had died before today. Sthenno and Corydon carried the body of Sikandar – no, he would always be Alekhandros now – back to his city. The Trojans had cheered the fall of Akhilleus, but Memnon's troops were spent without their leader. And the last of the princes of Troy lay dead. The city looked at a future blank as a wall.

ύψιλον
TWENTY

Corydon was among those who mourned by his friend's bier all night. The wind howled outside the city like the voice of a crying djinn; was it Bin Khamal? Thinking of the djinn, Corydon began to compose a little threnody, a lament for his friend the shepherd boy; the song said that the boy had had to die long ago. But he also put in the triumph of killing Akhilleus, and a few lines of lonely lament for the hero; would he find what he needed in the Kingdom? Love, calm?

He was going back to Euryale's studio to see how she had progressed when he saw a hooded and cloaked woman coming out of one of the houses, her sobs ringing out on the night air, unabashed, hiccupping sobs loud as a toddler's. She cannoned into him, and her hood fell back, revealing a face glistening with tears. At first Corydon thought she was some girl who had lost her man in the war. Then he recognised her. It was Aphrodite.

With a gulp, she said in a voice blurry with tears, 'I can never have him now.'

Corydon was impatient. Sikandar hadn't wanted Aphrodite. He had wanted a hillside and his sheep and his friends. At the end this had been deformed into a wish to be a hero, a wish that had killed Akhilleus. Aphrodite had not been part of the equation.

But she suddenly threw back her head and laughed.

'You think that, Panfoot, but he did want me. He did. He just didn't know it yet. As men grow to be men, they begin to want me. How else can they escape manhood? And I begin to want them, to be able to give them respite.' Her sobs increased. 'But now he belongs forever to the world of men and of battles. Though it will not be sung so. Men will sing of him and of me, and they will forget.'

Probably. Corydon had already seen how people could annihilate in recollection. Medusa was remembered now as just a monster. Abruptly, brushing aside his own sudden hot tears, Corydon asked, 'Are you still going to help me?'

'More than ever. Did you see those arrows? Guided by cold-hearted Athene.' She almost spat the word. 'She's always favoured Odysseus.' Corydon was surprised. Odysseus didn't look too carried away by the Olympians. Somehow he was – homely and sensible. If Akhilleus – Corydon thought of him with a pang – had been like a monster in his self-knowledge and violence, Odysseus was more like the Minotaur, a man who just wanted to be at home. Corydon also thought of his father when he thought of Odysseus; they both had a simple delight in tricks.

'Athene likes to trick people too,' said Aphrodite

bitterly. 'And Odysseus lets her help. I hate him too. But don't worry. I have many plans for him. And I will help you with Zeus. I will.' She put her hand on his arm. He wanted badly to snatch his arm away, but prudently made no move. Drawing her cloak over her head again, she drifted off into the street, one among many mourning women whose sobs filled the night air.

Euryale was at work, cursing the bronze, cursing her assistant, cursing the statue. It was an inferno of heat in there; kiln, melting metal. It also stank because Euryale was keeping herself going with bites from a deer she had taken that morning and hadn't had time to cook properly.

'Shouldn't you share that?' Corydon asked.

'Not *now*,' she snapped, taking another mouthful. 'Come back in a few hours and I'll show you something.' She moved around to steady the slave as she began to pour the bronze into the vent. A river of liquid metal, brighter than the sun, lit the room.

'Where's the Snake-girl?'

'On the roof,' screamed Euryale. 'Go away, Corydon.'

So he did. He climbed the ladder to the rooftop, to find the Snake-girl coiled up in a corner, wrapped in an old quilt, watching the stars.

She looked up as she heard Corydon's step. 'It can't go on much longer,' she said softly. 'One way or another. Akhilleus is dead. Sikandar is dead. Hektor, and Penthesilea, and in a way Gorgos. Is there anyone left to fight? Just the daimons, and old men, and monsters, and women. It must end soon.'

Corydon thought of Sthenno's disc. There would still

be a battle of earth, and a battle of fire. But Sthenno had sometimes misread things . . . And it was clear that the Snake-girl at any rate had had enough. He sat down beside her, and they stared in silence at the wheeling stars. Corydon felt the light touch of her shoulder against his. Awkwardly, feeling he was soothing a scared animal, he patted it. 'Why don't you go?' he asked. 'Go back to the island and look after the baby? There are still boats further down the coast.'

She was silent for a while. 'I think of it,' she said. 'But I want to stay with you.' Corydon felt a huge warmth invade him. He put an arm around her. She hurried on. 'It's not only you, it's the gorgons. And the Minotaur, too; he brought me some honey only yesterday and he's so unhappy here. And the sphinxes. I feel – not at home, but befriended. But it's mainly you. I know you aren't really – I mean, it wasn't – but I sometimes pretend that the baby is ours.' She looked at him anxiously to see if he minded.

He felt the warmth spread still further. 'I'd love to help with the baby,' he said simply. 'I'll always feel as if it were mine. It seems funny to be a father,' he added. 'And it will have some very strange aunts. But we'll all love it and it will comfort the gorgons now Gorgos has grown beyond us all.' He gave her a gentle kiss on her pointed chin. She settled into the crook of his arm, spreading the quilt over them both.

The pink light of dawn found them asleep in its soft light. Corydon was sleeping so deeply that at first not even the loud thudding noises woke him. Then he sprang into wakefulness; was it the gates? What was it?

Men were running and shouting. Again. Tired men woken from tired sleep. Panicking. What were the Akhaians doing? How could they avert the new peril if they didn't know what it was? It wasn't even a thumping so much as a sussuration, as if the whole city were somehow shaking like a jelly, trembling at the approach of the Greeks. He ran to the street side of the roof, followed by the sleepy Snake-girl. Looking down into the street, at first he saw little; the light was still greyish, and most of the running men were in more distant streets.

But then he saw it.

A small mound of what looked like sand, moving. Was it a wounded djinn? How could sand move? Then an arm with a spear burst out of the mound. A second arm with a shield. And a fully armoured Greek hoplite leapt out, followed by another. More Greeks emerged as Corydon watched; he saw that they were Akhilleus's old ant-men, now truly running like ants from an anthill.

He must warn the army. Instinctively he crouched beneath the parapet, then began working his way along to the ladder.

'Get down,' he hissed to the Snake-girl. 'We must warn them. Can you go the back way? I'll try the front door.'

'Be careful,' she said. 'They are right outside.'

'I'll get Euryale,' he said. 'It will be all right.'

Perhaps it would have been. But when they reached the studio Euryale was nowhere to be seen. Perhaps she had gone out for more onyx stones; a half-finished eye for

Zeus lay on the table in her workroom, uncanny and staring without its iris and pupil, but with long gold lashes.

'We'll have to risk the streets,' he said grimly. 'I still have plenty of kleptis skills. Come on.'

They opened the great wooden door a crack. As they peered out, the noise increased. A last hoplite, resplendent in glossy black armour, seemed to pour out like a snake slithering from a hole, rearing up to strike as it emerges. And yet it wasn't Akhilleus; he lay dead, and this man was different. Corydon caught a glimpse of furious eyes, *red* eyes. And the Snake-girl froze beside him. It was the man she feared, the father of her child. Akhilleus's son, Neoptolemos.

Stealthily they crept out. The Greeks, including Neoptolemos, were heading to the right. So Corydon and the Snake-girl went left, sliding silently from doorway to doorway.

They were almost at the end of the street, when the Snake-girl mistimed her slither into a doorway and set the gate rattling hard. Corydon didn't even need to see; he could feel Neoptolemos turn, feel the hard red stare piercing the street.

'Men, go ahead!' Neoptolemos cried. 'Remember, open the gates. No more for now. I will remain to make sure no one warns the palace.'

He began moving down the street towards them at a brisk run.

Corydon frantically grabbed the door handle, but it was locked. They would have to run for it, chased by that terrible tower of metal. He seized the Snake-girl's hand,

and they tore off down the narrow street, then quickly Corydon saw a narrow alleyway – was it a blind alley, though? No time to see; they turned, hoping it might fool Neoptolemos in the grey light of dawn, but the hard metal feet came on, turned too. The Snake-girl was breathing hard. Luckily, the alley led to the main street, which was full of anxious Trojans. Corydon and the Snake-girl burst out into a whole group of them, and clutched them with relief.

'It's the Greeks,' cried Corydon. 'A tunnel, or something. One of them is right behind us. Akhilleus's son.'

But when he turned Neoptolemos had vanished. The Trojans began hunting through the streets, finding the ant-men, and dispatching them angrily. But not their leader. He had simply vanished.

Had he gone back into the hole? Or was he hiding in the city?

They heard the trumpets blare as Agamemnon's forces attacked the gates. There were few enough by now to answer them. Corydon saw boys younger than himself strapping on play-thing bows. He told the Snake-girl to go home; he feared for her with her former master abroad in the streets. He caught the arm of Euripylos, the new leader.

'I'll get the Minotaur,' he said. 'We'll find him.' He knew he would need help if he found Neoptolemos.

Euripylos frowned. 'I do not need help,' he said arrogantly, and Corydon could see he saw himself as like his grandsire Herakles, standing alone against earth and heaven.

'Yes, you do,' he said gently, and ran off to get the Minotaur, who was sitting alone in his small garden, ignoring the chaos.

When he saw Corydon he stood up. 'Is it time?' he asked, sounding worried.

'Not yet,' said Corydon. 'Euryale is still at work. We have another task. We must find Neoptolemos. He has concealed himself somewhere.'

The Minotaur was already hurrying into the street. 'We need the dogs from the palace to help. I can scent as I must, and so can you. Do you have anything of his?'

Only his child, thought Corydon. *And the babe is not yet born.* Had he come for that? Somehow Corydon didn't think so. He thought Neoptolemos was the kind of man to forget the Snake-girl when he had used her. Aloud, he said, 'No.'

They went back to the earth-floored street where Corydon had seen the Greeks emerge. They tracked Neoptolemos easily until the large strong feet reached the cobbles. Then the footprints vanished. It was as if Neoptolemos himself had also vanished away.

They combed the street for signs. But there was no trace of a Greek hero. Corydon was exploring the edges of the cobbles for the ninth time when he idly noticed the curving trail of a small snake as it slithered through sand. There were still snakes in Troy; did this one come from the Snake-girl? Then he remembered that she had said she could no longer make them, while pregnant. So what was it doing?

A sudden hiss alerted Corydon to its presence. It was slithering towards him down the street. It was an asp, its teeth glinting and its eyes were . . .

Corydon halted. Could it be . . .? But that would mean that . . .

The black-scaled snake reared up, twisting higher and growing arms and legs, its tail growing shorter, armour bursting out from its body, and the red eyes glinting, glinting with satisfaction at seeing the horror and amazement in Corydon's eyes as it prepared to thrust its spear. Corydon leapt aside and called for the Minotaur.

The bull-monster turned and ran towards Corydon, seeing Neoptolemos complete his transformation from snake into man.

The man in front of Corydon grinned. 'When she blinded me, I was healed by bonding with snakes. There were some useful side-effects. I can coat my weapons in venom whenever I want to. And I can turn into a snake,' he said, then lunged with his dripping spear.

The Minotaur's charge took him in the side. He was flung through the air, but with a graceful twist found his feet again. Corydon saw his arms fasten to his sides as he began to shrink back into a snake again. *Quick!* With bursting lungs he flung a market vendor's basket over the snaky, writhing form.

Neoptolemos was trapped, unable to make whatever writhings were required for his transmogrification into human form. Breathing hard, the two monsters faced each other across the basket.

'What shall we do with him?' asked the Minotaur. 'We

cannot leave him within the city. Should he escape he would be a terrible danger.'

Corydon was silent. He thought briefly about killing the hateful hero while he was vulnerable, then dismissed the idea. No. It would be too cruel. He eyed the glossy black snake, through the small chinks in the wicker work.

'What if we take him outside and pay someone to carry him far away?'

'It would be putting them in danger. If he regrows into a man . . .'

Both of them looked fearfully at Neoptolemos. He could do that now and burst right out of the basket.

'Throw him from the walls,' said Corydon reluctantly.

'The fall would kill him.'

'Not from the gate side. You saw how well he jumped.'

'All right.' They carried the basket hastily up to the wall. And flung the contents as far as they could, both feeling uneasily like murderers. The advancing Greeks were therefore amazed to see Neoptolemos rise up before them like an angry basilisk . . . with a broken basket on his head. Corydon saw him shake it off furiously, and knew that they had further roused the rage of an already angry man.

'Was that the earth-battle?'

'Maybe.' The Minotaur shook his great head. 'Maybe.' He looked grim. Corydon wondered what he was thinking and put out a timid hand. The Minotaur enfolded him in a hug, then went back to watching the Greeks coming, and coming, more and more across the great wide plain.

'And there are so few of us,' Corydon sighed. 'Why is it always like this?'

'Because of the Olympians, perhaps. But also because men are evil. Not all men. Not always. But enough are like that man we threw from the walls. Bullies. Mindlessly angry.'

'Will it change if we defeat Zeus?'

'If men have a place that belongs to them it might be different. A place that they belong to. I am happy when I have my bees. You are happy when you have your hillside, your sheep. That is enough for most of us. But there will still be men who want the heady excitement of destroying what matters to another man. Who will kick over hives and steal or kill lambs.'

Corydon was silent. He had stolen many lambs himself. Was he like that? Suddenly he thought about how poor the farmers he had stolen from had been. He *was* like that.

'Yes,' he said. 'I did that myself. But I had no army. It is that Zeus loves men like that and gives them power. Without him they would be bullies with stones. With him they are a vast horde with spears.'

'Then let us go and see if Euryale has done her work,' said the Minotaur. 'I would like to help the city now. I do not think there is much time left.'

When they entered the studio, they saw two bronze wonders. The first was Euryale, curled up asleep in a ruffle of sharp feathers. When had he ever seen Euryale sleep, unless enspelled? He hadn't thought she could.

The second was the statue. Gleaming, silky, robed in

green and white, its eyes dominated the room, their hard onyx stare and long gold lashes seeming to hypnotise everyone.

The Minotaur shook Euryale's shoulder. 'Wake,' he said in his soft rumble. Euryale did wake. Her own bronze lashes lifted.

'That was remarkable,' she said. 'Mortal sleep! A whole new subject for art. Well, what do you think of him?'

'It's awesome,' said Corydon. 'It will fill everyone with amazement.' Tactfully, he didn't ask how he was to carry it.

'Do not fear, mormo,' said Euryale, with a wide yawn. 'It has been enchanted. Sthenno has wrought greatly. You may make it shrink to the size of a mannikin, and with another word you may make it grow to godlike dimensions again. Look!' She said a word, then lunged for a piece of dried barley bread Sthenno had left behind.

The statue shrank to the size of Corydon's forearm in a great rush, like a fountain going backwards. Corydon picked it up. It was still heavy, but it did not carry its full-sized weight. The Minotaur took it from his hand. 'This I will carry,' he said, and Corydon was grateful. He was grateful to Euryale too; she wrote down the magical word to make the statue grow, and she and Sthenno had also prepared a pack of food and a waterskin for each of them; some wrinkled apples in another bag were the last of their store. The Minotaur had brought a honey cake to share.

Now Sthenno herself fluttered in, feathers stiff. 'Mormo,' she said sharply. 'Mormo. Listen. The city will fall. Look at the disc.' Only the fire battle was left, 'and that may be the fall of the city itself,' she said. 'Do not fear for Gorgos,' she added kindly. 'He is with the goddess.'

'We will go,' the Minotaur rumbled softly. 'The ship is ready at its moorings, south of the city.'

Corydon hesitated. 'I must say goodbye,' he blurted, and ran to find the Snake-girl.

Her face had grown puffy and her body was now swollen with the coming child. As he watched, she slept with a terrible stillness that told of her exhaustion. There were blue circles under her eyes.

He bent and kissed her, very softly so as not to wake her. She did not stir. Then he was gone.

Sinkingly, he knew he would probably never see her again. He hoped the gorgons would help with the baby as they had with Gorgos. As he and the Minotaur moved wraithlike through the streets of Troy, Corydon found his gaze sharpened by his awareness that he was looking on a great city for the last time. He had never noticed the daimons much, but now he saw them, one playing with children, one or two simply floating, drifting past houses and men. He noticed the great ornate fountains in which soldiers would wash themselves after battle. He noticed the way the smallest children's limbs had grown sticklike with hunger, though their faces still smiled with a cheer that couldn't be quenched. One was carrying a tiny bunch of weed-flowers, which she placed carefully at the feet of a Lar who stood in the gateway of her house. Corydon saw the Lar smile, and could see too his own longing to protect reflected in the Lar's expression. The girl returned the smile and the Lar waved. It was hard to imagine that Zeus had once been like that.

The city was looking war-worn, some houses dilapidated because their owners had been killed. And there were lone women, watching the children play from under black veils of mourning. But it was still precious. He wished he could save it.

'You can save something,' said the Minotaur comfortingly, and Corydon saw that he too had been watching the children. 'We can save the idea of a great city. Or so Sthenno says.'

'Gorgos will lead some of them away,' said Corydon, as they walked. 'And they will build again somewhere else. Somewhere remote.'

'Faunus told me,' said the Minotaur, 'of his country. It lies many leagues from Hellenic lands. It would serve. It has vines and olive trees. It would be a beginning.'

Now they had reached the tiny side-gate of the city, guarded night and day. Corydon looked up at the walls, put his hand on them, wondering if Bin Khamal's relative slept within, also ceaselessly watching. Or had his power been exhausted? He had not warned them of Neoptolemos's invasion, but then Neoptolemos was plainly endowed with magic as dark as Styx had been. Then he dismissed the problem.

The guards stood still, not talking, their eyes watchful. Their armour was battered and it did not shine much, and they looked lean and hungry, but their discipline had not relaxed; they had not surrendered. They saw Corydon and the Minotaur approaching, and saluted.

'We have orders to let you go,' said one. 'But I must beat to quarters so my men are ready in case the Greeks have placed a watch on the doorways.' Corydon suddenly thought that he hadn't heard the Trojans call their enemies names, not once. They had no special words for Greeks or Akhaians. He remembered the way the Shells and Dolphins had abused each other, and marvelled. He smiled at the man with additional warmth.

Then the gate opened, and he and the Minotaur left Troy behind. Neither looked back. Neither could bear it.

ΦΑ

TWENTY-ONE

Following the furrow again ... the small fishing smack was very like the boat that had taken them some way to Atlantis. Once more they were heading due west, the setting sun in their eyes every day like a streak of blood. Four days from Troy, Corydon saw stiff billows of cloud on the horizon. Was it a storm?

'That is Olympos,' said the Minotaur. 'It is a lonely mountain. And always shrouded in cloud.'

'Can they see us?'

'If they wish,' said the Minotaur. 'But their eyes may be turned elsewhere.'

With a jolt, Corydon also wondered what had become of Aphrodite. He fingered his Pan-pipes. He had his own ideas if she failed them, as he half-expected her to do. She had said she would see them on Olympos.

The cloud was a solid wall of white ahead of them. It was a fluffy cloud, not a storm, but it was utterly and unnaturally still; it should have been blowing and shifting in the light wind, but instead it was a fortress around the mountains of the gods. Its soft surface belied an unnatural strength.

He could see no mountain within, but the cloud was itself shaped like a mountain. The boat drove forward. They could see a shallow bay ahead; they beached the boat, and leapt onto the land. It was a smooth stretch of sand. No seabirds called. The beach sloped sharply, and they laboured up the soft red slope. At the top they could see a path, which led into the cloud. It was little more than a goat-track, but along it were small, crude altars, on which men had sacrificed oxen. The piles of skin and fat for the gods stank a little in the warm sun.

'It's that stink of death they feed on,' muttered the Minotaur.

'I thought they ate nectar and ambrosia,' said Corydon tentatively.

'They do. But it is the smell of our mortal deaths they love.'

The cloud-wall was directly ahead. The cloud leaned over them, like an over-friendly uncle about to ruffle a sulky boy's hair.

'What is nectar?'

'Just a drink made with their honey. Very sweet and smooth. I make mead. You have tasted it.'

'But it does not give eternal life,' said Corydon with a wry smile.

'Why should anyone want eternal life? Sthenno and Euryale have lived time out of mind, as long as this mountain. They do not want to die. No living thing wants to die. But they would not have chosen the long years they have seen. It is only that few can choose to end them.'

He extended his stick, and prodded the cloud-wall. It did not seem solid. The stick was intact.

They walked into the cloud. A moment of drenching grey. A sense of pent forces. A faint flicker of blue lightning. And then they were, astonishingly, through the cloud.

They came out into the hard yellow-white light of a brilliant sun. The grass was spangled with dew. Tiny wildflowers, rich purple, clambered over rocks. A few pale primrose orchids drowsed in the sun. The Minotaur saw a bee, its belly heavy with pollen, swooping on a flower cup. The silence was entire and unbroken. No birds sang. There was no wind to shake the green grasses or disturb the flowers. Only the droning bee could be heard.

They looked up. The mountain dreamed above them, its wall looming over their heads, its peak capped by glinting snow. There were no clouds to blur its terrible outline.

No clouds anywhere. What had become of the mountain's thick cloak of storm? Corydon looked around, his gaze sweeping the clear horizons. It was impossible to imagine unquiet weather here.

Curiously, Corydon turned. The clouds through which they had come were gone. Walking backwards, he retrod his own steps, until he had taken double the number that had brought him out of the cloud.

But there was no cloud. There was not even the memory of cloud. The grass was dry under his feet.

Which meant that they were trapped. There could be no going back. They were held in Zeus's fist of cloud, and they could not return unless they defeated him.

Where was Aphrodite?

Corydon turned his eyes to the heavy wall of mountain again, splurges of snow spilt on its flanks. There was no point in waiting. They must manage without her. Towards the peak ran a little path, stony and obscure, a goat-track. *For me,* thought Corydon, ironically. Along its way they could see stone altars, very like the one they had passed just before they plunged into the cloud. But these bore no weight of meat. They were as bare as the peak that rose above them. They had, however, been tended; the grass had been pulled away from them, leaving bare circles.

Without a word, Corydon and the Minotaur clasped hands, and began to walk towards the mountain. Neither wanted to break the thick silence.

Their feet made little sound on the stony track. Keeping their eyes fixed on the peak, they plodded on. Their packs already felt heavy. The grass smelt sweet, though, and the scent of flowers drifted up to them. It was a place so calm that Corydon felt more than ever a monster, as if his Pan-leg was an unwarrantable disturbance. The Minotaur's shaggy head and furred body looked wrong in the smooth enamelled landscape. And although it was like a dream of pasture, there were no browsing animals – no goats, no sheep, and no men or girls to guard them. It was perfectly clean and neat. The heat of the sun was ideally pleasant, without being oppressive.

And yet somehow its very perfection became a kind of burden. Corydon began to long for something real – some dung, some flies, a dead bush. Anything that wasn't manicured. This was not natural: it was a terrible garden, a smug and hateful parody of the wild pastures he loved. He began to hate it.

And the mountain's baldness cowed the landscape before it. It was so much fiercer; it was as if all the life of the landscape had been sucked into its powerful, sheer slopes. As it grew nearer, Corydon began to sense a menace. It was as if the mountain had eyes. The mountain was utterly silent. A few thin streamers of water ran down its face, but they made no sound.

It also looked entirely impossible to climb. It was virtually a sheer wall of rock. Corydon knew about climbing – it was one of his kleptis skills, and it had been honed in the White Mountains on the Island of Monsters, which contained their share of rotten rock and chimneys and exposed walls. But this mountain was far larger than anything in his experience. It seemed to stretch forever. It was a shining pinnacle of impossibility.

He pointed, and turned left. Perhaps there would be an easier ascent on the other side. Or on one of the flanks. The Minotaur plodded after him dutifully.

After an hour or more of roaming through the same jewelled meadow of purple and yellow flowers, he was forced to give in to his rising sense of hopelessness. The mountain was like an anthology of difficult climbing. As well as the fierce face they had rejected at first, they had managed to discern an avalanche funnel bigger than any he had ever seen, a whole packet of overhanging ledges, a cluster of couloirs, deep gorges surrounded by vertical rock, green ice making the surfaces gleam slick in the sun.

There was no easy way up this mountain. And the sun was westering. It was time to make camp for the night. They could not build a fire; there was nothing to burn. So they ate some hard biscuit ration, drank from a mountain stream so cold it made their teeth shriek in agony, and pulled their sheepskins around themselves.

Corydon was glad of his skin; it smelt real. He and the Minotaur slept back to back. But it was obvious that nobody would come, neither animal nor man. The land was as empty as a ragpicker's pocket.

The next morning they woke at dawn. It was a rich pink flush that made the mountain snows look as if they were stained with blood. But they must now attempt to climb.

They reached the mountain's foot only an hour after first light. Now it was so high above their heads that they could only see the summit by bending back their heads. They unrolled a rope and tied it round their waists, connecting them so that if one fell, the other could try to pull him back. Corydon himself knew he would have little hope of saving the heavy Minotaur if there was a disaster; he also knew that the great monster's weight could bring him to his death. But the rope at least gave both a chance.

Corydon knew, too, that his Pan-foot could find vital holds. It acted almost like a hook, securing him to rock and ice. His other foot he therefore safeguarded with a special shoe that Euryale had made: it was light thin bronze, very hard, and covered in thin hook-like spikes. It tied onto a snowboot made of soft leather. The Minotaur had a similar device for each of his huge furred feet; they too were bound like lightning-studded sandals over a thick furry buskin boot with a smooth leather coating that would keep his feet dry. Wearing them, he looked like a child with bedroom slippers. Corydon almost laughed, but the hush of the mountain oppressed him.

They began to climb. Each step was a calculation: find a spur of rock, reach it with a hand, hold on, place a foot near the hand, swing forward, swing out, swing down. Place the next foot. The next hand. Confront the next problem: a bulge in the mountain's face. Work out how to traverse it. The next: an overhang. The next. The next. Slowly, but with rhythm. Slowly, but with grace. With momentum. With cunning.

It was tiring. It was hard work. And it was also a mere nothing. It required only application. Due diligence. There was nothing impossible here. And Corydon knew that there would be impossibilities to come.

They met their first real difficulty after they had been climbing steadily for three hours, ascending dizzyingly above the smooth grasses. There was no wind, but there was no cloud either to soften the spectacle of the sheer precipice below. They came to an overhead ledge; Corydon pulled himself up, then helped the heavier Minotaur to use his strength to reach it too.

They could see into the mountain's secrets now. Ahead

of them and to the left was the sleeping ice bulk of a glacier, its snows dirty and ugly. And its surface was not smooth: it was serried and crazed by hundreds of crevasses, so that it was scaled like the back of a crocodile. Some of them would be hundreds of feet deep and dozens of feet wide.

But they could not go to the right. Beside the glacier, rock had been pushed out to form an overhang that couldn't even be reached from their precarious ledge. It was impossible to traverse it.

They would have to attempt the glacier.

They set out. The first dozen or so crevasses they walked around, treading carefully on slippery ice. The next half-dozen or so involved nothing worse than a long step across a deep darkness that seemed to call to them.

But then they came to wider crevasses, too wide for a step. The first was bridged by a terrifyingly thin span of snow and ice; Corydon ran lightly across, but the Minotaur's greater bulk made the bridge shift with leathery groans. Cracks appeared. As the bridge collapsed, the Minotaur flung himself onto the other side of the great gulf's gape. His bronze-spiked foot found a secure hold, and he levered himself gasping onto the damp snow.

Still neither spoke.

But now Corydon realised that they were surrounded by a deadly maze of wide crevasses. It was as if the mountain had lured them into its lair in order to cage them in shivering death. The nearest one wore another light snow-bridge, thinner than the previous bridge. It could not be attempted; the risk to the Minotaur was too great.

Instead, Corydon and the Minotaur chose to try to find a way through the maze; they walked on their spiked feet in a wild world of emerald and turquoise ice, seeing dizzying vistas to the mountain's heart opening before their feet, swerving, dodging, weaving. It took over two hours to travel a hundred feet in the direction of the summit, because they had to cross and crisscross their line of direction. The hard sun beat down. And there was still no sound except the dripping of the ice. Corydon began to feel as if he had gone deaf.

At last, legs aching, nerves in shreds, they staggered off the glacier's edge. Corydon could see only too clearly what lay ahead. It was something far more deadly than the ice-maze they had just survived.

It was a couloir, a narrow chute bounded by rocky cliffs on either side. It was tilted at a ferocious angle and furred with snow, deep and powdery beneath, but on the surface sleekly iced, green and glossy and bluish. Here and there rocks protruded from places where the snow had thinned in the brilliant sunlight, then frozen to treacherously light verglas in the night, the thin and fragile coating of ice too delicate for the many deaths it had caused. It was impossible for the small ice-axe each held to get a good hold on verglas; it was so fragile it would simply shatter when a spiked tool was applied to it.

Again, neither said a word. It had become an unspoken superstition. If they did not speak, they might survive.

Perhaps both remembered that if they did not send

word the gorgons might come for them . . . But *could* they? Could they penetrate the cloud? In his heart Corydon knew they were alone here, as alone as they had been in the underworld; no, *more alone,* for there they had faced the hordes of the dead. Here was nothing.

Each looked hopelessly at what lay ahead. At last, they sat down on the ridge at the top of the glacier. The Minotaur reached into his pack and brought out a hunk of bread. Corydon shared his waterskin, which was almost frozen. Both felt their icy clothing like a weight of armour. Still neither spoke.

Then Corydon drew in a deep breath. And as the mountain loured above their heads, shining and terrible, he suddenly felt a bubbling impulse he didn't try to deny. He began to sing. It was a song about the mountain itself, a song that told it of its own splendour, its ferocity, its hardness. Its cold. A song of death in snow, of lonely climbers buried in its deep and icy heart. Of the warm human and animal bodies that had clung to its sides like baby animals holding a mother's fur.

In putting the mountain into words, he captured its strength. And the mountain seemed to know it. He couldn't say it looked docile now, but the dread of its awful silence was broken, dissipated. It was not conquered, perhaps would never be conquered. But it was indefinably less alien. Less, well, monstrous. Suddenly he sang of Sthenno and Euryale, condemned to live for years out of mind. The mountain was like them. Gods rose and fell, men were begotten, born and died. The mountain was almost immortal. And yet it was fighting its own slow battles – against the rotting of rock, the collapse of stones. One day it would be level with the plain. Corydon remembered that Gorgos had once said that stone had its own impossibly slow language, taking centuries to utter a syllable. Was he in danger of mistaking that long slow word for silence?

But the word this mountain was saying sounded like a fierce word. His song helped him, but it did not make for communication. The mountain was a monster, and it devoured, but it did not or could not choose to know itself. Yet.

He stood up. It was time to attempt the couloir.

They progressed with agonising slowness. Each step had to be cut in ice with the axes. After a few laborious hours of jagged ice steps that gave when they put their feet on them, splinters of ice that seemed aimed at their eyes, fierce shards of ice that stuck in clothes and boots, feet that slipped treacherously, things got worse.

The slope grew steeper. Now it was not a slope at all. It was a cliff of ice. Now they had to use small bronze pegs to secure handholds, attach rope to them, and haul themselves up. Inch by inch. Below them the glacier crevasses yawned.

Each bronze peg had to be retrieved after use. They had only twelve – 'one for each Olympian', Euryale had said lightly – and they could not afford to lose even one.

Then, just as Corydon felt his hands and feet would never stop aching or uncramp themselves, they were almost at the top, and he drew a deep breath.

Here, however, things got worse. Again.

The ice had been hard, crisp. That had made driving the pegs into it with only a small hammer an ordeal, especially when dangling by one hand from a previous hold. But now they reached a patch of softer ice that didn't hold the pegs at all. Melting ice from the top of the ridge had softened the ice here, making it into unstable slush. They tried driving pegs into the rock itself, but it was granite, and the pegs simply bent and buckled.

Corydon had no idea what to do.

They couldn't traverse to somewhere better. The couloir was a narrow defile between rocks they couldn't climb, rocks that hung out over the valley.

Then he had an idea. He wasn't sure it would work, and it was very risky, especially with the Minotaur. He tied one of the bronze pegs to the end of a slender skein of rope. Then he flung the peg-end desperately at the ridge-top he could see, frustratingly, only a body's length above him. He gripped the other end tightly. His first throw missed; the peg didn't lodge. His second was also a failure. After repeated tries, however, he felt the bronze peg grip the ice; the rope, once slack, went taut. He tugged it. It seemed secure.

Now he had to trust his weight to it. With a glance at the Minotaur which bade him hold his position, he slowly detached feet and hands. Now he was dangling from the rope. It reminded him of the time Gorgos had rescued him on the cliff-edge. But here there was no irritating Gorgos to help.

Slowly, painfully, his shoulders screaming, he began to

inch his way up the rope. Hand over hand. It held, but it also burnt his palms with icy pain. Inch by inch. One hand. Another. His feet desperate for a hold. Hand. Over. Hand.

The ridge had one final test for him. Its edge was an overhang, and he had to manoeuvre desperately to get his foot up past it. At last, though, his toothed boot caught on snow. He managed in one wriggle to hurl himself onto a narrow ridge. And lay, panting, winded, for a minute, ignoring the deep soft snow making its way onto his skin, ignoring the quest, ignoring everything but his labouring lungs. After much longer than usual, his breathing returned to normal. He peered down. There was the Minotaur, waiting, patient and sagacious. Corydon knew the great monster was not agile enough to do what he himself had just done. Nor was he strong enough to pull the other monster up.

Quickly he attached the bronze pegs to the rope he had used, at intervals. He lowered it down to the Minotaur, having checked that its end was firmly embedded. The Minotaur began to try to climb, but it was obvious to Corydon that it wasn't going to work. He couldn't make any use of his legs; he dangled helplessly, and not even his great arms were strong enough to pull him up.

'This can't work,' he gasped. The silence had been shattered by Corydon's song, and both felt able to speak at need now. Corydon could see his great laboured breaths forming clouds of vapour.

'What—'

Suddenly Corydon tugged at his pack, pulled out

his sheepskin, and began tying together his ropes to form a crude sling. Carefully, he lowered it. The Minotaur eyed it.

'Is it – can you—?' Corydon saw that he was close to being paralysed by the vertiginous drop behind him.

'I can't—'

'Just climb onto it,' Corydon said, trying to sound encouraging. With a desperate heave, the Minotaur flung himself into the sling. The weight tugged hard at Corydon's arms and hands.

Now how was he going to pull up his friend?

The Minotaur would have to help himself. The sling would stop him from falling, but he needed to dig his spiked feet and hands into the ice to lever himself upward. The ice kept collapsing into slush, but he pressed his feet desperately against the rock beneath.

'You have to climb!' he shouted. 'It's not far! I'll pull you as well!'

The Minotaur gritted his teeth; Corydon saw them flash. Then he swung himself closer to the ice, and pressed a furry toe into its blue sheen, a hand. Corydon pulled, and the Minotaur raised himself as the sling pushed at his body. Another careful climbed step. Another.

It had to work. Surely their combined strength would be enough.

It was working. The Minotaur's foot slipped once, and they lost some of the height they'd gained, but then he took another giant step, another. Corydon could see his furry head, his eyes bulging in fear like those of a calf who smells the butcher. Then his arm shot out, made a hold on the top of the ridge, and with a scramble and a cry he rolled himself out of the sling and onto the icy shelf so quickly that Corydon had to clutch at him to stop him sliding on the ice.

They gave each other brief, hard hugs. Neither wanted to give way to the tears welling inside, or even to the relief flooding them. There was still far too much to do. And the sun was shedding red light over the snows. Corydon realised now that the whole mountain was a blood-altar, with himself and all those who aspired to its summit as the sacrifices. And perhaps he was to be among them, for a new peril was declaring itself.

As the chariot of Apollo Helios galloped for home, streaking the slopes with scarlet streamers, it was getting colder. While once Corydon had been able to see his breath in clouds, he now noticed that it froze as soon as it touched his pack or his clothes. His clothes themselves – chiton, cloak – were so stiff and heavy with ice that he felt as if he were wearing a full hoplite panoply. The Minotaur's fur grew stiff with white ice too. His thickly furred chin was hung with a long white beard of ice, so that he looked like a parody of Zeus himself. As Corydon watched, he saw the great monster give a shiver. A few small icicles fell off him. Corydon's ears were searingly painful, his nose a deep ache.

'Must – dig – shelter,' said the Minotaur, reluctant to open his mouth because the cold set his teeth aching.

Corydon began to dig, but it was soon obvious that the ridge was no place for a shelter. The unnatural stillness of Olympos meant there was no wind, but it was still exposed. The ice, too, was impenetrable. It was obvious that they must go on to find shelter before nightfall.

They laboured up the steep ice-cliff with fingers too frozen to test holds. There were many heartstopping slips. Just as Corydon felt his feet had no sensation left, he saw a small outcrop of rock, and in its lee was a patch of snow warmed to blood-red by Apollo's last glance. He shouted, his cracked lips splitting, stinging.

They turned aside. And they blundered into a thick, wet patch of soft snow; it gave way under them, they slid, helpless toboggans, then jerked themselves upright, found holds, began the painful climb again. And at last, as the mountainside turned blue, they reached the rock, and found a wall of soft snow behind it.

Almost exhausted, their monster-strength drained, they dug themselves into it, made a hole big enough for both. Their warmth filled it with the drip of melting snow, and they caught some of the moisture and poured it down dry throats. Then they found harsh stale crumbs of food in their packs and wolfed them down. It was pitch-dark: they could not see their hands, or each other. They hunkered into their sheepskins, which felt as thin as Sthenno's parchments, frail against the onslaught of ferocious cold that drove water into hard splinters of ice. The air too seemed somehow thin; it hurt to breathe. They lay close, needing each other's warmth, and finally fell asleep.

XL
Twenty-two

Corydon dreamed, following a mocking voice down nightmare halls of ringing ice into the heart of a mountain. Zeus Almighty laughed from his immensity as puny monsters tried to scale him, fleas attacking a great shaggy lion. Could they catch him? The mountain was him, and it was huge and strong beyond imagining. How could they persuade him to abandon all that strength and come into the nothingness of an eidolon? And yet Corydon knew they could. The mountain was too big to see the little that assailed it. One day it too would fall – to the small drips of water, the burrowing of plant roots, the gentle grip of frost and ice on its severe rock. Its song was a song of loss, of failure. So would Zeus's be.

But then the dream changed. He seemed to plunge down through layer after layer of ice and snow, searching, searching for something . . . a faint crying . . . As the darkness deepened, the last rays of greenish light illuminated the face of a child, crying as if his heart was breaking – deep sobs, choking, tearing. The child put a hand over his mouth, as if he was frightened of being heard, then gulped out another sob. Before Corydon could put a comforting hand on his arm, the child vanished. But Corydon could hear his cries change to terrified screams somewhere, somewhere in the mountain . . . He himself turned for the surface again.

He woke with his heart full of hope, to find them walled in by the ice created by their own breath, which had formed a solid blue wall before them. Corydon felt panicky at first, but then as he turned to rouse the Minotaur, he put his ice-axe effortlessly through the wall; it was thin, like an ice-leaf, and no snow had fallen to reinforce it. Did snow ever fall here?

The Minotaur rumbled softly, and woke too. Rummaging in his pack, he pulled out a crushed honey cake wrapped in a leaf, and held it out mutely to Corydon. Corydon took it, but broke it carefully in half, and gave half of it to his friend. The simplicity of sharing their meagre food was enough for now to raise his spirits.

'Do you think it ever snows here?' he asked. He recalled the swirling flakes of Hades' lands.

'I think it did once,' said the Minotaur. 'Long ago. But now I think Zeus has come to hate change. Spring, summer, autumn, winter. All change. Even wind. Change violates his will. He wants to keep everything, always. Always the same. So there is no weather.'

'There are night and day,' Corydon pointed out.

The Minotaur considered. 'Apollo Helios is his son,' he said. 'Perhaps he wants his son to be part of what he has made.'

'Or perhaps night and day remind him of the mortals he controls,' said Corydon grimly.

The Minotaur took a mouthful of melting snow as drink. 'It isn't real,' he said. 'This isn't the real Olympos. It's Zeus's idea of a mountain. Because it is all mountains, it is in truth none of them.'

Corydon pondered, as he too made his teeth scream by drinking the slush. Zeus lacked a local habitation and a name, because he wanted to rule the world. If they could reduce him to being merely local . . . 'Was the real Olympos his land once?' he asked, as they began preparing for the climb once more.

'It was once the seat of the king of the Titans,' said the Minotaur. 'Zeus's father. You have met him. Kronos.'

Kronos! Corydon remembered the old man and all his books. 'How did Zeus take his father's place?'

'It is a long story.' Both felt a disinclination to leave the snug snow-cave. 'Kronos and Rhea had many children. But Kronos was given a prophecy that one of his own children would kill him; it was given by the Furies, who love strife. So he ate every single one of his children. And Rhea managed to hide only one, who was kept safe on an island. The boy was made to hide whenever the Titans came in sight. He grew up in shivering fear. Then one day his mother told him what had become of his brothers and sisters. He knew one day Kronos would remember him. To prevent himself from being devoured, he poisoned his father with a deadly herb. His father was in agony, and in his pain he vomited up four of Zeus's siblings: his sister Hera, his brother Poseidon, his brother Hades, and his sister Demeter of the lovely hair; these two alone still loved their father, and had absorbed some of his power over time because they were within his belly for longer.

'So began the war between the Titans and the children of Kronos. The Titans were mighty – remember Vreckan! – and many thousands of men died. Yet Zeus and his brothers learned that Kronos had imprisoned an army of monstrous smiths because they had refused to serve him. Zeus decided to free them and win their allegiance.'

'So he wanted to free monsters?' Corydon was amazed. 'Was he kinder then?'

'Yes. He was once the great leader he now only believes himself to be,' said the Minotaur. 'They descended to the deepest pits of Tartaros, where the Kyklopes and the hundred-handed giants lay groaning amid a realm of licking fire. Zeus and his brothers freed them. The monsters had great cunning, and they offered to make him and his brothers invincible weapons: a helmet for Hades, a trident for Poseidon, and for Zeus the lightning itself, the power of storm.

'You remember Hades' helmet. That is the means by which Medusa died.' For a moment his soft voice caught on an old grief. 'Poseidon's trident gave him dominion over the seas. And Zeus was given rule over all the air, and all that lives in the air. All. It was too much for him. It gave him power to escape his own fear. And when he had power to save or damn, he used it to dispose of enemies and allies alike. The many-handed monster-smiths were freshly penned in a volcano, forced to labour night and day to make weapons for the Olympians. They had to make crowns and jewels and regalia and thrones, so that Zeus might seem rich in his own eyes. Now he will only feel safe – from his father – if he is the only power remaining on earth. None will be allowed to stand against him. Not monsters, and not men.'

Hidden in a snow-cave, Corydon could understand Zeus's longing for security. He felt certain it was the child Zeus whose crying he had heard, deep in the heart of the mountain. Had Zeus imagined a gentle, peaceable realm once, but found himself ambushed by his own fears?

'So he *did* once truly rule on Olympos? What was it like then?'

'It was his country. As each Lar has a family. As each dryad has a tree. It was a real mountain. With rocks, and weather, and animals born and dying. It was not as clean, nor as deadly. Once he loved it, too. As dryads their tree. But he tried to make it too safe, and to do that he had to kill everything about it that mattered to him.'

Just like his brother Hades, thought Corydon in surprise. *Hades wanted the Lady back. What does Zeus want?* As he thought this, he thought of Zeus as a tiny baby, in the night, a child crying for the light, but with no language but a cry. 'But now he has no country.'

'Yes. And no one can be happy without a country.'

Suddenly Corydon saw it. 'Perhaps . . . if he becomes a Lar . . . We must somehow use the statue to give him back his country!' he exclaimed.

Then he had another idea. 'What became of his mother?' he asked.

'She lives with *her* mother now. With Gaia.'

'And where is Gaia?'

'Everywhere. She is the earth entire.'

Corydon was used to unhelpful answers, but this topped his worst guesses.

The Minotaur was strapping on his pack, examining the ropes for flaws. 'She might be a lion,' he said. 'Rhea always loved lions.'

And a memory flooded Corydon, the memory of a mother lion stretched out dead, with her dead cubs at her side. A mother.

No, it wasn't possible. That had just been a mother lion. A loving mother lion who had been a mother to everyone she met, but a lioness, that was all.

But just suppose—

Just suppose Zeus's son had killed the one thing he had been looking for through eternities. Would he even know?

Suppose he could be told? Might it break him?

Strapping on his own pack, Corydon promised himself to hold it all in his mind, let it mature like a cheese hung up to strengthen as its whey drained off.

He and the Minotaur crawled out of the cave. It was already plain morning. The rockface loomed above them, a vertical wall of grey rock, the snow and ice seeming to vanish from it. And Corydon saw why. This stretch of rock was vertical with a slight overhang at the top. The rock was solid and smooth, the worst possible rock to climb up. But they would have to do it.

At least it didn't look crumbly.

Out on the mountain again, Corydon and the Minotaur

were once more reduced to silence by the enormous landscape. Looking down, they found they could see all the way to the verdant grass far below, its gloss paled by distance. The grass stretched to the horizon, its enamel interrupted only by what looked like clouds but were actually flowers. Only two kinds. Yellow and purple. Not a cloud broke the blue monotony, not a tree interrupted the green grass, not a hill, not a tussock.

It chilled Corydon's heart. It was like a bad painting of a much-loved face. Impatiently, he almost called out, 'Father!' his heart aching for the shaggy roughness of Pan's lands, his own thick fur and beard. The Minotaur understood, and put a warm arm briefly around him. Corydon saw for the first time that the great beast did resemble his father in his wild, rough, loving friendliness.

'We shall go,' he said, his soft rumble the warmest thing in that hard and hating land.

Their bronze spikes were useless once more; the hard rock defeated them, bent them back and refused their entry. Corydon saw that the only way was to climb using natural fissures and cracks in the rock.

There were plenty once you were close enough. There almost always were. Clinging to the wall like a lichen, fingers spread, Corydon found he could manage well if he used his Pan-foot as a kind of anchor while he searched for other holds. He led the way, telling the Minotaur to follow exactly where he led, climbing as slowly as he safely could to give his friend time to assess. Sometimes, though, a hold was too small for more than a second's rest of finger or hoof, and then he had to move on quickly.

'Do just as I do!' he ordered. 'Same speed. Everything.'

The Minotaur was not tiring; his strength had always been immense. But the test of nerve and skill was telling on him. When they were about two-thirds of the way up the sheer wall, his foot slipped, and only Corydon's lightning reflexes saved him from falling. A few hundred yards later, and it happened again; this time he fell the length of his body before he could be retrieved, and Corydon had to climb back to where he clung grimly to the wall in order to lead him upward again.

Then they came to a stretch where there were very few hand- or footholds at all. The rock was as smooth as glass. Only tiny cracks appeared. Corydon and the Minotaur were forced to climb fast, as every minute handhold gave purchase only for a second or two. Many were rimed with ice and they made tortured fingers ache and throb. As well, they were slippery. Then they came to an easier patch, with a big ledge on which they could rest. They looked down the long cliff and drew in their breath and stretched cramped fingers and toes. Corydon's Pan-foot was aching. It was as if this land were inimical to it.

The Minotaur spoke in a whisper, as if he had little breath to spare.

'I hinder you,' he said, sombrely. 'You would be safer alone.'

'I would despair alone,' Corydon whispered back.

'I think I should leave you,' the Minotaur whispered.

'NO!' Corydon had not meant to shout. But he had suddenly felt as helpless and abandoned as the baby in his dreams.

There was a sudden sound. Afterwards, Corydon thought that it had been like a crack, as when a stick breaks when you stand on it, but very much louder. As loud as a drum-roll. It was followed by a whooshing noise. And above them they saw it coming. The ice-white end of everything. A thick roll of snow, roaring like a beast. Was it miles wide?

They watched it advance. It was no use running. No use hiding. The only hope was to hold fast to the mountain's face; perhaps it might slide over and past them. Perhaps. They could feel the aching ice-cold wind it blew already. They could feel the mountain at their faces. They braced themselves.

Luckily they were clinging to a near-vertical slope when the stinging power of the avalanche struck them. Most of it soared above their heads, billowing around them, blinding and choking them. But the edge protected them from its full might. It had broken above them, and what they felt was merely its eddies and surges.

These were bad enough. Corydon's face and eyes were thickly coated in snow. Snow was in his hair, his eyelashes. The Minotaur's fur was so thick with snow that he looked like a snow-demon. Both were heavy with the pouring waves of snow. But it did not dislodge them. They had managed to hang on. And now the snow made their upward progress worse. Coating the incline with unstable powder, it made handholds almost impossible to find. When they did put tentative fingers out, their fingers slid on the soft snow. The handholds were thickly furred with it too.

But they kept on, their bodies cold and aching. What else was there? Corydon felt as if he had been climbing this face for days. For years. Each hand- and foothold took minutes. And already the sun was westering, diving behind the mountain. The shadows blued. And the snow began to ice in the shadows. Corydon kept going. They must reach shelter before full dark. Shelter. There was no shelter up here. Nothing but the mountain's own bareness. It did not want them. Its absoluteness defeated their blundering monster-bodies. It was icily perfect. They could never climb it. Never.

Left foot. Right hand. And then they were at the top, and Corydon could see the bleak bald summit just above them, flat as an unfriendly face.

He would have given anything for a hot meal. Lamb stew. Warm bread. Sthenno's arms around him. Medusa's fierce hugs: the oddity of being cut off was that she seemed just as near as the others. But there was the Minotaur. Shyly, Corydon put out a hand, and the Minotaur extended his. They stood like that, only for a moment, then they turned to the task of building a snow-hut that would shelter them for the night.

They nibbled a harsh crumb of dry bread as they climbed into it. Corydon thought of Gorgos's birth: the snow-hut felt like a mother's belly, as if he and the Minotaur would have to be born anew in the morning. He thought of Gorgos's rebirth, and wondered if Troy still stood, or if now was the time to lead its people to safety. Suddenly he felt panic-stricken – how long had they been here?

They had to reach Zeus before the city fell, before the survivors set out. This was their only chance to thwart Zeus's plans. Corydon wanted to spring out of the cave and run for the summit now. But he knew this would be madness. Restlessly, he tossed and turned, his growling belly reminding him of how good it would be to be back in Troy. The Minotaur didn't sleep easily either. He lay still, but his great dark eyes were open.

Was there still a Troy to go back to? Corydon's dreams were a river of burning and running, the screams of women and the shouts of warriors. The whirlwind-djinn entered Troy, summoned by the walls, and somehow turned their fury on the burning town. The orange fires had no power to warm him. They only made him shiver more. Then he saw the firelight shining on Neoptolemos's scaled tail, and knew his intent face was that of a hunter; he sought the Snake-girl and her belly laden with his child. He sought her pain, intent as a prowling cat. His serpent tongue lashed out curiously.

Beside him, the Minotaur too woke, and slept, and woke again. Once they woke together.

'Did you see—'

'Yes. Gorgos. Leading the Trojans. And the remnants of our people too.'

'Do we see truly?'

'How can we tell? It may be that these dreams are from the coldness all around us.' They lay down again.

Outside the snow-hut, something about the light had changed. Instead of the hard and merciless dawns to which they had become accustomed, the light never grew in strength. Instead, what lay around them was . . .

'Snowlight!' cried Corydon, and burrowed out to see the mountainside thickly veiled in heavy curtains of snow. Snowflakes danced as if possessed all around them. Blinding, dazzling, they swirled and jumbled, they confused and bewildered. Corydon looked up to where he knew the summit was, just a few hundred yards away. But he could no longer see it. The snow had cast a cloak about it so that it was hidden.

'How can this be?' he shouted, into the wind. His mouth filled with snow and his teeth began to ache.

'It can be,' said a cold voice, 'because I choose that it *shall* be.'

Corydon turned. Behind him stood a white figure. Tall, impossibly tall, taller than the Minotaur, she stood on the edge of the precipice. She was cloaked in thick white fur, but as she raised her arms and shook her cloak hem, thousands more whirling snowflakes poured from her. Her hood fell back, revealing a white face. On her head was a diadem of ice. Her hair streamed down, silver and white.

'Do you know me?'

Corydon took a step towards her. 'Are – are you winter?' he asked tentatively.

'I am more,' she said, 'but I am winter, too. I am the cold that eats the heart. I am the hunger that kills love. I am the number that destroys all difference. I am the answer that ends all questions. And you are Corydon Panfoot. You are a shepherd, so I have long been your foe. I suck the breath from the newborn lamb before it can reach the teat.'

'You are a monster, then,' said Corydon. Behind him, the Minotaur nodded. 'And if you are a monster you are of my kind.'

The white-clad lady laughed. 'Nay,' she said. 'I am not of your kind. My world is pure. No creature can live in it. Only mind. Numbers. Ideas. Logic. No bodies. Nobody. I am alone. I am always alone.'

Now she sounded a little sad, but it was a fierce kind of sadness. Corydon was unexpectedly reminded of Medusa.

'Do you ever make up songs?' he asked.

'Songs! Of what use are songs?' she asked him, snowflakes flying from her robes. As she lifted her cloak again, Corydon noticed how very thin she was, almost ill-looking, her bones showing hard through her fine white skin. 'What good is it to sing? Do you know the beauty of prime numbers? Do you know of the elegance of geometry? Each of my snowflakes is a perfect equation. Each is an integer in a long and secret simultaneous equation.'

Corydon spoke politely. 'I'm afraid I don't know what that is.'

'I know you do not,' she said. 'But he does.' She pointed with a long white finger at the Minotaur. 'He knows. And he will belong to me. His mind will be cold as my snows. Cold as ice. And we will talk of Planck's constant, and of Gödel, and of numbers so long that they can be wrapped around all the mountains and yet never speak to other numbers. In such talk we will make something more beautiful than any song.'

The Minotaur took two steps forward, and for a moment Corydon trembled. But when he spoke it was his deep, steady voice, furred, rough, and warm with life.

'I must get back to my bees,' he said.

'My snowflakes are like bees,' she said.

'But they make no honey,' he said, shaking his heavy head. 'To be like is not to be the same.'

'Honey is for babies,' she said, and it was as if she had been stung.

'Honey is for all who live,' said the Minotaur. 'We may love numbers. I do love them. I love to know them. I love to make things from the knowing. But bees know numbers too, and they are better friends than you would be. They sting. You would devour.'

Her face grew even whiter. 'You refuse me?' she whispered.

'I want only to reach the summit and see Zeus, lady.'

Corydon watched her raise her hood. Something about the gesture awoke his memory. She raised her eyes fully for the first time, and he caught the steely-flash of grey. And he knew her.

'I know you. You are Athene,' he said. His voice was flat.

She smiled, a slow smile, her thin lips stretched over sharp teeth. 'I am one way of seeing her,' she agreed. 'And you are yourselves but integers in a long equation, which great Zeus will solve. Now,' and her smile became more mocking, 'now, try to reach him. Go on. Try.' With a whirl of her cloak, she was somehow caught up in the thick snow she had made. And then she was gone.

If it had not been for the urgent visions of the night, Corydon would have crawled back into the snow-hole. The temperature was clearly dropping, and the summit invisible; moreover, he could feel the needle-like gaze of Athene of the snows between his shoulder blades, and felt sure their progress to the summit was unlikely to be simple. The Minotaur, shoulders bowed, looked tired. But Corydon skidded over to him and seized his hand, trying to tell him how glad he was that the allure of numbers had not overwhelmed his loyalty to the monsters.

'The Waters of Lethe. The hazary,' said the great beast softly. 'So many ways to release ourselves from the torment of knowing who we are.'

'Aren't numbers a kind of truth?'

'Of the head. The heart also has its truths. And my heart tells me we must reach Zeus today. Now.'

They set off without further talk.

ΨL

TWENTY-THREE

The snow around them seemed to form a moving wall, constantly blocking their progress and stopping them from moving towards the summit at more than a wounded man's pace. Corydon felt as if he were dragging his own dead body. His legs ached, and his hands were pulses of cold pain. It was as if his monster-strength was gone, just as it had been in Atlantis when he had worn the false body of a human boy. Now his own body felt equally alien.

'It's the mountain,' said the Minotaur grimly, reading his thoughts. 'And now the snow. Unnatural. We are as far from ourselves as a hawk from the moon. And we may never find ourselves again.'

They were lost, as in Atlantis. It was ironic. Away from all they loved, they must entice Zeus into incarnation. With no place, they must find a place for him. But Corydon thought that in an odd way their plight was helpful. He himself felt an odd mixture of helpless rage and childish longing. Perhaps Zeus felt the same all the time.

They were on the last ascent. Suddenly Corydon wondered why he had thought Zeus would be up here. It seemed unlikely that he would crouch on a snow-slope in a freezing snowstorm. He had never seen Zeus, but he remembered Poseidon's terrible wave-forms, his awe, his power. What must Zeus be like? But still he kept going.

And now they had reached it. The summit of Olympos.

But there was nothing here but rock, and snow. And nothingness. Not even a lichen grew.

His heart plummeted. He closed his eyes. They had done their utmost, and it was nothing.

The Minotaur drew in a heavy panting breath behind him. Corydon's eyes opened again. Automatically, he flinched from opening them into the cold.

But there was no cold. A pale light was gathering around them. Pale gold, sleek, expensive light. And the cold was being displaced by warmth. The stillness was present, dead air, but now it was heavily and expensively scented. He looked down. They no longer stood on snow, but on a level floor, pale gold stone, stretching around for hundreds of yards. Corydon found he could move. Taking the Minotaur's hand, he shuffled forward, his feet still wet and almost frozen. He could smell a strong smell of – was it honey?

'No,' said the Minotaur. 'Not honey. Ambrosia.'

It smelt even more dead than the mountainside. Plainly nature had had nothing to do with it. It smelt false, like –

was it sweets on a festival day? No, an older, staler, stronger smell.

He felt suddenly sick. He was hungry, but he would rather die than eat that stuff.

'Quite right,' said the Minotaur, reading his thoughts from his disgusted face. 'It would make you immortal, though.'

'It would make me immortally dead,' said Corydon fiercely. 'I don't want to stay alive forever. In nature nothing stays alive forever, not even the stones.'

'Not true,' said a voice from behind him. 'I stay alive forever. I eat this every day. And that is why I shall always win. Because I can never change or be destroyed.'

They turned. There stood what seemed to be a tall man, impressively robed in grey and purple and white, elegant robes with just a hint here and there of gilding. His long hair was neat, shaded with silver; his beard was immaculate, his face not unlike those of Hades and Poseidon. Corydon could tell that this was Zeus. He reeked of old power, even though he was not displaying it.

'Yes,' he said, bowing. 'Yes, you speak truly. But you also know how weary it is to live forever as an Olympian.'

To his surprise, something did flicker at once in Zeus's eyes.

'It is true that mine is a burdened life,' he said smoothly, 'for I must plan and execute the destinies of all who live on earth. Just now I am preparing to blot out a city that troubles me with its cleverness, its energy. I envy its vitality. I am menaced by its intelligence, for intelligent men will one day put us all at risk. So I shall burn it with everlasting flame.'

Everlasting flame?

'The fire of men's ambitions, the fire of their greed. I channel all that is worst in them. That is why you are an annoyance. You are not all man, and so I cannot control you. But you have interfered in what was fated to happen. The chthonic powers should have vanished from the earth by now. They have been superseded. They were just a phase in the evolution of religion. What should come next is monotheism. The worship of one god. Myself. And yet somehow you, with your little rebellions, have managed to sustain the old gods. And now they have a new champion in your friend Gorgos, who may sustain them for many thousand years.'

He sounded both rambling and petulant, old man and toddler.

'Maybe you need to try something to bring it about,' said Corydon fearlessly. 'Your own worship above that of all others.' This might be his chance. The Minotaur was already unrolling his pack. He produced the cloth bundle containing Euryale's statue. Corydon knew he would need all his cunning kleptis wits to convince Zeus.

Just as he thought this, there was a thud behind him. He looked around. Aphrodite had abruptly materialised on the stone floor.

'You silly boy,' she said. 'Obviously I'm not the mountain-climbing kind. But I could have persuaded a daimon to bring you here if you had asked me. It's sooo – well, chthonic of you to have climbed all this way.'

Zeus looked surprised. 'What is going on here?' he asked.

'I'm here to talk to you,' said Aphrodite, dimpling seductively, and swaying her hips. Corydon's heart sank. Would Zeus really like this approach? He felt a premonition of disaster.

Zeus looked at her. Aphrodite swayed her hips again. 'Hello, aunt,' he said very dryly. Corydon's lips twitched, and the Minotaur gave a surprised chuckle. 'Now, stop it. Go and do some shopping.' He waved his hand.

'But I have to talk to you,' she pouted. 'You know,' she went on, 'it's always been so disappointing that you don't really have – you know – a body. A *real* one.'

Zeus motioned to the walls, which instantly filled with paintings and tapestries showing him mating with a very wide range of nymphs. He was a boar, a bull, a golden rain. In the most ominous picture, he was a gigantic black thunderhead placing a paw of cloud on a nymph's back.

He smiled wearily. 'No god enjoys more of your realm than I,' he said. He didn't sound exultant, merely tired. Corydon could see why. The pictures kept multiplying. Now there appeared to be thousands of them. Zeus was different in each one.

Aphrodite put a sinuous hand on Zeus's arm. 'I *know,*' she said, intensely, looking up at him. Zeus shrank back slightly. 'I *know.* But I want you to have so much more. All these disguises. What would pleasure be like if you were just yourself?'

Zeus smiled. 'Aphrodite,' he said. 'If you know as much as you pretend, you would know that in these moments no one is simply themselves. Everyone is a fantasy self. Someone they long to be, not someone they are. Now stop bothering me. I need to deal with an evolving problem.'

Aphrodite beamed. 'It's so sweet and funny when you talk like that. An evolving problem.'

Zeus frowned. 'Go away, dear,' he said, absently patting her arm.

Aphrodite ignored him and threw her arms around him. 'You are my best-ever nephew,' she said. *Nephew?* thought Corydon in astonishment; this grey-haired patriarch couldn't be a diddy nephew – except he could, of course. How confusing immortality was. 'And I want to give you a special present. A special one. It's a really good present.'

'Thank you, no,' said Zeus firmly. 'Aphrodite, I don't want the present you have in mind. Millions of men would long for it, but I'm not a man. Please, go and bother them.'

'But you *could* be a man, Zeus darling. A man just for one day. To feel the longing and the sweat and the ferocity you haven't felt for years. Centuries.'

Zeus smiled. 'It sounds charming,' he said. 'But today I have other plans. I have a city to destroy. And I must also make sure that the draggletailed remnant of its people do not escape.' His smile was quite empty.

'Why not celebrate?' Now Aphrodite was entwined around him.

'Because I haven't done it yet. The city has begun to burn. The heroes are rampaging through the streets. But there is still one obscure group of Trojans who keep avoiding them. And I have to make sure they are' – he gritted his teeth – 'annihilated. No shred left.'

'But darling Zeus,' said Aphrodite, her light voice laden with honey, 'dearest Zeus, that will not make you happy.'

Zeus shrugged. 'I have not been happy for millennia. What is happiness? A bubble, a dream that the humans chase. I will not be happy. But I will be free. I will destroy the last of the monsters, the last of those who sought to destroy me.' For just a second, one of the pictures of Zeus embracing a nymph morphed into the portrait of a screaming baby staring up at a multiple-headed Titan with jaws agape. 'I will not be happy, but I shall be safe. Then the stage will be set for my final battle. The last battle. My battle with my father.'

As he said this, his voice suddenly shifted from a triumphant trumpet-tone to a cracked flat note of fear, and Corydon could see that there was real dread in his eyes. He too felt terrified, for he had seen a battle between the gods that destroyed a city. This battle might end the world. But he couldn't see that Kronos was frightening.

Aphrodite put her hand on Zeus's arm again. 'And of course you shall,' she cooed. 'Of course you shall. But before that, let me give you a night of pure oblivion, freighted with the easy pleasures only bodies can know. Pleasures that fall into the hands, like ripe fruit. Pleasures you need not pursue.'

Now both monsters could see that Zeus was interested and attracted. Aphrodite went on. 'You are the king of pleasures, lord,' she said, her voice like a dove's soft cooing, the sound of a blissful summer. 'But you rule pleasure. You do not seek it or have it. Give yourself to me. Put yourself in my hands.'

Zeus murmured something. Then he said it louder. 'Perhaps. Perhaps this would be a way. To make war on my father. Books. Always books. He reads too many books. He cared only for books. The dry whisper of paper. And if we interrupted him he pushed us away. A dry, bookish old stick. Perhaps a red-blooded body—'

'Of course, lord,' Aphrodite's voice thrummed. Corydon looked at her, and noticed she had somehow begun to shine golden, as if a golden cloud were forming around her. After days of blue-white ice, it was almost shocking. The king of the gods had apparently forgotten Corydon and the Minotaur in his bewitchment. Instead, he stared at Aphrodite. The golden cloud began to envelop him, too.

'Quick!' hissed Corydon. 'The eidolon!' With fingers that still fumbled after days of cold, the Minotaur undid his pack, and unrolled the statue that Euryale had made. It looked small and crude, but the Minotaur rolled it dexterously forward, so that it tumbled over and over to Zeus's feet.

'See, lord, what I have for you!' Aphrodite cried. 'It does not look much. But it was made by a great witch of Thessaly, one of the greatest, many years ago. She foresaw this moment.' Corydon tried to hide his grin. Aphrodite was a good liar. And a storyteller, he suddenly saw, just as he was. In the exultance of her lie, he also saw a kinship to Medusa. He only hoped Zeus hadn't seen Euryale at work on the piece.

The king of the gods was frowning at the eidolon, puzzled. 'It looks somehow familiar,' he said. 'Have I seen it in dreams?'

'Doubtless, mighty one,' said Aphrodite. 'Dreams of your own happiness. And it has a magic you may not have recognised.'

Zeus frowned. 'Show me,' he said.

Aphrodite intensified her smile. It made Corydon feel a little sick.

'Mighty and refulgent lord,' she said, stumbling a little over the word refulgent, 'this tiny statue could not be a worthy body for you. Behold! It is in truth the size of a human body.' She waved her arms at the statue. It did not change. Corydon quickly muttered the spell as quietly as he could, hoping his voice would carry to the statue, but not draw him to Zeus's attention.

Luckily it worked. The statue quickly bloated to a full-sized man, a muscular kouros with a deep chest, strong arms, and softly tousled curls. The long bronze eyelashes lay on the cheeks. The beard was combed as accurately as a battle line of men. The statue wore an elegant white chiton.

Zeus seemed hypnotised. 'Well,' he said, 'if a god must take flesh, this flesh looks perfect.'

'And you must indeed take flesh,' said Aphrodite, her voice now cooing again, 'if you wish to be happy. Happy, Zeus. Happy. You have forgotten the word. Your power has not made you happy. And yet no one deserves happiness more than you, great one. Why not lay down your burdens, just for a half-day?'

'And I would be human . . . just for an hour . . . or a day . . . And when I have a human body, men will worship me. Me only. Because I have chosen to be incarnate, to share their lives . . . the age of the One True God will dawn . . .'

Corydon held his breath. He felt that if he made the very slightest sound, Zeus might change his mind.

But Zeus's eyes were bright with eagerness. He stepped towards the eidolon.

'What do I do?' His voice was that of a little boy, half-scared, half-hopeful.

'You take my hand,' said Aphrodite, her voice like honey. 'And then you jump. Like a child jumping into a puddle. Jump into the statue.'

'Just jump?'

'Just jump.'

Zeus took Aphrodite's hand. He seemed to have forgotten Corydon and the Minotaur completely, preoccupied with his own troubles, his life, his need to escape.

Corydon saw his knees bend. And he jumped.

Slowly but surely, he began to sink into the statue. Little streamers of golden light ran up those parts of his body nearest the statue; at the same time, the statue itself was changing, from a greener gold to a dark gold.

It was working.

But as Corydon watched, there was a hard black screech. A figure burst out from somewhere behind them. 'Zeus! No!' she shrilled.

But it was too late. The statue and Zeus were melding more and more. Zeus was melting into the statue, the statue bleeding into Zeus. They were one flesh. There were a few blurred moments, and then Corydon saw a single bronze figure, upright and stalwart.

He looked at the eyes, and saw the surprise in them.

'Zeus!' The black-clad goddess pushed Aphrodite out of the way. 'Zeus! You are trapped! You are in an eidolon! Can you hear me?'

It was plain that Zeus could hear her, from the way the eyes flickered. But it was also plain that he could do little about it.

'Break him out!' she moaned. 'Help him. Help.' Now her cries died away. She sat down hard on the hard floor. Hard, hard. Her eyes were hard. And Corydon knew her, even though her face grew old before his eyes: Hera, with the golden hair. She smiled a mad smile, and she began to sing:

'Zeus, mine own Zeus,
  Lying so lowly,
Thou in thy nothingness,
Shelterless, comfortless,
See'st thou the thing I am?
Know'st thou my bitter stress?'

For a second or two, Corydon thought her voice was following another that he could almost hear, the heavy voice of another woman calling her grief to the sky. His eyes were briefly shrouded by a vision of heavy curtains of flame and smoke. The gods, he thought, can only mock humans. They can never be human. Hera was trying to take Zeus's hand in her own, but the gesture was made clumsy by the inflexibility of bronze; like so many of the gods' movements, it spoke of toddlerish anger, not adult persistence.

Hera flung back her black hood. Her eyes sought the one to blame, as a snake seeks the warmth of the mouse. Tears spilled down her now-withered cheeks.

Then she saw Corydon and the Minotaur. Aphrodite had vanished. Her eyes caught on the Minotaur's opened pack. The snake seemed to coil, ready for a quick pounce.

She turned her head stiffly, like a hunting animal.

'So,' she said. 'You have made of him a creature like yourselves.'

'We have given him a body. His statue will be set up at Olympos. The world will come to him. Isn't that what he wants?'

Hera laughed, a sound like wind in the last leaves of autumn. 'Perhaps it was, stinking little shepherd boy. Perhaps it was. But it was not what *I* wanted. No. I wanted to rule the world. I wanted him to rule it. For me. For our children. Forever.'

'What children?' Corydon spoke with a sense that his life would soon be over. 'Ares? Or Hephaistos, whom you neglect and kick and despise?'

Hera smiled. 'My children do disappoint me,' she said, looking at him more intently. 'Even you, Panfoot.'

'What do you mean?'

'I mean *you*, Panfoot. You. You are my son as well as

your father's. You have nothing mortal in you, except for his love of things mortal. I seduced him. I knew he could father a child who would overthrow his father, and rule the earth as Zeus did the heavens. He thought I was a pretty nymph. I was myself, all queen. In the end, he knew. Oh yes, he knew. He has always known.

'Those funny little dreams of mummy making bread! They used to make me laugh. The woman you lived with as a baby lived in my shadow. She put you out like a stray cat when I told her to. You've never had one second of real love from any mother. Not me. Not your foster mother. No one. You may think you've won. But you can only ever be a loser. All my sons are losers.'

The content of her statement took a while to reach Corydon. He heard her words, and they lodged in his mind. And suddenly they seemed to explode in a terrible burst of flame, like one of Lady Nagaina's weapons, burning his world, burning his idea of who he was. But there was one small forlorn post of hope that he clung to. One cool refuge.

'Not true,' he said, through stiff lips of pain. 'There was always Medusa. She was my true mother. Because only she loved me as a mother.'

As Hera opened her mouth to reply, there was a rushing boom as a wall of cloud burst the windows of the gods' palace. A gale crashed in, and Corydon and the Minotaur were caught in its giant fist. As Corydon fought it, he saw Hera snatch up the eidolon of Zeus. But for him it was too late to hold on to anything. They were both swept out into the onrushing wall of cloud. Like a child dropping a toy it no longer wants, the wind let go of them. They were falling from the summit of Olympos.

In fact, there was no mountain anymore. Zeus's over-controlled dream land had vanished. And the raging storm clouds, released from his control, were bringing it back to wildness as they screamed for their master's loss.

At first there was no sensation of falling, only of plummeting through the air. But as they fell, Corydon could feel himself caught in a terrible wave of ice that made his skin feel as if it was about to fall from his body. His mouth was full of warm iron, and he realised he was bleeding – from the nose, the mouth, even the eyes. Then they hit the cloud itself. It was like a night when all the stars had been quenched. They could see, hear, feel nothing.

Corydon felt something that must have been some ice hit him on the arm. Then a powerful gust took him, and he found himself spinning higher and higher. When it released him, he began the tumbling fall again. Several more ice stones hit him. Then another gust, sending him up once more. He could no longer tell where the Minotaur was, and a panicky fear seized him. He was alone. Alone.

ωμεγα

TWENTY-FOUR

Corydon was spun around by eddies of wind; bruising ice struck him again and again in the face. He had no thoughts. He lived, survived, from second to second. But his heart ached for his aloneness even more than his body ached from the ice.

A finger of warmth touched him. And did he truly hear a voice? 'My son, do not fear my wildness. This is intense, but it is as clouds should be. Storms are what we know. We are shepherds.'

Corydon felt the warmth steal around his heart. Yes. Yes, he had seen storms. And now he understood. These storms had been released from Zeus's hand, when he went into the eidolon. They were running wild because they were like animals who had lost the touch of a master. And that was something he understood.

But terror was still all around. It was the storm clouds' own fears he was picking up. He knew frightened animals can communicate fear to a boy, and it was partly that, but there was also plenty to dread.

Corydon suddenly found he could see again, but what he saw was horrific. He had entered a tunnel in the cloud, one that pointed straight down, spinning furiously. Corydon couldn't run, or flee. He could only toboggan helplessly. The lumps of ice which had bombarded him when he couldn't see now struck him repeatedly as they tried to push past him in their desperate rush to reach the ground.

The darkness closed around him again. Now it was absolute.

Then a blue blade of light split the sky. The sound that it made hit Corydon like an immense wave, and sent him tumbling. Which way was down? Which way was up? He knew only the terrible, sickening motion. He guessed this was how thunder felt within a cloud.

Blue waves of light broke the cloud open again. More waves of air rolled him. The motion was like a very rough sea; he was amazed to find himself being violently sick. As he straightened, more huge hailstones struck him. He prepared for more hailstones, only to feel himself struck by a wall of water that drenched him in a second. The water pounded him almost as ferociously as the hail had. His whole body ached and shivered, and was tossed lightly as a leaf before an autumn gale.

Then there was sudden light.

He had fallen through the bottom of the cloud.

What he saw was angry blue-grey water, storm-tossed as himself. It stretched out foamy fingers to grasp him. Corydon could do nothing to save himself. He plunged on, downward, and hit the sea surface. It felt like slamming into a rock wall. The water was cold with storm-surge. And he had no energy to fight this last battle. He let the waves take him. He could do nothing else.

As he sank slowly into the water, he remembered what the sphinx had said about the cost of saving a world. 'What it always is,' she had said.

Medusa had died in saving the underworld. Now his heart accepted that to save what was left of Troy and the monsters he must pay a price, and the price was everything. He knew he could fight harder, but his legs and arms refused the knowledge. They could not struggle to lift him up to breathe. It was terrifying to find himself short of air and unable to reach for more, but he also watched the terror from somewhere far, far away, somewhere that saw a shepherd boy dying far from home, far from land, far from friends.

Dying. He was dying. His mind held the word as his body sagged.

He wished he could see his friends once more. Just once more. But it didn't make him fight the sea.

Dying. This, then, was the end of all things.

With a jolt of pain, he thought of his mother, who would not miss him; he wished he could die in the arms of a mother who had loved him truly. He wished he could die on land. In battle with his friends. In his own city. In his father's arms.

This lonely struggle was like his life.

Like his life had always been. Alone.

As his burning lungs became a red agony, his drifting mind shaped a last fragment of song: 'Sea-lord, you are at long last the victor, But I no longer care to win.' And he didn't care. His mind fled his body, down a long dark corridor, a piece of labyrinth that was at last leading to an exit, an exit made of brilliant light and warmth. As he saw it, he smiled as his body convulsed in a last agony. And then it was over and his mind was free.

The Snake-girl's body opened after long red struggling. There was a cry from Euryale.

'It's a girl,' she said. The infant slithered out, fierce and bloodstained, roaring with fury at being forced from her warm nest. Euryale flopped her onto the Snake-girl's scaly belly. The Snake-girl put out an incredulous hand. The baby's roars stilled.

'She's lovely,' said the Snake-girl. The baby was black and thickly furred all over, with a small squashed face like a monkey. She didn't look like Neoptolemos, or like the Snake-girl either. She looked like a dog-monster of the line of Kerberos.

'She's mine, anyway,' said the Snake-girl, and began nursing her. 'All mine.' Her eyes were fierce.

The other monsters stood around her bed, protecting her. The ship rocked slowly. It was packed to the gunwales with refugeeing Trojans, boys and girls, men and women. All that Gorgos had salvaged. In another corner of the hold, a family prayed to the tiny Lar they had brought with them. A girl wove a seaweed garland to the Nereids. The people of Troy had brought their little gods with them into exile. The air was heavy with the escaping daimons, blue as violet petals.

'So to a new land,' said Gorgos. 'We will build a city greater than Troy there. As great as Atlantis. And we will build it with ideas. With the ideas of the little gods. We will find other peoples there, and we will not take their land from them but invite them truly to share it. Their little gods will join ours. And in our city there will be no kings. No Olympians. There will be government of the people. By the people. For the people. And it shall never perish from the earth as long as we remember Troy. In this way, all that we loved in Troy will live and cannot be burned.'

Sthenno smiled; she had been listening attentively. 'Yes, my Gorgoliskos,' she murmured. 'This shall be. The city shall be called Roma. And it shall be eternal. Men and monsters will err, and the city will not always be as you hope. They will give you the wrong name, calling you Aeneas, making you a prince of Troy. They will rename all of us. But your city will live. *Roma eterna*. Its flame will light the world forever.'

Gorgos turned to Sthenno. 'That is the language of the Graeae,' he said. '*Roma eterna*. Should it be our language?'

Sthenno pondered. 'It seems fitting,' she said. 'For the Graeae were the memory trace of Troy. In their language may Troy be remembered best. But I still mourn the city's fall. As the Graeae would say, *sunt lacrimae rerum*.'

'What does that mean?' asked the Snake-girl. Her baby had dropped a sleepy head on her arm.

Sthenno sighed. 'I suppose it could mean something like this: there are tears of things. Or there are matters about which all we can do is cry.'

All of them were silent, remembering the last hours in Troy: the burning city, the screams, the ferocity of Neoptolemos as he led the last assault.

It had happened so quickly. They had refused the stupid wooden horse, standing dumb in the plain. It was obviously a trap. But the Greeks had simply made a breach in the walls using their new and terrible catapult, based on an old design the Minotaur had discarded. They had been firing from it all day, when suddenly one stone had struck a vulnerable patch of wall, and the wall had crumbled. The djinn had risen wailing into the sky. The daimons had fled. The people of Troy knew the moment of doom had come.

And yet the Greeks had not profited as they expected. Neoptolemos had seized upon the royal family, certain that they were most important, and so had missed the departure of the fleet led by Gorgos, heavy with Trojan treasure, Trojan ideas, and Trojans. The monsters had expected some action by the gods, but there had been nothing. The red, smoke-filled sky was silent. As they stood out from Troy, Sthenno pointed to the north.

'Zeus's hour has come. The high gods have fallen,' she said. Afar off, there was a distant rumble of thunder.

Euryale chuckled joyously. 'Zeus, Zeus,' she said. 'Eternity in a bronze cage. Demand no direr fate. It is you who are the Trojan horse, but for you there will be no escape. Incarnate forever.'

'Men to come will build him a great shrine at Olympia,' said Sthenno.

'Misguided fools,' said Euryale. 'Do they think he still has power?'

'So he does,' said Sthenno, surprising them. 'Olympia will for a while be his country, and he will have the power of a little god. But it will be a while before men truly see that they are alone with the little gods under free stars.'

She looked up through the hatch. The first stars had prickled into a nightblue sky. 'The heavens are free,' she said, and gave a great sigh. All of them looked upward. The ships sailed on.

It was the Snake-girl who broke the silence of remembering.

'Ah,' she said. 'But what of the Minotaur? And Corydon?'

'The Minotaur lives,' said Sthenno. 'But someone had to pay the price. The price of saving the world.'

'And what is that?'

'What it always is,' said the deep voice of a lapis sphinx. 'Life. Only life can buy life. Your baby was born and at the same moment your friend died.'

A single tear drifted down the Snake-girl's cheek. She brushed it aside. Her heart ached, patient, unsleeping, the immortal heart she would always carry. It would always be empty now, except for her daughter.

'Do not weep, and do not fear,' said Sthenno. 'He has died and he has saved his people. And he has found father and mother, and he sleeps between them. They are the family they were meant to be.'

'His mother?' Gorgos looked up.

'Gorgos,' said Sthenno. 'You and your mother were star-crossed. It was Corydon who was the son of her heart. You know that, though you also know she loved you. So too Corydon's birth-mother was not the mother of his heart. Now he and Medusa may walk together and make songs for the Lady of Flowers. This is not something to fear, or mourn. This is the destiny you wish for us, though in another shape. This is freedom.'

And for just one moment, all of them saw it. A shepherd boy, alone on a hillside, watching his flock. There came to them the faint sound of pipes playing a tune of glowing joy. Corydon had come home.

Resources We Used:

Arabian Sands (1959), by Wilfrid Thesiger.

The Marsh Arabs (1964), by Wilfrid Thesiger.

The *Zend Avesta,* sacred Zoroastrian text.

Confessions, St Augustine.

The Outlaw Josey Wales, film, Clint Eastwood.

For a Few Dollars More, film, Sergio Leone.

The Good, the Bad and the Ugly, film, Sergio Leone.

And, of course, the Morricone scores.

The Arabian Nights: The Thousand and One Nights and a Night, Richard Burton's translation.

Butch Cassidy and the Sundance Kid, screenplay by William Goldman.

C. P. Cafavy (1863–1933), *Poems.*

Virgil, *Aeneid.*

Quintus Smyrnus (4th century), *The Fall of Troy.*

Ovid, *Fasti.*

The Homeric Hymn to Demeter.

Euripides, *The Trojan Women,* translated by Gilbert Murray.

Leonardo Da Vinci, *Leonardo's Machines: Da Vinci's Inventions Revealed.*

Joe Simpson, *Touching the Void.*

Heinrich Harrer, *The White Spider.*

Jon Krakauer, *Eiger Dreams: Ventures among Men and Mountains.*

Gavin Pretor-Pinney, *The Cloudspotter's Guide.*

Gladiator, film, Ridley Scott.

Glossary

As we promised, just as our first book represents archaic Greece and our second book represents Greece in the age of the polis or city state, so this book represents Magna Graeca of the Hellenistic period, though it is not set in the time after Alexander the Great but many centuries before. What made the Hellenistic world distinctive was Greek cultural fusion with the East, especially Persia. In this book Corydon begins in the desert, a space of wild magic for the peoples of the East, and then visits Troy, a city where the extreme West of Atlantis fuses with the pre-Moslem East to create a different kind of magic from that of the Greek pastoral. In the great epic *The Iliad*, Homer dramatises this clash of worlds.

But people still tend to think of Greekness as much too much like Romanness, much too Western, even Germanic, missing the highly-coloured bright oddity of it. This mistake is apt to get worse when children's authors retell Greek myths based on nothing but other dictionaries of Greek myth: the bare bones of story with no clothing culture to give them taste and smell and substance. Those white statues were painted in azure and gold and red, and often dressed in clothes. We think we're performing an act of restoration here. The matter of Troy is much odder than most people think.

Iliad. This is Homer's poem about Ilium, another name for Troy. It's an odd poem because in it Troy doesn't fall, and the main character, Akhilleus, doesn't die. But his anger with the Greeks is the poem's main subject, and so are the battles – many battles, most of them futile. Homer wants to show us the way war is the best thing men can be, and the worst, and also the most boring and silly; fabulous heroism is often wasted, and dogged dullness is sometimes more successful. In Homer the point is sometimes for things to have no point.

Homer. We put Homer in our story as an act of profound reverence. He was born in Ionia, in Khios, and he was blind, and he did have a boy-servant who was probably learning how to be a poet too. That is all we know – and we don't really even know that . . .

Leonardo Da Vinci. Is the origin of the machines the Minotaur makes. He too was trying to save a walled city-state, Firenze (Florence) in Italy.

Troy. May really have existed, a great and glorious port city (think San Francisco or Sydney, Marseille or Mumbai) which was a gateway to the East by ship and by caravan. Our Troy was once an Atlantean colony, so it has towers, though not such high towers as Atlantis.

Lar. The eventual Roman name for the small gods of each family. Probably not really Greek, but Virgil (see below) insists that the Trojans fleeing the sack took their Lares with them. In our book they are the smallest of all the small gods because they represent a person's immediate family. They want to resist war (just as a family does) but they don't have much power (just as families can be completely crushed).

Djinn. Plural of jinni, but we thought jinni sounded too unfamiliar and odd, and 'genie' is really from French translation and just means 'spirit'. Before Islam, the Arab peoples believed in spirits of vanished ancient peoples who acted during the night, and could change shape into animals at will. There were many different kinds, including the ghoul (night shade), and the efreet, who are especially strong. These are the monsters of the Arab world. Our djinn partake of the desert but are shapechangers.

Camels. The royal road in Persia was the fastest messenger service in the ancient world, entirely staffed by relays of dromedary camels. They are tireless racers, capable of easily outdistancing most of the small horses of the ancient world.

Bedouin. Our kleptis gang is based on T. E. Lawrence and Wilfrid Thesiger's encounters with the nomads of Arabia. So courteous that starving tribespeople will ply a guest with more food than he can eat, they are sadly often treated as monsters because they are nomadic.

Tashkurgan. We made this up, though physically it's based on the cities of the desert, like Petra. We made it up out of names like Tashkent, and *Narnia*'s Tashbaan, which we always loved a lot more than C S Lewis wanted us to (because the food sounds great).

Winged lions. Tashkurgan is also Venice in its role as an Eastern city of darkness, and so we gave it winged lions, but made them real and rather bossy. Lion-demons are common in Egyptian myth.

Cassia birds. Ancient Arabia has a rich fauna which made it hard to gather the spices for which it was famous. Cassia, which is a kind of cinnamon, used to be guarded by cassia birds who used it to build their nests.

The serpent-god. Our attempt to represent the problem of dualism, which came into Greek thought from the East. Roughly, dualism says that the world, the flesh and the devil exist and are bad, bad like Sauron – that is, all bad. Good exists to fight against them. This is the basis for a lot of fantasy narratives, but it's dull and untrue to life.

Ahriman. The representation of evil in the dualistic religions of Zoroastrianism, the religion of the Persians. A destructive spirit who is chaos and is surrounded by evil daevas, spirits who love to destroy. See *The Serpent-god.*

Ahura Mazda. The Creator of the universe in Zoroastrianism. He is the ultimate truth and creation, the ultimate good. Believes that everything can only be achieved through deeds. See *The Serpent-god.*

The marshes. At the Tigris Euphrates estuary live the Marsh Arabs, where they have lived since Corydon's time.

Akhilleus. (Romans wrote his name as Achilles.) The greatest of all the heroes, because his divine mother held him in the waters of Styx, making him all but invulnerable. But that's not the main reason he's remarkable; Memnon is similarly invulnerable, and he is less remarkable. Akhilleus is also very intelligent. And there's not a lot he hasn't seen. He's aware of the gods and their plots, as aware as any monster, as aware as Corydon. But like Corydon, knowledge does not mean escape.

Odysseus. (Romans wrote his name as Ulysses.) The other great hero of the war. In Plato's *Republic*, heroes of the Trojan War are asked to choose the form in which they would like to be reincarnated. Agamemnon chooses to be an eagle. But Odysseus says he wants only to be an ordinary man. Normal. Joe Public. In a way, this is what he always is: an ordinary man with exceptional strength, intelligence, and what the Greeks call *metis*, which is low cunning and trickiness. He knows about the gods' plotting too, and he too can do nothing about it.

Memnon. He isn't in the *Iliad*; Memnon's story comes from Quintus Smyrnaeus, a later Homer-imitator like us. Memnon comes from Africa. He is the son of the dawn and her mortal husband Tithonos, before he unfortuntely became a cicada or cricket (see Tennyson's poem). Having a cicada for a father isn't a problem for Memnon, but that and his raven-black skin make him an outsider, a little bit monstrous. He is also a staunch friend of the Trojans, especially Prince Hektor.

Hektor. The Trojans' chief indigenous warrior. A prince of Troy. Homer shows that he goes completely berserk while fighting, which makes him formidable. But he has none of the self-awareness of Akhilleus or Odysseus.

Paris. Or, for us, Sikandar. Sikandar is the Eastern form of the name Alexandros, which was Paris's real name. (People called Alexander the Great that too.) Most pro-Trojan versions of the Trojan War stumble over Paris, usually portrayed as a long-haired dope who can't fight and can't help kidnapping a girly girl and thus dooming his people. That Paris is so awful that we decided he was a kind of monster . . . And in legend he is a shepherd, like Corydon.

Penthesilea. Also not in Homer but in Quintus Smyrnaeus. Penthesilea and her Amazons come to defend Troy because they too are monstrous and because they too have Atlantean origins. In legend Akhilleus falls in love with Penthesilea, but only after he has killed her. There's a German play about it, by Hölderlin.

Helena. In our story, a Big Excuse, but in Homer she really is something the Trojans won't give up; it's as if she represents the power of sex itself. In Euripides the real

Helen has been in Egypt all along, while an eidolon takes her place in Troy; this is our story too, and one day we might write about the real Helen's life in a desert kleptis gang.

Philoktetes. A hero who carries the bow of Herakles, and its arrows. Was going to the Trojan War when he was bitten by a snake sent by Hera, which poisoned his foot, causing him to go lame and smell so badly that his men abandoned him on a nearby island. In Sophokles' play, *Philoktetes*, after the death of Akhilleus, the Greeks send Odysseus and Neoptolemos to bring him back to help them kill Paris and defeat the Trojans, but we've put him on the Trojan side.

Neoptolemos. Purely horrible. Violence itself, incarnate. Virgil says he looks like a snake when killing Priam.

Agamemnon. Not a big character for us. Cursed to a destiny of kin-slaughter, he's only interesting because he's like a Zeus-on-earth.

Khryses. Homer's priest of Apollo. Ours is an illustration of the limits of institutionalised charisma. Huh? Well, most religions have charismatic founders. But then they die and are replaced by a hierarchy of priests who lack charisma themselves, but represent the charisma of the founders. It's all in a book by a man called Max Weber.

Apollo. In Homer he comes down from Mount Olympos to the plain of Troy, and the plague-arrows clatter on his back. Apollo is also the god who drives the chariot of the sun, Helios. He is on Troy's side, as is his sister Artemis. But for us he is a trickster, Apollo Loxias or double-tongued.

Hera. As we all know by now, wife of Zeus. As we all know, not pretty. Miserably in need of Zeus but also in some ways his enemy.

Athene. As we also know, Zeus's daughter in every sense. No one is more oppressive than the dutiful daughter of a tyrant.

Aphrodite. Not love, as in romance and Valentine's Day, but absolute psycho-madness that leads you to behave badly and embarrassingly. But also the lure of self-forgetfulness that such desire entails.

Zeus. Zeus is the CEO, the chief, the leader of the giant global conglomerate that is the Olympians. Okay, not every bad thing the gods do is due to him, but (as with Enron) someone has to swing for their crimes. Having amoral but extremely powerful gods gives earthly rulers the worst possible kind of role-model. Look not only at the Roman emperors, but also at the Athenian empire.

Dryads. Each tree has one, so they are quintessentially local and not global. They don't fight any more than trees do. The dryad's defeat is about the powerlessness of natural beauty to resist war.

Faunus. An obscure Roman god, very like Pan in that he's a part-goat country dweller. Our idea is that some Roman gods come from Troy with Gorgos/Aeneas.

Virgil. The great poet of the fall of Troy is this Roman epic writer, author of the *Aeneid*. He likes the Trojans, not the Greeks; for hundreds of years everyone else liked them too because no one read Homer anymore. Chaucer and Shakespeare liked the Trojans best too. Virgil does pathos brilliantly. Homer never does pathos.

Aeneas. The hero of the *Aeneid*, and his story is that he escapes Troy to found Rome as a sort of New Troy. We equate him with Gorgos. Interestingly, medieval British writers came up with another Trojan refugee, Brutus, who went further and founded Britain, as a sort of New Troy *and* Rome. Another reason English writers like Chaucer and Shakespeare were always on the Trojan side.

The Greek words. γνοθη σεαυτον, as Corydon says, means 'know yourself', and was inscribed on the Temple of Apollo at Delphi, source of the most famous prophecies in the ancient world.

The Latin words. 'Farra deae micaeque licet salientis honorem/ Detis et in veteres turea grana focus', (You may honour the goddess with spelt, and dancing salt/

And grains of incense on ancient hearths) et cetera, spoken by the one-eyed old women. They come from Ovid's *Fasti* (Book IV), a totally and unjustly neglected masterpiece about the rites and festivals of the Romans. It's a description of the rites of Ceres, aka Demeter.

The rites of the Thesmophoria. Everything that happens to Corydon and Gorgos to prepare Gorgos as a vessel for the little gods is based on the Thesmophoria, a festival of Demeter so secret that men were not allowed to enter. In the festival, women symbolically relived the anguish of Demeter when her daughter Kore/Persephone was abducted. It featured insults, piglets, rotting flesh, a snakepit, and a day-long fast. Greek religious practice (as opposed to the tidied up versions that we know as myth) is usually very dark, and salvation costs blood.

Caves. Many Greek mystery religions took place in caves; the best-known were those in Samothrace. A mystery religion is one involving death and resurrection.

Palinurus. Helmsman of Aeneas's ship; as the price for the safe passage of Aeneas and his people after fleeing from Troy, Venus/Aphrodite offers to Neptune/Poseidon the death of Palinurus. So Corydon too must die, carrying on his back the wrongs of the world.

Priam. King of Troy, who sees his sons (fifty, according to some versions) die one by one and is finally butchered himself by Neoptolemos.

The three old women. They are the Graeae, who shared one eye and one tooth between them. Traditionally, they come in the story of Perseus, but he doesn't really deserve them, so we put them in here.

Trojan horse. Makes the Trojans look like idiots. Not in our version, though. It might have been the first time people chose quantity over quality.

Olympos. This is the tallest mountain in Greece. When the Greeks imagined the gods living on it, they didn't think of it as icy, snowy and real, but so high that its top was effectively 'heaven', or at least the dwelling-place of all the gods who didn't have other homes to go to. Olympos is actually a very easy mountain to climb, but the Olympos here is not the mountain you can find on a map, but a mountain in Zeus's mind, so we based its topographical features on the north wall of the Eiger, which is one of the hardest climbs in Europe, and in the world.

Mountain terms. Couloir: A steep gully, usually full of snow. Verglas: Ice so thin it breaks when you stand on it; so you can't get a hold with (for example) a pin or axe.

Planck's Constant. A physical constant discovered by the German physicist Max Planck, which describes the sizes of discrete packets or quanta or electromagnetic radiation – one of the founding discoveries of quantum mechanics.

Gödel. Kurt Gödel was an Austrian-American mathematician and logician, one of Einstein's closest friends, whose principle work was on the incompleteness of mathematical theories.